Crescent of Darkness

By Virgil Thornton II

For Coach Boone and Pokie

Published by ***Weird Disciple Publishing***
Edited by ***Marrisa Thornton, Articulate***

© 2014 Virgil Thornton II
© 2018 Virgil Thornton II (Final Version)
ISBN (e-book): 978-1-7326548-0-8
ISBN (paperback): 978-1-7326548-3-9
ISBN (hardback): 978-1-7326548-7-7

This is a work of fiction. Names, characters, businesses, places, events, locales, and incidents are either the products of the author's imagination or used in a fictitious manner. Any resemblance to actual persons, living or dead, or actual events is purely coincidental.

TABLE OF CONTENTS

TABLE OF CONTENTS

PRELUDE

~ ~ ~

Exploding cars aren't always cool. Years ago, however, I would've never said that. It was a chilly winter's night, and my parents had made my sister Samantha and I bundle up before getting in the car with them. I was on the way to my grandmother's house in Canada without a care in the world. It was cold outside, but with my family, there was warmth.

The radio played softly. No one had spoken for quite some time, because nothing interesting sparked up a conversation. Out of the blue, Sam asked, "Hey Dad, why did Grams move to Canada in the first place?"

"Well," Dad stated, eyes flicking once to the rear-view mirror, "Ever since… the incident with Grandpa, Grams couldn't stay in her house in Huntsville. It got too expensive."

The grief of my grandfather's disappearance was still fresh in my mind at that time. It was about a year after he vanished, and back then I thought it was near impossible to live without him. His winsome smiles, hearty laughs, and valuable advice always picked me up and kept me going.

I'd never forget the call we received. His assistant's voice was filled with something I couldn't identify. Regret? Panic? Dread? Maybe all three. He simply told us to rush over and that something had gone wrong. From that day forward, it had felt as though my grandfather's disappearance had taken a piece of me, or at least a piece of my joy. As I sat in the car and thought, I could feel my face turning red; tears began to form at the corners of my eyes.

Faint blankets of sadness began to settle over me, but before I could be pushed to tears, Sam's soft question interrupts my thoughts.

"What's wrong?"

She must have noticed.

"N-nothing," I lied, trying to relax myself.

There was a long pause, this time filled with awkward silence, and I used the scenery of the distant city lights to calm me. The moonlight shimmering off of the sugar-coated cliffside set me at ease, and the soupy darkness that lied just beyond the guardrail transformed some of my sadness into fear. I waited a bit longer, and then decided that I should bring myself to speak again.

"Hey Sam," I said enthusiastically, "You want to go for a few games of *Swords and Shanties* tonight?"

She hesitated, seeming a bit confused, then, "Sure! I've been waiting for a chance to reclaim my title as Pirate Queen!" She added a smirk and a little more confidence to that last part.

To our surprise, Dad suddenly laughed, still staring at the highway.

"You both know I'm going to win this time." He challenged, joining in on the suddenly competitive mood.

"None of you are," Mom said sternly, more in Dad's direction than anybody else's. "It's eleven o'clock right now. By the time we get there, you two in the back will hop right in the bed. You guys will have to postpone your little game until tomorrow."

Sam and I sighed in disappointment. Mom was right, though. I could already feel my eyes stinging, and my body longed for the smooth sheets of a bed. The car started to settle back into silence when all of a sudden, a pair of tremendously bright lights came around the corner, sending a jolt up my spine. They were headlights… from a truck, approaching us head on, driving on the double-yellow lines.

We didn't have enough time to cross to the left side, so Dad quickly smashed the horn, slowed down, and attempted to position the car to squeeze by on the right shoulder. Disbelief and panic arose in me as the driver swerved, full speed, directly towards us. Right before they rammed into us, Dad yelled something that sounded like "Guitar", but that couldn't have been it because Mom screamed in anger at whatever he said.

The impact was insane; it threw the world around me into a tumbling, spinning, blurred mess. I felt the car skip off of the road and burst through the guardrails. Terrified energy surged through me as my head was filled with the odd sensation of being thrust upside down. In the moment where we were still flipped, where my feet were hovering above my head and the trinkets on the floor began to rise to the ceiling, only one thing was going through my mind. *I'm not breathing, am I.* It wasn't the seatbelt choking me.

The whole car was floating, or falling rather, while still upside down. My feet forced tight under Mom's chair and my death grip on the armrest were keeping the seatbelt from putting too much pressure on my chest. I wasn't hyperventilating. Right before the car slammed into the ground, I realized what was happening. I was bracing myself for death.

In a sudden bright flash of light, the first slam was over. It almost seemed like the car didn't smash into anything, but rather, it slid off of something. We rolled right side up and then began to tumble down the hill. It was more of a throwing motion than a bouncing one. I was constantly slung away from the window, towards Sam, with a nauseating dance of blood rushing between my head and my torso.

Each rollover felt like my last. At any moment I knew a jolt would break something crucial, or debris would strike a fatal blow. I was expecting a quick, horrific, painfully painless death at any moment. Suddenly, I was back with my feet above me again, but now we were hanging instead of floating. We were alive?

From behind my blanket of shock and dizziness, I could feel the bitter cold from outside on my face. I could hear the air hushing and car pieces clinking down the hill after us, and the night wind rustling through frosted tree needles. The windows were broken. No airbags?

There was silence, but luckily everyone appeared to be alive. I was so stunned, it took a few slaps from Sam for me to realize I should probably unclick my seatbelt. I reached down-up, but before I could free myself, the car jolted. A crunching noise began to grow, and I realized we were sliding.

The snow must've been frozen beneath us. We had tumbled for a considerable distance. There was only so far that we could go before we'd careen off of a ledge too high up to survive. I had a good feeling this was that ledge.

Some emotion rose in me. Not sadness, not fear. Dismay? No, it was disappointment. We survived all of that just to die there. I didn't know what I wanted to do with my life, but having it end so early was not on the agenda. My mind was surprisingly blank. Unlike the usual countless thoughts swirling in my head, I had only three. *This is how we die. I hope I make it in. Grams is going to be really sad.*

Dad laughed a sort of "well this sucks" laugh, and then said in a croaky voice, "Never forget that I love you. John 15:13."

I didn't have time to respond. That same, unnatural, gold-tinged white light from before filled the car. The strongest forces I have ever felt pressed on me with incredible strength. Everything around me was suddenly split in two, and then invisible ropes wrapped around me, tugging me violently through the missing trunk.

I was in the frigid air, flying backwards towards solid ground. My eyes instinctively closed. I prepared for impact and slammed hard against the wet snow. I opened my eyes just in time to see the night sky filled with a million stars, and at the top of my vision the car gracefully slipped out of view.

I quickly rolled over and sat up, horrified. Was I the only survivor?! I concentrated hard in the darkness. The moonlit snow was too dim, and my head was still swirling and pounding from the fall. Were those silhouettes? Please be silhouettes.

It happened abruptly yet predictably. There was a loud, distant crunch sound and then a great explosion shook the ground beneath me. The flash of light surprised me, but it also confirmed that those were silhouettes. But I only caught two.

A rolling cloud of fire rose up from the edge, twisting and twirling as it reached the end of its life, and the hot flames revealed that Sam and my mother had made it out with me.

CHAPTER 1

MOVING DAY

~ MATTHEW ~

Today was a really boring day... well, at least the first part was. The moving truck is full of silence as we coast down the interstate. I've explored every other aspect of my brain at least three times already during this never-ending car ride, so I'm not surprised when Dad starts to come to mind.

It's been around three years since he died, and almost a year since my grandmother died. Wow… I just realized that means everyone on my father's side is gone (oh, excluding Uncle Gyro). After the accident, if I can even call it that, weird things have been going on with Mom.

She, like Sam and I, was depressed, but somehow, Mom found Dad's wedding ring in her pocket after the crash. That really messed her up. To this day, she sometimes cries out his name while she sleeps, and when Sam and I go in there to check on her, she's usually tossing and turning roughly while clinging onto her comforter.

Sam and I gave her plenty of weeks before we started to ask her about "Guitar" or "John 15:13", but the only response she'd give was either stomping off in complete rage or acting like we hadn't said anything. We stopped after the second attempt and try to avoid the topic when conversations grow quiet.

I frown at those thoughts, but then remember my old therapist's joke '*It seems like you don't want to be here, so just know; a smile a day keeps Dr. Psi away.*' Try to focus on other things. I attempt a smile, but who am I kidding; my body is overflowing with boredom. Where I'm sitting doesn't make it any better; I got the half-chair half-armrest put in the middle of all moving truck front seats.

We've been on the road for almost five hours, and I feel a headache slowly growing in my temples. Sam and I don't even know where we're going; we just know we're moving to somewhere in Alabama. I was suspicious that it was going to be my grandmother's old house, but it can't be. That thing was huge and probably costs a fortune.

I look down in my lap to find my portable console. I had been playing something earlier, but nearly forgot about it. After one lackluster glance, I close the gaming device. In the moment, I just wasn't interested in playing any more, but if I knew what was to come, I would've had a game marathon.

Instead, I sluggishly roll my head over to Sam to check out what she's doing. Bummer; it's the same thing she's done since we first got in the car. What she calls '*multi-tasking*' is composed of listening to death thrash metal or whatever you call that deafening stuff, absently chewing on clearly used-up gum, and scrolling through posts on her social media page. How can she do that for five hours straight?!

Samantha Blue is my 14-year-old sister. She's a born blonde, but prefers her hair dyed black. Mom just rolls her eyes every time. As of now, Sam's hair is shiny and smooth, and it reaches down just past her ears. From my angle, her hair is covering one of her aqua green eyes.

Her skin is the color of peach and everyone says we look the same for some reason, disregarding the tiny black mole she has on her left nostril. Her lips have a light pink tint, but she wears purple lipstick (looks weird if you ask me). She's both pure awesomeness and evil, somehow managing to get on my nerves one second and have me laughing the next. She is wearing her trademark soft dark blue hoodie, probably with some edgy rock band t-shirt underneath, and dim gray shorts.

In an attempt to humor myself, I comically toss my head over to look at my mom. It works, and I get a few idiotic giggles out of myself before sinking back into hazy boredom. My mom is Rebecca Kelvin-Blue and she's in her late thirties (38 maybe?). She has bouncy cocoa hair that flows down to her shoulders from a widow's peak. Her crystal blue eyes are trained on the road, but they take a quick glance in the side view mirror just out of habit.

After five solid hours, Mom's gotten pretty good at driving this thing. Her skin is peachy and she doesn't wear make-up often nor does she have any blemishes. Sometimes, rose blush fades in and out with her emotions, matching the color of her lips.

She's really understanding and kind, but can easily get strict, and seems to stay stressed all the time. She is wearing a cyan colored shirt and navy-blue jeans. Around her neck hangs a bright gold chain with Dad's dull silver wedding ring looped in it. She toys with the ring while she drives.

I finally stare forward at what seems like a never-ending three-lane road, worn and gray against the forest's orange autumn mood. I suppose I might as well describe myself now. I'm Matthew Blue and I am 12 years old. Yes, I know my name rhymes. I've been reminded a bajillion times.

My skin color is my mother's, and so is my hair. I've been told I have a wispy, ruffled, curtained hair look, and everyone used to joke about my forehead because of it. That's not why I have curtained hair though; it's because I'm too lazy to put real effort into brushing it.

My eyes are sort of like Mom's, but a creamier blue; not as sharp as hers. They're probably bloodshot right now because I'm too sleepy to stay awake yet I'm too rested to sleep. Suddenly, I am aware of what I'm wearing; a red shirt and blue shorts today. A tingle rises on my lip and I scratch it… bummer; still absolutely no signs of facial hair. This is a sad, sad thing indeed.

We coast along the barely populated road, and as I feel Mom easing onto the brake, I force myself upright to see what's ahead. What? We've reached an interstate exit at last?! Sam just so happens to look up, and we both gaze at the approaching green and yellow sign.

My face lights up as I read it, '*Exit 340B East 565 Huntsville Exit Only*'. Isn't this near the place where Grams used to live before she moved to Canada? What was it… Madison! I let a manic smile play across my face. I used to love visiting Grams; living near her old home is going to be awesome.

When I was little and went over her house during the summer, I remember I thought she was the coolest because she used to play video games, watch movies, and eat snacks with me. It was actually pretty great, and I always remember being surprised at just how good she was at some of those video games.

We glide through a network of streets and hills, pass by shops and fields, and finally enter a neighborhood. I didn't really catch what the sign said, but I glanced just soon enough to see what looked like '*Cove*'. After turning right past a clubhouse (nice!), we coast down a surprisingly steep hill. I look down the slope and see that it leads to a turn next to a clearing with a lake. As the impossibly familiar houses pass me by, I start feeling jittery.

We ease down the hill and stop at one of the last houses approaching the bend. I could recognize that light gray brick palace from anywhere. It's not as big as it was when I was a kid, but it's still pretty large. My head is full of excited screams; we're actually moving into Gram's house?! Mom rolls the truck into the driveway, and Sam and I promptly rush out just as we come to a stop. The two of us shake and stretch, breaking free of the stiff molds we'd become over the trip.

Mom marches up to the door, takes a deep breath, keys the lock, and swings open the door. Sam and I go to file in behind her, but she stops. Before either of us ask what's wrong, we notice a dark, hooded figure in the middle of the living room. It seems to look up at us, holding a pose like a deer in headlights. Mom, Sam, and I freeze as well.

After an infinite second of this, Mom reaches into her purse, but then the intruder bolts at us. As the figure moves closer, I can tell it's a guy. Mom and Sam back away, but I stand my ground, half out of fear and half out of defense. Well, since I'm here, I might as well fight. He's instantly in my range and I throw a surprise hook. It's too slow, for he ducks under it with ease and tackles my legs. With the force from the tackle, he causes me to fall forward, the world flipping around me.

I quickly put my hands out to break my fall, and while the rest of my body hits the porch first, my arms shield my face. Pain runs through my body like falling dominos. With a clattering noise, my game system slips out of my pocket.

From behind me, I hear Mom shout, Sam grunt, and then what sounds like two people hitting the ground. Did he just throw them both down at the same time? Suddenly, the intruder's feet come into view. I watch as an arm reaches down and snatches my game. Hey, that was a gift from my father! As a last resort, I swing my leg around and kick his shins. Satisfyingly, he trips, banging his face into the railing and twisting roughly down the small porch stairway.

All of us are completely stunned for a good 3 seconds, and then we begin to chase him.

CHAPTER 2

HE THREW A WHAT?

~ MATTHEW ~

I leap off the porch and over the steps, hitting the sidewalk and stumbling into a run. There's a slight twinge of pain in my ankles, but I ignore it; I'm too angry right now. Sam is hot on the thief's heels as well. She throws something, her MP3 player, and it hits him in the back of his head with a thud. Before it can fall to the ground, he spins around quickly and grabs it. His hood flips off, revealing his cinnamon skin and mess of brown hair.

"Freaking thief!" Sam shouts angrily, apparently not noticing my ruby red game system in his right hand.

The two of us continue to chase him down the middle of the street, luckily downhill, so all three of us have an extra boost of rather hazardous speed. We sprint towards the lake and pass a man rolling a stroller, who casts us a confused look. There is a group of girls giggling and chatting by the water's edge; they also shoot us concerned looks as we thunder and shout after the intruder. Suddenly, I hear Mom's voice. It's tired and somewhat distant but shrill nonetheless.

"Don't let him get away!" She commands.

I look behind me to see her running, but steadily falling behind, still on the sidewalk while we're about to turn around the lake. I guess flip flops were bad selections for this occasion. We start to round the lake; it appears this guy is going to try and take us for a loop and ditch us in the woods after we tire out. To my relief, I see a group of high-school aged boys on the other side of the lake near the street. They're running around the lake too, but they're headed to meet us straight on.

The thief sees this, reasons that the boys are probably out to stop him too, and makes a 90 degree turn straight for the tree line. Sam is still close behind him, stubborn concentration plastered on her face, but I'm starting to feel the effects of being out of shape. My lungs burn and my throat feels like fire, but I'm not about to give up so soon. My legs are fine, so I decide to pursue the thief and my sister into the woods.

Almost moments after we enter the forest, I forget the way out. The woods are much thicker than we had imagined, and all three of us are slowed because of it. Thank the Lord; more swatting and less running is doable for me. The bandit looks back a few times, then hops on a fallen tree and performs a massive leap straight up in the air. Heaps of cyan leaves forcefully spray from his shoes and fall to the ground. Wait, those aren't leaves. Those…

Those are flames! At first I thought he had jumped on some hidden springboard, but when Sam stopped running and I realized he was steadily moving up, the added possibility of a leaf blower jet-pack also disappeared from thought. How in the world is he doing this?! I can see Sam a couple of trees in front of me, frozen and staring up in awe at the flying bandit. He slowly turns in the air to face us, but Sam ducks behind a tree and I do the same right before we enter his line of sight.

All I hear are trees swishing and the odd 'fwoosh' of gushing fire, and then, a hissing noise comes from where he is. It grows closer, and then I see something bright, turquoise, and the size of a football dart past and into the grass.

Once it hits the ground, it splashes into wisps of flames that quickly change from green to orange. Wha- he can throw fireballs too?! This is just ridiculous! I notice the smoke from the fire trailing towards me, and I realize just how dangerous it would be to keep standing here. Luckily, there is an oddly placed rhododendron beside the tree I'm hiding behind; he won't see me if I change location.

I sidle over as quietly as possible, then sit down and force myself to relax. This must be a dream. Gah, I'm still breathing heavy, my mind still racing. I grip the floor of dead leaves and take a deep breath. My pulse is a thumping drum; I can faintly hear it. I do my best to quiet myself, and when I succeed, absolutely nothing happens.

The smell of smoke is still in the air. I can hear the faint crackling from where the fireball landed, the swish of leaves overhead, and the scared silence of the forest. I can feel the warmth from the weak fire, the pain in my throat, and the soreness of my lungs. I open my eyes and let out an astonished chuckle. This is real. Somehow, I'm actually fighting a video game boss. Boy, will I have a story to tell

Mom!

I quickly realize that I am not at home; if I don't act wisely, I may not live to get there. Now sobered, I scan my surroundings, just in case there's an aperture deep enough to hide in. Unfortunately, the ground looks pretty solid under these leaves. As I'm looking around, I notice that some other shrubs and trees are kindling. This adds being caught in a wildfire to my list of worries. My darting eyes catch Sam, and as soon as I spot her, I remember that she's with me.

She's looking off somewhere else behind a small hill of uprooted earth. I'm not exactly sure why, but seeing her face filled with confusion and a hint of panic drains me of any confidence I'd had prior. How are we supposed to get out of this?

"Can you guys not?" A voice comes from the thief, or at least from the little I saw of him; I can't say it fits.

He's very frank, a little nasally, and surprisingly calm. It's quiet, as neither Sam nor I are stupid enough to reply. He grunts out the next couple of sentences.

"Like seriously. I'm going to be honest with you, I don't even know where I am right now. You shouldn't have followed me. You shouldn't have seen any of this. I shouldn't even be saying anything right now. I've screwed up so badly."

That last sentence was more to himself than to Sam and me. After his little monologue, there is just more grunting and a slowly growing hissing noise. I sit up straight against the rhododendron's waxy leaves. For some reason, I get a feeling that Sam and I just opened a really big can of worms. The way this guy is talking… and those fireballs. We're in some serious trouble.

Why is he grunting? Did he somehow get wounded, or is he just tired? Why can he control green fire? Where is he from? Wait, how did he get in our house in the first place?! I violently shake my head. No, that's never good. I'm asking myself too many questions; if I keep doing that I'll start to panic. For right now I just need to figure out how I can get out of this alive. Oh, and Sam, too.

I turn my head silently, peering through the leaves and white flowers. The bandit is crouching behind a fallen tree, holding a bright green ball of fire in front of him like it's a glass egg. I can only see his curly brown hair and a little of his cinnamon face, for the rest is hiding behind the tree. Well, except for his arms, which are reaching over the tree to hold the fireball.

That ball of fire looks different than the one he threw earlier. The one earlier looked as though he'd just thrown something at me that was on fire, only for me to realize that it was fire and nothing else. This looks like a deliberate ball of flame, like a basketball *made* of green fire.

The fire is oddly bright. It should look dull and normal in the noon sunlight, but even though it is daytime, the ball still shines harshly. Whatever is going on, I don't think I need to stick around it any longer. My eyes dart from the thief and quickly scan my surroundings to spot Sam in her blue hoodie again. She's looking in my direction… at me! I wave, and she starts waving too, but not in the *'Hey'* fashion. It's more like *'Run'*.

I nod, mentally preparing myself to bolt off into the woods. My eyes dart towards my potential exit plan, the thief, Sam, and back at my exit route. Three, two, one. In a loud shuffle of leaves, I get up to run. Instead of looking where I'm going, I immediately glance over my shoulder to see if the thief had heard me. He must have, because he falls back in what looks like surprise. Maybe he heard us and thought we were rushing him.

The ball of bright green flame rolls up and out of his hand, making an odd, spinning descent towards the ground. I turn back around, just barely missing a tree, and begin pouring on speed. Through the wind in my ears I can hear what I hope to be Sam running as well, but before either of us get far, a crashing, hissing noise cuts through the forest.

Before I can hide, jump, duck, or turn around to see what it was, I'm ambushed by agonizingly hot wind and strands of green fire.

CHAPTER 3

TERRIFYING PURPLE NURSE

~ MATTHEW ~

When I open my eyes, I'm engulfed in cool air as opposed to fiery winds.

"W-where am I?" I half-stammer, half-think. I blink my vision into focus. Surrounding me is a dim, white room with some medical equipment in it. I don't know if I'm just being delusional or not, but something about the equipment seems oddly high-tech. The way it glows… just doesn't seem normal. The only exit I can see is a stairwell on the far side of the room, letting in a pool of lime sunlight, which is the only source of light in this room.

My eyes swim upward and are greeted with an IV stand. A bag of what seems to be clear fluid is hooked on it. I don't have to look down to know that the IV is linked to me. I can feel a powerful, chilly medication slowly seeping through me, making me disoriented. In a confused state and without looking, I try to remove the cannula, but I can't move at all.

"Where's Sam?" I blurt out to the room, losing control of my loudness. "Sam, where are you? Help me! Somebody help me! Please, get me out of here!"

I flail around in my bed, violently spewing insults and thrashing to break my restraints. My body responds sluggishly; sweat beads on my skin as I waste more and more energy. No good; the restraints are solid.

Giving up seems like my only option, so I do so. My eyes meet the white-plated ceiling, and my ears tune in on the silence of the room. If I concentrate hard enough, I can hear a bird or two chirping outside. With a sigh, I close my eyes. Sleep returns quickly.

Where did this light come from? I lift my heavy eyelids, and sure enough, an overhead lamp is generously shining yellow light down on me. Something about the light, maybe the color or maybe the intensity, makes me want to throw up. I try to look away, but the way my eyes feel also sickens me. Suddenly, a soft, purple hand gently places itself on my forehead, sending a jolt of surprise through me.

"Hello Matthew." A feminine voice sounds from behind me.

I let out an exclamation; of what, I'm not sure. The lavender, gloved hand is too small, soft, and delicate to be a man's. The hand smoothly slides from my forehead to my cheek, and it's actually kind of pleasing. Should I be afraid for my life? She continues before I can ask.

"You endured quite a beating from that sirocco earlier. It was very unlikely that most would survive. That cyber (says a V-word that I don't understand) wielder must've been very churlish… and quite experienced as well."

I don't know what half of that even means, so I remain silent. The nurse is silent too, probably noticing my confusion. In a flat tone, she states, "To begin, I am known as Nima Iyr. I retrieved your name from your sister, who is recovering well in the other room."

Relieved yet still a bit unnerved, I wait for Nima to say more, and she must have picked up on that, because she continues, "You'll recover within the next half hour. Do you have any questions for me? If not, I will depart and allow you time to heal."

I could ask where I am or how she found me, but just knowing that Sam is safe puts me at ease. The only real, oddly nagging question I have now is: "Could I see what you look like?"

I should have asked for literally anything else... No amount of bracing would have prepared me for this. I could've easily handled seeing a deformed person. I could've handled something more bizarre, like a robot (though that would make me uneasy). I could've even dealt with a ghost, which would've been better than a robot now that I think about it. But the frozen, curtsying "girl" in front of me? Oh no.

It... "she" is far from human. I guess she might've been able to pull off a painted girl, if it weren't for her head and shoulders. All of her skin that I can see is a jarring, benign purple.

Her hands, of course, look like a normal girl's hands, but since those aren't gloves I guess she actually doesn't have fingernails. To add insult to injury, her shoulder blades are sharper and more defined than normal, as if wings are going to grotesquely burst out of her back at any moment. Her head is the size of a human head, except it's a perfect sphere.

She doesn't have any hair, but she does have this wisp-looking thing coming out of the top of her forehead; like a C. There aren't even any ears on the side of her head; just two headphone-sized pale lumps with a few slits in them where ears should be.

My eyes shift to her face. I see her two eyes with small eyelashes and lips, all enclosed within a pale circle. No nose. No eyebrows. I got a glimpse of her eyes before she closed them for the curtsy. At first I thought they were white, but I can only guess that they are milky gray. The light above me makes everything shadowy.

Since her head is a perfect sphere, though, that makes her eyes uncomfortably far apart and her mouth oddly wide. I hardly notice what she's wearing; a skirt that reaches a little past her knees, a tank top, and a necklace.

Tears of horror build around my eyes, and everything in my body tingles with the urge to scream. My eyes train on her stomach, which is covered with the tank top. This is the only normal thing about her, and maybe if I look at it long enough, the rest of her will be normal too.

"Indeed, I foresaw this as a fiasco." Nima peeps, finally emerging from her pose.

Oh goodness she's actually real. She actually moved and spoke. I'm genuinely chained in a bed with some demonic creature in an underground torture chamber. After a minute, I remember that she spoke, and if I don't want this thing to get angry, I should at least pretend like this is okay with me.

"No n- I'm not scared. S'fine. Real… for real." I lie.

I constantly choke on my own words, trying as best as I can to act natural. Something that came so easily before is hard to remember right now.

"Inform me why it's so palpable that you are red, then." She challenges bluntly, looking straight at me.

My eyes meet hers, and I feel everything inside me lock up at once. My eyes roll into the back of my head, and darkness rushes in from all sides. If I'm dying right now, at least it isn't by the hands of this creature.

****

When I wake up, the first thing I notice is that I feel just fine. I'm not sure how long I've been out, but I can tell that it's nighttime, and I'm in a room that seems like my own, though somehow it isn't exactly. Things are a bit off; the room is a little bigger and things aren't placed in their regular spots. Oh snap, and it's a completely different color, too! Startled and confused, I roll over.

To my relief, I find none other than Sam, sitting in a chair beside my bed, head on her fist. At the mere sight of her, I internally let loose a relieved sigh. Maybe it was all just a really bad nightmare, and I passed out from exhaustion when we got to the house or something. Above all else, I want nothing more than to give Sam a huge hug, but she isn't the hugging type, so I decide to fake groan and rub my forehead instead.

"Where am I?" I ask her, hardly containing a grin.

"You're in your new room." She replies with sarcastic enthusiasm.

"I just had the craziest dream about a-" but before I can finish, Sam interrupts me.

"Nope, that was real. At least, if you were about to say something with a thief that could shoot fireballs and a purple alien woman."

I'm taken by surprise, so much so that Sam's bored face cracks a smile. Wait, that was real?! It couldn't have been… stuff like that doesn't just happen!

We both hear footsteps somewhere in the hallway, and then Sam changes the course of the conversation, "Mom flipped out since we were gone for so long, and she told me it took the police quite a while to calm her down. A bunch of people helped her get the house squared away, and Aunt Alice actually came from a few towns over to help out." She explains as she looks at me a few times and then at my room.

The footsteps must've led into a bathroom or something, because they were followed by a door closing and the sound of a bathroom fan coming on with the light. I guess we have to keep beating around the bush.

"That's pretty nice of them." I reply, realizing just how selfless our neighbors are.

"Yeah, they pretty much had the housewarming party right after. We have a ton of food in the fridge."

That person must've only washed their hands or something, because they are in the bathroom for a rather short time.

Sam starts to guide the conversation back to where it should have been, "We didn't find our stolen things. Mom was sort of mad, but glad we're okay."

"Great, that jerk still has my game." I complain softly.

Samantha must've heard, because she comments, "Yeah, I'm royally pissed over that punk stealing my MP3 player too. Good thing that guy didn't get his hands on Dad's ring, though!"

I nod, giving a knowing chuckle. That would've been bad on a totally different level. Sam looks out in the hallway, then smiles and waves, apparently making eye contact with whomever that was. She watches them until it sounds like they're descending stairs, then she looks back at me.

"Hey, we did get these. They look pretty sweet." Sam informs as she pulls out a necklace concealed under her shirt.

The necklace Sam is wearing has a shiny bronze string holding a flat, circular, dark purple stone. Imprinted deeply in the stone is the shape of a star. The depression is filled with a bright yellow, glowing, liquid-like material that sparkles and glitters. She smiles under the faint light of the strange amulet.

"Sick, right?" She asks. I nod in reply, dumbfound at how awesome that necklace looks.

"You have one, too!" She adds.

I look down, just now realizing the weird weight on my chest. Mine has a silver string, and the stone has a strange crevice in it. The depression is in the shape of a yin-yang, with the circles popping out. In one wedge, a bright liquid swims around, sparkling with glowing whites, silvers, and pale blues. In the other, an indigo-black swirls moodily.

I tip the amulet upside-down and no fluid falls out. I go to touch it, but instead of feeling something wet, I feel a smooth glass surface teeming with energy. A grin spreads across my face as I dwell on the feeling of luck that I have right now.

"How did we get these?" I ask.

Sam looks like she's about to answer me, but then a mischievous smile grows on her face.

"Wait a second, let me try something she told me…"

We both look at each other expectantly, then she asks, "Slap yourself?"

I raise an eyebrow and so does she.

"Uh, what?" I ask.

"No wait it has to be convincing… There is a bug on your face, so you should slap it."

Before I can ask what she's getting at, my hand comes out of nowhere and flies hard across my face. I sit up, more startled than hurt. Sam lets out a laugh, looking delightfully surprised.

"What in the–"

"Doctors say the best way to recover is through moving around, so you should wiggle your arms around."

Like an itch, a sensation begins to grow in my arms until I realize I'm flailing them manically.

"What in the world is going on?!" I ask, somewhat amused but mostly terrified.

Sam is having a laughing fit, "Okay okay you can stop now."

I gain control over my arms almost instantly and, to my surprise, I can simply lower them to my sides.

"How did you do that?" I ask.

Sam wears a satisfied grin, "I'll… let you know in the morning. For now I want to get in the bed. Dragging your unconscious body through the woods for twenty minutes was a bit tiring."

I simply watch her leave, then lay back in my bed and look up at the ceiling. Do I feel violated? Scared? Grateful? I'm not sure.

I just keep staring at the ceiling until I fall asleep again.

CHAPTER 4

THE DECISION

~ MATTHEW ~

I **have the craziest dreams.** One was about Sam and me with a group of well-dressed teenagers fighting skeletons. We had amazing powers and I was fighting a blue wizard swordsman whom I felt a lot a hate toward.

The dream was so vivid, so precisely detailed, that although impossible things were happening, I couldn't convince myself otherwise. Most of the other dreams I forgot when I woke. Unfortunately, I remembered this next dream very clearly.

Its skin was a dead gray with unearthly blue fire serving as its cloak. "How foolish. You chose the Forest of Death, and you did not expect its namesake?" What in the world was it talking about? In the distance, bright lights began to flicker. I start to crawl towards it, but then the voice speaks again, "True light is beyond your reach. Now sink into darkness." Suddenly, I was not surrounded by black. Bright red and orange was rushing past me at all sides. Torn, demented souls reached out to pull me in. The smell of burning and death overcame me as the sounds of unearthly screams became background music. I was in Hell.

I spring up from my bed, gulping masses of air. My fingers are curled tightly around the edge of my covers, which I must have kicked into an untidy mess. As I pant and sweat, absolutely horrified, I can still hear some of the tormented screams bouncing around in my head, pleading for help.

"Matthew! Are you alright?!" My mom asks me, appearing at my side as I continue to wheeze.

If I open my mouth, I know I'll start crying. Instead of embarrassing myself, I just stare at her, in shock. She hugs me then hands me a glass of water. After I regain my breath, I chug it and then lay down again. Well, I certainly won't be sleeping again anytime soon. Mom asks me about my dream. I explain it all, without missing a single detail. She studies me, and an '*I am still concerned yet disappointed in you*' look forms on her face after I finish my story.

"You're telling the absolute truth?" She asks, suspicious. I nod.

"And what is this?" She holds up the amulet Sam showed me last night by its strings.

At first I'm confused, because that doesn't relate to anything I just said, but then dread fills my stomach at the thought of Sam. The way she took control of my mind like an evil magician or hypnotizer… I'm certainly not letting her do that again.

"It was Sam's fault! She–"

"This is no time to blame your sister." My mom interrupts.

She explains to me how she heard me talking in my room and investigated to find me asleep. Then, I started gasping and she pulled back the covers to find my amulet too tight around my neck. I really don't know how that could happen, because it fit comfortably last night. Anyway, she promptly untangled my amulet and took it off.

I keep silent, so she continues her rant, "Maybe your dream came from the fact that you were choking! I can't believe you slept with a necklace on… that's just doomed to end horribly! Where did you even get this?"

She studies it a bit longer, looking at it as if this **is** the first time she's ever given its appearance any real thought. She gets an odd look on her face, then looks at me, then back at the necklace.

"…you can wear this, just take it off before you go to sleep, okay?" She asks kindly.

I nod, and she smiles.

"Well, breakfast is ready, and if you don't hurry up, Sam is going to eat everything!"

My skin grows cold at the mention of my sister. Before I can warn Mom about Sam's sorcery, she disappears from my room. Reluctantly, I slide out of bed and push my feet in my slippers (which are conveniently bedside). Sighing and absently touching my neck, I go out of my bedroom door into the tan hallway.

Smells of breakfast and memories of this house remind me that the kitchen is downstairs. I peer down the steps and sure enough, Sam is down there. As she hungrily scarfs down whatever sandwich concoction she made with her omelet, bacon, and waffle, I descend the stairs with apprehension, half wishing I had a shield. But, without one, I bravely walk across the white-tiled kitchen floor and sit opposite of Sam.

I eat a piece of bacon and pick at my omelet. I'm surprisingly not hungry, which is just slightly more terrifying than sitting across from a possible witch.

I try not to make eye contact with my sister, but it's unavoidable when she finishes her meal and asks, "You going to eat that?"

As I slide the plate to her, I ask, "Are you going to explain yourself?" I immediately know I could've said something cooler.

She gives a half-hearted chuckle and replies, "Persuasion." Then she has a long chat with me (only broken by pauses to eat) explaining the amulets. The necklaces she showed me last night are named vira, and Nima gave them to us. Sam briefly glosses over Nima, so I guess she didn't have as big of a problem with her as I did. Then again, my sister is the closest to fearless that I've seen someone get.

Anyway, vira are special talismans that give the owner… well, magic. There are two types of vira; honor and cyber. Honor vira are real vira, which are super rare and have bronze strings. Like a fingerprint, each one is different, and even though they can be interchanged, they work best with their original owner. Sam demonstrates this by taking off her necklace and giving it to me. I put it on, and I immediately understand what she was talking about. I can only describe the sensation as like trying to push two of the same poles on a magnet together. It just didn't feel right to have on.

Honor vira have a number of different abilities, from summoning tools to giving premonition dreams to even invoking persuasion. She smiles at that last part, which brings feelings of both revenge and uneasiness. *Cyber vira* on the other hand are manufactured, fake copies of vira, which have red strings and can only spray green fire, nothing else. The fire guy must have had a cyber vira, as Nima had said, but his must have had some modifications done to it.

Since my amulet has a silver string, Sam said Nima was pretty confused as to what it means. She was intrigued that it fit me and wondered what it could do, since it apparently isn't an honor vira or a cyber one. The thought of having to meet Nima again makes me uncomfortable.

Sam's right in the middle of voicing her disbelief of the whole situation when Mom walks downstairs.

She immediately switches to a lying mode, "Even after what happened last night it's still hard to believe magic … is the only way to defeat that fourth boss in *Heal Bound: Phoenix*. It's going to take some work, but you can definitely defeat him with enough wind spells!"

She uses her TV commercial voice, and I instantly start struggling to hold back laughter.

Following along with Sam, I do my best weatherman impression, "Oh, thanks Sam! Hey Mom, I didn't see you there."

Mom raises an eyebrow, "I'm taking it you two are on good terms?"

We both nod, grins on our faces. Mom's face goes blank for a second as she seems absorbed in somewhat concerning thoughts, but then she shakes her head, laughs at herself, and claps her hands. This sudden change of moods, especially with that loud clap, startles both Sam and me.

She gives us a funny tilted gaze, smiles oddly, puts her hands on her hips, and says, "Well, that's great. At around 2, we're going over to visit our neighbors. You know, say hi and everything."

Sam shrugs off Mom's weird behavior, and so do I. Instead of chores or something productive, Sam and I play video games for two hours straight, well, after we change clothes. Although it may seem like we've made up, I keep some distance from my sister. I don't want her experimenting with her amulet anymore, especially since I haven't figured out how to work mine.

After the gaming marathon (in memory of my stolen handheld), we meet Mom downstairs, go outside, and walk down the sidewalk to our neighbor's house. Before we can ring the doorbell, we're met with a paper sign taped on the front door. *At the clubhouse.*

The three of us look at each other, not really wanting to walk up the rather steep hill to the clubhouse, but then Mom states, "It's not that far… and it's a pretty nice day today."

After the five-minute trudge, we reach the clubhouse. As soon as we round the side of the building, I remember that I forgot to see what the other side of the clubhouse sign read. Meh, if I'm going to be living here, I'll probably read it one day.

Mom enters the key code (she learned it last night at the housewarming party) and we sidestep the small gate. We are greeted with a pool, but instead of seeing just a few people swimming around like I expected, the place is packed. Cheery music rolls over the mass of people swimming or lounging in pool chairs. A group of older gentlemen laugh and joke around the smoking grill. On the far side of the pool is a basketball court, and it looks like both sides are having intense games.

I was about to wonder why there were so many people here, but then Sam comments, "This is one heck of a family reunion."

"How did you know it was a family reunion?" I ask her.

She looks at me, baffled, "Didn't you read the giant purple banner outside?"

Huh, I guessed I must have missed that, too. There is one thing I don't miss, however, and that's how awkward our arrival is. Everyone here is African American, so Sam, Mom and I stick out like sore thumbs. A few people adjacent to the basketball court begin staring at us, concerned, and some people playing in the pool give us confused glances.

"Um… you sure we should be here?" Sam asks Mom. I can hear the embarrassment in her voice.

"Well, I thought that we… oh, here she is!" Mom looks toward an approaching middle-aged woman and her husband.

"Rebecca! How are you?" The woman greets.

"I'm doing great, thank you! I just wanted to stop by so I could introduce my kids to yours."

The woman's smile turns from forced to relieved, "Oh good! Why don't you stay for a little while? We have plenty of food…"

Mom raises her eyebrows, then turns to Sam and I. Sam raises her eyebrows in a similar way and looks at me. This is too socially awkward for me to handle, so as a default response, I nod. Sam and Mom both smile, but I can't read what type of smile it is.

"Great. Come on inside."

We follow them inside, where swaths of other middle-aged women and elderly people are sitting back and talking. The conversations grow a bit less chatty once we enter, but they continue nonetheless. Mom, Sam, and I are treated to their buffet spread of chicken, macaroni and cheese, collards, and other cookout foods. We load our plates and sit down with the woman and her husband. Mom and the woman talk a lot about the neighborhood and such, while Sam and I just focus on finishing our food.

Once all three of us finish our delicious meals, we follow the woman and her husband back outside. To my surprise, introducing ourselves is actually not that bad, and after we've met the young and old around the pool, I feel much more comfortable. Mom is saying her goodbyes to the woman when, in the distance, I hear a splash. I ignore it since I'm too caught up in the basketball game on the other side of the pool, but it must have caught Sam's attention. Her eyebrows raise in disbelief.

"Matt… let's go over to the pool really quick." Sam commands.

I glance at the host lady and my mom, then follow Sam to the pool's edge. Swimming around there is a familiar looking guy who we hadn't been introduced to. He wasn't in the pool before, so he must've been inside or something, earlier.

Wow, he looks really familiar. He was… one of the teenagers in my dream?! No, wait, yes! Yes he was! Although it's hard to recall, I'm positive he was one of the well-dressed people in that weird skeleton fighting dream I had last night. This is so bizarre; he's right here, swimming in front of me and chatting with family members. This is crazy.

"I know this is going to be weird to say, but that guy was in a dream I had." I whisper to Sam.

Sam and I slowly turn our heads until our eyes meet.

"You creep!" Sam spits, her face filling with disgust. I start to feel embarrassed, but she smiles and slaps me on the shoulder.

"I'm just playing with you. He was in my dream too." She says, then adds, "This is just too bizarre."

The boy turns around. He has big brown eyes with strange, gray outlines, and chocolate skin. His lips are pulled back in a friendly smile, revealing some of his milky white teeth. He's lean, with pretty decent arms and abs. I can't see through the water correctly, but his legs are probably toned as well. He has beady, midnight black hair and green swim trunks. At first, I thought he was treading water with no hands, but then I realize he's standing.

"Hey, how's it going?" The guy asks. He has a kind, rich voice.

I look back at my mother, who is seemingly running on fumes with her goodbye.

Sam notices too, saying, "Good. I'm Samantha and this is Matthew… we'll have to catch up later."

He nods saying, "I'm Yoseph by the way. See you around."

We return to Mom's side, and almost a second later, we're back out of the pool gate. Mom relays how interesting her conversations were with Yoseph's mother as we make our way to our next neighbor. Those neighbors have a pretty small family, but I met a new friend, an Asian guy named Aaron.

****

This week, things were mostly normal. The day after our neighbor visits, Sam and I went back to get Aaron and Yoseph's contact info. Sometimes we'd chill with the two of them at the clubhouse, other times we'd play video games. On Wednesday, we spent the day at an outdoor mall down in Huntsville with Yoseph.

Everything was great until today, Friday. Yoseph, Sam, and I are biking through the forest. Aaron would've come, but he felt sick. Our parents let us do this, but loaded us with safety; cell phones, GPS, snacks, water, first aid, and extras of everything. We start off by coasting down the neighborhood's steep hill, then ride along the sidewalk, pass the shimmering blue lake, through the pretty lower half of our neighborhood, and then onto a forest trail.

We ride diagonally; I'm leading the pack, Sam's in the middle, and Yoseph's at the back. We ride for a good mile, enjoying the earthy forest air, the sparkling sunlight peeking through the treetops above, and the calm breeze brushing our faces. Everything rushes by so smoothly thanks to this surprisingly even trail.

After about fifteen minutes, I start to think I hear a noise. It's like a bird cawing… no, those are words. Someone is calling out for us? Who could it be? It's not Aaron, because it's a female's voice. It's not our moms' either, because it's not mature enough. It's more like a teen girl's.

At first, I think I'm just making something out of nothing, but then Sam asks, "Hey, do you hear somebody?" I hear the light squeak of brakes and follow suit, slowing myself to a stop. Sam coasts by me, then brakes herself. The three of us look off into the distance, trying desperately to figure out what that noise is or what its saying. However, after one more cry, it stops. All that's left is the sound of wind hushing through trees.

I look at Sam, who looks just as perplexed, then Yoseph says, "Yo guys, what the heck?"

We look in the direction he's looking, which happens to be the direction we just came from. A purple and green figure is seemingly gliding on air towards us. I look back at Sam, who perks up. Oh boy, here we go again. As soon as Nima gets in earshot, she begins walking while she speaks. I'm not quite sure what she was doing before, but it sure wasn't walking.

"For an instant, I had believed that I would have to amplify my voice indefinitely!" She says.

A wave of discomfort washes over me as the alien comes into detail; she's just, not… right-looking. The fact that her voice sounds like a text-to-speech program just makes things more uncomfortable. I see Yoseph's face; wide-eyed and smeared in terror and confusion. Her milky gray eyes catch mine for a brief moment, and then she looks at Sam.

"I adjure… recommend you pursue me. The amulets I gave you have special abilities, and I will need you to use them and assist me with preventing a catastrophe."

With that, she walks off into the woods. Sam looks at Yoseph and I, shrugs, and then follows Nima, wheeling her bike at her side. I take one look at Yoseph and I can tell he's as equally doubtful of this situation as I am.

In this moment, I made a decision that will not only affect my life but the lives of everyone around me forever. With this single decision, I threw my very existence into one of adventure and horror alike. If I were to have followed my gut and stayed on the trail with Yoseph, we could have lived normal, safe, enjoyable lives.

But I didn't. Instead, I reassured him. I don't even remember what I said to him because I didn't believe it myself, but it must have worked. Next thing I know, the two of us are walking our bikes through the woods, following the girls. Such wild things are ahead of us.

Nima and Sam round the base of a hill, cross a gurgling brook, and after a clearing or two, we are greeted with an enormous dome of vines. It's about the size of my two-story house. Nima and Sam vanish casually behind the curtain of green, but Yoseph and I stop dead in our tracks.

"Uh, do you really think we should follow them?" I ask.

"I don't know," replies Yoseph.

After a long pause, Yoseph mounts his bike and says, "Well, you got me this far. I'm not about to be the one explaining why everyone else is missing."

He bikes off into the jade hemisphere. I'm almost compelled to bike off after him with that logic, because I would hate to see the bad side of his sweet and friendly mother, but something stops me. I stand there for a while, debating if I should go with my friends or wait for them to come back out and retrieve me.

Even though Yoseph has a good point, I just can't muster up the courage to enter the vine dome. Forget it; I decide the safer option and start to wait. I'm watching a squirrel make its way around the forest floor when suddenly, there is a rumbling blast from inside the green dome, and a shockwave then washes everything outward in a blue hue. What was that?! Out of curiosity, I look behind me to see the most unimaginable thing.

The color is being sucked out of the forest. Tendrils of emerald, brown, blue, and a thousand other colors swirl and streak across the sky. The sky itself rapidly gets darker, as if it's approaching nighttime, yet the sun stays right where it is. Even the trees are bursting into swarms of color, and the vibrant particles that result are being sucked into the vine dome.

WHAT.

My heart hammers in my chest as adrenaline courses through my veins. Before I know it, I am back on my bike and into the dome. I can't see anything but green-blue vines raining down and patches of white on the ground, but I can still feel the rumbling. Bobbing and weaving through jade columns, my bike whirs loudly at its top speed.

After a while, the ground takes a sharp decrease. I pick up a dangerous amount of speed. The wheels begin to protest even louder as my speed increases, gravity working in harmony with my vicious pedaling. I would usually take my feet off the pedals because at this point they would be going too fast, but with all of the energy in me right now, I manage to pump as fast as the bike tells me to. I can't think up an excuse for this. It's too complex for a dream and nothing else explains it.

I finally clear the dome and start riding back on flat land. Looking wide-eyed, I see this extremely elaborate tree house with Nima, Yoseph, and Sam standing next to its trunk in a small patch of shaded flowers. Near them is a colorful, impossibly two-dimensional oval, violently swirling and suspended above the ground. The others urgently beckon for me to hurry.

I look up in the sky and spot a spinning diamond ring. This ring isn't just any diamond ring. It is literally a ring made of diamonds, and on the top is this golden pearl, in which all of the particles of color from earlier are being sucked into. I would actually consider it a bracelet, because it's so big, it could probably fit around my wrist.

The sky is almost black with the sun still shining harshly. Stars litter the sky, although it's around noon. Patches of the ground dissipate into pixel-like clouds of color, being sucked into the ring soon after. What's left behind is only blank, white sand. This doesn't make any sense. All I can do is just keep pedaling.

I ride my bike as fast as humanly possible, with more white sand replacing the forest floor around me. Yoseph, Sam, and Nima turn towards the oval, heaving their bikes inside and then leaping in afterward. So, the oval's a portal? Alright, good. Now, instead of hellish confusion, I have a goal; just get in that portal. As soon as I decide this, the portal's surface begins to waver like it's a pond that had a stone thrown in it. Oh great.

Whatever is left of my surroundings are a blur as I hurriedly reach the portal. My bike becomes lighter. I look back to see my hind wheels starting to flow away with the rest of the color. No! I quickly jump off of the bike. In one fluid motion, I pick the thing up with inhuman strength and chuck it into the portal. I leap up myself and hook my right arm into the portal. Before I hoist the rest of my body over into this nonsensical pit of colors, I look behind me to see what has become of the forest.

Everything as far as I can see is flat, snow-like sand. The bleak landscape is void of anything, and the only thing aside from the sand is the black sky, filled with more stars than I thought existed. It looks nice, but I'm not sticking around any longer. I throw myself into the portal, falling about 50 feet into a sea of pink dots.

All around me are pulsing, bright colors fading between lime green and pink and electric blue that twist into black infinities at any angle I look. I look upside-down at my friends, who are flailing and floating forward. Purple and indigo hexagons flicker across the existence of what could be this place's sky… or it could be the ground… or both, and different flashes and shapes seem to press textures into my eyes. I feel super dizzy and groggy, and the impulse to faint is like trying to hold back throw up. Nothing feels real; I can't feel the dots, but yet I can. At this point I just hope I live through this.

The last thing I see is a blinding flash of yellow in the far distance, a big shockwave, and then the dots began to swirl crazily, flipping me violently in a wide spiral.

CHAPTER 5

A WHOLE NEW WORLD

~ SAMANTHA ~

The first thing I notice as soon as I come to is that my back is killing me! Even though it feels like I'm lying on the ground, I'm actually on a bed of leaves. The leaves feel like finished wood, but flexible… a bit too flexible to make a bed out of. I am lying on my back, of course, with my arms to my side and my hair tickling my neck. My backpack serves as a very uncomfortable pillow. I silently sit up just a little to stretch my neck and get a better look at my surroundings.

It looks like I'm in a brownish-green tent with a pretty big rock in the middle, playing the role of a main support shaft. It takes me a few moments to realize that the tent is made of enormous leaves, much larger than the skateboard-sized ones I'm lying on. That must explain why there is a rock as the support shaft. The opening to my left invites in harsh daylight.

I blink a few times and look around. Yoseph is curled up near the opening and Nima is resting on the other side of me. I can't see Matt. I go to crawl out of this… hut, but then immediately go back to being rigid as I hear footsteps outside of the tent. Oh crap.

I move my head to look at the entrance and it ruffles my backpack. I only have seconds to decide to fake sleep before the leaf wall on my side is flung back. Although I try as hard as I can to resist, my eyes flash open.

"Stop messing with them you stinking animals!" The boy commands, standing over top of me.

He stops his random brouhaha when he notices there aren't any pests, just me, staring at him. A relieved smile quickly replaces his scowl, but I keep my surprised look. The boy is moderately tall, with a soft face the color of coffee beans. His large eyes are a curious brown, and surrounding them is a thin layer of indigo. He's near bald, with a tiny layer of curly, onyx hair to make up for it. He has on some gray pajamas, and a random band of lighter skin runs across his forehead. Must be a birthmark or something. We stare a little longer, and then he says,

"Y-you're awake?"

I give a small nod, trying not to stare at his odd birthmark.

"Are you feeling well?" He asks politely. I nod.

"Do you speak?!" He questions, making a big, table-flipping gesture with his hands.

I laugh lightly, and he decides to sit down next to me. The discoloration slides up his forehead as he kneels. That's not a birthmark, but rather… a really faint ring of light? The ring slowly floats down after him, then stops around his forehead like before. Is that… a halo?

He probably must've noticed my look, because then, "Oh… yeah. I'm… I'm sort of dead." He replies as if he was admitting to slacking off or something.

Icy cold sweat stabs through me. Did I die in that portal... or can I just see dead people? Nevertheless, creepy dread fills the pit of my stomach; I can just hear him saying '*And so are you*' in a hollow voice. He speaks again, cutting off my worries.

"You're not crazy! Trust me; other people can see me, too. I'm kind of real, see?

He holds out his palm. I press mine against his, connecting them. I sigh in relief, though I'm now confused.

"I would lie to you and say I'm an angel, but I'm not. I'm actually a spirit from Hades… care if I explain?" He asks.

"Go right ahead." I reply, interested to see where this goes.

"Okay, so I died, right? And I was doing what all dead people do, sleeping and waiting for… um… actually, that might be a little too heavy for you. Don't worry about it kid, okay?"

We both share an awkward laugh, then he continues, "So I'm in this amazing nap and then suddenly *BAM*. The warmth and darkness and beach noises are gone and I'm standing in the middle of some throne room with this woman dressed as a queen smiling at me. So obviously I ask her what's going on. She tells me if I want to go back to sleep, I have to shake her hand. Biggest mistake of my afterlife. She'd never employed a spirit before, so the terms for my release were super general. Apparently, I have to do either one-thousand good things or ten bad things to decide whether I go back to Hades or get sent to Gehenna, which is a fiery, torturous pit of eternal suffering."

I grit my teeth at his rather extreme fate, and he laughs.

"Yeah, great thing to wake up to after a few decades of sleeping. Just this random woman gambling your entire existence so that you must 'do good in the world', which was really just her way of making me spend time with her daughter. I mean, she's a nice kid, so I guess it isn't too bad."

"Isn't it hard keeping track? Well, if you're going down the not-fiery path?" I ask.

"Oh wow, you're actually paying attention! Most people just tune me out. But to answer your question, no. I just keep doing good things and one of these days I'll return to that nap."

I nod, and then silence ensues as I digest this information. A dreadful thought enters my head, and then I decide to go ahead and cut to the chase.

"Am I dead too?"

He stares at me with a solemn look in his eyes, and his lips curl into one of those regretful half-frowns. An empty disappointment starts to fill my chest, but then he cracks a smile. I look at him, confused, and he lets out a few chuckles.

"No, you're not dead. I just wanted to see how you'd react!"

I give him a scornful smile as he chuckles a bit more, then we both look off into the distance.

Suddenly he says, "Oh right, you must be hungry. Would you like for me to catch some fish for you?"

I go to naturally and politely decline, but then I realize the newly growing pain in my stomach and accept instead. He rises and walks off, and I take this opportunity to reflect. This ghost dude seems like a pretty nice guy. He doesn't scare me as he probably will scare Matt or Yoseph. I mean, I became pretty chill friends with Nima and she's... something else. The unknown has never really been that terrifying to me, I like it actually. I'd make the perfect horror movie candidate, wouldn't I?

The sounds of nature and distant splashing from Ghost Boy are the only things to occupy me. Instead of blankly staring off into the forest, I decide to think back on the crazy stuff that happened back in Alabama. Nima was rummaging around her awesome treehouse looking for something, and as soon as Yoseph showed up, she found it. It was this weird looking jewel bracelet.

She also found yet another honor vira and gave it to Yoseph, then she told the two of us about the bracelet, and how it was a special ring called the *Mundatorite* that was thrust on her by an evil prince named Kyndule Yatniv. She said she brought us into the forest because the ring had mystic and dark powers, and something else about assembling heroes to destroy it. I don't know, I sort of spaced out.

I distinctly remember Nima walking it over to us so we could get a better look, but as soon as it got close, the pearl part of the Mundatorite let loose a shock wave of blue energy. It sliced out in every direction without warning, throwing us back and destroying the room's windows. After having a warped, violent flying spasm, the ring darted out one of the windows, and the three of us headed out of the treehouse.

Outside, the Mundatorite was spinning incredibly fast and absorbing… like, color itself or something. I don't know exactly what the heck was happening, but Nima said that "the essence of the planet was being captured" so I'm assuming it was bad.

Forceful spikes of pure color blasted up from the ring from time to time, but it would only last for a second before a spike was sucked back in, spraying rainbow sparkles everywhere. Although the ring was stealing our planet's essence, which is a bad thing, it looked pretty freaking sick.

So anyway, Yoseph and I grabbed our bikes as the ring started to vibrate. A color spike shot out of the ring and exploded onto the ground, melting into an oval instantly. Then, thin as a sheet of paper, it flipped up and locked in place, suspended in the air. Needless to say, if I wasn't confused before, I was then.

Nima tried to explain that it was a portal that led to her home planet, Arret, but it was near impossible to catch what she was saying over the sounds of colors being sucked out of everything. Matt zoomed out of the tree line, tailing us as we filed through the wormhole.

I look up to see Ghost Boy coming back from wherever he'd gone, carrying three wriggling and purplish fish with some sticks tucked into his belt. He cradles the unwieldy animals as he shuffles his way over to a small campfire I'd just noticed. He barely gets to the firepit before the fish slip from his grasp, but luckily, they plop right onto the dying embers. With a large hiss of steam, the fish stop moving. Ghost Boy looks at the fish, horrified, then glances at me and tries to put on a confident smile like he meant for it to happen. I laugh, and then he begins to prepare the fish and revive the fire.

While he's cooking, I decide to take a look around. Everything looks normal; there's a reddish-orange fall forest with taller, brown, jungle trees in the background, bright blue skies, fluffy white clouds, a beautiful sun, and a seemingly deep lake with calm, green-brown water. I head over to Ghost Boy and ask him where we are. He tells me we're a few kilometers outside of Hillsgatha, *Fiponik*. I've never heard of Fiponik before, and I let him know that. For some reason, Ghost Boy seems surprised by this, because he says Fiponik is one of the most influential countries in the world. Out of curiosity, I ask the name of the planet, and he looks at me with a strange look.

"It's Arret." He says as though that's common knowledge, which I guess it should be.

I can recall Nima talking briefly about Arret after she'd talked about Yatniv. It's a planet in the same galaxy as Earth but nowhere near it. Oh snap… so that must mean that ring, the Mundatorite, actually sucked up the entirety of Earth. Like, the whole thing. Yikes, that's bad.

Ghost Boy finishes cooking and serves me the fish. I devour them. Either they were really good, or I was really hungry. He advises that we get some more fish for the others since they should be waking up soon, so we do. While we're fishing (well, he's fishing with his bare hands and I'm just watching) I get to know his name; Virrel.

Once the rest of the group awakens, Virrel explains to them what he explained to me. The fact that he's a ghost doesn't really faze Matt, and Yoseph seems more freaked out that we're on a different planet. The whole ordeal kind of confuses Nima; she doesn't seem like the paranormal type.

After Yoseph and Nima calm down, Virrel goes on to explain why we were so hungry when we woke up; we've been out cold for two days. He was originally in these woods on a mission to chase down a destructive monster and stop it from returning to his employer's homeland. Once he found us knocked out in the middle of the forest, he thought he'd look after us as well.

Of course, we ask him what the monster is like and where it went, but Virrel has never seen the beast. He only knows that it's mindlessly destructive and it lives extremely close by. Needless to say, that puts the rest of us on edge. I have a feeling we're going to be involved in that confrontation.

The others finish their fish-on-a-stick, and then Virrel kindly offers us a job. His employer is the daughter of the queen who summoned him; she's the current empress of some nearby islands. They always have more positions open in her group of guards. He does his work for free, but *living* employees are paid very well, apparently. Matt, Yoseph, and I aren't quite sure what we're supposed to be doing aside from maybe finding that Mundatorite ring or something, so we leave the talking to Nima.

"Actually Virrel, we have a quest of our own to complete. Before our friendship continues any longer, you must know this one fact; we are aliens."

Virrel blankly stares at Nima, then looks at me and a lightbulb goes off (or in his case I guess it would be a halo).

"So, is that why you'd never heard of Fiponik?" He reasons.

"Precisely." Nima answers for me.

"You four look pretty normal for aliens… but I guess whatever suits you works for me." Virrel concludes.

Nima pulls a map from her back pocket and unfolds it.

"Here marks our current location." She says, pointing to a section in the lower left corner.

As soon as I get a glimpse of it, I start blinking madly. At first I thought the holographic-looking red dot on the map was a trick of the light, but Nima confirms that the red dot represents us. Just like Virrel had said, we're in a place called the Hillsgatha Territory, right next to the blue dot that is Hillsgatha Lake. If we were to travel a town or two north, we would reach the border of a providence called Saint Markus. That providence has three big cities: Tapadim, Quepora, and Markus Square.

Smaller towns swarm them and trail off into the more uninhabited blank space. There is also a blacked-out town called '*Hillsgatha Square*'. It's so far left on the map that it's nearly cut off by the country border. To our east is Mirthoaten Gulf, which is massive and littered with about a dozen islands. Virrel leans in and points to one of the biggest islands, Peritari. That is his employer's homeland.

Night falls, and at first we think about going into a nearby town and trying to get a room at an inn, but then we remember that we have no money (or at least no valid money). Because of this, we decide to just camp out here, and Virrel joins us.

****

I relax in my part of the tent, scrolling through the notes on my phone. Two weeks have gone by in a flash since we first landed on Arret, and before we start our journey to get back home, I want to take a moment to actually digest all of it.

My phone's battery is dishearteningly low, but that doesn't worry me like it normally would. I obviously have no signal and no WiFi, so it's pretty much only useful for notes and pictures. Speaking of which, let's see what we have here.

I went ahead and split the weeks up into four parts, since that's luckily how they seemed to work out in real time. I'm not sure if someone planned it this way or if it just happened, but nonetheless, here we are.

Week One Part One:

- Not a dream? Freak out a lot
- Two moons? Continue to freak out
- Not freaking out? Double anti-freak out?

Even though no one is awake, I can feel my face reddening with embarrassment. Yeah, the first part of week one definitely wasn't the best. Yoseph, Matt, and I were pretty calm on the initial day because we hadn't really processed everything that was going on. I'm not sure about the boys, but I personally thought this was all a strange dream or something that would somehow blow over.

I remember that first night. I had a weird mixture of panic and empty reassurance in my mind, and I was trying to laugh and joke a lot until this whole thing returned to normal. I noticed how bright it was for night and looked up. Glowing in front of the countless, unfamiliar constellations was not one but *two* moons. I can't remember the moon phases right now; I know one was full, and the other was a... waning gibbous I think. Either way, I was really fighting panic then.

Going to sleep and waking up the next morning still on Arret didn't go too well for our psyches. Lots of crying, screaming, cursing, flipping out, that sort of stuff. Looking back on it, I actually feel pretty sorry for Virrel and Nima. They just had to sit there uncomfortably for like four days straight and watch us have breakdowns and existential crises (crises? crisises? crisii? I don't know).

Strangely, on the fourth day, all of our panic went away. I distinctly remember it, waking up to a brisk morning and feeling… peace? I don't know what it was or why it happened, but when I left the tent and surveyed the dew-covered forest, I felt calmer than I have in quite some time. It's like, I don't know, I just *understood.* I'm not sure it's possible to describe, really. The boys woke up feeling the same way, and the three of us have been quite normal ever since.

Yoseph said he'd been praying a bunch, so maybe it was that. Or maybe something inside us broke and we're all crazy. Honestly, I think it might be a bit of both. We were so calm that we actually started to panic about not being panicked.

Nima and Virrel were surprised and probably a little concerned too, but nevertheless, we moved on to the latter half of the first week.

CHAPTER 6

CASUAL MAGIC WEAPONS

~ SAMANTHA ~

eek One Part Two:

- Persuasion gets free food
- Matt and Yoseph are crybabies
- leri Tropo map is sick

I can feel a devilish grin growing on my face at this, and it almost makes me laugh. The persuasion ability our amulets give us (they give us a lot of powers, really, but I'll get to that later) should have never been entrusted to me. On the fourth day, once the weird calmness had settled over everything, Nima and Virrel decided to discuss their plans with us.

A big part of the plan was going around and gathering as much info as we could on current events. No one knew where the Mundatorite went after the whole Earth fiasco, so Nima wanted to go around locally to see if any news or rumors had spread about it. Virrel used this time to gather info about his monster as well.

We spent most of the time during those days traveling on foot, having chats on people's porches, and making grocery store runs. It was also during those days that Nima showed off just how awesome our persuasion is. During the conversations, she would word her questions perfectly, and information would flow out of our hosts, sometimes even to their confusion.

Apparently, all of the food we'd eaten over the past week had also come from the persuasion ability. Nima had used it to convince many of the nearby grocers and restaurants to give her any food they couldn't use or didn't want. That explained why we always had oddly normal food like bread and milk for meals instead of, I don't know, grass?

She let us know that, unfortunately, persuasion doesn't work very well in instances were money is involved or if there are multiple people, so she could only score us some bottom-of-the-barrel, next-day-it's-rotten food. I didn't mind, though, and the boys didn't seem to either. Virrel also helped us catch crabs and fish in the lake, and they were certainly delicious.

At night sometimes, Matt, Yoseph, and I would go outside and gaze at the sky. We would have put our feet in the water, but the lake was too cold, so we just sat next to it instead, talking about our families all the while. Cheesy, but I admit: I missed my mom (and still do), which makes me want to find this Mundatorite ring even more. Speaking of the lake, it's grown and now actually surrounds us, so we're technically on an island. Virrel and Nima seemingly shrugged this fact off, so the rest of us did too.

Under the starry skies and with the toasty warmth of the fire glowing at my back, those nights by the lake and the days before them helped Yoseph, Matt, and I adjust to our new environment.

We got to see how normal this planet is, how regular all the people are, and how fathomable our goal is, even though we really didn't know it back then.

Speaking of goals, that's where the Ieri Tropo comes in. It's pretty much a GPS on paper. I remember at the campfire before the second week started, Nima pulled out the map she'd shown us on the first day and explained it to us. She'd had it way back when she'd first lived on the planet, but she didn't use it often. Pretty much, the Ieri Tropo is a magic map that helps people by showing them routes to take, clues to think about, and items they should get.

It's really trippy to look at, since when I do, all of the information pops off of the map like I have 3D glasses on. According to Nima, it only works for people with honor vira (I guess that's yet another power to the list!), which explains why Virrel says he doesn't see anything outside of a country map. I spent most of dinner that night drinking in all of the information.

I remember a red marker in the forest, which indicated our position, and a golden ticket called the *Golden Taste Ticket* floating right beside it. Under the title were stats about the item itself and details about the item's location. It even had a distance counter and a wobbly, holographic compass at the top that turned when the map did. A dashed line led from the ticket to one of the big cities in Saint Markus, Tapadim, where a bowl of rainbow orbs sat. After that, the line trailed off towards what looks like a giant cloud… or maybe a big forest? I'm not sure, but I do know that I call dibs on map holding for the rest of the journey.

Week Two Part One:

- Just follow the Ieri Tropo
- Yatniv is big bad guy
- Weird alien stuff everywhere

My eager smile fades as I recall the start of last week. Nothing particularly bad happened, but we did receive a lot of info on the world around us and the plan for getting the Mundatorite back. Virrel and Nima thought it would be pretty important to fill us in on the culture of this alien country, Fiponik, so that we wouldn't stick out like sore thumbs.

First, Nima wanted to solidify our plan of attack. She suspects that that evil prince she told us about, Great Sir Kyndule Yatniv, is behind all of the Mundatorite madness, so we'd probably be confronting him in the latter stages of our adventure to get it back. He's actually the dictator of the country we're in, so that's a thing too I guess. She told us not to panic, though, because if we were to follow the Ieri Tropo to the T and pick up what we need, everything should work out (relatively) fine.

Just so that we understood how terrible of a person Yatniv is, Nima told us the story about how he destroyed her home village. Well, she didn't really go into detail, she just pretty much said that it happened and she was the opposite of happy about it. I remember Yoseph was super confused that Yatniv would destroy a part of his own country, but Virrel and Nima told us that yep, Yatniv is just crazy like that. Great, of course the Mundatorite wouldn't end up in the hands of a sweet old lady or something. I guess that would make life too easy.

Virrel explained that Yatniv did a similar destroy-his-own-territory thing to one of the oldest villages in the world, called Hillsgatha. Apparently, these vira necklaces that we have grow on super rare, biennial magic trees, and Yatniv had a nightmare about one. Subsequently, he thought "*screw it, I'm the dictator*" and destroyed all the ones in his country. Hillsgatha was a bit too protective of theirs, so he wiped out the town with it. Nima looked oddly uncomfortable during the whole story, but when we asked her, she said it was because that was the tree she'd gotten our vira from.

Around the middle of last week, Nima and Virrel explained some of the cultural aspects of this planet, since our adventure is bound to take us through the heart of the nation. One of my favorite "lessons" was about the diversity of intelligent species on Arret. I know it sounds boring but it was actually pretty bizarre.

This planet's original inhabitants were, get this, blue humanoids with pink hair called the woodish. I swear I'm not making this up. Anyway, after a long, undisturbed supremacy, these guys encountered the democs, which is Nima's race. The democ planet (I forgot its name) had just been annihilated by some scientific cosmic phenomena (forgot that name too) and all the democs were begging for the woodish to let them stay on Arret. The woodish allowed the democs to stay but, surprisingly, the democs became the suppressed race and have been getting the bad end of the stick ever since.

A few generations went by and then humans showed up. No one really knows how we got here. Nima agrees with the theory that humans evolved from some local animals, but Virrel believes we came to Arret via supernatural means. Despite our origins not being clear, we aren't seen as mysterious, but rather, adorable. Socially, or at least in a few Arretian countries (namely Fiponik), humans aren't seen as people, but as the equivalent to children, even throughout adulthood.

What really baffles me is that we've somehow been perfectly fine with that for the thousand or so years we've lived here. So that means once we get to civilization, people will look at me like I'm a little girl? Trust me, I will punch the first person that stops me to play "Peek-a-boo".

Anyway, the population across the planet and in Fiponik is pretty even, with about 35 percent woodish, 33 percent democ, and 32 percent human. Each species also has their own races, so it isn't rare to see both interracial and inter-specie relationships; things get a bit confusing if we get too technical. When we were canvasing the area for info, I saw a few democs, but I'm honestly kind of excited to adventure out and see what else we can find on our way to the Mundatorite.

Week Two Part Two:

- Switchblade = shield
- Mental punch = star coins
- Mental stretch = hover star

My smile returns as I read this. The last few days have been absolutely sick. Mainly because Nima showed us how to summon *freaking weapons from thin air.* Yes, absolutely epic, I know. Well, they aren't 'weapons' per say; Nima called them 'tools' because "our abilities should only be used for good, and while 'weapons' are used for destruction, our 'tools' should be used for construction". Lame, right? Because I was *definitely* looking forward to killing millions with my new powers.

The grin on my face grows as I remember the day in crisp detail. Nima had told us to concentrate on an "engaging emotion", so I was standing there thinking about that one time a few mean girls from two grades up tried to jump my friend Juliana back in middle school. My blood was boiling almost instantly, and then it felt like my body was a switchblade and I just pressed my own button. In an odd rush, I felt the air shift around my left arm. When I opened my eyes, boom, it's a freaking shield.

I thought it was going to be something lame like a gardening spade or sonic hearing, but I was delightfully wrong. The shield was shiny and black with silver swirls hugging the edges and a bright, reflecting, neon yellow star in the middle. Purple 'S's surrounded the star, making a pentagon. I remember it being a comfortable weight; not too heavy yet not too light, and it's slightly top-heaviness seemed perfect on my arm.

I took a few threatening swings and listened to its heavy whoosh, then tried to fight back a witch's cackle and looked around to see what everyone else had. I was pretty jealous when I saw Yoseph, beaming, holding a 6-foot wooden pole with a flaming blade at the end. Then I looked over at Matt and almost crapped my pants. My little brother, to my horror, was casually holding a wickedly sharp machete. The entire thing was made of solid white ice, mist spiraling slowly in the breeze, and what looked like little sparks of electricity were bursting here and there around the blade. It was, and still is, the stuff of nightmares.

Nima summoned her tools for us to see. Surprisingly, they were two long, dangerous-looking green sickles. They don't look like they fit Nima at all. She's smart and cunning and looks like the type of person to use a ranged weapon, like a spear or bladed frisbee. But the way she twirled those incredibly dangerous sickles gave me the impression that she knew what she was doing. To make our tools disappear, we had to "internally desire" for them to go away. As an example, Nima casually looked at one of her blades and it vanished.

Out of nowhere, it reappeared as a white silhouette for a second before snapping back to normal. She explained that after we first learned to summon and retract our tools, doing it again would take little to no effort at all. We simply had to think it back into existence. I did as she said, telling myself I didn't need my shield anymore, and sure enough, it simply wasn't there. Surprised, I thought about the switchblade feeling again and my shield appeared immediately, white and then normal. Absolutely sick.

We played around with our wea… I mean tools for the rest of the day, and then ate dinner and crashed. When we woke up the next day, everyone was hype that their powers were actually real and not part of a weird dream. I know it seems like we should've just went ahead and accepted reality at face value around that point, but hey, stuff like this is still pretty hard to wrap my head around. Even now I don't believe it, and I've been using my powers for three days!

Anyway, the second day of weapon training focused on our secondary power. As I said before, our vira gives us a stupidly high amount of abilities. I'm still smiling now because I can't believe just how loaded we are! So Nima tells us that the secondary powers aren't as straightforward as the tools, so we'd have to figure them out on our own. Bummer, right? Wrong; we figure them out in like ten minutes.

Yoseph's, unsurprisingly, is shooting fire out of his hands and feet. After a few tests, each gentler but still as hazardous as the last, we determined that he shouldn't do any more practicing in the grass or by the trees. As for me, it was pretty weird. Through very embarrassing, excitement-drunken attempts to lift things with my mind, partially as a joke, I discovered that I can shoot star-shaped coins of light out of my hands. I can do this by… well, punching beyond my body. It's like a mental punch, except I'm imagining myself continuously pushing forward out of my body and through the air. Yeah, it's pretty trippy.

Matt doesn't seem to have a secondary power (thank goodness!) and Nima already showed us hers on Earth, which was the cool levitating wind thing she did back on the bike trail. While on the topic of powers, Nima describes our last ability: immunity. Our amulets grant us invincibility to the element we control. That means Matt can't get frostbite, Yoseph can't get burned by fire, and I… well, I don't really know. Maybe I can stare at the sun now or something; I haven't tried.

Yesterday was our last day in camp. On that day, Yoseph and I taught ourselves how to fly. I know, it sounds ridiculous, and to be honest, we were just joking around at that point. Our thought process was, hey, we can do all this other stuff, why not fly? Yoseph's was obvious: rocket feet. We were all still pretty surprised that it worked.

Mine was different, though. Soon enough, I found out that if I imagine myself as one of the star coins, then mentally stretch out all of my limbs, I could control the star coin's size. I can also guide its direction with my mind, too, by simply plotting out where I think it should go. So, in conclusion, I can make a big, star-shaped boogie board that floats around in the air. I've only ridden it like three times because it's terrifying, but I can do it nonetheless!

So that means, all and all, we can summon tools, use secondary powers, have premonition dreams, invoke persuasion on people, resist the element we control, *and* read the Ieri Tropo. On top of that, Yoseph and I can *fly*. Overpowered, right? Honestly, I don't think this Yatniv guy is going to stand a chance!

We'll have that Mundatorite back before we know it.

Chapter 7

Water Lasers

~ Samantha ~

This is probably the last time I'll be able to use my phone. I scan over the list of notes one more time before shutting my phone off.

Week One Part One:

- Not a dream? Freak out a lot
- Two moons? Continue to freak out
- Not freaking out? Double anti-freak out?

Week One Part Two:

- Persuasion gets free food
- Matt and Yoseph are crybabies
- Ieri Tropo map is sick

Week Two Part One:

- Just follow the Ieri Tropo
- Yatniv is big bad guy
- Weird alien stuff everywhere

Week Two Part Two:

- Switchblade = shield
- Mental punch = star coins
- Mental stretch = hover star

With a nod, I press and hold the power button until the screen abruptly goes black. Something about that, about shutting off my phone for good, a device that I used to use so much, makes the full weight of everything hit me. Wow, today we actually start our journey to get the Mundatorite and go back home. This is actually happening. Time to go.

I slowly move the leaf from overhead as I let my eyes become adjusted to the light. I then stand up and yawn, taking time to blissfully stretch in every direction. Although it's brisk outside, today is a beautiful day. A melancholy feeling grows as I look at the campgrounds we'll be leaving behind.

I look over to the area where Yoseph and I did our flight training. In that patch of flowers is where I finally beat Virrel at finger jousting (yes, this planet has finger jousting, and it's surprisingly popular). Close by, near those bushes, is where I taught Nima her first cartwheel. I look to the bank on the opposite side of the big lake. Matt and I sat together on that bank, crying and talking about our fears for the future. Last night was a lot more emotional than I'd like to admit.

I give the landscape a sad smile, mentally wishing it well. Soon, everyone else is up; we take down the tent and prepare to leave.

"Alright, before we depart, we require the Golden Taste Ticket." Nima informs, looking at the Ieri Tropo for reassurance.

I remember the Golden Taste Ticket from the map; it's one of the items we'll need on our quest. Though I'm not sure of its purpose, we have breakfast and start searching for the ticket anyway.

After a solid thirty minutes of searching all throughout the woods, we find it sitting peacefully under the rock we used for the tent's support. Needless to say, we all felt incredibly stupid.

The ticket sat upright in what looks like a money capsule someone would use at a bank drive-thru. Since Matt has the most space in his backpack, he carries the capsule. Once he slings the bag over his shoulder, he looks at me. He has a bit of trouble meeting my eyes due to some of the stuff we discussed last night, but I give him a smile and it reassures him.

"Hey, you have the medical supplies, right?" He asks.

"No, Yoseph has them." I report, and Yoseph gives a thumbs up as confirmation.

Our medical supplies are pretty much a pack of alcohol swabs and some gauze.

"Outstanding. I possess the Ieri Tropo. We will depart in... said direction." Nima commands, pointing northwest to a part in the trees.

We take a minute to make sure we have everything before walking to the river's edge. Yoseph, Matt, and I wheel our bikes alongside Nima. We take a few steps before we notice that Virrel is still sitting over by the tent rock.

"What's wrong? Aren't you going to join us?" I ask him, confused.

"I can't. I've got to get rid of the monster and then head back to my empress." He states sadly.

We all stand around in silence, needing to go but not wanting to leave Virrel behind.

"Okay then… we'll help you find the monster. You know what kind of things it likes?" Yoseph tries.

"Well," Virrel starts, "I know it likes shiny things… oh, and wriggling toes. That's why it keeps biting people's legs off first."

We're all stunned silent, and Virrel lets out a chuckle.

"Yeah, this thing is serious."

We all ponder silently until Yoseph tries again, "Aight then. Um, where did the attacks happen?"

Virrel thinks for a bit, then says, "Normally they'd happen to groups of people on the coast. All reports came from people that were near some rock formation at sea. Some people say it's a red beast, but almost everyone says that they hear loud splashes right after an attack."

Matt jumps at a brilliant idea, "What if the beast is a fish? That could explain why it splashes and no one can see it!"

Nima chimes in, somewhat intrigued, "That would also explain the creature's fondness for bright and reflective objects as well as wriggling items it could identify for food."

Virrel shakes his head, "I thought the same thing, but that can't be the case. In some instances, instead of one person being bitten in half, whole groups of people would be found dead in puddles of mud with abrasion wounds on them. Also, if it were a fish, then why would its home be the forest?"

I suddenly become hyper aware of my surroundings and notice the lake in the background.

"Uh, guys… how far is the coast from here?" I ask.

Virrel and Nima look at each other, then Nima says, "Maybe a kilometer or so out. Why?"

"What if it takes a tunnel from the beach to this lake?" I ask, and as soon as I do, I realize how stupid my idea is.

Everyone looks at me in silence, and I can't tell if they're trying to roast me or if they're actually considering what I said. Soon, Virrel chimes in.

"Well, it's worth a shot."

He outstretches his arms towards our tent rock and it begins to float. Right, I forgot. Since Virrel is a ghost, he has telekinesis. I guess that would make sense now that I think about it. Anyway, the rock moseys its way over to the big lake, rises slowly and silently above it, and then suddenly falls.

It connects with the watery surface a few moments later, resulting in a monumental splash. We wait, but nothing happens.

"At least we tri–" before I can finish, there is a distinct tremor in the ground.

It isn't a was-I-the-only-one-who-felt-that tremor but more of an I'm-surprised-I-can-still-stand tremor. As we stumble around, the island jets upward. For a second our feet leave the ground, and when we touch (or flop, rather) back down, the ground starts to bob.

"Y'all gotta chill with this." Yoseph says, panic in his voice.

Everyone stands back up, frantically glaring at Virrel for some morsel of information.

"Oh joy… it's a *Grave Digger.*" Virrel says simply.

Whatever that is, I don't want to stick around to see it!

"You aren't referring to..." Nima immediately calls forth her twin sickles, backing up rapidly to the center of the island.

Virrel yells a huge "RUN!" and we wholeheartedly comply. Yoseph, Matt, and I completely ditch our bikes and sprint to meet Nima in the middle of the island. I then whip back around, trying to look in every direction in search of this Grave Digger thing, but everything seems unnaturally still. I begin to gather thoughts, but they scatter as I witness what happens next.

This enormous, multi-colored whale about the size of a semitruck springs out from the lake's depths and up towards the sky. Cold water blossoms from the jump, raining down on us as we watch in fear. Red and silver scales flash on the whale's body, and a floppy, cyan, mane-like appendage stretches from between its eyes to its purple dorsal fin. It lets out a roaring screech through thick, pink lips, and then crashes back into its pool with the biggest splash I've ever seen. Holy crap.

The island begins bobbing, then starts to jerk as if something is knocking into it from below. I'm so busy looking at the ground and the water for any signs of Grave Digger that I'm caught off guard when Virrel yells, "You guys need to get out of here, I can take this!"

"We refuse to leave you, Virrel!" Nima instantly shouts back as things begin to grow oddly calm again.

Uh, I don't know, Nima. I'm feeling a little half-hearted on this one. Virrel is technically dead, so he's… good, and I am in no condition to fight, seeing that my legs won't stop wobbling enough for me to stand properly.

The island has stilled out significantly, and for a moment, I begin to think the whale retreated, but then the giant fish bursts out of the water again, this time from one of the other three lakes that surround us. Without warning, the entire world flips from beneath me and my face is in the grass. Stunned, I struggle to stand, realizing that the monster must've just tilted the island.

A large shadow flickers overhead, mist sprays, then a giant splash sounds near the other end of the island. I shudder violently, then nearly laugh at the ridiculousness of this situation. I guess fireball wielding super thieves weren't enough; now we have to fight an acrobatic rainbow whale… what is my life right now?!

"Get ready to make a move, everyone! I think it's about to attack this time!" Virrel warns.

My terror is mixed with dread as I press my internal switchblade button. My shield appears onto my arm, and I ready it with a surprisingly still grip. I look at the shield, taking note of its mystic aura and tough finish. Just looking at my tool gives me a much-needed boost of confidence.

Everything stills out again and I notice that my friends are steeling themselves, prepared with their respective tools as well. It seems like they also got a confidence boost, because no one looks like they're on the brink of tears anymore. Things remain motionless for a little while.

"Did it–" Matt is interrupted by a third burst of water at a different lake. I flinch, then get angry at myself for doing so. Now fueled with some self-anger, I raise my hand to shoot some star coins at the whale as it flips through the air. To my surprise, nothing comes out. For a second I panic that I'm losing my powers, but then I remember my training.

Aside from immunity and reading the Ieri Tropo, which is always active, we can't use more than one of our abilities at the same time. I debate trying to will away my shield in place for star coins, but before I can, the beast somehow spins, still airborne, and shoots this thick, pressured beam of water from its mouth.

The beam violently ploughs through the ground like it's wet season. It rushes forward, much faster than I had anticipated, and as it speeds closer, I can see how much deadly force is behind that water stream. Smartly, I decide to spring out of the way rather than block it, and the death beam barely misses me, sending mud and sod exploding from the land. It leaves a three-foot-deep trench in its wake.

At this point, I honestly think we're screwed.

I expect to hear the splash of the beast returning underwater, but I don't. Looking where the whale would have landed, I see it hovering just over the water. Huh, this can't be right. I focus harder on the whale to see if it overshot its landing and got caught in a tree or something. Matt keeps saying Virrel's name, but it takes me a few seconds to figure out Virrel's doing this. He stands near us, straining his face off with his hands outstretched like he's pushing a boulder. Oh, right, his power! I keep forgetting that. He heaves the monster whale with an invisible crane onto the island, making it lean under the whale's weight.

"Now will you run?" Virrel asks as he cautiously approaches the behemoth.

I don't know about everyone else, but I take off. While still running top speed, I get rid of my shield, make a hover star, and angle it over the river separating us from the mainland, planning to use it as a springboard to get across. Hearing footsteps behind me, I decide to leave the star there after I'm done for whomever else. I run, jump on the star, and then leap off of it, luckily clearing both the thin river and a beam of water. Instead of landing gracefully, I basically collapse on the ground, forgetting the fact that the island's tilt is higher than the mainland. That doesn't stop me though; instinctive fear forces me to get up and keep running.

We sprint through the forest, and I count the footsteps and breaths behind me. There are two others. Our feet heavily pat down the trampled dirt trail. We run so far we almost reach a town; just thumps and huffs and the sounds of wind rushing by. Abruptly, all three of us stop for some unknown cause. I don't know why; I'd love to keep running. Turning around, I see that my two followers are Matt and Nima.

"Do you think maybe we should've stayed and helped them?" Matt asks between breaths.

Probably. My irrationally high terror is dying down now, and I'm thinking I definitely could've kicked some whale butt.

"By no means. Just have faith in them." Nima states, sounding somewhat worried. That certainly re-enforces her super brave quote from earlier.

After about ten minutes, Yoseph and Virrel appear at the far end of the trail. As they come closer, I can see that they are strapped with our equipment. I can also see that they are soaking wet. Our three bikes ride perfectly straight behind Virrel, almost as if they have invisible riders on them.

Virrel decides to travel with us for a while so he can "find a quick route back to his employer" but I doubt he's going to be paying that mission very much attention. The two of them distribute out our backpacks, which are damp from where they had been on their backs, and when Virrel moves out of the way for us to get our bikes, I see that mine is splattered with mud.

"Sorry about that. I tried my best." Virrel apologizes, but I easily forgive him.

It isn't a big deal, and besides, the bike looks kind of sick this way, like it's been through some stuff. Yoseph, Matt, and I mount our bikes (which, luckily, have dry seats) and ride through the shade of the forest. As we ride, Virrel glides alongside us, making use of his telekinesis, while Nima does her small wind gliding thing, helping her travel faster.

We follow Nima into a forest town, then deeper within towards what looks like an amusement park sky ride station. All the while, familiar faces look out from cabins and market windows, waving as we pass. The sky ride station is surprisingly just that. Matt and Yoseph have equal looks of confusion as we approach the colorful pods cycling past one another along telephone-like wires.

Nima explains that this form of transportation, air lift, is quite common in rural towns. It's a free service that takes you in a direct line either away or towards the nearest city.

We enter the station, walk through the turnstile, and since the boys want to stick together, I board one of the colorful seated pods with Nima and the bikes.

CHAPTER 8

GHOST STORIES

~ YOSEPH ~

That whale fight was crazy. The slowly passing autumn treetops go pretty much ignored as Virrel and I fill in Matt on how the fight with that giant fish went. Admittedly, Virrel did all the heavy lifting, both figuratively and literally. He kept having to redirect the water lasers (which looked dope) while I threw a few fireballs at it.

Honestly, I was kind of scared, so none of my fire actually made it far enough to hit the thing, but hey, I tried. Eventually it just died from... suffocating in air? I really don't know how to describe it, but we beat it, that's for sure. I've never been in a real fight; I'd have to say that was a pretty wild introduction.

We reach the first stop, but Nima told us to get off on the second one, so we stay on. Since no one really has anything to say, I start to notice the calm fall breeze and the masses of red leaves around us. I look at Virrel, whose eyes are lost deep in the treetops outside. My gaze shifts to Matt, who is sitting opposite from us, twiddling his thumbs. This pod seats four people, so our backpacks are piled beside Matt.

After more silence, I decide to engage the two of them.

"Virrel, do you mind if I ask you a personal question?" I start.

The ghost turns around, intrigued, and I notice Matt out of the corner of my eye, similarly interested.

"Go for it." Virrel invites.

"Okay, um, so this might be weird, but how did you, like…" I draw a finger across my neck.

Virrel lets out a chuckle.

"Nice question Yoseph. Back in my day, Great Sir Yatniv… well, I guess they both have the same title, so Gentarh, who was Kyndule's father, ruled Fiponik. Like Kyndule, he wasn't highly favored, even though he was a very good ruler. Taxes were fine, there were lots of free public services, and the quality of life was quite high."

Virrel shakes his head, "But then he started wiping out cities just for fun, and kidnapping people's wives and stuff; that's where most people drew the line."

Matt and I raise our eyebrows, and Virrel nods, "Oh yeah he was crazy, and Kyndule is just like his father. They think just because they are good rulers they can toy around with their power. Smart, but sickening. Oh, and side note, they are both kind of racist because all the good jobs keep going to the woodish, and us humans and democs are left either unemployed or with…"

The ghost lets out a sigh and puts up his hands, "I digress. So, to make a long story short, there was a little bit of a raid… I guess it was a small invasion since my island, Peritari, is part of *Mirthoaten Islands* which is technically a different country…"

Virrel shakes his head and laughs, "See? I can never stay focused!

Okay, pretty much, I was the leader of my providence and all of the young men wanted to go to this raid. I tagged along too, even though I was 68. Let's just say, Gentarh was tipped off about the raid and we were all blasted into oblivion.

"If it weren't for my employer, the empress, having some clashes with Kyndule, then to this very day I would have still thought Gentarh was alive and still the Great Sir. Yet, Gentarh wasn't killed by the raid. He actually died a few years ago, allegedly in an accident somewhere far from here."

Matt and I dwell on the story for a few moments, then I notice that the treetops are steadily beginning to rise.

"Wow," Virrel says, "That was pretty fast! Ready to head out?"

Matt and I both nod and collect our stuff. In a few seconds, the air lift pod slides into a landing, and we shuffle out of it. Samantha and Nima are waiting at the exit of the station, bikes ready. The city around them is much more reserved and suburban than I had expected. It's definitely got more hustle and bustle than the other two towns we skipped by, but it only has a few high-rise buildings.

As we come into earshot, Nima begins to speak, "We must take lansit transportation to our next destination. We must act with haste, for the lansit follows a strict schedule."

Matt and I heed her warnings and hop on our bikes. We follow Nima's swirling wind thing to the lansit station. The five of us weave through two blocks, passing dozens of shops and offices along the way, then take a long straight down a hill.

As we bike down the side of this street, which seems like it's probably this city's main street, I still don't get a glimpse of any of the societal stuff Nima told us about. There are mostly democs here, but humans aren't rare or anything. A few people wave as we coast past, but for the most part, no one bats an eye.

There isn't a lot of foot traffic here, so we can glide down this hill without much of a problem. Most of the traffic is on the street. Cars… well, wheel-less, hovering cars, are almost bumper to bumper, slowly weaving their way in and out of lanes to try and get places a bit faster.

I guess Arret and Earth aren't that much different after all.

Suddenly, the lansit station is upon us. It looks exactly like a train station, both on the outside and on the inside. As soon as we dismount our bikes and go to wheel them inside with us, there is a loud scraping noise followed by a snap. The five of us stop and look at Matt, who is looking down at his bike's hind wheel. The rubber part is trailing off and one of the spokes is broken.

"What happened?" Sam asks him.

He looks at his bike, confused, but then a look of realization washes over his face, "Back when I was running from the Mundatorite, I remember that some of it had gotten my bike. I guess that's why this happened."

"No need for concern," Nima states, "We have arrived on time."

Matt says a final goodbye to his bike, then ditches it in front of the station doors.

Once we enter and Virrel pays our entrance fee (it was really cheap but none of us had any money to begin with), it takes Nima no time to find our platform. Almost thirty seconds later, what looks like a monorail gently slides to a stop in front of us. We board it, and in another thirty seconds, we're off.

Whoa, that was close!

The monorail… sorry, "lansit" coasts past the city buildings, and as soon as we begin to reach the outskirts, we pick up speed. Once we completely leave the city and are surrounded by plains on all sides, the lansit starts going ridiculously fast, somewhere over 200 mph. Tall, pale fields of reeds rush past us in a blur, and eventually they give way to rolling meadows as far as the eye can see.

Golden grass and a rainbow of different flowers fill these plains, all zipping by at relentless speeds. I scan the open, blue sky, looking at the masses of fluffy clouds drift by in the distance. I'm lost in the beauty of the landscape for a bit before Matt turns around in front of me.

"Hey, I have a weird question for you." He starts.

I nod. He shifts a bit in his seat and an odd smile grows on his face, "I've been trying to figure out how to describe this, but I just can't. What would you say it feels like to summon our tools?"

Dang, that's a good question!

"Um… it's kind of like an internal jerk or… like pressing a spring-loaded trigger."

Nima chimes in from the isle across from us, "I would describe it as a psychological actuation based on a coalescence of volitive and instinctual inputs via one's environmental conditions."

Matt and I stare at her, absolutely lost, and then Sam chimes in,

"What are you guys talking about?"

"The sensation that arises when one commands their tool into existence." Nima answers.

"Oh, I call it switchblading… because it feels like your body is the hilt and then your tool is the blade." Sam says casually.

I raise my eyebrows at that spot-on description, then turn to an equally impressed Matt and shrug. The rest of the ride is spent staring at this new city's passing buildings.

We get off the lansit and get a glimpse of the next city from the platform. This city is *actually* a city, filled with flashy shops and tall buildings, but we don't get to have a look around. As soon as the lansit jets off to its next destination, we take some stairs under the railing and then begin walking out into the plains.

I would ask Nima where we're going, but I'm taking it that we're headed towards the floating stadium in the sky. Yeah, I'm not kidding. The sun is angled oddly above it, so its upper rim casts a shadow on the rest of it. I can see banners and flags on its side, but I can't make out what they read.

With nothing else to do, we start walking towards the huge, droning sky stadium. It's silent except for the swishing grass, creaking bugs, our footsteps, and of course, the hum from the coliseum. The noises from the city are too faint to notice.

Virrel looks at Nima, then at Sam, Matt, and I.

"So… are you guys liking Fiponik so far?" He asks us.

"Yeah, it's pretty nice." Sam replies, absently looking off at the incredibly distant mountains.

"It's more chill than I thought it would be." I admit.

Matt is silent for a bit, then he says, "Yeah, I'd have to agree with Yoseph. I don't think I've seen any woodish people yet… well, at least in person."

Nima raises a finger, "Good observation; we are currently in the more democ- and human-centric areas of the country, therefore the woodish population will be low. However, it is sure to increase the further northeast we go."

No one talks for a little bit, and then Virrel asks Matt, "What did you mean by that last part?"

Unsure of who Virrel is talking to, both Nima and Matt respond with "What do you mean?" nearly at the same time, which causes a little laugh to go through the group.

"You'd said 'at least in person' when talking about woodish. So, you've seen them before?" Virrel questions.

Matt scratches his head, "At least I think so. From the way you and Nima describe them, I think I've seen them somewhere in a dream before."

I know exactly what Matt is talking about, and so does Sam. Apparently the two of them had the same dream on the night before my family reunion; it was about fighting skeletons in a ballroom with a bunch of fancy people. It was a hot topic for a while back in Alabama, but then the three of us kind of moved past it. Now things are starting to piece together a bit.

Nima is oddly quiet, and then says, "Thank you Matthew for reminding me of that. That dream will work in conjunction with the

Ieri Tropo to help guide us along our journey. Due to our vira, we had a shared premonition. This means that the individuals we witnessed helping us will inevitably be individuals who we will meet along this quest. Remain vigilant for them."

The rest of the walk is pretty much quiet as we digest that information. Well, at least Sam, Matt, and I digest it. Virrel just gazes off into the meadow, trying not to look as confused as we know he is. Fifteen more minutes pass and we're nearly beneath the stadium. The low hum it's emitting now surrounds us, but it's pleasant, so it doesn't bother me. We all come to an unspoken stop, and I gaze up at the floating stadium to size it up.

It's pretty impressive. The banners and flags read the stadium's name, which must just be "Skyling Stadium", the game that's being played, which is "*kaxahhe*", and the teams that are competing, which are the "Saint Markus *Serbuds*" versus the "Terramosa Turtles".

The entire stadium, looming and concrete, is about 50 or so feet in the air. Not as high as it seemed from afar, but I surely don't want to fly that high up.

"Yo Nima, how are we supposed to–"

But the alien shushes me. She, Virrel, and Sam seem to be staring down something in the not-so-far distance. Matt is still frantically searching the meadow grass, trying to spot what the others are.

It takes me a few moments before I see it. About 15 feet away, there's this horrifically bizarre creature staring us down. I can only describe it as a cross between a giant cobra and an alligator, with its eyes, mouth, back, and tail being the cobra part, and alligator making up the rest of it.

It's got sleek, green scales across the entirety of its body, and it's crouched in a pouncing position, frozen and almost completely camouflaged among the autumn grass. My eyes wise up, and I can see that two of its buddies are not too far behind it.

Nima does a downward pushing motion, and Sam places her bike in the grass. I do the same. Nima then looks back at us and points up at the stadium. Her eyes flick past us for a second, then grow wide and she points to the stadium again, more frantically this time. Sam exchanges a worried glance with me, then wordlessly shoots one of her star bullets into the air. It stretches out into a hover star big enough for two.

It swooshes back down to pick her up, and as soon as she coaxes the terrified Matt onto it, I hear rustling in the grass. The creatures are crawling towards us. Virrel locks the first one in place with telekinesis, but he must not have noticed the other two, for they continue to scurry towards Nima.

Nima sprints towards me and I turn around for her to piggyback. As soon as I do, I catch sight of two more cobra-alligators quickly approaching us, but these are slightly bigger… and covered with reddish-brown scales instead of green ones. Fear overcomes me, but I'm knocked out of my stupor by Nima jumping on my back.

The moment her legs hook around my waist, I blast into the sky, easily jetting off much higher than I ever have before. Once I'm safely out of the creatures' reaches and somewhat stably floating in the sky, I look down to see if Virrel had made it out.

He did, and the creatures are now in a huddle around our bikes, glaring up at us. Before I can breathe a sigh of relief, the two red ones yawn up at me… and then fireballs start shooting out of their mouths! What?!

Sam and Matt are far above harm's reach, and the first two fireballs pass harmlessly over me and under them. Then the creatures seem to get better accuracy, and the next thing I know, a volley of fireballs is arching straight up at me. Nima's grip around me fearfully tightens even more, and I tighten my grip around her legs to reassure her.

The first fireball gets too close for comfort and I dodge it as best I can, making sure to turn Nima away from the heat. It takes me a moment to gain balance on my weak streams of fire, but then another volley of microwave-sized flaming orbs are spat at me. I fly higher to avoid a few, then kick the last one out of existence. I forgot Nima makes me unbalanced, so we nearly flip out of the sky because of it.

I feel terrible for nearly killing us both, so before any more shenanigans can almost claim our lives, I force myself higher into the sky. The creatures shoot a few more fireballs, but those fall too short and completely miss Virrel.

Shaking and unstable, we barely reach the entrance booth before we collapse into a huffing mess. I suppose Sam had just as hard of a time carrying Matt, because her hover star disappears right as we get to the booth. Virrel seems just fine. Now that I think about it, couldn't Virrel have just carried Nima?! Oh great.

The guy behind the ticket booth, looking very concerned, gives us a minute before questioning,

"Do you guys need some water?"

I close my eyes and shake my head, and I suppose the others do too, because nothing happens as we continue to try and slow our breathing.

"Those were dragers," Nima says between breaths, "They are a common predatory species here in Fiponik. The green ones are typical for plains, but one would usually spot a red drager in the desert."

There is more silence, and then the clerk begins to speak again, "I… kind of just want to let you guys in for free because it's impressive that you, what, flew here?"

We nod and start to laugh, realizing how insane our stunt back there was.

"Unfortunately, though, I've got to charge something. Tell you what, if you guys don't have tickets, I'll charge you half price. You know what? Quarter price."

Matt digs out the Golden Taste Ticket capsule from Grave Digger's lake and hesitantly hands the entire thing to the clerk. The clerk twists off the top, looking half amused and half skeptic as he takes the large ticket from its cell. Curiously, he takes a bite.

At first I thought he was smelling it, but no, he actually bit half of the ticket off. I guess that's how they take tickets here? Judging by Nima and Virrel's expressions, I don't think so.

"Wow! Well, all of you, step right on in!" The clerk exclaims.

CHAPTER 9

ROYAL STARING CONTEST

~ YOSEPH ~

The stadium is stupefyingly (if that's a word) big. The field in the middle is like a large indigo tennis court without the net, with random floating indigo pads here and there. A red line runs horizontally through the field, making it look even more like a tennis court. Countless rows of chairs surround its edges.

My grumbling stomach makes me notice a concession stand sitting at one end of the field. On the other side is a press box, with the score board floating right above it. Man, they must really like hovering things here; hovering cars, hovering stadiums, and now even hovering score boards?

The others start to walk down the main set of stairs, and I blindly follow them. Instead of paying attention to where I'm going, my eyes are lost in the playing field. Whatever game it is, we have nothing like it on Earth.

There are a little under twenty people on the field, with eight on each side of the line, and they all have scoopers on their arms. A surprisingly fast ball with a trail of yellow light is being flung back and forth between the opposing teams, occasionally hitting the ground or a wall and ricocheting off of an invisible ceiling.

I've got to follow the others up a set of stairs, so I look away from the game. The stadium is packed, so we climb quite a ways to find five empty seats lined up for us. I plop down next to Virrel at the very edge of the row. Virrel turns to me like he's about to explain something, but then Nima leans forward and begins shouting down the row.

"This is kaxahhe! This sport is played all across Arret, and it is as popular on Arret as international football is on Earth! Enjoy the game, and we can talk during the quieter break period!"

With that, I sit back in my chair and enjoy. The contestants are wearing opposing uniforms (green vs. white) with a blue circle on some random place on their uniform, commonly on their sides or shins. All around them, the yellow glowing ball bounces. It bounces off of a player's scooper, then the ceiling, then the back wall, and then it makes a huge angle against the floor.

The ball rockets towards a white player, who scoops it out of the air in one fluid motion, spins violently, and slings his arm harder than I've ever seen someone do. The ball almost disappears, slamming on the far wall and ricocheting off to hit a green player in the back. There's a ding noise, and the green player looks up at the score board. I follow his gaze. Green is at 21 and white is at 18. In a bit of a fanfare, the eight rolls into a seven and the crowd roars. So… they count down? A bit confused, I continue to watch.

The ball buzzes around, hits a green player again, and then the white team's score drops to 16. Okay, so points are bad in this game. The white team is doing pretty well, but then suddenly one of the floating platforms turns from indigo to orange. A green player immediately scoops the ball from the air and redirects it at the platform. The ball hits the pad and turns from yellow to orange while the pad goes back to indigo. At this, all of the player's eyes start to widen and the crowd erupts again. Dramatic music starts to blast from above, and I start laughing at how little sense this is making.

The already fast-paced game seems to pick up speed, and now the ball is almost a blurry line as players from both sides hilariously duck and dodge out of the way. Eventually (and to the crowd's dismay), the ball hits a white player, and I immediately look at the scoreboard. Comically sad music plays as the team's score goes from 11 to 14. Ah… so the orange pad adds points.

The game continues to capture my interest, and it seems as though the green team is having a really difficult time getting their score down. One of the white players bounces the ball off the side wall and it hits a green player in the side, right where the blue circle on their uniform is. Curious, I look at the scoreboard.

Fanfare sounds again as the white team's score drops from 12 to 10. I guess the circles take an extra point. Instead of the game starting up again, there is a bit of music, and then a break is announced. With this, a lot of the roaring from the crowd dies down into excited chattering as people get up from their seats and walk around.

I look down the row at Nima, who asks Sam to open her pack and distribute food. Once we're all munching on fish, fruit, and bread, Nima explains her final plan. She thinks that finding everyone from the dream should be just as important as following the Ieri Tropo.

She admits that, though she would like it to be a civil meeting, the shared dream of the skeletons in the ballroom suggests that we'll be fighting Great Sir Yatniv.

Nima guessed (and Virrel supported her) that the scuffle would take place at the *Celestial Conference.* The Celestial Conference is the only place where we can find Yatniv, the Mundatorite ring, and a portal back to Earth in the same area. Also, it happens every decade so… let's just say we can't afford to miss it.

Having a large group would not only give us a physical advantage but also a political one. Everyone is thoughtlessly nodding until Nima says the word "political", and then everyone stops, including me. Nima explains that it will be an important part of our leverage against Yatniv.

We have a little vote to decide the leader of our group, which is, unsurprisingly, Nima, and then we decide to make up a title for ourselves. Instead of going about it diplomatically, we just shout out whatever random name comes to mind.

We shout out names like "Here Comes the Thunder", "Herculean Beauty", and "The Boys in Blue", but then Nima suggested we try something that actually fit the group. After a bit of silence, Matt suggests being called the *Earth Pirates*, and everyone half-heartedly agrees. There's a bout of silence between the five of us, and then one of the people sitting in front of us turns around.

"Are… are you guys planning to overthrow the government?"

As soon as he meets eyes with Sam, his face goes "uh oh". He goes to get up, but then suddenly Sam reaches forward and angrily slams him back in his seat. The rest of us start, surprised at her random outburst, but before any of us can say anything, she says forcefully, "MP3. Handheld. Now."

The guy looks at her for a moment with an expression of terror and confusion, but then she shakes him violently and he caves.

"Alright, alright I'm sorry." He says as he reaches into his pockets.

To my absolute amazement, the guy pulls out a pink MP3 player complete with earbuds from one pocket, and a red handheld game system from the other. What in the world?! Matt's face is a combination between my complete shock and his sister's odd anger. He snatches the handheld from the random boy's hand, looking as though he's about to slap him in the face. All of us suddenly notice the awkward quiet and disapproving stares flooding in from every direction.

Nima decides to break the silence.

"You three are somehow familiar?"

"Yeah! This is the jerk that landed us in your infirmary. He stole our stuff the moment we stepped foot in our house, so we had to chase him through the woods. And the fact that he pretended like he didn't know who we were… oh my goodness I just want to *wring your freaking neck.*"

The boy flinches as Sam leans forward, but Virrel reaches out and holds her back.

"Identify yourself." Nima commands.

"I'm…" he pauses, obviously trying to think of a fake name, but then realizes that that wouldn't be a wise choice and reluctantly admits, "I'm Bacoj Leewig, from Quepora."

Bacoj looks around Matt's age, with curly, dark brown hair puffing up like a small, messy afro. His eyes are a syrup color, and his skin is a little lighter. A faint mustache curves over his pinkish-brown lips, which are turned into a shameful frown. Around his neck is what Nima and Virrel described as a cyber vira, and honestly, they gave a pretty good description. I can tell it's not a legit honor vira like mine because of the red string and bluc outline.

Nima then asks Bacoj oddly, "Why are you still here?"

Virrel, Matt, and even Sam give her the same shocked look that I do. Did she just roast him?

"What?" Bacoj asks.

"Any non-motived individual would have fled as soon as the threat was detained. But you are still here, and you even admitted your name. Why is this?"

We're all silent. That was a pretty good point.

Bacoj is slow to respond, "I... was going to see if I could join your team."

"Why would you want to?" Nima asks again with the same amount of cold curiousness as before.

After a moment of hesitation, Bacoj tells us that he used to be in a rebel group himself. He believes that some of his actions caused him to end up on Earth in the first place. He was on a mission to gather some information on Yatniv's palace for some sort of planned raid, but then he was caught by guards. He thought being a kid would get him a pass, but it didn't. Instead of being executed or imprisoned, Yatniv decided he wanted to fight Bacoj himself.

Initially, he smiled at the opportunity, but the tyrant turned out to be a swordsman as well as a magician, and he was way more powerful than Bacoj expected. Bacoj remembers desperately trying to retreat back to his group, then coldness on his head, then suddenly appearing in the middle of a living room in some random house. He didn't know where he was or what magic just happened but he knew he was far from where he started.

When Matt and Sam walked in on him with their mom, his brain went into panic mode. He thought that he would have to start a life of his own where he was, and he immediately made a dash for their electronics, so he could sell them and get some money. After trying to hide in the woods and seemingly blasting Matt and Sam away, he stumbled around the forest for a bit before being recalled back to Arret.

Apparently, his teammates knew something crazy would happen to him, so someone placed a hex on him that activated over time. Once Bacoj realized that his rebel "buddies" knew that the operation would end up with him getting captured, he decided to leave that group and take his services elsewhere. To him, we seem like just the right bunch.

The five of us glare at him, caught somewhere between doubtful and accepting. I would be hung up on the whole "magic" piece, but that honestly doesn't seem farfetched compared to everything I've seen so far. After some time, Nima wordlessly extends her hand and Bacoj shakes it.

"Welcome to the team, Bacoj. No more stealing." She says.

Bacoj flashes a grateful smile and nods in agreement. After that, Nima takes a few moments to discuss the quest with Bacoj, and then all six of us review the Ieri Tropo.

"It says we are to secure the '*Eonia Sprites*'." Nima states.

"Where's all that stuff at? All I see is a map of the country." Bacoj questions, stretching and twisting to try and get a good look at the map from his seat.

"It's a map that only works for honor vira users." I tell him, also stretching to get a good look.

"Any clues?" asks Virrel, looking at Sam instead of the map.

"The Stairwell of Curiosity." Nima replies before Sam can.

Without questioning her, the six of us collectively look to the left at a strange staircase, made from a different material than the rest of the stadium. At first, I thought it was an odd design choice, not worth a second thought, but now it seems special. The stairs go up beyond the overhang... and I wonder where it leads.

Just then, a sort of electronic chime happens, like an elevator arriving or something. The giant, floating scoreboard changes from a green 17 and a white 10 to a wall of text. The top part is in English, and the bottom is in Kraues, which Nima says is a common democ language. The part that I can read says,

"Don't forget to buy your *Applestirk Dayz* paraphernalia at the concession stands! Go *Serbuds*! We also have a special guest from Mirthoaten Islands, it is Empress Rigm herself! She has come to enjoy the kaxahhe game and all of its festivities, so please visit her at the large booth under the concession stands."

Twenty guards begin to march down from the entrance. They all surround someone who I can only assume is the empress. The guards, suited in black, all have black-gray bracelets on their wrists, along with an assortment of other high-tech stun weaponry I wouldn't want to deal with.

I can't make out what the empress looks like, but I can see that she is shorter than I'd imagined (though I only learned her name ten seconds ago). She wears a long, white kimono with a yellow circle on the back, and its rays indefinitely expand from its center.

At her side is a brown-haired woman dressed in a shorter, plain yellow kimono. This woman holds a yellow parasol over the empress, hiding her face and shielding it from the sun. I can't tell what it is, but something just… feels off about this. Uneasiness seems to hang like a cloud around the empress and her guards; the fancy air around them is failing to mask their suspicion.

"Well…" Virrel says as he stands, "It's been fun. I hope things go well for you."

He sidles past me and makes his way down the stairs towards the empress, seemingly upset.

Bacoj looks like he wants to take Virrel's seat, but he glances at Sam and rethinks his idea.

After some silence, he decides to speak, "That's nice; I never knew that island lady was also a kaxahhe fan. I would've imagined her to stay home and watch the game."

"I concur… this is a rather strange situation. Anyhow, I have formulated a plan." Nima states, "Yoseph and I will depart and converse with the empress. Our quest may intrigue her, and we could use her assistance."

Wait, what? I nod before I embarrass myself, trying not to let my nerves get to me. Why do *I* have to go talk to the empress?

"Matt and Bacoj, I want you two to attempt to discover what lies beyond that stairwell and hopefully retrieve the sprites."

They nod and run off, apparently eager to end their curiosity.

"And Samantha," she says finally.

Sam looks up.

"You remain here and surveil everyone's progress."

"Will do." says Samantha, trailing the '*do*' while leaning back and twiddling her thumbs.

"Good, we should all be back relatively soon. I will leave the map here."

Nima looks off into the distance, as if caught up in her own thoughts. Then she heads down the steps. I follow. The game starts up again as Nima and I are heading down the steps, but to my dismay, that doesn't deter her. She simply slides past all the ascending people, and I reluctantly do the same.

We reach the pathway in front of the stands and begin to circle the playing field. I slide my hand against the ash white railing as we approach, closer and closer to the empress's booth. Not many people are along with us, probably because they don't feel very comfortable under her authoritative gaze. I ignore the excited arena and the even more exciting game, staring at the ground the whole walk there. Nima and I soon reach a short line and I look up at the empress.

Empress Rigm has long, straight, ink black hair, with narrow eyes nearly the same color. Her skin is a soft pale and her lips, painted red, move rapidly as she speaks with those who dare to approach her (which are mainly reporters). She raises her left hand to do a gesture, and I notice a rope-like bracelet connected by an amber stone on her left wrist. As she carries on her conversation, I stare at her, trying to recall her from somewhere. Huh, doesn't ring a bell.

I continue staring at her, at first double-checking to make sure I don't recognize her, then taking in every detail about her elegant outfit, then just zoning out. I'm startled when she raises her hand to her mouth, letting out a regal fit of laughter.

"Nice job; no one's ever beaten me in a staring contest before! Whatever you have to say, I'm certainly listening."

It takes me a moment to figure out that she's talking to me, and when I do, embarrassment engulfs me. I can't believe I spaced out on her face! I must've looked like such a creep! I attempt to say something witty, but it just comes out as a nervous laugh.

I can imagine myself saying something offensive and being shunned or something. Virrel and Nima taught us about broad social topics, but I have no knowledge of these guys' customs or political works; anything I say could mean something negative. The weird silence makes my blood turn cold.

Lacking the words, I look at Nima, which is the best decision I could've made.

CHAPTER 10

INSANE WIZARD DICTATOR

~ YOSEPH ~

"Your Eminence, I am... Ms. Iyr and this is my companion, Mr..." Nima places a hand on my shoulder.

"Hollingsworth." I mutter.

The queen and Nima both nod, then Nima continues.

"My friend Yoseph comes from Earth. His planet's essence was stolen by a ring, which I suspect is the Mundatorite, and Great Sir Yatniv's doing. I have decided to put together a union of heroes to help them get to the Celestial Conference and restore Earth."

Dread fills my stomach. We have got to sound like crazy people; I'm just waiting for her guards to brutally arrest us.

"I see. So, what would you like for me to do to help you?" Empress Rigm asks casually.

Wait, what?! Was... did she hear us correctly? Nima just told her I was an alien and one of her fellow politicians stole an entire planet with a piece of jewelry, but she is totally okay with that?

"Any support possible." Nima replies, continuing this somehow normal conversation.

"So, it's settled, then." Says the empress.

Nima and I look at each other, and then ask in almost perfect unison, "What's been settled?"

"My head guardian Virrel and I, Empress Rigm, shall join your heroes' group and try to restore Earth."

A blossom of relief springs in my chest. Virrel tries to hide a grin, but Rigm proudly displays hers. Nima and I subtly high-five, which surprised me because I thought Nima wouldn't know what a high-five was. Man, that was really easy!

"But Empress, who will lead Mirthoaten Islands while you're gone?" Asks a woman about the empress' age.

She's a little taller than Rigm, with overcast gray eyes and dark brown, flowing, curly hair. She was the one carrying the parasol from earlier.

"Good point Neldyma." She pauses, then says, "Or, should I say, Empress Ploppo?"

All of her guards, as well as Virrel and this Neldyma woman, all look like they are choking on air. Finally, Neldyma finds words to speak, "Did you just… abdicate… to me?!"

"At least until I come back." The former empress says nonchalantly, standing up from her seat.

The new empress seems to calm down a little at that, then gets a curious look in her eyes and asks, "Why are you doing this?"

Rigm's expression changes from delighted to serious.

"Someone needs to take control of the political situation in this country. Yatniv was a good leader, but he lacks conscience."

Her expression softens again, "And besides, Ms. Iyr reminds me of a very kind person I used to know."

The empress then turns to her group of guards and asks, "So, who will follow me?"

The guards look at one another, and then all of them put their hands up in unison. What?! This is incredible; we just went from five people to almost thirty! With this much power we'll never lose to Yatniv!

"Alright," Rigm says, her face serious again, "Nel… Empress Ploppo. Will you lend assistance to us, seeing that all of my financial assets have just been frozen?"

The brown-haired woman nods, "Of course."

Rigm starts to walk towards Nima and I, but then in a flash, all of the lights in the stadium go off. The crowd is hushed into a shocked murmur, and I look back to see that the game has stopped.

The only source of light aside from the shining sun above is the oddly bright scoreboard. I take a few steps back to see what's on it. Instead of colored numbers or a wall of text, it's an image… a video rather.

In the image is a woodish boy dressed lavishly in royal regalia. He has a heart-shaped face, and plastered on it is a devious, calculating smile. His blue skin is two shades darker than the sky and his straight, pink hair wisps dramatically down from his white crown.

His piercing, hazel eyes gaze down on us like a hawk on prey. Something about this guy feels corrupt, yet also dangerously… magical. I can't really describe it, all I know is that it's the opposite of warm and fuzzy. Gasps and shrieks ripple from the audience, and many people begin crying and wailing. My goodness, I guess this guy is no joke. I am almost completely sure that this is Yatniv.

"I thought I'd drop in to make things interesting. How did I do?" The boy asks in a disturbingly regular tone.

His only reply is more screaming and crying, but then a response comes from the overhead speakers.

"Great Sir Kyndule Yatniv, Master Wizard of the Bulganaura. What is going on here?" Rigm's voice asks.

I look down at her throne in confusion, but she isn't there. I look around for a bit until Nima taps me and points towards the press box, where Virrel and Rigm are huddled around a microphone. How did she get up there so fast?!

Either way, I let a frown play across my face. I thought Yatniv would be older, for he looks almost my age, but I guess he's a bad guy nonetheless.

"I just wanted to remind you who is in charge. Why did you think you were invited to a kaxahhe game? For your amusement? Of course not, I needed to smoke you out of that palace of yours."

"Why? What is your objective?" Rigm asks, trying to put a soft edge to her voice. I can tell she wants to roast this guy, but I don't think anyone knows what he's capable of, and she doesn't want to put these people in danger because of her anger.

"I just told you Rigm, to show you who has the real power here. Do you know what I could do right now? I could drop this entire stadium from the sky. I could kill you and all of these people, too."

A sickening grin spreads across his face as he surveils the horrified audience. Goodness, this guy really is a terrible person! His intimidating eyes scan the crowd, then he does a double-take and squints in one direction.

I follow his gaze and find the only other source of light in the stadium. Standing at the end of our row is Bacoj and Matt. Bacoj holds a bowl with what looks like glowing, rainbow ping pong balls, and both of them look up at Yatniv with an awed expression.

Is that what we were looking for?

"Are those… the Eonia Sprites? Wait…" Yatniv leans closer to the screen, squinting even more. Bacoj, Matt, and everyone in that section of the stadium shrink back as a result.

With a laugh, Yatniv says to himself, "Hey, I fought that one on the left… I'm surprised you're still alive, little man."

He then grows quiet as he presumably looks at Matt. Abruptly, he sits back in his seat, an angry smile replacing his devious one.

"Brown-haired boy, that looks an awful lot like the *Crescent of Darkness* Amulet around your neck. If that's a costume, I'm interested in how you ever learned about such a thing… and in all of my years as ruler I've never been so angry at an act of defiance.

"Whether that's real or not, you have only yourself to blame for what's about to happen next. I can't take any chances, and honestly, I never liked Rigm anyway."

The screen blacks out, and then a moment after, a horrid sensation rises in my stomach. A monumental rumbling begins in the ground under me and screams of absolute horror come from the stands as the same sensation washes over them. My feet just barely lift from the ground, and so do Nima's and everyone else's. The…

stadium is falling?!

As soon as that thought enters my mind, there is a deafening crashing sound, and I crumple to the floor hard enough to knock me clean out.

CHAPTER 11

DARK REFLECTION

~ NIMA ~

A medical professional urges me to stay awake, and then I fall asleep again. Swirling, comfortable darkness pulls me upwards towards a foreboding, ethereal song, but then anchors of the physical world drag me back down. In a gasp and a burst of cold, my eyes flash open. But… I'm still met with darkness.

For a moment I believe that I am permanently blind, which I accept with a frank disappointment, but then my eyes adjust, and I realize that I am in a *florma*, which can be best described as a healing pod.

Since Arret has far more superior technology than Earth (no offense), our medical profession is extraordinary. Recoveries from near-death experiences are fixed in hours, and broken bones take minutes. All because of the florma; it is a capsule one sits down in which is full of medicinal fog.

This fog contains nanobots. One breathes in the fog, then the nanobots painlessly enter their body and repair damages. Combined with nanobots, the fog also contains anesthesia, so that one remains asleep while the robots restore broken bones and circulate blood.

I suppose my procedure wasn't that long. I sit in the sweet-smelling chilly darkness as my thoughts run wild. My companions; Yoseph, Samantha, Matthew, and Bacoj, are they still alive? Let me not forget Rigm as well. That was such a destructive and devastating fall… I am surprised that even I survived. The chances are very slim that the others did as well.

Things have never appeared so grim. If the Inter-Planetary Supernatural Helper Association *(IPSHA)* would bring themselves to action against Yatniv, then none of this would be an issue. But he's too clever, too tactical, and everything gets tangled in a mess of political tape. Nothing on this planet can stop him.

I'm so foolish. I should have went to Earth's IPSHA. One call and they would have put a stop to this, or at least helped me destroy the Mundatorite. But I didn't want to be a bother! How moronic of me! Gambling the safety of an entire planet on children I don't know, all because I didn't want to make a scene! Oh, how I wish I could travel back in time!

So many mistakes, all at the worst times. Even after we failed to destroy the Mundatorite, I was naive enough to think that I could make an impact. Win Earth back; really? From Yatniv? So what if I had the Crescent of Darkness at my side. He could very well be dead now because of my idiocy.

Sad whirring arises in my throat, the democ version of crying, as I realize what I've done. I have failed, not only myself, but also the entirety of Fiponik and Earth. I wasn't smart enough to outwit Yatniv. I should have ventured to find the Eonia Sprites myself. Maybe then, this entire fiasco could have been avoided in the first place.

We should have hid the moment things seemed awry. I should've made the call back on Earth. But I was foolish.

I had friends for once, and one of them was even the Crescent of Darkness. I thought I could do it. I thought I could avenge my family, relieve Fiponik, and save Earth, all in one fell swoop. But I couldn't. I am not good enough… and I was never good enough.

A wrenching hook of sadness tugs at my gut, and I double over in purring. My swirling cry grows louder and louder, and simply hearing myself sob makes me feel even more pathetic and worthless. I bawl for what seems like a short eternity, thinking about the potential friendships and adventures I could have had.

After I've coaxed myself into a whimpering, warm ball, trying to keep my mind as blank as possible, the door to my florma opens. I look up to see a nurse, surrounded by harsh light. He reaches in and helps me up. I get out of the pod, disoriented and ashamed, and I simply ask, "How many survived?"

The nurse looks at me with a frown, "We don't know. We confirmed at least half… died on impact."

My throat is already sore, but the whine begins to creep in again. The nurse gives me a smile and puts a hand on my shoulder.

"It's going to be okay. Someone is going to come around one of these days and fix this. I just know it."

His statement just makes me want to cry even more, but I hold back the whirring and pretend to be reassured just to satisfy him. It must have worked.

"Don't worry about it. If you have any belongings or are looking for someone, you can probably find them at the front desk."

I nod, and he walks away. Just to humor myself and justify more self-pity, I make my way over to the main desk. I know where it is from the wild commotion coming from its direction. When I round the corner, I'm met with a mass of people all crying and hugging and yelling at nurses.

I take one sad look around the crowd, and then lock eyes with Samantha. She looks brand new, her skin a fresh shade of ecru pink. All of the fading black dye in her hair was obliterated, replaced with healthy, shiny, golden hair (with a hint of brown).

The mole on her nose is gone, and all of the marks and blemishes that were on her have vanished as well.

CHAPTER 12

CASUAL NAPPING

~ NIMA ~

I **have never embraced someone so hard.** Alternatively, I have never been hugged so tightly. When she pulls away, she looks at me with an almost frantic expression.

"We need to leave, now. I talked to a few people and found out that the others might still be alive, but they'd be at a hospital across town."

I nod, as I now notice Bacoj at her side. He looks at me expectantly, but I just pat him on the head.

The three of us quickly exit the hospital, then we follow Samantha's directions. We are making our way down the sidewalk with haste, and when we turn the corner, I almost slam into Matthew full force.

He jumps, startled, and since Yoseph was not too far behind him, he does the same. Matthew and Samantha look at each other, simultaneously release sighs of relief, and then embrace one another.

Immediately, Samantha begins rubbing her knuckles into Matthew's head, which causes him to flinch back, and then they both laugh. Yoseph looks amused, but Bacoj seems just as confused as I.

Samantha pulls the Ieri Tropo out of her back pocket; the map is heavily damaged, with wrinkles all throughout it and a large tear running almost all the way down the middle. Even though my prized possession is ruined, we continue on.

The five of us walk silently through the city, following the Ieri Tropo towards our next destination; the Tapadim Regional Airport. After a while we begin to spot some road signs, and those prove to be slightly more helpful than the wide-scale national map we are using.

"So…" Yoseph starts after a bit of silence, "You guys hear anything interesting at your hospital?"

"Actually, yeah. Bacoj and I talked to the empress and she gave us some… rather interesting news." Samantha then looks at Bacoj, who laughs.

"She's a true politician alright, because she said that from now on she'd be travelling 'parallel' to us. I guess we're just a bit too dangerous to be around." He mocks.

I sigh, both relieved and stressed. This is good news because it still means that we have her support, but it's bad because it's auxiliary and not direct. Suddenly, my entire mood shifts, and I can't help but let a smile come across my face.

I guess having an auxiliary team is great, seeing as though I thought everyone was dead just a few minutes ago.

I remember the conversation at hand and decide to contribute.

"Did you gain any information at your infirmary, Yoseph?"

"Well," he starts, "Matt's got a giant bounty on his head."

There is silence between the five of us, because this information is both quite extreme but also predictable.

"Oh," Matt adds, "And there are supposed to be thunderstorms tonight."

****

We arrive at the airport after traveling another 15 minutes. My feet are sore; I can tell everyone else's are too, but we're still in high spirits. Our arrival is marked by a jet taking off in the distance. However, on Arret, commercial airliners are much different than on Earth. Our commercial flight vehicles are actually rather quiet, and the noises they do make are distinct yet pleasant drones.

We enter the somewhat empty airport and make our way to the entrance booth. Matthew stuffs his amulet in his pocket, as well as avoiding eye contact with the staff members, so we get through without much of a problem.

The airport has a relaxed, tranquil, almost thoughtful air about it; I'm only disturbed by the impressed look the clerk gave once Bacoj handed him the Eonia Sprites from Matthew's bag. The bowl they were in broke, so Bacoj had to take them out one by one, and each time, the clerk reacted with surprise.

We make our way past the front gate, and then look at the map.

Samantha scans the Ieri Tropo and raises her eyebrow, "It just leads to a big cloud. Are we supposed to go into that thunderstorm Matt was talking about?"

Bacoj looks at Samantha like she's inferior, but then I give him a look and he remembers that she isn't from this planet.

"No, Samantha. That is Safemill, another provincial region within Fiponik."

Bacoj spots our gate, and we spend about twenty minutes waiting for our flight. Those minutes started off tense, but once a security guard saw Matthew and didn't react at all, I let go a sigh of relief. Everyone around us is just as apathetic, staring at their personal devices and not once looking up.

Whomever is commanding the musical selection list for this airport is quite the listener. These songs are very relaxing. As I watch people walk about, talk to shop vendors, or roll their clacking luggage behind them, I feel at ease. Everything is so normal here.

We eventually board our flight. The plane is a bit smaller than I expected, and once the others situate themselves, I realize that all the seats are taken. I walk up the row and then back down it, but before I can panic, I notice a seat open next to a quiet boy.

It's relatively close to the others, and he seems nice enough.

Chapter 13

Clipped Wings

~ Nima ~

The boy lets me sit next to him, and after a few awkward moments, we decide to introduce ourselves to one another.

"Hi, my name is Chirus." He states.

He has muddy blond hair and dull, olive-green eyes. Chirus doesn't seem like the most athletic of individuals. In fact, he probably does not venture outside often. His skin is a pale-apricot color, and he has faint, plum-colored bags under his eyes.

His pink-pale lips form a welcoming yet shy smile. His appearance seems shaggy and sleepy, like he has not rested well for a few days. The plane takes off, and we decide to go ahead and start a conversation with one another.

Apparently, Chirus is going to Safemill to find more information on a glowing tambourine that he found. It randomly appeared next to him one morning, so he believes that it is special somehow (aside from the glow), and he wants to find out where it came from.

I tell him that some friends and I are on a journey to visit some unique locations, and that he might want to tag along if exotic information is something he's searching for. He admits that he is on his quest just to occupy himself, so he decides to join.

We nod, and then look off to our respective destinations. Chirus has the window seat, so his gaze is facing outside, while I have the aisle seat, so I gaze at my hands. I decide to actually look down the aisle to see lines of still, cocked heads. Taking a nap does seem like a nice way to pass the time.

The emotional and physical fatigue from my day catch up with me, and I soon drift off. I open my eyes to see an oddly poetic sight: black and white. The ground, stretching toward the horizon, is made up of white sand. Beneath this sand is more sand, and it continues until it forms the entire planet. Even though I can't see this, I just know it.

Then there's the sky, which is a deep and wonderful black abyss, filled with billions of glittering stars. The sun shines the brightest, looking like a terrifyingly close version of the countless ethereal lights in the distance. I follow the elaborate, sidereal patterns in the sky until I notice the horizon again… and Yoseph, Samantha, and Matthew. They look as awed as I, but with hints of confusion.

"We are currently in the astral plane. This is a feature of our amulets' premonition abilities. Our exact location, however, is something I have not deduced."

"We're on Earth." Matthew replies, "I remember, because this is what it looked like right before I hopped into the portal after you guys."

"Is that so…" I comment, mystified at Earth's obliteration and the power of the Mundatorite.

"Good Lord, this is horrible." Yoseph whispers.

Samantha looks at him, and he continues, "I mean, of course it's pretty, but this is what our planet will be if we don't find that ring?"

The four of us float there for a while, staring out onto the clashing expanses of blank whiteness and colorful blackness. I can feel the mixed emotions from the others. They feel fearful, mystified, intimidated, and multiple other emotions that I can't quantify. I know this because I feel the exact same way.

There's a sensation on my shoulder, and I look over to figure out what it is. Abruptly, I'm awake again, looking at Chirus instead of the beautiful expanse of space. I am startled and confused, not only because of my sudden transition, but also because of the tears building around Chirus' eyes.

I notice that there is a lot of noise on board as well; people are talking loudly and quickly to one another, but I can't understand what's going on because they are talking over themselves. I overhear the people in front of me, however.

It is what sounds like a scared mother reassuring her crying child.

"What is happening, Chirus?" I ask as worry begins to replace my sleepy confusion.

"They're going to shoot down the plane. It's a shame we didn't get to go on that adventure. You seemed like a great friend." He replies, his voice shaking in a quivering mess.

Bewildered, I look past him and out the window. I can see an airport and a town around it maybe one hundred meters under us, but we're circling instead of landing for some reason. Then, something incredibly threatening comes into view.

I've only seen them in movies before. They've got caterpillar tracks, and their body is composed of a birdlike tank with a cannon spout for a head. Whatever it is sits in the middle of the runway, blocking our landing point. I believe they are called *Mortar Pers.*

The Mortar Per tilts itself until its spout is pointed at us. Dread fills my stomach, and I know what's about to happen. No, please, it looks like just a few more meters until we can land. The plane shudders as our pilot tries desperately to turn, speed up, and land all at the same time. It is in vain. There is a flash of light, and a thick, light blue laser beams through the dusk air towards us.

A second later, there is a flash, and in a horrific mess of flames and debris, the entire front of the plane is blasted off.

Pressure, wind, shrapnel, and fire swirls and rushes throughout the cabin, and the flipping horizon is the last thing I see before our half of the plane slams into the runway.

CHAPTER 14

UNFAIR RAIN LADY

~ SAMANTHA ~

First, it's the ringing, then the soreness. I look around me, trying to figure out what just happened. For some reason only my left eye will open. Matt is lying motionless next to me, and someone is screaming their head off a few rows up. Closer to me, one seat away, in fact, is mumbling.

The floor is actually the side wall for some reason, and the only thing to illuminate my surroundings… are the flames outside? Oh… oh no. The plane just crashed, didn't it? The ringing in my ears is making it near impossible for me to focus. I sit there for a bit, tasting the blood in my parched mouth and watching the flames flicker against shattered glass and debris.

****

When I wake up next, I'm alone and surrounded by odd-smelling fog. Huh, I must be in another one of those florma things. Relief fills me as I realize I can open my right eye again. Phew! That was certainly intense. I stare into the darkness around me, waiting for nothing, and then I begin laughing.

We literally almost died twice in one day. How do we keep surviving this crap?! First the stadium, and then our plane gets shot out of the sky? That Yatniv guy really wants us dead! Wait… oh no. Oh that's horrible.

So many people have died alongside us. Oh my goodness. There had to be tens of thousands of people in that stadium, and that plane we were on was at max capacity. A shiver goes up my spine, but it isn't from the coldness in my florma. Yatniv really is crazy, isn't he…

Just then, the door to my florma opens, and it's Nima. Thank the Lord she's still alive too. At the sight of her face, I am reminded of my baby brother, and before she says anything, I blurt out, "Where's Matt?"

"We- sorry, he's right here." She moves out of the way and Matt gives me a cartoony grin with a thumbs up.

I roll my eyes and try my best not to laugh.

"Yes. So, I wanted to relay to you that we need to depart immediately. Some of the medical staff let me know that law enforcement was going to show up tomorrow morning to detain us if we were to survive."

I nod, feeling a bit disheartened. They aren't going to give up, are they?

"They recommended a local hotel whose prices are quite cheap, and it's rather close to the hospital. It is currently half an hour past three in the morning, so leaving during the cover of darkness is the best idea."

I get out of my pod and enter the overly bright hospital. Goodness, couldn't they be a bit easier with those lights? As soon as my eyes adjust, we're back outside in the darkness. On top of that, it's pouring down raining. I'm talking sheets of rain, like the rain that makes the little roof thing above us sound like static. Fan-freaking-tastic.

"Do we really have to do this?" Asks… some boy I've never met before.

"If we do not, we will be captured and more than likely executed." Nima reassures him.

"Um… not to be rude, but who are you?" I ask him.

The boy looks at me, and either the hospital light behind me is messing with my eyes or he is really pale.

"I'm Chirus. I joined you guys to find out some info on my tambourine, but I guess I'm an enemy of the state now."

He seems more nonchalant than angry, so his comment doesn't faze me much. We all introduce ourselves, then get back to the task at hand.

"Yo, how far away is this hotel again?" Yoseph asks Nima.

"The nurse said it was two blocks south." Nima says, pointing to the left.

Suddenly, parts of the ground that I thought were made of grass flicker bright blue a few times, and then a low, almost soothing thunder sound follows.

"Chill! What was that?" Yoseph asks, beating me to the punch.

Nima opens her mouth, but then Bacoj stops her.

"Actually Nima, I think I'll explain it." Says the thief with a mischievous grin. Immediately, I doubt whatever is about to come out of his mouth.

He pauses, then says, "Over eons, the clouds gathered and solidified around this one rock formation, and eventually, Safemill was made. That's why every time there is a thunderstorm, you can see the lightning through the grass and feel the thunder in your toes."

Chirus lets out a short laugh, but Nima stares at Bacoj with an unamused expression.

"Enough jokes. We need to depart."

At her command, all six of us duck down and sprint off into the surprisingly ice-cold rain. The city seems to be active a bit further away, so there is absolutely no one out here. We make it a block before I'm proven wrong.

Standing on the corner, right in front of our path, is a woman. It's already creepy that she's out here at three o'clock in the morning, but on top of that, she's willingly standing in the rain... and she is standing just beyond the streetlight so she's shrouded in darkness.

Thinking quickly, I softly tell the others that we should just cross to the other side of the street. However, as we are moving, she moves along with us, still standing in our way yet still hanging back in the shadows. Halfway across the street, Nima stops defiantly, and the rest of the group does too.

"Who are you?" Nima yells out at the woman. She's standing about twenty feet away.

"Edihi Amini. I can offer hot meals and shelter, would y'all like that?" The woman… or girl, rather, asks.

She sounds a bit older than Yoseph, maybe a year or so shy of adulthood, and what really gets me is that she has a sort of Southern drawl. She is completely still behind her veil of darkness, leering at us mysteriously.

Nima takes the liberty of speaking for us again, "No thank you. We are currently on our way to shelter."

The girl finally steps out of the shadows. Edihi has a narrow, fox-like appearance, with a shiny, sun-kissed tan and a few syrup-colored freckles. Her eyes are a pretty mix of hazel, gray, and blue. She has back length maple oak hair, which is matted against her due to the rain. Her beige lips are pursed in a concerned frown, and her long-sleeve plaid shirt with jeans are drenched.

"I insist. I got more than enough food for everybody, and I live alone, so there'll be plenty of room for y'all to sleep…"

Bacoj takes a step forward when Edihi said '*food*', but that's about the only movement there is.

Suddenly, I hear the new kid, Chirus, murmur from behind me, "What are we waiting for?"

"We're enemies of the state, remember? This is probably a trap." I reply, following what my gut tells me.

"Come on," Chirus persists, "She lives alone! What is she going to do against the six of us?"

"I thought the same thing," murmurs Yoseph, "but if she lives alone, why does she have so much food?"

Chirus is silent, and then Bacoj suggests, "Why don't I just run up and rob her?"

"I have not finished scanning our surroundings yet. I want to ensure the area is safe before we split up for attack." Nima peeps.

"Attack?" Matt questions, "Why do we have to attack her? Isn't the hotel right over there? We can just walk past her!"

"That is very observant of you Matthew, but this is not a time for passive actions."

Then Nima does something I didn't expect. She outstretches both arms and suddenly her sickles are in each hand, first white and then their green colors appear.

"One does not stand in the rain at three o'clock in the morning just to take in weary travelers. She is an assassin." Nima concludes.

Edihi lets a malicious grin play across her face, and the six of us collectively take a few steps back.

"Would ya look at that? Aren't y'all cleverer than a county detective?"

"What are you going to do without a weapon?" Bacoj calls out to her, and he's immediately jabbed in the side by both Nima and Yoseph. I would have done it too if I was close enough. That certainly isn't something we need to mention.

Edihi looks at him, then begins laughing to herself. We all exchange glances, and from the light of the streetlamp I can tell that this cold rain is now the least of our worries.

Just then, the thick sheets of water that have settled beneath our feet begin to rise. The water raises as a sheet, and as it does, it begins to take away all the moisture in our clothes. I watch, dumbfounded, as the water raises above us all just to give way to air underneath.

The sheet of water continues to rise far above our heads, and then it curves out to make a dome. Rain continues to fall around us, but this dome of water protects us. Now completely dry, the six of us continue to stare down Edihi.

"Y'all like that lil party trick?" The assassin asks sweetly.

"What the heck is happening?" I hiss out of my teeth to whomever will listen.

"She's a *kupua*, isn't she?" Bacoj asks Nima.

"That she is." Nima replies.

"Hold up, I remember that name from a project I've done..." Yoseph then gets a weird look on his face, "She's a Hawaiian demigod?"

"It is different in this context." Nima says, and I can hear her voice wavering. Out of all of us, she is probably the tensest.

"Some of y'all must've not done your homework." Edihi teases, now beginning to slowly circle the group.

"Allow me to explain. You got three types of power sources in this world. First are like y'all, you get your powers from items. Unlike the other two, y'all don't really have fancy names or anything. Next are magicians, who, of course, get their powers from magic.

"The third are people like me, kupua, who just have power and don't got to rely on spells or items. We're the ones you wouldn't want to mess with. And right about now, you're on my bad side."

"What do you want from us?" Chirus asks, clearly intimidated by all of the strange terms and magical floating water.

"All I want is that little brown-headed boy there. Yes, you in the red shirt. You got a bounty on your head, little fella. But that ain't why I got to get you. It's 'cause my boss says so."

"Who is your boss?" Nima asks.

"Well," Edihi crosses her arms, then raises a finger to her chin and thoughtfully looks up.

"I have multiple bosses I guess… IPSHA is pretty funny, ain't it?"

I want to use my persuasion ability, but all of this tension is getting to me, so without thinking, I just blurt out, "IPSHA? What in the world are you going on about, lady?!"

Edihi looks at me, then raises her hand to cover her mouth and giggles, "Huh, I don't think I was supposed to say that much. Looks like I'll have to take all y'all out."

Suddenly, a beam of water comes out of the dome's wall and slams into my side, blasting me off my feet. I hit the ground hard, and then I hear everyone scatter. There is a swooshing fire noise, so I think Yoseph retaliated, but then I hear a grunt and a thud, so she must've struck back.

I get up and switchblade my shield onto my arm. At the sight of my tool, an angry, determined seriousness overcomes me. Everyone is apprehensively circling the assassin. Well, all except for Chirus, who is distancing himself from the assassin as much as possible.

Suddenly, Edihi lunges at Nima, kicking by her face and making her flinch. The assassin then smiles as she stares down Nima while the rest of us are frozen in indecisiveness. Nima could easily take the swing and cut this woman, but she hesitates, and Edihi punches her hard in the face as a result. Nima's hands instantly shoot up to her face, and then the assassin kicks her in the stomach.

Chirus yells for Bacoj to watch out, but then Bacoj is knocked back by a blast of water like I was. The part of the dome over Yoseph's head opens up, showering him with ice cold rain, and as soon as he moves out of the way, the rain forms into a bubble and slams into Matt's feet.

My brother trips, hitting his head hard on the ground, and as he begins to writhe in pain, Edihi makes a beeline for him. Does this chick really think she can get away with that?!

Enraged, I take off towards her. For some reason she doesn't seem to know that I'm approaching her, and right before she reaches my brother, I violently tackle her. The two of us crash on the ground with me on top, and I immediately rear back and punch her as hard as I can in the face.

This stuns her, and I'm still furious, so I punch her again, harder this time. Her face gets red and she returns a crippling punch to my gut. She then tries to wriggle me off, but rage overcomes me and I grab her hair. I feel like my body is engulfed in flames, and instead of punching her like I'd intended to, I viciously scratch her across the face.

She raises her arms to block her face. I tug on her hair to get her to move them, but when that doesn't work, I let go and instead grab her arms, trying my best to slam them into her face.

"Duck!" Chirus yells at me, but I don't understand what he's saying and I'm rammed with a hard blast of water. She successfully pushes me off, then stumbles back into a loose headlock from Bacoj.

The assassin immediately head-butts him and elbows him in the stomach. He backs away, and then she kicks him excessively hard in the crotch, causing him to crumple to the ground. Yoseph runs up to Edihi, holding his wooden spear with the flaming blade intimidatingly close to her face.

Of course, the assassin knows he isn't going to do anything, and the dome opens up above him. This time, Chirus gives Yoseph a head's up and he dodges the shower of rain. He twirls his staff until the non-burning side is pointed towards Edihi, then mildly pokes her in the stomach.

"Yoseph, hit her!" I scream, annoyed at his chivalry, but it's too late.

Edihi rips the staff from Yoseph's hand and jabs the blade of fire into his chest. Of course, it does nothing but shove him back, but her intent to kill cranks my anger back up to a max. I leap to my feet, rear back while she's turning around, and swing my shield as hard as possible at her face.

She ducks, then shoves me hard. I stumble back as she begins to approach me. The smug grin on her face is driving me crazy, so I come back around, lower and harder this time. She chooses to take the hit to the arm, and frustratingly, she takes it pretty well.

The assassin punches me in my face, but I'm so angry right now it feels like she hit me with a pillow. Filled with rushing heat and rage,

I decide to tackle her again. She tries to push back, but a surge of energy overcomes me and I manage to drag her onto the asphalt.

Instead of blocking, she attacks, taking countless swipes at my face. I try to pin down her arms, but she's too violent. Without warning, she stops swinging, and a second later, both of us are drenched in icy water. It's such a sensory rush that I am stunned long enough for her to slip from under me. Instead of attacking anyone, she starts to hobble towards the dome edge.

Nima comes out of nowhere, uncharacteristically knocking the assassin in the top of her head with the back of her sickle. Edihi immediately puts a hand on her head and stumbles away from Nima, then retaliates with a beam of water. It crashes into Nima and causes her to fall on her butt.

To my surprise, Matt runs up to the assassin next, machete in hand. Edihi looks at him halfheartedly, then takes a grab at him, but she is sluggish, so he easily dodges. He has the perfect opening for an attack, but just like Yoseph, he stupidly doesn't do anything because she's a woman.

The assassin hobbles to the edge of the dome, then waves her hand and the whole thing crashes down on us. I don't let the cold water stun me this time, and instead, I get up and take off after her. The cold water feels good against my hot skin, and I use my refreshed feeling as a speed boost.

However, after a few steps, I realize that she isn't hobbling towards the empty darkness. No, instead she is headed towards a group of silhouettes. She looks at them, then her shoulders bounce and she shakes her head. They nod, and then start running towards us. Oh boy. I turn around to retreat but suddenly a man I've never seen before is there.

He raises his hand, and in a yellow flash, I pass out.

Chapter 15

Sing Well or Die

~ Samantha ~

I wake with a violent start, looking around in every direction at once. Instead of being in some type of government holding cell or something, I am lying on a green sofa in the middle of a cozy living room. Sizzling noises and light talking are coming from an adjacent room, and I can smell delicious breakfast scents drifting from there.

Confused, I sit up and take another look around. There are a few paintings of forests and beaches hung up on the wall. The large windows to my right let in warm daylight. We must be in an apartment or something, because outside I can see the tops of shops and such.

Lying in the corner near the empty fireplace is Chirus, Matt is asleep in a recliner, and Bacoj is on a couch across from me. There is a small table in between my sofa and Bacoj's, and on it lies a note. I reach forward silently and pick it up.

Good Morning Crescent and friends. As courtesy for last night's violence, we have provided you with new backpacks, clothes, and an open range to this apartment's food resources. However, we have not forgotten our original mission, and law enforcement will arrive to detain you at midmorning today.

Enjoy your freedom while you still have it.

I glance around for a clock and find it on the far wall above the fireplace. It's almost 12:15. As I learned earlier, Arret has 26 hours, so midmorning was about three hours ago. Panicking, I spring off of the couch and dash into the adjacent room, which is the kitchen. In there are Yoseph and Nima. Nima is cooking scrambled eggs on the stove, and Yoseph is cutting up some oranges. As soon as I burst in, they stop talking to one another and look up at me.

"We have to leave, now!" I say, horrified that we could be arrested at any moment.

"Do not panic," Nima says simply as she goes back to cooking the eggs, "That note was but a false alarm."

"What?" I ask, a bit confused.

"On the back of the note is tomorrow's date, so this message was, essentially, put there simply to scare us. At first Yoseph and I believed it was planted to lure us into a false sense of security, but law enforcement would be incredibly punctual about our capture."

"Besides," Yoseph chimes in as he cuts another orange wedge, "They wouldn't give us new stuff just for us to be arrested."

Feeling even more confused and a bit stupid, I take a seat by Yoseph. He hands me an orange slice, and I bite into the thing. It is juicy and way tastier than it should be… probably because last night's dinner was just a few knuckle sandwiches and some ice water. Alright, I apologize for that.

I slurp the fruit down in no time, then ask, "So, are they on our side or something?"

"Optimistically speaking, yes. However, when we take realism into account, more than likely no." Nima comments.

"Nima and I were just talking about it. I'm thinking that they realized we were chill and want to help out but had to leave that threat here as a formality. Nima thinks that they're waiting for us to gather a bigger group, then arrest all of us at once so that they could take away as much political momentum as possible."

Yoseph raises his eyebrows, then adds, "Honestly, Nima's theory sounds like the right one."

I stay silent, waiting for breakfast to be finished. Yoseph finishes with the oranges and begins to prepare some type of pastry; drizzling what looks like syrup over some rolls. Maybe a crafty French toast? Nima scrapes the scrambled eggs into a container, and then starts putting meat cubes onto her skillet. The skillet must be hot, because they immediately begin to sizzle.

"Yo Nima… remember when we first got out of the hospital last night and Bacoj made that joke about the city being made of clouds?" Yoseph starts.

"Indeed." Nima replies, flipping one of the meat cubes.

"What's the real story behind Safemill?" He asks.

Nima shrugs, "Frankly, I do not know. Most people do not. But, although I am ignorant on the topic, I am not gullible enough to believe such a fantastical tale."

Just then, the person in question bursts into the kitchen.

"We've got to get out of here, guys! They're going to arrest us any second!" warns Bacoj.

"Read the back of the letter." I tell him nonchalantly.

Puzzled, he slowly makes his way back into the living room, and then we hear him say, "They were joking?!"

He quickly walks back into the kitchen to search our eyes for some type of explanation, but the three of us almost shrug in unison.

"Actually, yeah, that's our best guess." Yoseph explains.

Bacoj laughs, balling up the note and throwing it away, "So they just attacked us and then gave us free supplies?"

"Essentially." Nima replies.

The thief lets out another astonished laugh, then reaches in his pocket. His face lights up, and he pulls out a red wallet that we all know isn't his.

"I also plucked this off that assassin lady last night. I don't think we should have any money problems for a little bit, because she was loaded!"

Yoseph and I look at one another, shocked, but Nima congratulates the thief.

"Wait, how did you get that?" I ask him, honestly confused.

"When I went to put her in a headlock, I simply slipped it out of her pocket first. She didn't notice a thing."

"So that's why your headlock was so loose?" I ask.

The thief looks off, then says, "Sure."

A rush of annoyance fills me, and I sit up straight in my seat.

"See, that's the kind of stuff that pissed me off last night. Both of you, and Matt in there, are a bunch of softies."

Yoseph turns around from his syrup rolls, looking puzzled, and asks, "Wait, me too?"

"Yes, you too! You were the main one!"

"What are you talking about?" Bacoj asks, swiping an orange wedge from the table.

"The fact that you wouldn't hit her! Whatever that she's a woman, the most important thing is that she's a freaking assassin!"

Yoseph and Bacoj both look at one another, embarrassed, and then the flood of excuses come.

"Well, I mean, I'd already stolen her wallet…"

"She was outnumbered, so, I wanted to be fair…"

"It seemed like all I needed to do was just dissuade her…"

"What was she going to do with water powers, anyway?"

Nima cuts them both off with a bout of genuine laughter, then scrapes the meat cubes into a container and says, "Wow, you two really are softies!"

Once Nima and Yoseph finish making breakfast, we wake up Chirus and Matt, fill them in on what happened, and absolutely destroy Nima and Yoseph's cooking. The meal they prepared was quite honestly the most delicious thing I have ever tasted, and I don't know if it was because they are so good at cooking or if I was just that hungry.

After breakfast, we all get changed and review the Ieri Tropo. By this point, the other half of the map has fallen off and all of the lines are faded from water damage, but we are still able to tell where we need to go. Instead of it being that Celestial Conference, a pyramid is our next destination.

We assume that everything in the apartment is up for grabs, so we load up our backpacks something fierce. There are some bandages in the bathroom that Nima says act like portable florma, so we take all of them and dump them in Yoseph's bag, along with soap bars.

Nima stuffs her bag with miscellaneous accessories that we find around the place, and Bacoj puts a brick of knives into his bag. I get the food like last time (Nima made some extra wraps just to fill up space). Chirus puts his special tambourine in his bag, and at the sight of the instrument, he seems to get irritated.

Matt asks what he can carry, but Nima decides that it would be best for him to hold on to any of the special items we get along the way. Now that we're all suited up and ready to go, we exit the apartment, making sure to leave the door unlocked just in case we need to return.

Outside, the day is brisk and chilly. Luckily, the six of us are dressed appropriately. Also luckily, none of our clothes really stand out, so no one bats an eye at us. It's a relatively easygoing walk to the pyramid.

The city streets are busy, and there are a considerable amount of woodish people here, but they just wave at us or smile in adoration. At first I'm confused, but then I remember that societal thing Nima taught me a while back about humans being seen as children. Weird.

Almost everyone is wearing gleaming, plastic-like rings around their palms (they almost look like brass knuckles but pushed further down) and doing weird stuff with them. Some people walk around talking with their hand on the side of their face, as if they were trying to politely convince a headache to go away. Others press holographic buttons appearing on their forearms, pausing to think about what to press next.

Nima sees my face and comments, "Those are the Arretian equivalent to cellular phones, called *shuza*. When one places their palms against their cheeks, one is sending or receiving a call. The holographic buttons on one's arms let them carry out text message conversations."

Chirus and Bacoj show us theirs, and then proceed to check messages on them. As the six of us approach the pyramid, we also find out that it has a wall surrounding it. Like, a very big wall. It's made of cement and painted with ancient colors (under the graffiti); a huge contrast to the fairly modern city around it.

It sits in a small park with a few benches and trees, and there are a few people hanging around, walking their pets or staring at the wall. There is also a giant, gleaming sapphire gate sitting at the front of the pyramid, serving as the only entry point through this wall. Beside it stands a wooden info sign.

We walk up on it and give the sign a read.

"Here stands the Dazus Pyramid. It is rumored to have many treasures and dangers inside, but despite attempts from local, provincial, and governmental forces, the pyramid refuses to open or be demolished.

"This pyramid dates back far before civilization, when Safemill itself was still being formed. Some historians say it is actually a part of Safemill, thus giving it its invincible and mystical properties. We urge citizens to avoid affiliating themselves with the gate, for those who have tried to climb its walls or open its gate have reported extreme misfortunes happening the same day."

We all take a moment to soak in the information, and then Nima asks, "Is there a hint on the Ieri Tropo?"

I pull the flimsy, faded, half sheet from my back pocket and give it a look. What it says doesn't make any sense, so I read it out loud to the others.

"The instruments of your spirit will part the gates." I say.

There is silence, and then Matt says, "It sounds straightforward but at the same time I have no idea what it means."

"Can I give it a look?" Chirus asks, and I hand him the map.

He studies it, and Nima peeks over his shoulder. Abruptly, he hands it back to me.

"Yeah I have no idea what that means." He admits.

"Maybe we have to use our tools? That seems like a spirit instrument to me…" Yoseph suggests.

"But once they're out, what are we going to do with them?" I kindly challenge, "The thing is invincible, so it isn't like we can break it open."

"She's right." Bacoj says, "This thing has been around for eons. Countless people have probably tried to open this. If we want to come out on top, then we're going to have to think out of the box."

"Maybe we have to… express ourselves somehow? Like…" Matt pauses.

"What, reciting a poem?" Chirus jokes.

"Maybe screaming in unison?" Matt adds on, and they both laugh.

Yoseph gives it another shot, "What if it's like some type of spiritual journey that we have to go on? Like a spirit challenge that we have to face, and we've got to meditate or something to get there?"

Everyone stares at him, and then Bacoj peeps, "You're overthinking this."

"I mean it's so straightforward… maybe we have to use actual instruments?" Matt suggests.

"That is a clever suggestion Matthew, but the only instrument we have is Chirus' tambourine… perhaps the other instruments are our voices?" Nima proposes.

There is a bit more silence, and then everyone agrees that Nima's idea makes the most sense. Well, all accept Chirus, who is a bit pessimistic.

"We're going to sing the gate open? What if it doesn't work?! Then we'll have that misfortune curse, and we'll probably die."

"Well, you better sing well." I respond, and everyone chuckles except for Chirus.

"So, what, acapella-style?" Yoseph asks, "If so, I can beatbox."

"Yeah that sounds awesome. I'll whistle or something." Matt suggests.

"I've got a mad hum if you guys want to hear it." I chime in, feeling the groove of everyone's excitement. Now that I'm starting to think about it, I'm beginning to feel more and more confident about our plan. I actually think I saw something similar in a show once.

"If you don't mind, Chirus, I could do some serious damage with that tambourine of yours." Bacoj comments.

Chirus hands over the tambourine, and Nima rubs the side of her arm. Nima and Chirus look at one another, and then Nima lets out a nervous chuckle.

"To be completely transparent, I am incredibly inept with regards to musical tasks." She admits.

"What's wrong?" Matt asks, "Just follow along with the beat. You don't have to sing or anything… heck, since we're standing on this pathway, you can just scrape your foot on the ground."

"If we can pull that off, it would sound pretty dope." Yoseph adds.

The alien takes a few steps back and her eyes fall downcast, "I do not feel comfortable participating in this task, for I feel my weaknesses will detract from the efforts of the team and thus lead to failure. Continue without me, and I will join in again once this challenge is surpassed."

There is some awkward silence, and then Chirus says, "I guess I'm singing then."

We all look at each other, waiting for someone to start, and then suddenly, Bacoj puts his head down and starts rattling the tambourine. One two three *four*… that's a nice beat! He's shaking the tambourine on the first three beats and hitting it on the fourth.

Yoseph, unannounced, comes in with some freestyle beatboxing, which he is surprisingly good at. His beatboxing along with Bacoj's tambourine sounds admittedly pretty sick, so we all fight back laughter as the two continue.

I look at Matt who looks back at me expectantly, and then I start my humming. I hum as low as I can, doing so in short bursts that sound like they would belong with the beat that Yoseph and Bacoj have made. It does, and then we all look at Matt.

Instead of whistling, he looks at Nima, raises his eyebrows, and starts rhythmically scraping his foot against the ground. Yoseph was right, this does sound really nice! The four of us then look at Chirus, trying our best not to let grins overtake us. His face is a weird mix between confused and horrified, and then with a large sigh, he begins to sing.

"Gate, we ask that you open. Gate, today we plead and try. Gate, gate oh please just open. I don't want to see my new friends die."

Chirus is more so melodically talking as opposed to actually singing, but there's a bit of passionate flare in his voice that makes it sound impressively good, so we keep going.

"Gate, come on man I'm begging. Gate, just do it super please. Gate, we're being deadly serious. Look, I'll get down on my knees."

He does, but the gate still doesn't open. I'm starting to run out of breath, but the others don't stop, so neither do I.

"Gate, you're starting to scare me. For all that's good just open. Gate, we're losing our breath here. Well, here is the bitter end."

The others get the cue and dramatically end their musical parts, but even after silence has settled upon us, nothing happens.

CHAPTER 16

LOTS OF EXPLOSIONS

~ SAMANTHA ~

In an ear-splitting crash, almost as if an explosion went off, the gate suddenly splits apart. Under the watchful eyes of both us and passersby, its sapphire doors slowly roll inward, letting loose a long, stony, grumbling noise. What? We did it?!

Stunned remarks come from all around us, and I quickly realize that we're surrounded by a crowd of bystanders. They look into the dark abyss beyond the pyramid's entrance, and then after taking a few pictures with their shuza, they begin to disperse.

I gaze back at the others, and everyone has an astonished look on their faces.

Nima clears her throat, then says, "Well, let us proceed."

Everyone except for Chirus moves forward. We continue for a moment, then look back at him in confusion

"No." He says, arms crossed and nose pointed high.

"Wait, seriously?" Yoseph asks.

Chirus nods stubbornly. We all look at each other, unsure of what to do next. Should we use persuasion on him?

Matt asks what everyone is thinking, "Well, why not?"

Chirus heaves a sigh, "I joined this group so that I could find some more info on that tambourine, but aside from using it just then, no one has made an effort to look into it."

I look at the others, unsure of what to say or do. I figured Chirus joined us just because, but I suppose that isn't the case.

Nima heaves a sigh, then says, "Bacoj, hand me the tambourine."

The thief does so, and then Nima walks over to Chirus.

"I was the one who made the promise, so I will fulfill it. Chirus and I will go and learn more about this tambourine. Do you four believe that you can handle whatever is in this pyramid by yourselves?"

I glance at Yoseph, Matt, and Bacoj, who are looking among one another with curious expressions.

"Sure thing." I assure Nima.

She smiles and nods, and then she and Chirus walk off towards the rest of the city. The four of us turn around and are met with the looming wall of darkness once more.

"Uh, Yoseph?" I ask.

"What? Oh, right." He says, and then a second later, his hand is engulfed in flames. The fire throws flickering orange light against the cement walls. A second later, Bacoj activates his cyber vira, casting more light in the tunnel.

The green and orange contrast one another and weakly fight off the expansive, hungry darkness around us. I soon start to feel paranoid, so I switchblade my shield onto my arm. Matt does the same with his machete, and the four of us continue our apprehensive crawl through the pitch black.

The air grows hazy and warmer as we continue onward. The faint smell of gunpowder begins to grow stronger, and soon, we start to find strange, glowing stalagmites alongside our path. Yoseph suddenly stops, and so do the rest of us.

"Y'all see those?" He asks quietly, which scares me more than it would if he were to panic.

Frantically, I scan the tunnel floor, and then I find it. Just at the edge of the combined firelight, I see something black. It kind of looks like three sprouts of ivy coming out of a lily pad. The harder I look, the more of these "ivy pads" I can see.

"Bacoj," Yoseph whispers again, quietly and calmly, "You know what these are?"

I hear the thief swallow hard, and then he says, "It's too dark to tell for sure, but they look like *Jade Spinsaws*."

There is silence, and then Bacoj continues, "Oh, right. Jade Spinsaws are notoriously aggressive plants that will slice you up if you aren't careful."

I look over to make sure Matt is still there, and he is, but he's scared silent.

"What should we do?" I ask

Bacoj thinks, then says, "They're provoked when there is movement nearby. If we had anything to throw, we could lure them out of this state and make them vulnerable to fire. I'll use one of the knives in my bag…"

Before Bacoj can unzip his bag, I stop him, remembering my star coins. As soon as I do, I realize that I should've used them on Edihi last night.

"I've actually got a few projectiles of my own." I say, now a bit upset at the thought of the assassin.

I focus on that feeling of punching beyond my body, and as expected, a bright yellow star-shaped projectile shoots out of my hand. It travels through the dark air, throwing a cylinder of light against the floors, ceiling, and wall.

As soon as it passes over the Jade Spinsaws, the plants violently tremble, and cute little flowers pop out of the top of them.

The four of us scream, but then we all calm down as we realize what we're looking at. The flowers have four petals connected to yellow circles with smiley faces in the middle. They start to sway back and forth, almost like they're dancing gleefully.

Yoseph lets out a lighthearted laugh, and I playfully nudge Matt in the side. He looks back at me, letting out a relieved sigh.

"Shoot another one." Bacoj says, absolutely stoic.

Beginning to get worried, I mentally prepare myself to shoot again. The punch travels forth from my palm in the form of star-shaped light. As it zips above the patch of dancing flowers, horrible egg cracking noises begin to fill the tunnel as their faces fold open. Four-foot vines snake up from the holes that were their faces, and what sprouts from the top sends goosebumps prickling along my neck.

They're human tongues. Yes, pink, taste bud covered, human tongues that wriggle disgustingly in the air and somehow make choking noises. Little sparks like bang pops go off around them, throwing quick bursts of light in the blackness of the tunnel.

Green, spiky leaves flip up from around the tongues, spinning violently like they're helicopter blades. I'm only awestruck by these horrific abominations for a second before Bacoj suddenly unleashes twin rivers of fire onto the plants.

Bright green fire gushes out of his hands, immediately engulfing the Jade Spinsaws and causing them to thrash about violently. Bacoj stops his assault, breathing heavily, and the four of us continue to watch the group of plants writhe, crackle, and shriek. Their weird plant flesh turns glowing pink and floats away with the flames. Soon, all that's left are shriveled ashes and stagnant smoke.

"You think there are any more of them?" Yoseph asks Bacoj.

"Probably not. I heard somewhere that they need a lot of water to grow, so it baffles me that there were so many in one place. We should keep moving though. I'm getting creeped out."

"Wait," I say, noticing a single stalactite glowing in the smoke, "Do you think that's important?"

I point up and everyone looks. Yoseph raises his flaming hand a bit higher so we can all get a better look.

"It's the only glowing spike on the ceiling, and it was over a bunch of those plant demon thingies… sounds important to me, right?" Matt comments.

"Worth a shot." Yoseph says, and then he switchblades his staff into his hand.

As he's swinging at the spike and missing more than he's landing, Bacoj turns to me.

"Uh, just what exactly are we looking for again?"

I whip out the flimsy map, and Bacoj apprehensively holds his fireball a bit higher so I can see better. No need, for the hologram-like info that springs up off of the map is still perfectly visible in the dark.

"It says our next item is… the *Peace Per*?" I say.

"No way," Bacoj chuckles, then he takes a peek at the map before realizing it won't work with him.

"What's it look like?" He continues, and I hear a successful crack nearby, telling me Yoseph must've landed a solid blow on the stalactite.

I examine the holographic clue, then say, "It's kind of like a slab of golden rock with a big blue gem on one side."

Bacoj laughs in astonishment, "Are you joking?"

"What?" I ask anxiously, "Is that something special?"

Bacoj looks at me like I just asked the obvious, but then he remembers that we're aliens and have no clue what anything is.

"Right. Well, a per is a type of weapon… actually, the concept of a Mortar Per came from it… anyway, I'm getting ahead of myself. The Peace Per is a mythical weapon used by a folk hero named Teodusi. Whenever he put the gem in the path of the sun, it would shoot giant laser beams that made things explode."

"That sounds awesome!" Matt says, and with a satisfying crack and thud, Yoseph knocks the stalactite down.

"You're right. I don't know the full myth, but I think he ended up losing it in a bet or something to do with hubris. Either way, the point is, the Peace Per is a thing of legend."

"So, like an alien Excalibur?" Yoseph suggests, the broken stalactite now in hand.

Bacoj raises an eyebrow and shrugs. Right, I guess he wouldn't know what that is, would he? The four of us stand in slightly awkward silence for a bit, then continue on. Our path ends quickly and abruptly at a moldy wooden door. It looks pretty heavy, so I don't think breaking it down will work.

I look back at the boys, stumped, and they look equally as clueless. Yoseph raises the stalactite experimentally, and just like that, the door opens. We don't even have a chance to look at one another in astonishment before we're engulfed in blinding light.

It takes a few painful moments for my eyes to adjust, and when they do, I lower my arms to get a good look at the place. There is a massive square skylight at the top. The sunlight pouring in from above casts a deep shadow of something on a glass platform high above our heads. It looks like some sort of treasure chest.

I just realized that the floor is flooded with water. It's still, clear, and about ankle high. I can see the tan marble floor just beneath. Rising out of the ankle-high water are two cases of old, dark oak stairs. They spiral up the mossy stone wall, which is covered in reflected sunlight. Underneath the moss, the walls are painted with sharp shades of blue, lime green, and pink zig zags.

Bacoj groans, and I notice a second later what he's upset about. Four massive leaves sprout out of the floor, sitting still in the glass-smooth water. The leaves have white, glimmering dots freckled across them. Dozens of ivy pads litter the floor around it, completely submerged.

Oh great.

"Bacoj, is that what I think it is?" Yoseph asks, not daring to step into the water.

"I don't know," Bacoj admits "I've never seen a Jade Spinsaw this big… I've never seen any kind of plant this big."

We all stare at the calm pool for a bit longer before I decide that it's time to take charge.

"Alright guys, we can't stand here forever. Does anyone have any solutions?"

"Well, I know that as soon as we touch the water, they're all going to attack us." Bacoj reasons.

We're silent, and then to my surprise, Matt speaks up.

"What if I try to use my machete to freeze the water? Then we wouldn't have to worry about any of the smaller ones."

"You can do that?" Bacoj asks.

My brother shrugs, "I mean, I hope so."

Bacoj and Yoseph are silent, and then they nod approvingly. Matt looks at me. I give him a shrug, genuinely unsure, and he shrugs back. Holding his breath, he reaches out to dip the tip of his machete into the water.

The rest of us lean closer, eager to see what happens. Matt's machete gently pierces the silky-smooth water, and before a ripple can travel out, the water around his machete is suddenly ice. Soft crackling travels over the floor as ice seamlessly forms from the water before, until the whole thing looks like the floor of a hockey arena.

"There we go, man! Good job!" Yoseph pats Matt on the back.

Apprehensively, the thief places the tip of his shoe on the ice floor. Nothing happens. Bacoj gently shifts more and more weight onto the ice, but everything stays fine.

I look at my brother and Yoseph, and they both give it a shot too. The ice is solid and the big Jade Spinsaw still seems to be dormant, so I join them. The four of us tip toe over to the stairs, almost slipping a few times, and then we silently examine the stairwell.

It looks even worse up close, with obvious water damage and mold running all through it. There is no railing, and each step looks like it was loosely shoved into the frame rather than nailed into it. Bacoj steps on the first one, but surprisingly, it holds his weight. Delighted, the thief goes to climb the staircase, but the very next step immediately snaps in half, sending Bacoj crashing onto the icy floor.

"Well, that isn't going to work." Bacoj says as we help him up, "I guess you all will have to fly up there without us."

Yoseph and I share a nod, then I force out a star coin and mentally stretch it into a hover star. I hop on, and then the two of us begin a slow ascent to the glass platform.

We both just kind of stare awkwardly at the wall for a bit, and Yoseph goes to speak. Before he can start, there is a loud crinkling noise followed by a watery sliding sound. We don't even have to look down, for suddenly the noise maker is eye level with us. Oh my goodness. It almost looks like a venus flytrap, but it has a bulbous head instead of a flat one. Its flesh is veiny and sickeningly orange, and frost prickles here and there around its mouth. Suddenly, the creature's face splits open four ways, revealing a wrinkly pink mouth and two thrashing, bladed, magenta tongues.

The creature emits a deafening screech like a defective firework, and its cry is so loud that it sends waves of goosebumps across my skin. Yoseph immediately blasts higher into the air, and although the creature has no eyes, it seems to spot Yoseph.

It rears back and lunges, but only gets a face-full of fire in return. Yoseph looks down, and to our combined dismay, the flames did nothing to this thing.

"Uh… I'll figure something out; you guys get out of here!" He shouts, and then he takes off before I can reply.

The creature screeches again, apparently upset, and then it turns to face me with a surprising amount of speed. Its four lips curl menacingly, bearing sharp, needle-like teeth.

This doesn't look good. For a second, I glance down at Bacoj and Matt. Maybe it was to see if they had somehow figured a way out of this situation. Maybe it was just to look at how dizzyingly high up I am from the ground.

I'm not sure, but in the moment I glanced down, I could tell that the two boys were OK. Bacoj is trying in vain to light the creature's leaves on fire, and Matt is trying to saw into the stem, which has the width of a tree or two.

My eyes flick back up to the plant monster's curled mouth, and I make my hover star float to the left. If there is one thing I need in this battle, I know it's going to be speed. I've never fought a giant monster before, so all of this is pretty much assumption.

The creature opens its mouth wider and I expect it to lunge at me like it did Yoseph. I violently jet out of the way, which is still good, but the monster doesn't try to eat me. No, instead, it gags up a volley of… fireworks?!

Colorful missiles and glowing bolts spring out of the creature's mouth, zipping and spiraling before letting out deafening booms. Far away, fireworks always look sick, but this close up, I nearly soil myself.

"I think I'll call you Bang Mouth!" I shout, more to myself than anyone else. I don't know why I did it.

The thundering crashes and ear-ringing pops from the fireworks rattle the wooden staircases along the wall. Blinding, fiery, beautiful explosions of purple and green and red paint the air, leaving behind clots of black smoke and shimmering sparks.

Confused and honestly pretty freaked out, I decide to keep flying, trying my best to out-speed this thing. Bang Mouth continues to shriek and spew fireworks from its face, pelting the air around me with whining roman candles and exploding wheels. Searing wind lashes out from the blasts, spraying me with red-hot sparks and smoke. Thank the Lord this thing isn't accurate, but goodness, what I wouldn't give to be able to summon my shield right now!

Even though I've flown at least five circles around it by now, the monster continues to twist its head towards me like its stem is made of rubber. I swoop under and around an exploding shower of gold sparkles, then fake like I'm going the other way. My maneuver doesn't faze Bang Mouth at all, and it just lets out an unamused, growling screech before lunging at me. I jet backwards, of all places, and slam my back into the stairwell. Disoriented but still afraid, my hover star goes to the right and I dodge the creature's closing maw.

It bites down on the old stairs, and in one violent tug, rips the wood from the cement wall, chewing and crunching on it loudly. The wood seemingly dissolves in Bang Mouth's mouth, and then it raises its head to the sky and lets out an ear-piercing shriek followed by an intimidating display of fiery mortars and sparkling fountains.

Abruptly, a blue beam of solid light bursts down from above, going directly into Bang Mouth's maw. The plant glows for a split second, then its head violently explodes, spraying orange flames and colorful, sparkling pops into the air. Flabby hunks of plant flesh rain from the sky, fluttering while still aflame.

What was that?! I look up, and Yoseph is steadily descending with the Peace Per in hand. I shout for him, but for some reason I sound muffled, and he doesn't look up. I say his name, and I can feel the vibration in my ears but I can hardly hear my own words. Did… did I lose my hearing?

Oh, right. The thing was shooting fireworks at point-blank range and screeching non-stop, so of course my ears will need a break. I descend with Yoseph to the ever-approaching ice floor to see Matt and Bacoj staring up, looking equally as uncomfortable. It must've affected their hearing, too.

Yoseph and I wordlessly reach the ground, and then the four of us take one more silent look around before leaving. The trip back through the dark tunnel is completely quiet, and we're finally relieved when we exit. The city is active around us, but my ears still feel like they're plugged with cotton. Hardly any of the noise around me surpasses this constant ringing.

Bacoj quickly spots a park bench, and the four of us plop down on it. Yoseph's bag is full, so he gives Matt the Peace Per to hold on to. The four of us sit there, staring at the swaying trees or passing cars, letting our hearing slowly, steadily recover.

****

About two hours later, I wake to something rough poking me in the face. I take an angry swat at it. It was Chirus poking me in the face with a stick, and once I lock eyes with him, he starts laughing hysterically. Nima is behind him, and she's also uncharacteristically giggly.

My annoyance quickly fades into excitement as I realize I can hear again. It's still kind of muffled, but nowhere near as bad as before. I go to nudge the others awake, but they're already staring at the odd pair standing over us.

"You two alright?" I ask.

They look at one another, then chuckle. Nima replies, "We… are in an optimum condition."

Her speech is slurred, and it sounds weird especially since she uses so many big words all the time.

"Aight cool." Yoseph says, completely unconvinced, "You guys find out anything about the tambourine?"

They start giggling at one another and swaying like they're about to collapse, and then Chirus says, "Well, we were walking around for a looooong time… and then we found a librarian and she was kinda cute."

Nima looks at him, offended, and then they both break down into more laughter. When they finally stop laughing, Chirus looks confused.

"Yeah… what was I talking about?"

"You said something about a librarian." Bacoj offers.

"Oh right! Yeah, so the librarian was… librarianing… and then we asked her about the tambourine. So she takes us to the back."

The two begin giggling, and then Chirus continues.

"So we're in her office and she says to truly understand we need some… dilts."

At the word "dilts", the two of them begin laughing more, and Bacoj chuckles a bit, too.

"What are dilts?" I ask him.

"They're like these red vines that you can find in the woods, and if you eat them you get really giggly. They use them a lot in extreme surgeries and stuff where florma doesn't work. Apparently, they make people immune to pain."

I look at Matt and Yoseph. Matt is a bit too innocent to understand, but Yoseph and I share a bit of knowing laughter.

Chirus wheezes because he's been laughing so much with Nima, and then he continues.

"So anyway, we took the dilts and the librarian told us that the tambourine is called the… what was it again?"

"Uh… the…" Nima looks at the ground, thinking way too hard, and then says, "The *Ukob*! Ha, the Ukob."

"Right, right right right the Ukob. And the Ukob does something special when you play it and goes away after you use it once. So after she told us that Nima decided to–"

"Do not tell them *that*!" Nima half-shrieks, half-laughs.

She playfully shoves Chirus, and then they both fall to the ground, giggling themselves to an abrupt sleep.

I glance over at the boys, who are just as amused as I am. After we crack a few jokes about what just happened, Bacoj suddenly stands up.

"I'm going to go look around."

"Yo," Yoseph says, rummaging through his bag, "While you're out, can you see if someone can decipher this scroll? I found it up there with the Peace Per."

Yoseph hands the white roll to Bacoj, who scans the paper before rolling it back up.

"This is Shwedo, so somebody can definitely decipher this. I'll look around… and I'll make sure to avoid any pretty librarians."

The four of us laugh, and then Matt chimes in, "Can I go with you? Who knows what will happen!"

Bacoj gives him a concerned look, then says, "Well, out of the entire crew at the stadium yesterday, Yatniv only recognized the two of us. We'll have to be careful."

Bacoj walks over to Nima, who is completely knocked out. The thief rolls her on her stomach, and then opens her backpack and rummages through some things. He soon pulls out two pairs of sunglasses and complimenting beanies.

Matt nods excitedly, and the two of them walk off towards the city. For the longest time, it is just Yoseph and I sitting on the bench, watching cars go by and people walk down the sidewalk, listening to the muffled breeze run through the trees overhead, and feeling the lovely mix of sunlight and shade on our skin.

Eventually Yoseph sparks up a conversation about the fight we just had, and we spend the next 30 minutes talking sparsely about family and hobbies. After a while, Nima and Chirus begin to stir. Soon after, Bacoj and Matt return, and they look pretty excited.

The six of us gather around the bench, and after Nima and Chirus dodge a barrage of jokes and questions, the spotlight is on Bacoj and Matt.

"Okay," Matt says, sounding pretty stoked, "If what we learned about this scroll is true, then we're quickly on our way to being unstoppable."

Bacoj excitedly butts in, "Let me read verbatim what was translated."

He ruffles a secondary piece of paper, clears his throat ceremoniously, and then begins to read, "Since you have found the Peace Per of Teodusi, you are truly legendary. Employed unto you from the heavens above is the angle Junia."

"Angel." Matt corrects.

Bacoj nods, then continues, "This angel can be summoned in times of need, but be warned, she is so powerful that calling her could do damage to everyone nearby. To summon Junia, say or think the following words with the most conviction…"

We wait for more, but Bacoj doesn't say anything.

"Well, what are the summoning words?" Chirus asks.

"If I say them, I might summon the angel!" Bacoj warns.

Chirus nods, and asks, "So, what even is an angel?"

I raise my eyebrows in surprise, and Yoseph does the same.

"They are an element of religious iconography generally associated with Abrahamism." Nima explains.

"Weird, right?" Bacoj chimes in.

Nima turns to Yoseph, Matt, and I, "Religion on Arret is much less of a defining social aspect and more of a rare cultural observation. Due to this, many religions have no subdivisions, and are subsequently clumped into all-encompassing factions."

"What, is religion like a popular thing where you come from?" Chirus asks me.

I look nervously at Yoseph and Matt, but they look back at me, so I reply, "Um, yeah… things get spicy over it sometimes."

Nima continues on, "Bacoj, if you could so kindly pass those instructions around for us to commit to memory. In the event that the information is genuine and operational, we could most certainly benefit from added power."

Bacoj hands Yoseph the paper, and as he begins to read, Nima continues, "We will eat lunch and then depart to our next destination on the map. Samantha?"

I pull the damaged half-map out of my back pocket and give it a look, but the dotted line which we're supposed to follow disappears at the ripped edge of the paper. I show it to Nima.

"No need for concern, we will simply go to Malle Island and find the funds to retrieve another." Nima replies.

I zip open my bag and hand out food. Everyone grows silent for a moment, enjoying their lukewarm breakfast meals or wraps, and then they strike up sparse conversation again. As the others talk about how close the next city is and how many relatives they have there, I'm handed the angel-summoning scroll. I shift my wrap over to one hand and give it a look.

Oh! It's just the *Angel of the Lord* prayer! My father taught this to Matt and me when we were little, so I just show it to my brother, who scans it and nods, then give it back to Yoseph so he can keep rereading. It's oh so tempting to give the actual summoning a try. However, the warning gives me the chills, and the thought of summoning a freaking angel both excites and terrifies me.

We're soon finished, and we pack away the sparse leftovers so we can get up to go. Chirus and Nima lead the group, talking and joking with one another. It's about a ten minute walk, and our destination is, to my surprise, an escalator station.

At least that's what the sign reads outside of what looks like a really big bus shelter. I take a look around. The city ended a few streets behind us, and now there is just grassy field and sightseers. The ground abruptly ends not too far away. There is a fence curving at the very edge that runs behind the escalator station, but beyond that looks like open air.

As we approach the station, I notice what the gap in the fence is. Instead of it leading to a traditional escalator like I had assumed, it's a giant, square tunnel made of super thick glass that curves straight down and out of sight. To my horror, even beyond the glass, I still can't see the ground.

There are police officers in yellow jackets and soldiers in fatigues all hanging around the entrance and talking to one another. Of course, this puts all of us on edge, but as we pay and make our way through the entrance, it seems as though they didn't recognize us. They just look at us from behind their sunglasses, pause, then smile kindly and wave.

We hurry into the escalator before more tension can happen.

Right before any of us can let loose a breath of relief, we realize where we are. Instead of stepping on a stair, we're on a large platform with two chairs. I look out of the glass tunnel and see that the ground… is hundreds of feet beneath me?!

Shrouded in a distant blue hue, below us sits an expansive sea of autumn trees stretching out as far as I can see. Being able to look out and actually see the slight curve of the horizon immediately gives me vertigo, but since the walls are made of glass, the only safe thing I can think of is sitting on the floor.

Honestly, I want to curl into a ball while I'm at it, but I force myself not to. Goodness grief; I can see everything up here. There are towns tucked into coves of trees, and I can see another one of those monorail things snaking around between each village.

The escalator calmly and smoothly carries us downward towards a beach city. At first I thought it was lowering us directly into the shimmering blue ocean, but then I noticed the giant cluster of New York-like skyscrapers and the massive patches of suburbs making a half-circle around them.

"That is Semparus." Nima says, her voice echoing oddly in this glass tunnel.

Chirus suddenly collapses in one of the nearby chairs and lets out a massive sigh.

"I need to take a break. Too many emotions!"

"Same." Yoseph says, his voice quivering a bit.

The big guy sits down on my right, and then Matt plops down on my left. Nima takes the chair beside Chirus. There is no more sitting room left, so Bacoj sits on the platform behind us.

We are all silent, knowingly confused and relieved. It is obvious that sound travels well in this glass tunnel, for we can hear conversations from people above and below us on the escalator. Because of this, nobody talks about what just happened.

Through the quiet, there is a chorus of shrieks that echoes from the escalator below, and then we see futuristic fighter jets streak through the sky, coming dangerously close to the escalator. Our tunnel sways and shudders a bit, and the escalator temporarily stops before starting back up again.

"That was pretty close." Chirus comments.

Nima looks like she's about to say something, but then the jets bank in the distance and come back around. It all happens so fast. Almost quicker than I can notice, it looks as though a piece of one of the jets fell off. The object then violently and unnaturally shoots through the air. That can't be a missile, can it?

The object smashes into the escalator, erupting in a fiery splash of glass and escalator panels. Everything in me sinks as the tunnel we're in jerks harshly to the right. I, along with everyone else, slam against the wall, and then another explosion sounds closer behind us. I'm washed with heat and thrown against the ceiling, but instead of hitting the ground, everything starts falling at once.

Everyone is screaming, including me, as we plummet faster and faster to the rushing forest canopy below. Wind roars through my ears. Weightlessness and sunlight engulf my body. The glass walls around us are spinning apart into jagged shards. This is the end, I'm sure of it.

The ground is suddenly only a few dozen feet below us, and all I can do is brace myself for death.

CHAPTER 17

CRITICAL COUSIN

~ YOSEPH ~

I just barely finish my prayer before we reach the treetops. Immediately, my body begins to jerkily slow down, like a speeding roller coaster pulling into its station. Glass and debris flutter past me, not any bit of it touching my body. In a matter of seconds, I go from plummeting to my death to hovering a few feet off the ground.

My stomach gently meets the forest floor, and as soon as I gain control of my limbs, I whirl around. High in the trees and shining like the sun is the most beautiful creature I've ever seen. Its skin is made of light, and its hair is a shimmering river of bronze. Behind its head is a faint circle of rainbows. The white, glowing robes around its body float as though they are in water.

The being's eyes are an ethereal green, and they stare down at me with caring love and odd amusement. There are massive, feathery, silver wings sprouting from behind it, but instead of flapping to keep it in the air, they stay stiff and outstretched, as if it were gliding in place like a seagull.

This being looks very, *very* human, almost like a woman with an age I can't tell, but there are things about it that are too perfect and too otherworldly to be human. Despite its beauty and benign gaze, I'm absolutely petrified, frozen stiff in awe and intimidation.

I hear the shuffles of the others around me, standing up and staring at this angel.

It then speaks with a voice as powerful as thunder but as delicate as a bird's song, "Do not be afraid. Look upon my face, children, and remember it. I am Junia of Shamgar of Strength and of Esther of Perseverance and Courage. It is the will of our Lord that I protect thee, so go into the world joyfully and seek glory for our King. When the time of unbearable strife cometh, only then shall I be needed. May peace be upon thee."

With that, she is gone. She doesn't fly away or dissolve into light or anything. She's literally there one second and then gone the next. As soon as she disappears, I can finally breathe again. The sky seems to fade back into existence, and with it is the underside of Safemill and the swaying forest trees.

I look down and at the others, all of whom have their mouths dropped open and tears in their eyes.

"That's an angel?!" Chirus chokes out. "Oh, I'm sticking with you guys forever!"

"That was magnificent..." Nima manages, "Ethereal... incredible..."

"That... that's the kind of stuff I can get with." Sam says as she points excitedly into the sky.

Everyone starts laughing and hugging one another, and I can't help but to join them. What a miracle! Sam rushes over and embraces me, then says, "You did it, you saved us!"

What do I say? You're welcome? No problem? All in a day's work?

"Yeah no worries I got you guys." I say, trying to sound as cool as possible.

She laughs and lets go of me, then continues to look at me a bit longer before an irritated voice calls out from the distance.

"Hey! Where are ya? I just saw ya… there you are." The voice is deep with a thick northern city accent. He almost sounds like a club bouncer or mob boss that's still in high school, maybe from Brooklyn or Jersey City or something.

The six of us turn to the direction of the voice, and we see a boy trudging through the forest towards us. He's got curly brown hair, blue-green eyes, a casual red hoodie, and a weird silver glove on his left hand. A single strap runs across his torso and a stick pokes up from behind his shoulder; there must be a bag or something on his back.

He gets up to us and then looks up in the sky, but then a look of disappointment washes over his face.

"Whoa whoa whoa where'd that lady go?" He asks us.

"What, the angel?" Nima asks.

"I don't know, whatever that glowing thing was in the sky just then." He replies, looking up expectantly.

"That's…" I look at everyone else to see if I should say anything, but they look back at me.

"That's Junia. She's like a… really nice ghost." I say.

"Okay then, call her back up. I gotta borrow her for a second." The boy says simply, crossing his arms and shifting into a patient stance.

I take another glance at the others, but this time they look as confused as I am.

"We can only summon her in times of need. Why do you require her assistance?" Nima asks.

"Well, seeing that I was plummeting to my death a few moments ago and she saved us outta nowhere, I thought I could've thanked her or something."

"Us? There are others?" Nima asks.

The boy gets an *are you kidding me* look on his face, "Come on toots this is public transportation of course there are others."

Bacoj stifles back a laugh, and then the boy looks at him, "Ey, who are you? Matter fact, who are all of yas?"

We go down the line, starting with Chirus and ending with me.

"Okay, nice to meet you. My name's Kabel."

We stand there in awkward silence for a bit, and then Kabel speaks again.

"Uh, so you guys trying to get to Semparus or something?"

Nima chimes in again, "Yes. Do you know the way?"

"Bout a half a kilo north. Caught a glimpse back when I was descending into my grave." Kabel responds.

We trudge through the woods, passing the occasional group of confused and relieved citizens or giant glass shards, and all the while we ask Kabel questions. The first question out of Bacoj's mouth is about whatever is in the giant black rectangle strapped to Kabel's back. When the traveler answers with a smirk saying, "It's for emergency purposes only", we kind of get the picture to ask about something else.

We keep talking and find out that he's from the other side of the country. It's a strange, secluded providence that's spelled Áplestürc but pronounced Aplestroff. No one knows why, not even Kabel or Nima.

Bacoj and Chirus cringe at the name of the providence, and then Nima explains to us that his home is infamous for the extremely dangerous woods that border it. Kabel was in Safemill to show his aunt and uncle some of his new *Unkillable Rings*, which he kind of just glossed over even though they sound pretty dope.

While there, Kabel heard some rumors about an eating contest happening in a city that was right along his way home, so he decided to check it out. When the escalator attack happened, he lost all his Unkillable Rings, and so after the food contest he's going to go back home to earn more.

"Man, that's a lot of hard work tossed away. It's pretty impressive that you're so calm about it." Chirus comments.

"Thank you. Oh, and by the way I'M NOT CALM I'M ABSOLUTELY LIVID."

His furious voice echoes out into the woods and we all stop walking at once.

"LIKE SERIOUSLY I'VE TRAINED FOR SEVEN YEARS TO GET EM AND WHAT HAPPENS? THEY GET SHOT

OUTTA THE SKY." Kabel's city accent gets more and more intense as he shouts.

"AIN'T IT 'SPOSED TA BE A ONE INA MILLION CHANCE DA GOVAMENT TRIES TA KILL YA COMAAAN HEYA!" Kabel is beet red, huffing angrily and looking around with wide eyes, and everyone is kind of backing away from him.

I seize the opportunity, walking slowly to him with my hands up. He looks at me incredulously, then seems to realize what's happening and dispels all the anger from his face in one big sigh.

"My apologies. I don't usually get angry like this. S'just… you know, you work hard for something and somebody takes it away, you get angry, right?"

No one says anything, and then Kabel frowns and nods at me, "Thank you Yoseph. Pardon my outburst."

"Oh yeah no problem dude, I totally understand." I reply, feeling as though that would be the best thing to say.

Kabel keeps walking and I follow him. The others start to shuffle after me.

We walk in silence next to each other for a bit, all the while a risky idea stirs in my head.

"Something you wanna say?" Kabel asks.

"So… you want to do something about the government?" I ask.

He stops walking and looks at me, shocked. Before he says anything, he suddenly remembers the others that are behind him and starts to back away. An oddly charming smile comes across his face, and he raises both hands.

"I don't want any trouble now…"

Nima chuckles, nods at me, and then takes a few steps forward, "We're thinking about visiting Yatniv at the Celestial Conference and discussing some possible actions he could take that would positively affect the population."

I can hear Nima picking her words carefully, and I feel both relieved she stepped in and kind of bad for approaching the topic so bluntly.

"I believe Zteod is on our way. Care to join us for the time being?" The alien asks.

"Well why didn't ya say something earlier? Of course I'll tag along." Kabel says happily, lowering his arms. "You guys are in luck too. For a second I thought things were gonna get ugly."

The seven of us smile at one another, and then Kabel starts walking. We follow him. Chirus and Nima spark up conversation, and so do Matt and Sam. Bacoj remains silent, and then picks up his pace, walking up beside Kabel and striking up a third discussion. Huh… I guess I just got seventh-wheeled.

With nothing better to do, I simply look around, observing the beautiful sunset sky and the swishing forest atmosphere around me. Dead leaves and mulch crunch under my feet, and a rather cold breeze runs through the trees. That's right, don't the seasons change super fast here? It's so jarring that an alien planet seems so normal.

I quickly try to divert my mind elsewhere, because I know if I keep thinking like I am, I'll get homesick again. It used to be a big problem for Matt and me back in the beginning of our journey, but we learned to overcome it.

Wow, now that I think about it, that's pretty ridiculous! Just two days ago, I was chilling with Virrel in the woods… and two weeks ago my life was completely normal! I wonder what would've happened if I didn't follow Matt into the forest…

Soon, the seven of us reach a road. We walk next it, spotting a few homes positioned alongside it, before it gets too dark to navigate. Since we aren't in the woods anymore, there are streetlamps to guide us, and we walk aimlessly towards the shimmering city lights in the extreme distance.

After fifteen more minutes of walking, people start to complain that their feet hurt. I agree with them; my feet sting like something serious! Bacoj spots a little park a block away, and the seven of us stumble over to it. We all plop down on benches and kick our feet up, taking a moment to relax.

"Hey guys, I just remembered something!" Chirus starts, "I have a cousin that lives nearby… do you want me to see if she will take us in for the night?"

"Most certainly." Nima replies.

Chirus slides one of those cell phone brass knuckle things, a shuza, from his pants pocket, puts it on his hand, and starts dialing in his palm. Then he puts his hand to the side of his face, and a few moments later, he starts talking.

"Hey Ilone, how are you… I'm doing great! Hey could you do me a huge favor… so I'm with this group of cool people and we're in Semparus right now but we don't have a place to spend the night…

yes please… um, it looks like the corner of, uh, Tearney and East Jensin… yeah, it's a little park… sounds great... love you too… bye."

He takes the thin plastic circle from around his knuckles and puts it back in his pockets.

"She should be here in maybe forty minutes." Chirus reports.

"Excellent. I suppose we will relax until then." Nima replies.

It gets quiet, partially because everyone is tired and partially because there is nothing to talk about. The night is actually quite cool, but there isn't any wind, so it's tolerable. There are too many street-lamps to see the stars, but the double moons are still visible. There are also city lights from up in Safemill, making an entire area of the sky look like glittering stars surrounding a looming thundercloud. There are blinking red lights within the cloud itself; I guess those are for planes or something.

The receding pain in my feet is quite soothing, and the quiet and darkness are calming as well. Only the cold serves to keep me awake, and even then, if it were just a degree or two warmer, I would be out like a light.

In the first ten minutes we'd all perk up when the occasional hover car came by, but eventually we stop. The forty minutes seem to take forever, but when a modest, sedan-model hover car pulls up to the curb, I'm surprised at how quickly it came.

The driver's side window (which is on the right, facing us), slowly rolls down, and Chirus gets up and goes over to it. He has a faint discussion with the driver, and after a few minutes of nervous laughter and audible "uh"s, he waves us over.

Aw man, I was getting really comfortable! The rest of us get up from our seats and hobble over to the car.

"Yeah, so, it only seats five. Um, I was thinking the girls could sit in the passenger's seat and us guys will figure something out." Chirus reports.

Sam and Nima look at each other, then round the car to the passenger's side.

"Will I suffocate if I ride in the trunk?" Bacoj asks, walking over to the back of the vehicle.

"You aren't riding in the trunk, Bacoj. I know you'll steal something." Chirus says flatly.

Bacoj swears under his breath, and then Kabel comes forward.

"You could stuff *me* in the trunk." With a chuckle, he adds, "Wouldn't be the first time, either."

We look at Kabel, a bit concerned, and then Chirus says, "Um, I think you'd be too big. I'm not going back there… how about you Matt?"

Matt, half-asleep, jumps at his own name, "Huh? What?"

"Do you want to ride in the trunk?" Chirus repeats, sounding a bit amused.

"Yeah yeah sure." Matt replies groggily.

Chirus shrugs, knocks on the back, and a second later, it pops open. Matt climbs in it like a bed, and then Chirus closes it over him.

The rest of us cram uncomfortably into the back seat, and then the car pulls forward. We drive for a bit, turn down a main street, and coast towards the sparkling beach city. The driver turns on the radio, and some calming electronic music comes on.

"So," the driver says awkwardly, taking a glance at Nima, who's sitting in Sam's lap, "Who are your new friends?"

Chirus starts, "Okay so the democ lady up there is Nima and the blonde girl is… um, Sand, right?"

"You thought my name was Sand?" Sam asks.

"I don't know, aren't you like an alien or something?" Chirus replies.

Both the driver and Sam laugh, and then Sam says, "No, my name is Sam… with an M."

"Okay. And then, well, you can't see back here, but sitting next to me is Bacoj."

"Hi." Bacoj says.

"Next to him is the new guy… I forgot your name."

"Really? You gotta be kidding me, it's two syllables. Kabel."

"Right, that's Kabel, and then sitting behind you is…"

"Yoseph." I say, trying to cut Chirus some slack.

"Thank you. And in the trunk is Matt."

There is a bout of silence, and then the driver says, "It looks like you guys need some name tags."

We all chuckle, and she continues, "Well, it's nice to meet you all. My name is Ilone… and I'm Chirus' big cousin."

We all respond with a "Nice to meet you" or something similar, and then Ilone starts to ask about hobbies and such. She's mostly talking to the girls up front, so us guys have even more time to relax.

After about a half hour, the city starts to pop up around us. Streetlights and other cars quickly become more and more common until they're surrounding us. The once distant city is now a glowing environment of towers, restaurants, and shops.

I look over from the window to the rest of the car, and hilariously, Chirus and Bacoj are asleep. Kabel sits uncomfortably straight beside me, with his mysterious black rectangle laid on the floor. His eyes are glued on the road ahead.

Nima is looking forward like Kabel is, and Sam is still talking to Ilone, both of whom seem interested in their conversation. I don't know what Ilone looks like, all I know is that she has dreadlocks. I think they're brownish blonde, but the streetlamps wash everything in an orange hue, so I'm not sure.

After cruising through the city for ten minutes, we pull into a surprisingly empty parking space. The car glides to a stop, and then what must be wheels come down from the bottom to support the car against the ground. Ilone rolls down her window, letting in chilly night air, and types a code into some roadside kiosk. It beeps twice, and then she puts in another code, followed by more beeping.

There is a click, and then a loud hissing noise, and the parking space beneath us begins to lower into the ground. What is this, a car elevator? We slowly descend into a lighted tunnel, and then the parking space beneath us stops going down and moves to the left.

We continue to go through the tunnel, gliding left for a while, then the parking space stops again and the wall in front of us slides away. Ilone casually drives into a large, underground parking lot, and quickly finds a real parking space. Once the car has stopped and the doors are unlocked, we all shuffle out.

Ilone pops the trunk and I wake Matt while Kabel wakes the other guys. Watching Matt wake up is hilarious. At first he looks annoyed, then panicked that he's in a trunk, then confused as to why he's here.

"We're going to Chirus' cousin's house, remember?"

Matt looks like he's taking time to register, then says, "Oh yeah right, right."

He climbs out of the car and we follow Ilone to the normal elevators. As we make our way to her apartment, I finally get a good look at our driver. She's actually quite pretty. Her long, fluffy, hazel dreadlocks are tied into a ponytail behind her. From the brief moment we locked eyes, I saw that they were an odd, greenish-brown color.

The most shocking thing about her, however, is her skin color. She isn't pale like Chirus, in fact, her skin is caramel. It doesn't look like she just got a tan either. No, she's definitely mixed.

Her apartment looks familiar… oh! It's almost like Edihi's apartment back in Safemill. The only difference is that the color scheme here is an olive green as opposed to a light blue. Of course, she also has different belongings and pictures and such.

Everyone tiredly slings their bags against the wall and plops down onto Ilone's couch. She grabs a bar chair from her kitchen, and then comes in and sits with us. For a moment there is just silence as we all stare into space, and then Ilone speaks.

"So, you guys want to order something?"

"Do you guys have pizza here?" Sam asks immediately.

Everyone gives her a strange look and laughs.

"Of course, what do you think this is?" Ilone asks.

There is more silence, and then Ilone says, "I'll just get two plain and one with *shom*. Oh, and I like *imso* on my pizza, so I'll get one separate."

"Imso on pizza does sound rather delectable. Mind if I try?" Nima asks.

I have no idea what any of this is, but I go along with what's happening like I do.

"Go for it." Ilone replies.

Kabel sits forward, "I think you should get one plain and two shom. I can tell you right now I'm gonna eat a whole shom by myself."

"How about we get two plain and two shom? I mean, don't we still have Edihi's wallet?" Sam suggests, pretending to know what the heck everyone is talking about.

I silently thank Sam, though. I think plain pizza is probably just cheese, and I have no idea what shom or imso is. It's probably some alien goop for all I know. Or even worse: pineapples.

Bacoj is knocked clean out, so Nima gently slips the red wallet out of his pocket. She opens it and flips through the shiny bills.

"With a bit of cushion, this should be enough." She reports.

Ilone calls in the order along with some drinks. After a surprisingly short few minutes of conversation, the pizza arrives. We pay using the rest of Edihi's money plus a bit from Ilone, then set up the food and drinks across her kitchen table. The aroma easily wakes Chirus, Bacoj, and Matt. Ilone gets some square glasses out of her refrigerator (I guess they just chill the cups instead of using ice here) and soon we have a feast on our hands.

So apparently, imso is just spinach and shom seems like pulled pork. It also smells like it too, so maybe shom is like another word for ham or something. Sam and I are adventurous and try a slice... yeah that's definitely just pulled pork.

While everyone is quietly and hungrily munching on pizza, Nima suddenly speaks.

"Well, I suppose that since we are all here under one roof... it is about time to reveal the truth."

Everyone stops eating.

"Firstly, Matthew, Samantha, and Yoseph are aliens from a distant planet called Earth. Hence our group's name; the Earth Pirates. They have come here because Great Sir Yatniv has stolen the essence of their planet within the magical Mundatorite ring, and we are on a journey to the Celestial Conference to retrieve it."

There is heavy silence. Chirus and Bacoj nod as if this is common knowledge, but Kabel and Ilone look deeply concerned.

"Maybe they put a bit more than imso in that pizza of yours lady." Kabel comments.

"Secondly," Nima sighs heavily, then says, "Matthew is also the

Crescent of Darkness."

There is stunned silence from everyone as we all take time to register what she said, and then the kitchen erupts into shouting.

"What?! WHAT?! You brought the Crescent into my house?!"

"I didn't know he was the Crescent! Why didn't you guys say anything?!"

"You're the Crescent?! I thought you looked familiar!"

"Oh man. The Crescent of Darkness is in my house. Wonderful. Now I'm an enemy of the state. Fantastic."

"Oooooh, now that makes sense! I guess Sam gave me the heads-up a while back."

"So thaaaats why you asked me about the government that one time. You guys are… rebels!"

I look at Nima, panicking. The others don't seem to be taking this too well, and I thought we were going to try and keep that whole thing a secret. I mean, we'd have to tell the truth eventually, but she could've tried to be a bit gentler with it. Maybe, like, use the persuasion ability or something?

"Will you all continue to follow us on our journey?" Nima asks bluntly, as if she didn't just reveal that we're both aliens and government insurgents.

Kabel replies almost instantly, "Hey, you can count me in. I wanted to give Yatniv a piece of my mind anyway, and you guys were supposed to be dead, what, four times now? As long as we're still going to that food contest, I'm all for it."

We breathe a sigh of relief, and then look at Chirus.

"I guess I don't have a choice. You could've told me sooner though!"

Everyone looks at Ilone, who's staring at one central point in the kitchen.

After a moment of unbearable silence, she says, "Well, I've got nothing better to do."

We all laugh for a bit before going back to eating.

After dinner, the eight of us retreat back into the living room and talk. Nima says that our objective for tomorrow is to travel to Malle Island and retrieve a new Ieri Tropo so we can continue towards the Celestial Conference. She doesn't know how expensive the Ieri Tropo or the boat ride will be, but she asks us to stay high spirited. We may be able to get there using our persuasion ability, too. Kabel and Chirus say they'll see what they can do about covering us, but then Ilone chimes in.

Apparently, there's been some type of competition going on ever since the stadium crashed two days ago. A local professor designed some type of mechanized battle robot, and he'll give 1000 *nummis* to anyone who can defeat it. She stresses that the robot is incredibly lethal, so it might not be the best course of action.

Kabel immediately volunteers to take on the robot by himself as a *warm up* because, get this, he "hasn't had a good fight in about two weeks." No one really objects, so we just thank him and continue our discussion.

Nima brings up that we're on a time crunch to meet Yatniv before the Celestial Conference, which is the only place where we can find

Yatniv, the Mundatorite ring, and a portal back to Earth all at once. Ilone reassures her that we have about a week or two but suggests something that could save us time.

She thinks it would be best if Sam, Nima, and Chirus went into town and searched for a cheap boat ride to Malle Island while the rest of us supported Kabel during his challenge. Sam wants to go too, but none of the boys are willing to give up their spot, so she just pouts angrily at Matt.

We start a shower rotation. Chirus goes first and almost instantly falls asleep afterwards, then Kabel goes in. While he's bathing and Bacoj is gently nodding next to Chirus, Nima decides to discuss something with us.

While back on Earth, Sam, Matt, and Nima all had the same dream about fighting Yatniv and an army of skeleton warriors at the Celestial Conference. The three of them shared this dream because they're honor vira wielders and that is a part of their abilities. I would've had the dream too, but I didn't have my vira yet.

Even though she's new, it appears that Ilone also has an honor vira. It's turquoise with a wide, double T on the bottom and some squiggly lines on the top. After talking to her, she admits that she had the same dream as well around the same time we did, but she didn't know it was us. The showers are soon complete, and Ilone cuts off the lights.

Tired, full, and freshly showered, I let the comfortable darkness dip me into sleep.

CHAPTER 18

CRUISING WITH THE FELLAS

~ YOSEPH ~

Nima wakes up early, and after getting ready, we go our separate ways. Bacoj, Matt, Kabel, and I follow Ilone to her car and pile in, then we take the car elevator back up to the street and head off to the destination on Ilone's flier.

It's a relief to sit in a more comfortable position this time; now I can watch the scenery whizz by without someone else violently pressed against me. Kabel has his mysterious black rectangle up in the front seat with him, so it's pretty much in his face. He doesn't seem concerned though; the entire ride he just cracks various bones in his body and stares excitedly out the window.

We soon find ourselves in the more industrial part of the city, as the parking lots get larger and the now shorter buildings become few and far between. We make our way parallel to the glimmering ocean, and eventually, we reach a tan building with a decently filled parking lot.

Ilone drives to the front of the building's main entrance, then shuts the car off.

"Here we are. Are you ready?" Ilone asks.

Kabel hugs his black rectangle with a big grin on his face, "Of course. So where do I go?"

Ilone takes another look at the colorful flier next to her, "Uh, you're looking for the Makomax *RS-227 Xpressdeath* 4.0… what a ridiculous name… anyway it's going to be the side door on the left of the main entrance… I guess it's that red one."

We all look up, and sure enough, there is a big banner over a red door that reads, "Challengers Enter". Two democ guys are sitting outside, eyeballing our hover car with amusement.

"Well then," Kabel says as he opens the door, "If I ain't out in ten minutes, come in and wake me up."

He drags his black rectangle out behind him, closes the door, and slings the object over his shoulder. He walks up to the guards, has a faint conversation, and shares a few laughs. Then, Kabel grabs the stick that's poking out of his black rectangle, takes an excited breath, and barges in the red door.

There is a lot of whirring and buzzing, and we hear Kabel shout, "We're just gonna do it right now I see!"

A flash of fire illuminates the inside of the red door right before it closes. After a few moments, we hear a circle saw loudly cut on, and then it sounds like it's swinging around for a bit before emitting some horrid grinding noise.

There is silence, then an aggressive zapping noise. What sounds like high pressured water blasts against the door, and then the zapping noise happens a few more times. There is a long bout of faint, unintelligible noises before a thunderous crash. Everything goes quiet for a while.

The red door opens, and Kabel walks out, soaking wet and holding a silver briefcase. He has a smug grin plastered across his face, and the two guards stare up at him, absolutely dumbfounded. He cheerfully makes his way over to the car.

As soon as he opens the door he starts talking, "Bada bing bada boom I got the money simple and clean child's play really."

He's speaking so fast and his city accent is a bit heavy so I have to take a moment to register what he said.

"Great job Kabel! That was fast, too!" I congratulate.

"Yeah, what happened?" Bacoj asks.

Kabel plops down in the passenger seat, and since he's drenched, Ilone cringes.

"I'll tell ya all about it on the way back. For now, Dr. Keeko wants to speak with us."

We look out the window to see a man in a lab coat approach the door. He's tall but has short hair like mine, with dark skin and a faint goatee. He's seems to be in his mid-thirties, with a surprisingly sharp, athletic appearance. We meet eyes and share a nod.

"Good afternoon," he says, "I am Dr. Niejir Keeko. I was incredibly impressed by Kabel's display of fighting skill, and I would like to continue studying him for a company project."

The car is silent as everyone looks at one another for a response, and then I decide to say something.

"Uh, we're all kind of going on a bit of a journey… I mean it's up to you Kabel."

"I'm sticking with you guys to the end of it." He replies.

I look back at the doctor, "Yeah so, maybe afterwards?"

"Do you all believe there may be combat or action throughout this journey?" The doctor asks.

"Um," I look at the others, not knowing if they find that question a bit odd, "Maybe, why?"

The doctor smiles, "Well then I will simply travel alongside you and document your progress."

"What kind of project is this?" Bacoj asks.

"We're developing a super soldier armor suit, and I'm tasked with designing the Accelerated Combat settings."

The five of us in the car look among one another, impressed, and then Ilone says, "Well, I mean, my car is kind of full…"

"Not a problem," Dr. Keeko reassures, "I can provide my own transportation. If your journey takes you out of town, is there a place I can meet up with your group before you depart?"

"Where are we going next?" I ask the others lowly.

"It was Malle Island, right?" Matt questions.

"Well, I'm pretty sure we're coming back to the mainland for the rest of the trip." Bacoj reasons.

"We'll be at the ports." Kabel answers simply.

The doctor nods and says his goodbyes as we pull off. As soon as we begin down the road back into the city, Kabel starts talking.

"So boom as soon as I open the door it's like this black refrigerator with a glowing red eye in the middle and four giant, spindly arms, right? And the arms start to unfold from around it and one of the arms is a flamethrower and it shoots fire at me and I'm like '*Ok so this is how we gonna do'* and so then I whip out Sizzle–"

"Sizzle?" Ilone asks, choking back a bit of laughter.

"First of all I don't like being interrupted toots. Anyways yeah, that's the name of my weapon, *Sizzle Stick*."

"So… Sizzle Stick is in that black rectangle of yours?" Bacoj concludes.

"Surprise surprise," Kabel says flatly, "Okay, so I whip it out right and then–"

"What's it look like?" Matt asks, partially to pick with Kabel.

Everyone laughs as Kabel sighs in frustration, "You guys gonna mess around and get punched in the face. Ok… so Sizzle Stick is my sword, and I can press a button to make it heat up and burn stuff. It's made outta… um, what's that metal called… it's ah…"

Kabel closes his eyes and starts snapping, "Come on baby think now… it's ah…"

"*Temeotire*?" Bacoj offers.

"Dat's it dat's the one." Kabel blurts out.

"Isn't that what boilers and stuff are made from?" Ilone asks.

"Yeah, it's common sense," Kabel says, "Because the metal stores the heat from around it and then lets it go when you spark it– something like that. You all went to science class you know how this stuff works."

Matt and I trade a confused glance, and then Kabel continues.

"So I got Sizzle out right and the robot is steady unwinding, still spraying fire at me to keep me away. So then it's finally ready and one of its arms is a circle saw and I'm like '*Alrighty then time to play*'.

So it swings the saw and I dodge, and it swings again and I do a flip over the arm but I time it so that–"

"Hello?" Ilone asks.

Kabel shoots her an annoyed glare, but it turns out she's just talking to Chirus on her shuza, so the traveler doesn't say anything.

"Um, so that I land on the arm itself. And then I drove that sucker into the ground and cut it off. That old robot didn't like that, because he started to shoot lightning at me from his third arm. And then his fourth arm nicked me with some water so that the lightning would have an effect on me.

"But the idiot left his circle saw in the middle of the floor, so I dodged a few lightning bolts and then threw the blade at 'em. Boom, lightning arm came clean off. So it only has the flamethrower and the water now.

"So he's sitting there trying to figure out what to hit me with, and the thing musta thought I was just going to stand still and wait for it. 'Course I didn't. I ran up to the sucker, dodged a bit of fire, and then ripped that thing out the ground and chucked it against the wall. Boom, killed it in one hit."

"You ripped a giant robot out of the ground and threw it?" Bacoj asks, doubtfully.

"Did I stutter?" Kabel challenges.

"How is that possible?" Bacoj replies.

Kabel lifts his left hand, incased in a silver glove, and says, "This baby right here."

"What's that?" Matt asks.

Kabel rolls up his sleeve, and apparently his entire arm is made of the silvery, skin-like metal.

"It's a bionic arm. Super strong, and it blocks lasers, too."

****

Instead of stopping at the apartment, we go all the way to the harbor. As we approach the ocean, the stores and buildings get more maritime-themed. It's actually pretty nice, though it looks slightly out of place since it's autumn.

We pass what must be the public piers, and then Ilone pulls into a parking space and we all exit. Waiting for us at the docks are Sam, Nima, and Chirus. Next to them are a few… bodyguards?

"Good news you guys! We don't have to worry about a ship fare… or money at all." Chirus reports.

"Indeed. We arrived in enough time to meet Former Empress Rigm once again. Coincidentally, her group is traveling to Malle Island as well. However, they are venturing out in search for one of her old friends so that they can discuss some recent events.

"Monetarily, Rigm said that her friend and the current empress, Empress Ploppo, secretly allotted her group more than enough traveling funds, so she's willing to generously share."

The rest of us look over at Kabel still holding his briefcase.

He looks around, shrugs, then says, "Well, more for me."

"Alright now here's the fun part," Sam says with an evil grin on her face, "Empress Ploppo gave Rigm and her group two boats to travel on. The first is a public relations yacht called the Farewind, and that's the one us girls get to ride on. Since all the space is taken up, you guys… well, you'll see."

Sam gestures to one of the bodyguards, the Hispanic one, and he steps forward with a smirk.

"If you're going to Malle Island, follow me."

Chirus immediately asks Ilone for her car keys so he can sit and wait, but the rest of us follow the guard down the docks. We keep walking for a while, passing all of the towering yachts, fancy sailboats, and even more modest things.

After that, we start passing little motorized boats and even canoes until we get to the very edge of the docks. Bobbing in the blue water is a little brown boat that looks like it can sit three comfortably.

"My name is Rixave, and this, gentlemen, is the S.S. Barefoot. This is what will decide whether you're boys or men." Our guard, Rixave, says with a grin.

"How far do we have to go?" Matt asks.

Rixave points to the horizon. At first I don't see anything, but then I can just barely spot a white speck contrasting the dark blue line where the sea meets the sky. Oh nah.

"You've got to be kidding me." Bacoj comments.

"Nope." Replies our guard.

Everyone looks at one another with uncertainty as Rixave steps into the boat. We all expect Kabel to get into the boat next, but he looks back at us as if we asked him to eat a live rat.

"I don't do boats. I ain't no chump, but I ain't going first either."

Bacoj shrugs, sighs, and steps on board. He almost loses balance and sits down quickly. Sweat begins beading on his forehead, and he looks back at us with terror in his eyes.

"I feel like this is a horrible mistake." He says.

Matt steps in next, wobbling and sitting down abruptly just like Bacoj did. I look at Kabel, and he looks back at me.

"I've never been in a boat before." I admit.

He sighs, "We betta still be going to that food contest. I mean it's a boat; aren't we the Earth *Pirates* or something? I dunno…"

He lies on the ground and then quickly scoots onto the boat. The vessel violently rocks side to side, and everyone aside from our guard lets out a scream of surprise. Kabel looks up at me with teary eyes and starts shaking his head.

"Don't do it Yoseph," He laughs, "We're all going to die on this hunk a junk, don't do it."

I hesitate, but then Rixave gives me a look that challenges my pride, and so I defiantly step onto the boat.

I can feel the vessel slightly sink under my weight, and the weight of everyone else is the only thing keeping us balanced. I sit down, swallowing fear and saying a prayer.

"We'll be fiiiine." Rixave reassures, thoroughly amused, and then the boat suddenly jerks to a start.

I can hear and feel every individual wave slap against the underside of the boat. For the first few minutes, we simply coast out into the shimmering blue beyond, watching the docks shrink away and looking out at the other boaters enjoying themselves.

We spot the Farewind, which is cruising along pretty fast, and I see Virrel at the top. He sees us, and we both wave at one another before he retreats back into the yacht. Soon, we're around the half-way point. The waters around us are a darker blue, and both Sempa-rus and Malle Island look hopelessly far away.

I'm just now realizing how quiet it is, and how this little slab of sheet metal is the only thing keeping us from an ever-expanding blue abyss. Just then, our guard swears under his breath.

"What? What's wrong?" Kabel asks.

"Look overboard." Rixave replies as he fidgets with the motor.

The four of us apprehensively glance into the water, and I can spot large, dark ovals snaking alongside us.

"Don't tell me those are aquadragers." Bacoj says.

"Those are aquadragers." replies Rixave.

Bacoj and Kabel start to freak out, and I look at Matt.

"Aquadragers?" He asks me.

"It must be like the water version of the things we faced at the stadium." I reply, trying to put two and two together.

Matt thinks for a moment, then starts, "Those alligator-cobra things that we had to fly away from?!"

"Exactly." I say, realizing just how screwed we are.

Matt grips the side of the boat, and then there is a splash to our left. A horrific creature sails through the air, teeth flashing, but then it splashes into the sea again. That was ugly! It had a crocodile's body with a snake's face and fins for limbs. Its scales were blue like the water, and its eyes were piercing and fishlike.

Kabel takes the Sizzle Stick from its sheath, and I can't help but marvel at the sword. It's huge, with the blade alone about the length of my leg, and it's pretty much a solid, sharp hunk of metal in the shape of a trapezoid.

Another aquadrager burst from the water, and he smacks it out of the air like a baseball. It splashes back into the water, and then the rest of the aquadragers begin to circle the boat, churning the seas beneath us and making us turn off course.

Suddenly, Rixave cranks the motor to the max. It groans in protest, then spits out a column of water and throws us violently forward. The S.S. Barefoot shoots through the sea, skipping dangerously as we try our best not to fall off.

A large wave comes our way and we take it head on. The vessel shutters, then lurches forward. We rear back, slam into another wave, and then catch air time. Everyone screams as we weightlessly soar for a second or two, and then the boat crashes back into the water, spraying salty foam everywhere.

Wobbling, we slowly regain our speed, and then continue to skip towards the ever-approaching island. I have a death grip on my seat as the boat continuously bounces, and I'm trying my best to shield my eyes from the rushing wind and water.

The aquadragers are right on our tail, occasionally jumping out of the water like dolphins. They try to spread out and gain on us, but we're going too fast. All five of us are looking behind the boat, staring defensively at the leaping predators.

Abruptly, the aquadragers stop chasing us. Relieved, we all turn to one another to joke about what just happened, but then I notice out of the corner of my eye that we're gunning it at a ridiculous speed straight towards the sandy shore.

The others must've noticed, because they start shouting warnings as Rixave eases the motor off. We're still gliding way too fast, and everyone braces themselves for impact.

I close my eyes, and a second later, I'm violently thrown from the ship.

CHAPTER 19

A TYPICAL CONCERT

~ YOSEPH ~

Dazed and confused, I sit up and brush sand off of my face. In front of me is the S.S. Barefoot, sitting bravely on a hill of sand. Rixave is still seated by the motor, laughing his head off. Matt is sprawled a few feet away, groaning.

I continue to look around. Kabel is on his back, staring up at the sky with a look of shock on his face. Sizzle Stick is in one hand and his briefcase is in the other. Bacoj is still aboard the boat, dry heaving over the side. Goodness, are all boat rides like this?

It takes us a while to get ourselves together, but once we do, our guard leads us towards the docks. When we reach the Farewind, there are a few more guards and Virrel sitting outside the entrance. They are all either on their shuzas or quietly eating.

"Where are the others?" Rixave asks.

Virrel responds, "Oh, they went to Cici's concert. We already finished all of the shopping."

"Concert?" Bacoj asks aloud, then he turns to us, "I thought Nima said we were on a time crunch."

"She did, but Ilone said we had quite a bit of time until that Celestial whatever that we're going to. What was it, a week and a half?"

Kabel asks.

"Slightly more," Virrel says, overhearing our conversation, "and it's also a three-day event. You guys don't need to worry about a little concert getting in the way of things."

"Well, is there a reason they went? Not to knock whoever Cici is but," I scratch the back of my head, "I'd rather be early to the Celestial Conference than on time."

"Yeah, isn't their whole planet locked away or something? Sounds a bit more important if ya ask me." Kabel reasons, and the rest of us nod in agreement.

"I mean, we're just waiting for the concert to be over so we can talk to Cici." Virrel says with a shrug, "We can't move the Farewind, but if you really want to, you could convince the girls to get on the Barefoot with you and you all ride back to Semparus early."

Rixave snickers mischievously, and the rest of us unanimously decide against that option. I want to spend as much time as possible off of that rusty metal death trap.

Disappointed but curious, I ask, "Well, what all did you get when you went shopping?"

Virrel looks up into the air, thinking, "I know we got another Ieri Tropo… two actually, and they also got some new clothes."

We all nod, and then Virrel continues, "So that concert the girls are at already started, but I'm quite sure they'll let you in. The guys and I decided to stay here, though. I'm not sure about everyone else, but that music is too young for my taste."

The six of us share a chuckle, and then Virrel adds, "Now, if you go, you know you'll have to leave your weapons and stuff behind. We can hold on to them for you."

Everyone reluctantly does what he says. Bacoj slings off his backpack and hands it over, then hesitates before taking off his cyber vira as well. Matt hands over his bag with the Peace Per, and then he too goes for his vira, but Virrel stops him.

"You can just keep it tucked under your shirt. It's probably for the best, and I don't think anyone will notice."

Kabel plops down his briefcase of money, looks at us angrily, slings off Sizzle Stick, and places it in Virrel's lap.

"It betta not have a scratch." Kabel warns.

Virrel smiles and nods, and then Rixave speaks, "They're at the pavilion like last time?"

Virrel nods, and the five of us turn and leave.

"Wait, Matt, you've got to come with me." Virrel says, "Your leader suggested that you get a haircut so that people wouldn't recognize you, and I've got the perfect one in mind."

Matt hesitates, looking uncomfortable, and Virrel raises an eyebrow, "What, you don't want me to go with you?"

"Aren't you like seventy years old or something? I think you might be out of touch."

We all laugh, including the other guards, as the ghost looks astonished, "I'll have you know I was quite hip back in my day…"

"Sure thing old man." Rixave teases, and then we head off.

We joke around and follow our guard for five minutes. As we continue to walk, I notice music from afar. At first it's just the faint pop of a drum and the high notes of a guitar.

As we continue to approach, I can pick up on even more. Someone is singing… and there's what might be a… piano? The piano works even though the music is like some mix between metal and hip-hop, but what's even stranger is that they have pianos here to begin with.

That pleasing, deep vibration running through everything must be the bass guitar. These instruments grow louder as we approach an opening in the line of seafront luxury houses. We finally pass the last house and reach our destination.

There's about a thousand people crowded around a pavilion, all jumping to the beat of the music and shouting lyrics back at the singer. All the instruments I thought I heard are just futuristic versions of themselves, but there's one guy that's waving his hands violently in the air, almost like he's conducting. What in the world is going on with him?

"I'm going to go and get Matt after his haircut. You all enjoy the concert, and if you want to find the girls, they might be up front."

We nod to Rixave as he walks back towards the docks. Bacoj, Kabel, and I reach security, and they quickly check my bag of bandages and soap before waving us through. It's an easy walk there, but sidling through the countless rows of people to reach the front is pretty uncomfortable.

Bacoj spots the girls, and we slowly make our way over to them. Ilone and Sam seem to be having the time of their lives, gladly soaking up the crazy smoke and laser lights, but Nima is nowhere to be found.

"Yo," I shout to Sam, "Where's Nima?"

She stops jumping, "She's back at the Farewind with Rigm; they said they were just going to wait out the concert and do what they need to afterwards."

She looks at me, then Bacoj, then Kabel, then back to me.

"Where's Matt?" She shouts.

"Virrel took him to get a haircut, he'll be here soon." I reply.

She nods and goes back to jumping with Ilone. I look back at the guys. Kabel is right along with everyone else, jumping to the beat and pumping his bionic fist into the air, but Bacoj looks just as sympathetically interested as I am.

I can tell this genre of music isn't really his thing, so I decide to ask him a question.

"Yo Bacoj, what's up with the guy violently waving his arms?"

He looks up at the stage, then replies, "He's playing the theremin. It's what's making that" he imitates the sound "noise."

I nod in thanks. I was wondering where that other weird guitar was that I heard, but I guess this is it. For some reason, that instrument name sounds familiar.

The band finishes their song and starts talking to the audience as they catch their breath in preparation for another selection. It's mostly generic music break stuff like "Are you guys having a good time?" and "If you're excited make some noise," and a few jokes about how tired they are.

Suddenly, a wave of anger washes over me. I'm not sure why or where it came from, but for some reason, just being here is annoying me. I guess the band is feeling it too, because suddenly the guy on the futuristic piano says bitterly, "Really? That was pathetic; I could make more noise in my sleep."

"Talk about pathetic," says the drummer with a valley girl accent. She smirks as she points one of her sticks towards the back of the crowd, "Look at that late guy back there with a mirror for a head."

I, along with everyone else in the concert, turn around, and standing in the field between the security booth and the concert is Matt. From here, I can see that whomever cut his hair must've set the clippers to "almost bald." If I'm honest though, that's the cleanest edge up I've ever seen, so that definitely makes up for it.

His entire face is beet red, and he quickly scurries towards the edge of the crowd to hide from the attention. The drummer doesn't show any mercy, though.

"Look at him run; it's like he's got beard stubble on his head."

To my surprise, the rest of her bandmates laugh.

"Nah-ah. You either come up here and take the heat or walk right back out." The drummer challenges.

Matt freezes as comments ripple throughout the crowd.

"Come on Matt, get up there and punch 'er in da face." Kabel encourages.

"Wait, what?" I ask, turning around to face Kabel.

"Yeah I agree with him. She deserves it." Ilone chimes in.

"Look," Kabel starts as he shifts into a comfortable stance, "Nobody disrespects me, my friends, or my family. I don't care if ya nine or ya ninety, male, female, or anywhere in between. If you say something sideways imma punch you square in ya face it's as simple as that."

"If he isn't going to do it, I gladly will." Sam says.

There's some concerned silence among the group, and then Bacoj says, "Well he better do something quick before he's noticed, regardless of the haircut."

Another random wave of anger comes over me, and I want to shove Bacoj for his pessimism. Matt must have felt the anger too, because he balls his fists and starts marching up to the staircase on the side of the pavilion. The crowd erupts into shouts and "*oooh*"s as Matt continues to approach the stage. From the redness in his face and his walking speed, I can tell he isn't planning on using his persuasion ability when he gets up there.

"Uh oh," Kabel says, "He's getting too many eyes on 'em."

"We need a distraction." Bacoj says.

Kabel nods, picks up a random guy standing beside him, and throws him into the crowd behind us.

"Don't be shy!" Kabel shouts, then he smacks a woodish guy.

Ilone and Sam look at one another, then start wailing on people around them willy-nilly. I glance at Bacoj, and suddenly a stranger comes out of nowhere and tackles him to the ground. Someone shoves me forward, too hard, and I turn around to see that it's this beefy redhead guy I've never seen before.

I grin maniacally. I've been taking karate since middle school, and for years I've been waiting for an excuse to use it on someone. The guy takes a swing at me, but I duck and punch him full force in the nose. My fist connecting with his face is satisfying, and he's raising his guard too slowly, so I twist my body hard and hit him with a roundhouse. He's out like a light.

As soon as he crumples to the ground, I realize what I've done. Oh Lord, is he going to be alright?! I kneel down to check if he's breathing, which he is, and then stand up quickly. Everyone around me is either violently rolling around on the ground or uselessly grappling someone else.

Oh my goodness; this is a mess. We need to get out of here. Immediately, I look up to the stage, and Matt is shouting furiously at the drummer. Only he and the drummer are up there, so I guess the other band members are fighting in the crowd.

The drummer throws one of her drums at Matt, but he catches it and slams it onto the stage. The drummer suddenly stands up and they both walk towards one another angrily.

Once they're face to face, Matt goes to say something, but then the drummer kicks him incredibly hard in the crotch. Matt instantly crumples to the floor. To my horror, his amulet slides out from under his shirt. Everything in my body goes cold as the drummer seems to notice it. Oh no… our cover is blown.

I shove my way to the pavilion stage, and by the time I reach the bottom, the drummer is kneeling over Matt with an astonished look in her eyes. She then holds out her hand and a sai suddenly appears within it, first white and then gleaming silver. Did she just switchblade that?! So… she's a vira wielder too?!

She raises her tool to stab Matt, and thinking fast, I throw a fireball in her direction. She must've noticed it out of the corner of her eye, because she fearfully falls back. I put my arms onto the edge of the stage and then scramble up to my feet.

She stands up too, grabbing her first sai and switchblading a second one into her other hand. Okay, since we're going all out, forget persuasion. I'll switchblade my spear into my hands, too. Holding the smooth wooden pole in my hands, watching the fiery blade at its tip flicker and smoke, fills me with seriousness.

"This menace needs to die. And that bounty is mine." The drummer says.

We continue to stare down one another, tools at the ready. If I wasn't so angry and defensive right now, I might say she's pretty. Of course her ruffled cocoa hair and fierce onyx eyes continuously remind me that I'm getting ready to fight her, but her light brown skin and irritated face are somewhat attractive. Her features are odd; not as soft as Sam's, yet not as sharp as Ilone's, they're somewhere in the middle.

Suddenly, she throws one of her sais at me. I go to block it but it misses anyway. She then sprints towards me with the other sai in hand, raised and ready to stab. Instinctively, I smack her in the face with my spear. The drummer stops in her tracks. Her free hand shoots up to her nose as crimson begins to trickle from it.

What have I done?! Overflowing with guilt, I will away my spear and rush over to help her. I feel like such a terrible person; what is wrong with me?! I place a hand on her shoulder to console her, and she doesn't shove it off like I'd feared.

I bring myself to speak, "I am so, so sor–"

Before I can continue, she flings my arm off of her and drives the longest part of her sai through my backpack strap, through my shirt, and deep between my shoulder and armpit. Immediately, the most intense, burning agony I've ever felt flares to life in the entire left side of my body, especially where she struck.

I can't help but let out a horrified scream, and furiously, I head-butt her. Flames of pain sear away at my will as soon as I move to attack her. The hit connects though, and she recoils. I muster up all of my will and, ignoring the pain, I deliver the most aggressive side kick I've ever managed into her stomach. The drummer immediately folds over and falls on her butt.

I must've got her good, because all she can do is gasp and stare up at me with teary eyes. I'm just now realizing tears are streaming down my face as well, and a betrayed rage begins to replace my sympathy.

The drummer weakly waves her hand, and two things happen at once. First, her sai disappears from inside of my shoulder, which makes my wound feel like someone poured salt onto it. Second, something moves inside of her shadow. Suddenly, a perfect replica of her tuck rolls out of the shade her body is making.

It immediately stands tall and starts grinning maniacally at me. I'm in some limbo between confused, fearful, in pain, and enraged, so my body takes over where my mind won't, and I find myself backing up.

I notice that the clone doesn't cast a shadow, neither on the ground nor on the rest of its body, which looks really jarring. Before I can dwell on that, it rushes me. I stumble backwards more, but the clone slams me to the ground and causes so much agony in my shoulder that I nearly black out.

It pins me down, grinning evilly as it intentionally applies weight to the hole in my shoulder. Bright spots flicker in my vision, and I can feel my angry energy fading. The clone punches me across the face, and for a second I let my eyes dim.

As a last-ditch effort before I let the swirling darkness take me, I simply reach up with my good arm. My hand touches something soft and bumpy, and I immediately grab onto it. Whatever it is, it's bonier than it first seemed, and me grabbing it makes the clone stop attacking me.

The thing in my grasp starts to try and tug away, but I sink my fingernails deeper into it. My right eye stings too much to open, so with my left, I look to see that my fingers are dug into the clone's face.

An odd rush of panicky anger courses through me, and then my hand bursts into flame. The clone tries desperately to jerk its face out of my claw-ish grip, but despite the splitting pain in my shoulder and the brutal way I'm killing this thing, I don't let go. Soon, its hair catches ablaze and the whole clone dissipates into a wisp of steam.

I put my right hand back over my stinging, throbbing shoulder, and stare at the drummer with empty defiance. She looks back at me, still on the ground with her own blood smeared around her mouth, and then she switchblades one of her sais into her hand.

"He's my bounty." She grunts, then she beams the sai at me.

It twirls way over my head, almost like she was aiming behind me. Sure enough, I hear a hearty thud and an angry grunt behind me. I tenderly scoot so that I can look behind me, and standing at the edge of the stage is a skinny, light skinned woman.

She's got medium, wavy, black hair and steely black eyes rimmed with blue mascara. She wears a black leather jacket with a large white scarf that matches her shirt and contrasts her jeans. Her red-painted lips are curled in a furious snarl, and as I look closer, I can see tears in her eyes.

Matt struggles to sit up next to me, grunting and looking up at this random woman alongside me. For some reason, I just now notice the weathered, ancient book in her hand. It's flipped open to the middle, and the woman is gripping its spine intensely.

"Crescent of Darkness," she says, her voice cracking, "I am Taamré Noebo, Master Wizard of the Friorisis. My fiancé died at the Skyling Stadium because of you, and now you will pay!"

She raises her hand and opens her mouth to say something, but then her book flies right up into her face. Confused, she takes a step back, and she's suddenly thrown into the writhing crowd by an invisible force.

"Matthew! Yoseph! Cirovati! Are you all alright?"

I painfully scoot back around to see Virrel standing at the other side of the pavilion stage.

"Virrel! You know these people?" The drummer, Cirovati, asks.

"No time to explain, for now we need to leave before the police show up."

He lifts the drummer, Matt, and I all at once with telekinesis, and then he begins to run back to the docks, hovering us over the dying fight.

I'm too tired to see what happens next, and I pass out.

CHAPTER 20

THE FATED FOOD CONTEST

~ MATTHEW ~

What a day. First and foremost, that ride back to Semparus was super awkward. Rixave just kind of silently guided the boat along, trying to ignore the fact that everyone was bleeding while Bacoj and Yoseph were completely unconscious.

He would occasionally ask a question, and either Kabel or Virrel (he had to ride with us so that they could make room for the drummer on the Farewind) would answer with a simple sentence. Rixave would then reply with a passive "Oh, okay" and stay silent for a few more minutes before his next question.

When we got back to the Semparus docks, Chirus looked absolutely floored. He seemed somewhere in between concerned for our health and relieved he sat this one out. He apparently had some leftover "dilts" or whatever made him loopy back in Safemill, and we gave them to Yoseph to ease his stab pain.

We didn't have time for those florma healing chambers, but Rigm's guards patched us up pretty quickly, though, and after we got our stuff back from them, we parted ways again. They said they were going to Aplestroff or whatever, and that's one of the places we're going to as well, so that ought to be nice.

Before we could head to a lansit station and go to Zteod (so that Kabel could try his hand at their eating competition), we met up with an old friend at the docks; Dr. Keeko. Honestly, I'd forgotten he was going to join the group, but after Kabel explained that the doctor was there on behalf of a research project, Nima seemed pretty alright with him joining.

The lansit ride to Zteod took the rest of the day. It was really relaxing to see all of the autumn scenery whizz by at crazy speeds, and everything looked even more calming as the sun was about to set.

We found out Cirovati (or Cici as she's asked us to call her) is Rigm's best friend, so she made up with Yoseph and I fairly well. All the wounds from our fight had stopped horrifically aching, so we could finally look back at the whole thing and laugh. Cici said that she always wanted to do something big and political, so convincing her to join us was really easy.

While still on the lansit, Nima decided to gather up all the vira wielders in our group to talk about the skeleton fighting dream. Ilone already told us she had it, and Cici had it as well, so it seems like we're all destined for it. Nima reminded us, however, that our premonition powers show us the *possible* future, so we might end up avoiding a fight altogether, which is something she's really pushing for.

While on the topic of vira, Yoseph asked Cici how she did the clone thing. She explained that it was part of her secondary power. As vira wielders, we all have five powers: a primary tool, a secondary power, the element immunity, the persuasion ability, and the premonition ability.

Yoseph has his spear with his fire powers, Sam has her shield with her star coins, Nima has her sickles with the gliding whirlwind thing she does, Ilone has wooden fighting sticks called tonfas with water powers, and Cici has her sais with the cloning ability.

Cici can make up to six clones, and the more she makes, the less competent they are. If it's only one, then it acts with as much skill and cunning as she would, but if she makes six, they pretty much just stand around until they're hit with a killing blow. As far as secondary abilities, I stump everyone, because I don't seem to have any. Bummer. Anyway, they can't use primary tools and secondary powers at the same time; that's why Yoseph wasn't being skewered with six sais at once.

The conversation about vira eventually ends, and we reach Zteod after nightfall. Kabel had more than enough money in his briefcase to get everyone their own room, but he reasoned that saving up would be the best idea just in case something happens and we don't meet up with Rigm's group for a while.

Because of this, we only get two hotel rooms, one for guys and the other for girls. Dr. Keeko purchases his own room for the night. Chirus claims one bed, and Kabel got the other. Bacoj claimed the couch a second before I could, so Yoseph and I are banished to the floor. It isn't that bad, though. We're all full off of the food my sister packed from Malle Island, freshly showered, and our eyes are heavy from the long day.

I take one last tired look around the room before I close my stinging eyes. Kabel is melodically polishing Sizzle Stick on his bed. Bacoj is fast asleep on the couch. Chirus is intently watching a game of kaxahhe on the TV-wall (it's kind of like a projector but with a million times the quality and no projector).

Yoseph is watching the game as well, and he seems just as interested. Thinking about kaxahhe reminds me of that lady with the book earlier today: Taamré. If that thing about her fiancé is true, then I feel kind of bad. But it was more Yatniv's doing than anyone else's, so I don't let it bother me for too long. Soon, sleep overpowers me, and I welcome it.

****

The following morning, we all gather together and hike over to the food eating competition. Even though I'm usually all for stuff like this, I can't help but feel a bit antsy. That discussion at the docks yesterday has me kind of hoping this competition goes by quickly. Surprisingly, the contest shows up on our Ieri Tropos, so we know where to go. Sam has her map open and is in front while Cici has our second map in her pocket.

It feels good to be in a new set of clothes (however baggy they may be), and I've got a new backpack for the Peace Per, so that's nice. The others also got me some hair growth cream so that I'm not nearly bald, and it's working surprisingly fast.

The entire walk, we pump up Kabel in preparation for the eating contest. Because of the whole Safemill escalator thing, Nima is under the impression everyone that was around me back then is also being hunted. Fugitives showing up to an eating contest sounds like a recipe for disaster. I can't participate in the contest, sadly, and the only people that can aside from Kabel are Cici, Dr. Keeko, and Ilone. Dr. Keeko vigorously declines because he has to watch his blood pressure.

To our surprise, Ilone is completely on board, and so is Cici. Kabel signs the three of them up for it. The entry fees pale in comparison to the amount of money Kabel has in his briefcase. He has to part with Sizzle Stick again, which he does regretfully, and since the thing is so heavy, Yoseph volunteers to hold it.

The three put on their badges, sidle through the crowd, and take their seats at one of the many tables lined up back to back. In front of each seat is a massive party platter of hot wings with an empty bowl beside it, and at each seat's side is a pail, probably in case someone eats too much. I can smell the heavenly tanginess of the wings from all the way over here.

I guess the wings are on some futuristic hot plate, since they keep steaming as the seats eventually fill up. Soon, the competition is about to start, and my fingers are numb with anticipation. Cici sits on one side of Kabel, and Ilone sits on the other. The three of them have some pretty varied opponents...

An excited looking democ woman gets up on a pedestal before the contestants. She says that they all have 10 minutes to eat as many hot wings as they can, and whenever they vomit, wave their hand in defeat, or if the time runs out on them, they lose. Contestants can take their leftovers home.

The grand prize is a 100 nummis gift card to Slushere, the wing restaurant that is hosting the challenge. Ilone and Kabel glance at one another and trade a competitive nod, then Kabel locks eyes with Cici and the drummer giggles nervously. Kabel cracks his neck and back while Ilone re-ties her dreadlocks into a ponytail, then they both glare at their plates. Cici looks at them, then follows their lead, losing her grin and regaining the killer stare she had back in Malle Island.

Come to think of it, everyone is glaring at their plates, mouths devoid of smiles and hands poised to strike.

"Three… two… one… eat!" The announcer says.

There is a horn, and then the contestants dig in. The surrounding crowd immediately erupts into encouragement. Ilone and Kabel are shoveling wings into their mouths, thoughtlessly getting sauce all over their noses, cheeks, and fingers. Cici, on the other hand, is eating as though this is a normal night out at a restaurant.

Even though Nima said to keep a low profile, she sporadically starts cheering for the trio. Our group quickly catches on, and we all start shouting with the surrounding crowd.

People start dropping left and right, literally. Some people stop with enough time to wave their hand in defeat or sit back and shake their head, but others end up falling out of their chairs or vomiting into their nearby bin.

Once the clock reaches one minute, the numbers turn from green to red, and dramatic music begins to rise from the pedestal up front.

Almost everyone is gone at this point. People are laid out on the floor, some are slumped weakly over their vomit buckets, and others sit motionless in their seats, groaning.

Even the more heavyset challengers have tapped out, and all that are left are a few stragglers and the three from our group. Everyone is eating much slower now, well, except for Ilone, who is still eating like she hasn't had a meal in days.

One of the remaining opponents sits back in their seat, and then Kabel looks over at Ilone with disbelief in his eyes. She's still going strong, and it looks like she might even finish her platter. The last of the opponents falls onto her own vomit bucket, which is luckily empty, and it's just Cici, Kabel, and Ilone left.

The drummer is eating much too casually to pose a threat numerically, but Chirus' cousin is bulldozing through her challenge. The bionic traveler in the middle gently nudges Ilone in a *hey, you can quit now* kind of way, but she completely ignores him. His head lulls around like he's about to faint, then he violently shakes it and looks down at his food with renewed determination.

The clock strikes zero, and as the finishing buzzer sounds, Cici jumps and looks at the clock in a mixture of disbelief and disappointment. Kabel drops his half-eaten wing and abruptly lays his face down in his plate. Ilone tosses her last bone into the bowl beside her, then looks at her nearly empty plate in satisfaction.

Holographic numbers pop up over the bone bowls as the announcer surveys the contestant's tables. I see a lot of tens and fifteens, and some are even in the low twenties. Cici got 8, Kabel got

27, but then there is Ilone with an impossible 31. The announcer does one last check, then runs and grabs a bag from beside her pedestal.

She puts a bronze medal next to Kabel, a silver metal on top of some sleeping woodish guy, and then loops the gold medal around Ilone's neck. She also hands over the gift card, and Ilone takes it happily. The crowd then descends upon the contestants, helping them up and guiding them away. Yoseph, Bacoj, and I help Kabel wash his face of wing sauce and shame tears, and the girls clean up Cici and Ilone.

Luckily, the lansit station is a block away from the contest, so hopping on and heading to our next Ieri Tropo destination, Aplestroff, takes absolutely no time.

CHAPTER 21

CASUAL FAMILY DINNER

~ MATTHEW ~

The autumn trees rushing by outside go unnoticed as we talk about Ilone's victory. She sits next to Kabel, and they both lean in opposite directions of each other, wallowing in pain. Ilone nudges Kabel, then pulls the gift card out of her pocket and hands it over to him. They share a laugh, then they both fall asleep.

The lansit ride continues for hours, and I once again watch the sun grow orange and sink behind the vast forever of trees. Suddenly, we're engulfed in a mountain tunnel. Ten minutes go by as we look at the rushing inky blackness outside of our windows.

We must've been flying in that tunnel, because when we get out, we're in a totally different place. There is a long brown banner along the horizon in front of us and towering mountains slowly retreat behind us. Aside from that, desert stretches for miles on either side. Kabel suddenly wakes.

"We're in the deserts, aren't we?" He looks out the windows, and a happy grin comes across his face, "Ha ha! Almost home! I'm gonna introduce you guys to my ma! She'll love ya!"

"You have a family?" Bacoj asks.

The entire crew grows silent as Kabel looks back at Bacoj.

"Uh, well, yeah…" He forces himself not to say more.

Bacoj looks confused and scans the rest of us. We all nod. The thief then looks shocked and says, "Well, this is awkward."

Nima shakes her head and looks at the ground, "Do not feel isolated, Bacoj. I too have no family. Yatniv is responsible."

There is more silence, and then to our surprise, Dr. Keeko speaks up, "If it is any consolation, Yatniv is responsible for the disappearance of my family as well. I'll be an open ear if you need to talk about things that are bothering you."

The air is thick with discomfort and to break the awkwardness, Kabel suddenly says, "Look, at the end of the day, all us Earth Pirates are family. We gotcha back, Bacoj."

The thief thanks him, and then everyone kind of twiddles their thumbs for a little bit before Bacoj suddenly says, "Hey Dr. Keeko, we can talk to you about anything, right?"

The doctor raises his eyebrows, "Yes?"

Bacoj shifts nervously, then says, "Well, I was wondering if I could get a job at your place."

Dr. Keeko looks absolutely floored, "At Makomax? Why?"

The thief glances around the lansit at the other sleeping riders, and then pulls his cyber vira out from under his shirt, "I like magical weapons like these. I'm horrible with math and engineering and stuff, but magic like this, I can definitely do."

"How did you get one of those by the way?" The doctor asks, "They are almost as rare as the real thing."

"Er, I borrowed it. Anyway, is there anything you can do?"

Dr. Keeko thinks for a moment, then smirks, "I don't know, Bacoj. We have a lot of competition at our workplace. What makes you think you're better than the rest?"

Everyone chuckles a bit, but the thief looks excited to be asked.

"This cyber vira right here! A few friends helped me make some modifications to it, and now fire can come out my hands too instead of just the necklace itself."

"Quite impressive; I'll have to see it in action once we get into a better setting. If what you say is true, I just might be able to see if we can get you an internship." Dr. Keeko replies, amused.

Bacoj gets a curious look, "We're going to Aplestroff, right?"

Everyone agrees.

"One of my modding friends lives there… I haven't talked to them in forever!" Bacoj says.

"What's their name?" Kabel asks, "If you can remember, I might know where to find 'em.

"Ellia… I don't know the last name."

Kabel perks up at the name, "That non-binary toots? Half-human half-woodish? With, like, glittery rainbow hair and stuff?"

"Yep, that's the one!" Bacoj replies.

Kabel rolls his eyes, "You gotta get some better friends, Bacoj! Ellia's a nightmare!"

The thief laughs, shrugging and nodding in agreement.

Kabel continues, "I'm not sure where they live, but I wouldn't be surprised if I were to meet 'em tomorrow. Since I lost…"

Kabel, along with the entire team and Ilone, sit up in surprise as the lansit begins to slow like its pulling into a station. Incredulously, I look out the window, and sure enough, I can make out a station a few feet away in the evening light.

The brown banner that was once along the horizon is now a massive wall, towering pass the top edge of my window. The station we're pulling into is literally just that. There is the boarding platform, a station house that probably has bathrooms in it, and a tiny parking lot beside it. A long, two lane road curves from the distance, loops around the station, and streaks off into the horizon again. No cities or towns are in sight.

On the other side of this road is… whoa, I haven't seen that since we started this trip! It's that amusement park sky ride station, I think Nima called it an air lift. It is cycling colorful pods up and down, so high that I can't see where it goes.

The lansit glides to a stop, and at least half of the riders get off along with us. Lots of people crowd the restrooms or head over to the air lift across the street, but our team stays on the platform while Kabel calls his mother.

The conversation goes in circles for a bit, and there is a lot of excited screaming from his mother's end, but he finally convinces her to let his eight "cousins" spend a night or two at his place. With that, we walk across the street and board the air lift. The girls all crowd into one, and Bacoj decides to hang back with Dr. Keeko.

I get into a green pod with Chirus, Kabel, and Yoseph, and soon enough, we're being lifted into the sky. We continue to go up, slowly rising higher, and I watch as the station and ground beneath us shrink to a dangerous depth.

"So Kabel, which town do you live in?" Yoseph asks.

Kabel looks at him funny, then remembers that we're aliens.

"Well, the town is called Edge, but everyone just calls it Aplestroff because it's the only town in the providence."

"Really? Why's that?" Yoseph continues.

"There's a forest nearby, and the things inside it ain't too pretty. Long time ago they put up a wall around the forest to keep all the crazy stuff in, and they left some room for a town in the front. The wall became a border, and then Edge became a providence. 'Course the whole providence couldn't be called '*Edge*', so we named it after our town's founder; Ranten Áplestïrc."

The air lift crests us over the wall, which is pretty high and surprisingly thick. We float over it for a few moments before it gives way to a quaint little village. The buildings, which are engulfed in the wall's shadow, suddenly fall short, and there are fields of farmland for miles. In the distance, I can make out trees.

We begin to descend into the town, and Kabel continues.

"Those trees back there are the start to Drax Woods. Nasty place I tells ya. Been there three times, third time I lost my arm. Told myself I wasn't goin' back after that, but I guess I lied."

"Why did you go in the first place?" Chirus asks.

Kabel goes to explain himself, then does a double-take.

"Wait, don't you live in this country? Shouldn't you know?"

"Well I know about the hayride, but why would you do it?"

"S'why every Edgian does it: honor. Drax Woods is named after Raysgon Drax, Áplestirc's good buddy and one of the victims of the woods. Ever since then, it's been a yearly tradition for us Edgians to go out into them woods and show 'em who's boss.

"Used to do it in your own vehicle, then they figured it'd be best to stick together in a hayride. Started adding tracks after a while to find their way back easier. Only recently did the rest of the country hop on board with the televised broadcasting and the um, the... um... wassit called, the Applestirk Dayz festival!"

We finally reach the ground again, and Chirus breathes a sigh of relief. The four of us file out, meet up with the girls, and wait for Dr. Keeko and Bacoj to bring up the rear. Once we're all out, we follow Kabel down the main road. All the while I'm looking around me, and what I see is quite odd.

The town looks like a historical reenactment with a splash of futuristic themes. All of the roads are dirt and gravel, and there aren't any hover cars despite the town's size, but that's not to say that the shops and restaurants that surround the station aren't built with the same, hyper modern architecture as everywhere else.

Regardless of the building models, they're all made out of stone or wood, which looks really, really jarring. There are novelty stores and specialty shops and all sorts of different mom-and-pop restaurants; the entire place has a small town, rustic feel to it.

There is heavy foot traffic in every direction with tourists of all species and races. All it needs are the distant roars of roller coasters and this would make for a perfect amusement park. As I'm scanning the crowd, there is a particular area off to the right that catches my eye for some reason. I stare in that direction, confused, and then with a jump I notice the hooded figure beckoning for me next to the candy store. As soon as I notice it, it ducks down into the crowd and disappears.

I look behind me to see if maybe they were beckoning for someone else, but no one is looking in that direction. I glance back over at the candy store, but the hooded figure is still gone. Okay… maybe I might check it out a bit later.

As we keep walking, I make a mental note of where the candy store is. It won't be a hard trip back, since Kabel's house is a few blocks straight down the road. Once we arrive, Kabel looks back at us, grinning excitedly, and then simply opens the door, which I guess was just already unlocked. People must be really trusting around here! Kabel holds the door open, and everyone but Dr. Keeko files inside.

"I will come back early tomorrow morning to reconvene with you all." The designer says, and then Kabel closes the door.

We're all greeted with a cozy living room and delicious smells, then immediately after, a cute, young woman with brown-blonde hair and blue eyes comes from another room. She's wearing an apron with matching oven mitts. She must be Kabel's older sister.

"Kabel! Ya home!" She runs up to him before he can put down Sizzle Stick or his backpack and gives him a bear hug.

He hugs her back, and the two of them embrace one another before she lets go and gives him a kiss on the cheek.

"I see all the cousins are here too! I just got dinner finished; I can't wait to learn all about you guys!" She says as she retreats back into the kitchen.

"Thanks Ma, we'll be there soon." Kabel replies, and I'm instantly surprised.

That's Kabel's mother?! She's really young… younger than *my* mom! We all put our stuff down, then follow Kabel into his kitchen. As soon as I round that corner, tears come to my eyes. A feast is laid out before us. My prayers have been answered.

Soon, we're all seated at the table and eating. I decided to get one of the roasted pork steaks, some of those spicy yam curls, what looks and tastes like spinach lasagna, and of course, buttery rolls. All of it is delicious. Kabel's mom continuously surveys the table, looking at each and every one of us in a suspicious way.

"I didn't know we had democs in our family." Kabel's mom comments as she stares intently at Nima.

"She's Dondon's," Kabel replies with a mouth full of bread.

I glance up, and everyone is glaring down at their plates, constantly trying to stuff their mouths as to avoid conversation. My wandering eyes try to steal another glance at Kabel's surprisingly young mother, but she's already looking at me, so I'm caught red-handed. I smile sheepishly and she smiles back.

"You look familiar…" she says curiously, and the table seems to fall even more silent.

"Huh, you must be one of Rere's, aren't you?" She asks.

I can feel my face turning red, and I almost swallow my mouthful of pork too early, "Gah, yeah."

Kabel's mom looks at Sam, and it's like a weight has been lifted off of me, "You musta been that little girl she was havin… wow, it's been what, fifteen years now?"

Sam awkwardly bobs her head, "Just about!"

Kabel's mom smiles, looks over at Ilone, raises her eyebrows, and asks, "Kabel, was this ya cousin or ya girlfriend?"

Kabel and Ilone lock eyes across the table, staring at one another expectantly.

"My apologies, Mudda. She's… my girlfriend." Kabel says with a smirk.

Chirus drops his fork and clears his throat, glaring daggers at Kabel. Goofy grins start to spread across everyone's faces, and Bacoj has to put a napkin up to his mouth. Ilone stares down at her plate with an astonished smile on her face.

Kabel's mom continues, "I'm impressed son; she's real pretty. Maybe even a bit out of your league."

Now faces begin to turn beet red as the others desperately try not to laugh. Even Nima is forcing back a few chuckles.

"Thanks Mudda ya comment did wonders to my self-esteem." Kabel replies.

"You know I'm messing with you Kabel," his mother says, "You'll always be my little warrior…"

She pauses, thinks, and then says, "Did you show her ya Unkillable Rings? I thought that's why you left in the first place."

Kabel's face suddenly turns serious, and he puts down his fork.

"That's what I wanted to talk to you about in private. I think we should go ahead and end dinner first."

"What happened?" Kabel's mom asks, but Kabel stands abruptly.

"I hope you guys enjoyed the meal and thanks for having dinner with us. If you would like, you can head out into the town and check out some shops, or you could get ready for bed. Showers are through that room over to the right."

At the mention of shops, I remember the beckoning hooded figure from earlier tonight. Yoseph looks finished with his plate; maybe he can come with me.

The bionic traveler looks at his mother, still holding that oddly formal tone, "Of course you don't have to leave the table right now if you have ya plate to finish or any seconds you want."

"And I also made a *cocoina* for dessert." Kabel's mom adds.

Kabel nods, then asks, "Do they have a curfew?"

The young woman looks back at her son, then says, "Ah, if ya heading out, try to be back in an hour."

Kabel nods at the rest of us, sighs, and says, "Ma, how about we go in the kitchen? Let's get that cocoina ready for the family."

She stands with a worried expression and follows her son into the kitchen. Kabel closes the door behind them.

The table is completely silent until I force myself to speak, "Hey Yoseph, can you come with me to town?"

He looks at his empty plate, then scoots back and begins to wipe his mouth with his napkin, "Yeah sure thing."

"Where are you going?" Sam asks from beside me.

"Er, I saw a candy store and I wanted to check it out." I half-lie.

Sam nods, and then Cici blurts out, "Candy store? That sounds awesome! Can I go too?"

"Uh… yeah of course." I reply before I become too suspicious.

Cici smiles excitedly. The two are soon ready, and we leave. The town square is still packed, and my two friends follow me to the cartoony, pink-roofed sweets store. Cici suddenly gasps.

"It's like a dream come true you guys," she looks at us, "I'm going to drown myself in *lashytiers*… this is how I die."

We laugh, and she rushes through the glass doors. Yoseph goes to follow her into the sugary smelling lobby, but then I stop him. He turns around, and a gray cloth flutters down in front of me. A tan arm quickly loops the cloth around me a second time, and then the fabric violently constricts, pinning my arms down.

Yoseph looks surprised at whoever is behind me, then he switch-blades his spear into his hands.

"Well howdy do." A feminine voice says.

I look back, and sure enough, I'm pressing faces with the assassin we met back in Safemill.

"Edihi," Yoseph remembers her name, luckily, "Let him go."

"But you wouldn't hit a lil lady like me, would you?" Edihi's voice takes on a tone as sugary as the store in front of us.

With a face full of resolve, Yoseph angles the fiery blade of the spear at Edihi's thigh and jabs. The assassin waits until the very last second before violently jerking her leg out of the way.

"My my, yer a feisty lil feller now aren't you?" Edihi laughs, and I try to tug out of her grip, but she suddenly drags me until my balance is shifted into her steely embrace.

Yoseph and Edihi intently stare at one another, and I can feel my assassin's chest rise and fall behind me. Cici comes out of the shop behind Yoseph with a few lumpy sticks wrapped in white plastic. As soon as she realizes what's going on, she shifts the sticks to her left hand and switchblades a sai into her right.

Yoseph smirks, "Wassup with your little group from last time? They want to get messed up too?"

When Edihi responds, her voice is a lot more bitter than before, "I think you should mind your own business, hun."

She regains her composure, and then she leans her lips towards my ear. I can tell she's smiling again.

"If anything, y'all should be worried about your own group," she whispers, "I just noticed when y'all were walking in thatcha picked up a lil spy. Don't worry about it though, I'll take you into custody before he has a chance to do anything."

Edihi then lets me go for some reason. I spring forward, throwing off the gray cloth and dashing to Yoseph and Cici's side. When I look back, Edihi is wearing casual clothes, but her alluring eyes, maple hair, and kind smile are still the same.

"Haven't y'all heard the saying?" Edihi asks, "In Aplestroff, there are no enemies, only allies."

We don't respond, so she continues, "Y'all are safe now, but when you step foot outside these walls, I'll take all of you straight to the execution chamber."

A sour dread swirls to life in my stomach at such a serious threat, but then Edihi gives us a friendly wave and walks off.

Yoseph and Cici look at one another, then will away their tools and rush back to Kabel's house with me. Once we're inside, we're greeted with a surprisingly somber room. Kabel and his mother are nowhere to be seen, and everyone is silently sitting in the living room, eating what looks like chocolate pie. I can tell that Yoseph and Cici want to report our run in with the assassin, but for some reason, this doesn't seem like the right time to do it.

"What happened?" Yoseph asks finally.

Among the five, Ilone replies, "Kabel told his mother that he's going back into Drax Woods tomorrow morning to get another Unkillable Ring. She didn't take it well."

Silence, and then Sam asks, "Well, what happened with you?"

Yoseph goes to speak, but then Cici blurts out, "Some weird lady with a gray robe tried to kidnap Matt."

"Edihi, from Safemill." Yoseph adds, and everyone but Ilone reacts with surprise.

"Are you referring to the kupua?" Nima asks, and Yoseph nods.

"What?! How in the world did she find us again?" Chirus asks.

"I am unsure. However, knowing that the assassin is nearby is troubling news indeed."

"I have more," I force myself to say, "Nima, Sam, if you could come with Yoseph and I outside."

My sister and the democ look at each other, and then stand in unison. We file out the door, and Yoseph closes it behind us. We walk until we're at the edge of the road. I turn to the three, all of whom greet me with confused looks.

"Edihi said that we had a spy in our group." I say lowly.

The three frown and look at one another, then Nima asks, "Did she give any hints?"

"She referred to the spy as a he once, so I guess that cancels out Cici and Ilone."

"Then the only one it could be is… Kabel." Yoseph offers.

Sour dread returns as I look at the house in front of us, but then Nima interrupts my fear, "Do not forget Dr. Keeko. Did she indicate that the spy was in our group when she first met us?"

I think, then reply, "She did say she 'just noticed' the spy, so that could mean that she didn't recognize him from earlier."

"So Bacoj and Chirus are in the picture too?" Yoseph offers.

Nima nods, and then the four of us stand in silence.

"Let us go about this calmly. We should analyze each male member and proceed from there." Nima suggests.

We agree, and then Yoseph starts speaking, "First up is Bacoj. I know he's my homie, but he is kind of sketchy at times. I just… I don't think he's it."

"I was thinking Chirus," Sam says, "he definitely seems like someone who would put himself before the group."

"Remember, though, Chirus' cowardly nature has served as a distancing factor for nearly all of our excursions. In addition, he passed the perfect opportunity to have us arrested as soon as we reached Semparus." Nima defends.

"Good point," Sam admits. "Well, who do you think it is?"

Nima pauses, then says, "I believe it's Dr. Keeko. His sporadic manner of joining us puts him at a disadvantage. However, he repeatedly distances himself from us during our resting hours, which is where we're most vulnerable."

"So," Yoseph concludes, "it really is Kabel?"

"He just doesn't seem like a spy either. He's helped us out too much, and he seems too straightforward." Sam comments.

"Let us remember that Edihi is also a trickster. She warned us of impeding capture while we were at her apartment, but it was just a ruse. Perhaps this warning is another prank." Nima suggests.

We nod, and then Nima continues, "Let us go about our journey as if we are unaware, but remain vigilant."

We follow Nima back into the house and spark up a discussion with the others about tomorrow. The hint on the Ieri Tropo is literally just "Forest of Doom" and the item we'll need is also an Unkillable Ring, so it seems as though some of the team is going to have to join Kabel in the woods tomorrow. No one wants to make up their minds about it yet.

After that, we start a shower rotation. Soon, I'm showered and ready for bed. I'm not tired, but I lie on the floor until I drift off.

****

Yoseph wakes me up ridiculously early in the morning. At first, I go to tell him that we should be able to sleep in a bit longer, but I notice that everyone else is waking up too, so I stay quiet.

The morning is oddly serious and somber, and breakfast is eaten in silence as everyone, including Kabel's mother, stares at their plate. After we gather all of our belongings, Kabel kisses his mother goodbye, and then we all file out the door.

Dr. Keeko is sleepily walking towards the house, and when he spots us exit, he stops and waits. We walk up to him in silence, and then all of us follow Kabel through the town. Everything is peaceful, and there are very few people out, all of whom are carrying weapons and walking in the same direction we are.

Our team soon reaches an odd lansit-like vehicle. It's sort of like a combination between the lansit and the air lift. It's got individual roofless carts that can seat about ten, and they cycle around on a track like the air lift does. Instead of our destination being in sight, however, the tracks shoot far off into the distant morning fog.

There is no entry fee or station at all, so we simply wait for another cart to come from the mist, and then we all board it. The car whirs as it picks up speed down the track, and the town soon shrinks away. All there is around us now is harvested farmland, crisp patches of fog, and pink sunlight.

"Wait," Chirus starts abruptly, "What are we doing again?"

"We are entering the Hayride of Doom to earn an Unkillable Ring for the next location on our map." Nima says, but that's common knowledge since we briefly discussed that last night.

"What will we be fighting?" Sam asks.

No one answers, and then Kabel croaks, "We don't know. Changes every time. Some people started callin' em 'demons', but we try to avoid that term 'cause it looks like 'democs'. You know, politics."

We coast through the mist a bit more, then Chirus peeps, "We aren't all doing this, right?"

"Well, you know I have to, but if I make it out alive, I'm keeping the Unkillable Ring." Kabel replies.

"I believe the challenge is far more valuable than the reward. For the sake of research and for the group, I will venture into Drax Forest with Kabel." Dr. Keeko says.

I look over at Nima, who is trying her best not to look surprised.

"Well, I think this would be the best time to build my resume. I'll be right by your side, Dr. Keeko." Bacoj says.

"I can't let a little thief outdo me! Besides, this place sounds sick. I'm in." My sister declares.

I sigh nervously, "Looks like I'll be going too."

"Same." Yoseph mutters.

"I can't let you be the only girl, Sam. Let's do this!" Cici says.

"I am the leader; therefore it is my responsibility." Nima states.

Ilone shrugs, "Isn't that everyone? I mean, there's no use in staying behind I guess."

We all look at Chirus, who shakes his head.

"This is crazy, guys. You could easily die in this forest. The survival rate for this thing is like, what, thirty percent? What if one of you died? What if *all* of you died? Then what?"

"I guess you'd have a lot of responsibility to bear, wouldn't you?" Sam replies.

Chirus chuckles humorlessly, "I don't have any powers or weapons, I'm just me. If I'm the only one left, I can guarantee you Earth won't be getting saved."

Everyone is silent, and soon, we reach the end of the tracks. Waiting for us are four different hayrides bolted onto four of the dozens of tracks on the ground. The farmlands abruptly end at harsh, reinforced metal walls, and there is a hatch in front of each track. Those will probably raise later. Above it all is a huge banner that reads "FIGHT ON AND FIGHT HARD".

There are a surprisingly large amount of people here: about ten or fifteen. I thought it was just going to be us. Everyone files out of our little roofless cart, all except for Chirus and Nima.

"I suppose I will stay back as well," Nima mumbles sadly, "Never give up, and I expect to see all of you again tomorrow."

The cart makes a slow bank on the track, and then rushes off towards the fog and the town. I turn to the others, and everyone's faces are pale. The looming, ominous presence behind that metal wall is overbearing, even from the other side of it.

A few guys with clipboards walk over to us, and they ask for our names and ages. Surprisingly, when everyone starts flat out admitting their age, the guys don't bat an eye. I thought we would have to use persuasion or something, but even when I tell them that I'm 12, they don't seem to care.

We're assigned to one of the four hayrides according to last name. Sam and I get Hayride 1 (Winged Glory), Kabel gets Hayride 4 (Life Paladin), and everyone else gets Hayride 2 (Screaming Victory).

The sun continues to rise, and more and more people begin to arrive, bringing some chatter to what was once dead silence. I'm absolutely appalled by how steady of a stream this is. I've never seen so many futuristic weapons in my life, and everyone seems to have backpacks just like we do.

Hayride 3 (Lightning Halberd) fills up fast, and then the clipboard guys start to turn back riders who probably qualify for that hayride. I guess getting here early was a good idea!

Soon enough, a certain someone gets off of the roofless carts and makes her way over to us. It's Edihi. They sign her in and she heads directly towards our wagon. Each hayride has four wagons lined up one after the other, and most people are choosing the front one, but Sam and I are in the second.

The assassin climbs into our wagon and sits opposite of my sister and I, not saying a word but simply nodding. We nod back, and then I glance over at Screaming Victory. No one seems to notice but Yoseph and Cici. Yoseph searches my face for signs of distress, and Cici glares angrily at the back of Edihi's head.

My sister gives them a subtle thumbs up, and they both look off again. After another hour or so, all four hayrides are nearly full. I'm just lazily staring off into space, listening to the aimless chatter around me and trying not to get too nervous.

Suddenly, I spot a strange person get off of the roofless carts. From here I can see that they're wearing an eyepatch, and their hair is a trippy vibrant kaleidoscope, but it only reaches to their neck, so it isn't too distracting. I can't tell if it's a guy or a girl, because they look like they could be either.

Their sense of fashion is pretty contradictory to their hair; black jeans, gray hoodie, black boots, and a wickedly cool fiery grin on their mouth mask. I can see fingerless gloves on their hands, but I don't see them carrying any real weapons.

The person rushes over and signs in, then hops on Screaming Victory. For a moment, I prepare to return to what I was doing, but then Bacoj suddenly stands up and they hug each other. Huh… maybe that's Bacoj's modding friend that he mentioned back on the lansit… Ellia if I can remember.

A few more minutes pass, and then a group of four guys wearing all white come from the roofless carts. They're wearing bright red caps with what look like camera attachments, and I can see from here all of the medical equipment strapped to their waist. Each one of the guys hop in the dead center of each of the hayrides.

Suddenly, a loud click rings out from beneath all of the hayrides. All of the murmuring stops, and with a low whirring noise, the gates in front of our hayrides are drawn open. Beyond the threshold are a few gnarly trees and absolute darkness.

There's a hiss, and then all four hayrides simultaneously begin to roll forward on their tracks. A massive battle cry rings out from all of the riders at once, calling goosebumps to my skin and shooting a shiver up my spine. The cry is so loud that I'm certain the town heard it.

I take one last look at my surroundings before my sister and I are engulfed in pitch blackness. The noon sun shines bright and happy over farmlands and I can see the town in the distance. Fluffy clouds roll by lazily in the sky, seemingly waving at us.

There are a hundred people to each hayride, all screaming with their weapons drawn. I look over at Screaming Victory, and all of my teammates, including Dr. Keeko and the new person Ellia, are holding hands.

They shout along with everyone else, and right before the darkness overcomes me, I decide to do the same.

Chapter 22

The Hayride of Doom

~ Matthew ~

I can't see a thing, which is the only plus side, if there even is one. There are one hundred people on this ride but absolutely no one is making a sound. I'm not sure how fast we're going, because again, everything is pure darkness, but the wind brushing against my face tells me we aren't going too fast. I couldn't tell the driver to speed up if I wanted to. The entire thing is automated.

So far, so good. It's unnaturally dark, so much so that it looks like we're indoors. The weight of unknown fear bares down on me. It must be cold, because although I don't feel a thing, Sam is shivering beside me.

Nothing happens for a long time, maybe 10 minutes or so. Just when I start to think that this entire ride will only be darkness and tension, and that all the stories I've been told about certain death were just jokes, we are suddenly in a clearing.

I did not blink or fall asleep. The hayride didn't speed up or teleport. The clearing just appeared around us, as if it were there the entire time. There is a resounding jump of astonishment that ripples through the ride; everyone was just as surprised as I was.

The first thing I notice is the humidity. I couldn't feel the cold earlier, but I can definitely feel the warm, sticky, earthy smelling air. Something looks off about the sky… it's completely devoid of stars! The two moons above glow quietly as smoky clouds shift around them, but all the stars are gone. Wasn't it just noon a few minutes ago? I swear I didn't doze off, not even for a second.

As I continue to look around, I notice that there is no visible entrance or exit to this clearing; the tracks of the hayride go through one fence of dark trees over to the other. Speaking of the hayride, it has completely stopped.

In a stunned jolt, I realize something. I'm in the Forest of Death. Not just any forest of death either, but the one I had the dream about back on Earth last month. The one with the grim reaper and the one-way trip to Hell. What have I gotten myself into?!

Just then, noises come from the wall of trees surrounding us. For a few seconds, I can't tell what it is. It loudens until everyone can hear it and start to worry like I am. Then the sounds move toward us much faster, the hissing, scratching, and thumping rushing through the forest at a fearful speed.

I don't know whether to hide or run, but people begin murmuring uneasily, taking aim at the tree line with various guns and readying countless melee weapons; indirectly telling me that it's show time. It seems like as soon as I switchblade my machete into my hands, they emerge.

Spiders. Massive, brownish-black arachnids shuffle hungrily towards us, their four pairs of prickly, hairy, five-foot-long legs helping to pull them from the shadows. Their bodies are impossibly huge, almost the size of a regular adult's torso.

Instead of having grotesquely massive spider heads, they have the calm faces of sleeping dolls. Gray stripes run designs across their back. Their mouths violently and sporadically open as they grow closer, letting out hissing shrieks.

My heart leaps in my throat and terror pastes goosebumps on my arms. I almost drop my blade, but then snap out of my stupor and steel myself. This is what I signed up for; might as well take it like a champ. Suddenly, about fifty guns open fire from various riders, blanketing the spiders with lasers and bullets and darts.

The swarm of spiders continue to close in, but the gunners are dead set on defending the hayride. Some get a bit too close for comfort, and people with melee weapons start to jump out and cut them back. A spider shuffles in from my left and goes to jump on board, but we both spot each other at the same time.

The spirit of battle overcomes me, and without thinking, I leap off of the railing, soaring high as I aim to land on the giant bug. I'm holding my machete all kinds of wrong, with the blade facing me and my left hand crooked, but I don't really register it.

I embrace this sort of flight, and before I know it, my blade is lodged in the spider's back. It writhes as my tool sends electricity through its body. Sam pulls me back on board and tells me to never do that again, then shields us off from the fray. The spiders continue pouring in, and soon the gunners get confused on which ones are corpses and which ones are active threats, so many of them begin to sneak past and leap on board.

Lasers and bullets are flying everywhere, people are screaming, and a flash of silver from someone's swinging blade almost takes my ear off. One of the abominations must've dropped down on Sam's shield because she suddenly falls on me along with something else much heavier.

The creature flails its eight legs violently in the air, and then Edihi blasts it in the face with water. That stuns it for a moment and Sam quickly finds her bearings. My sister aggressively surges upward, and the abomination scrambles off her.

Sam readies her shield as it turns to face us, aiming that same calm doll's face in our direction. I realize that this thing doesn't have eyes, but instead, two closed mouths where eyes should be. In a burst of courage and disgust, I reach around Sam and slash the thing with my machete.

My tool must be really sharp, because the blade runs through this creature's skin with little to no resistance. It shrinks back, and then spasms until it stops moving. Another one leaps on from below, and Edihi immediately surrounds its head with a bubble of water. The creature begins violently swinging its appendages around and blinking, then it suddenly freezes and curls up.

One tackles me from behind and its spiny skin pokes through my shirt. I slam hard on the deck and my machete clatters away from me. A scream for help escapes my mouth, but Sam and Edihi are already rushing over to me.

Edihi goes to wave her hand and attack with water, but another creature leaps on the hayride and trips her. The abomination on my back looks up at my sister, then starts vibrating as it lets out a ridiculously loud and distorted screech.

Light washes over Sam, and she's suddenly petrified. I can hear the creature turn its attention to me; all three of its mouths breathe hot, fruity, garlicky air down my neck. In a burst of agony, it sinks its fangs into my shoulder.

I let out a scream, struggling in vain to get out from under the creature, and then suddenly, it's ripped away of me. I turn around as gingerly as my injured shoulder will allow and I'm met with a familiar face. It's Rixave, the guard that helped us sail over to Malle Island. He's still dressed in his SWAT-like guard gear, armed with an odd and terrifying spiked sledgehammer.

The guard rushes over to Sam, and then a few seconds later, they both rush over to me. Rixave kneels down to examine my shoulder, but then all of the spider corpses begin to rattle. The two of them look up, and then the creatures suddenly disappear from existence altogether. There is a bit of silence, and then everyone cheers for a bit before tending to the wounded. Rixave goes back to inspecting my shoulder, then he puts down his hammer and slings off his backpack.

Sam looks up, probably at Edihi, then walks over to her.

"What are you doing here?" He asks as he pulls out bandages.

"I was about to ask you the same thing." I reply.

"Well," says the guard, separating the bandages, "Rigm wanted to stop by for a little break before heading to Gumwood. I thought I'd take on the challenge and see what all the hype is about."

He gently pulls my collar to the side of my arm, and then tears the bandages open. They give off a little puff of dust.

"So… did anyone else come into the forest with you?" I ask, trying not to make this awkward. He presses the bandages tight over my wound, and pain stirs to life. The bandages are surprisingly cold though, so it feels kind of good.

"One of Rigm's girls, her name is Yera, decided to tag along. She's in Hayride 4 though, Life Paladin I think it's called. I also met an old friend named Kelsea. She's got sunlight powers."

"Huh?" Asks a voice behind Rixave, but he shakes his head.

I pull my collar over my shoulder and Rixave helps me stand. My vision gets a bit spotty; I must've stood up too fast. After the wave of dizziness passes, I look around the hayride. Everyone is bandaging themselves up and, surprisingly, taking quick water breaks. We lost a lot less than I'd thought; maybe none at all!

Sam pats me on the back, and I turn to her. Apparently Edihi just got a bloody nose from falling, so she'll be fine. The abomination bit me on my left shoulder too, so I'm able to keep fighting. Rixave introduces us to his friend Kelsea, who is a kind, cinnamon skinned girl with medium, dark hair. Oddly enough, she's dressed in seemingly cumbersome orange robes, and they make her kind of look like a Shaolin monk.

The people that were originally next to us are somewhere else on the ride, so Rixave and Kelsea decide to sit with Edihi, Sam, and I. With the five of us patched up and ready to go, along with everyone else on board, the hayride starts again. We slowly crawl towards the wall of trees, which seem to have a gap in them the closer we approach. Soon, the all-encompassing pitch blackness returns.

Unfortunately, it's all downhill from here.

The very next clearing had demonic clowns that got more grotesque and laughed louder the longer that they were left alive. After that was a clearing of faceless little girls, who were surprisingly minding their own business. Then after some of the gunners opened fire, the girls ran up and brushed their fingers against people. Those people then got a horrified look on their face before they just seized up and died.

After that was the Jack in the Box. We quickly figured out the thing moved every time anyone blinked. It started off deep in the woods and made a zig zag towards us. As it approached, the music got slower and the box seemed to grow larger and more intimidating. Luckily, we didn't have to face what was inside.

The clearings keep coming one after the other, some getting a bit too grotesque and others disturbingly calm. One clearing was just giant glowing eyes staring at us from the darkness. Another was full of snakes with human heads that let out blood-curdling screams for help but then viciously attacked us.

Deaths come and go through each clearing, and at first they are sickening, life-altering revelations for me, but soon, I begin to grow desensitized. Five clearings, ten clearings, fifteen clearings, eventually, I start to feel my confidence breaking. Is this ever going to end? Were we even supposed to survive this?

Of course, everyone has skill here, but this forest has little to do with that. The difference between life and death lies in split second decisions, which I feel is scarier than anything else. Run or stand still? Attack or show mercy? Any choice could either lead to me surviving or meeting a painful death.

The five of us are doing quite well for ourselves. All of our decisions have luckily been the right ones, and when it comes to fighting, we can definitely hold our own. Rixave and Sam are doing well with their weapons, and when it comes to Edihi and Kelsea, either their powers are super effective or next to useless. Luckily, it seems to alternate between the two of them.

We finish what must be our twentieth clearing, and then head into the woods again. Maybe half of the people we started with are left. When we abruptly emerge from the darkness, instead of seeing a tree-surrounded clearing and greeting our terrifying foes head on, I'm engulfed in harsh light.

When my eyes finally adjust, I realize I'm sitting on a little wooden raft in the middle of a lake. It's daytime, noon in fact, and puffy white clouds roll by in the baby blue sky. I look around wildly, and I begin to recognize my surroundings.

This is Alabama! Like, Madison, Alabama! This is my neighborhood! I sit up, and the raft rocks underneath me.

"Have a peaceful nap?" Someone asks beside me.

I look over… and it's my grandmother?! The wrinkles in her face, her happy, blue eyes, they're all so familiar yet distant.

"What are you crying for?" She asks me, and then she hugs me, which is just as warm and frail as I remember.

"Almost done out there?" Echoes a voice from the lake's edge.

The two of us look to see Sam beckoning for us.

"Lunch is ready! Come on, Mom's getting super impatient!"

"Just a minute!" My grandma yells back, then looks around the raft in confusion.

"Gah, where did our paddles go?" She asks, looking puzzled.

I look around too, more dumbfound at the entire situation than anything else, and then Grams laughs and says, "Huh, how'd they get in the water?"

We look at one another, confused for totally different reasons, and then she says, "Matty, could you grab that paddle for me? We wouldn't want Michael to get all worked up…"

Michael? Like, my dad?! In a mixture of confusion and excitement, I lean over the side of the raft and spot the paddle a little below the surface, seemingly stuck into the lake floor. I go to grab it, but then suddenly an equally familiar old voice comes from the sky. It's my grandfather's.

"Don't do it." He warns.

Startled, I look up, and to my surprise, the sun is completely black. Then the sky is black, and so is the lake water, and the raft, and everything, and then I'm suddenly back on the hayride in the middle of the night.

Instead of grass being outside of the hayride, there's only inky water. Everyone else on the hayride is murmuring quietly to themselves and letting out the occasional laugh. One guy bends over and reaches around in the water, and then something dark and curved slowly creeps out from under the surface. Is that a hook? It gently slides against the guy's arm, softly sinks its sharp tip into his skin (which he doesn't react to) and then yanks him into the water without a splash.

Oh… my… goodness. I turn to Edihi and violently ram her into the crowd of people beside her. She slams into them, and they all seem to snap out of their stupor.

"Splash everyone!" I scream, and then I turn to my sister, who is looking off into the distance with a doubtful, uncomfortable expression.

There is a massive gushing noise behind me, and I assume Edihi did her thing because people start immediately yelping and coughing. I waste no time, aggressively jolting my sister until the light returns to her eyes.

She looks around, confused, and behind her I see Rixave chuckling as he actually steps down into the water. In a rush of panic, I shove my way past Sam and Kelsea, desperately grabbing at the guard's clothes.

As soon as I get a good grip on him, he jets downward as if he was hooked. The force of the pull and his weight are much too strong for me, and I crumple down with him. Luckily, I feel quite a few people grab on to me, but my arms are still hungrily dunked into the dark water.

I don't want to let go of Rixave, and even if I wanted to, my fingers are caught under his vest, which feels like it weighs five hundred pounds. A black hook begins to slowly rise next to my arm, but then someone leans overboard with me.

It's Kelsea. She grabs a fist full of golden sunlight from thin air, and then slams it into the back of the hook. There's an explosion of brightness, and suddenly Rixave becomes extremely light. The people pulling me back into Winged Glory instantly have zero resistance, and so we all fall back on the hayride floor.

I look in my arms and Rixave's vest is the only thing that greets me. All I can do is stare at it, speechless. Kelsea sits down beside me, equally as breathless. The two of us just stare at the vest, and I can feel heat building behind my eyes. I was too slow. If only I had been a second faster. I… I was just too slow.

But the hayride continues on.

The next clearing we appear in is the oddest out of them all. It's about twice as big as the clearings normally are, so the signature wall of trees is probably forty or fifty feet from Winged Glory instead of twenty feet.

To our left is a tall, pretty woman. She's in a flowing, snow white gown that dances gently in a new breeze. Her skin is the color of her clothes, emitting a faint, ghastly glow. She sings into her cupped hands like there's an invisible microphone in them.

Her voice comes from everywhere and nowhere, her lovely, wordless song drifting across the grounds with the breeze and soft plucking from a choir of invisible harps. She's on a marble platform, almost like a stage, and there are various weapons driven into the grass between us, all covered in moss and rust.

To our right stands something that looks like a small, abandoned zoo, and behind its rusty bars lie massive piles of glittering trinkets. There is a big sign in front of it that simply says, "You've earned it!" and it looks like it might be written in blood.

The hayride stops, in that dreadful, finite way it always does, as if saying *Well, this is our final stop... forever.* However, people don't take aim at the tree line and ready their weapons. Instead, everyone starts sighing in relief and hopping off the right side.

This isn't an illusion. I can tell because instead of the deep confusion and empty hope that I felt back on the lake, this is just normal bewilderment. Some people are staying on board though, facing the singer. They are also abnormally casual, kicking up their feet and cracking open some drinks.

I look back at the dozens who went over to the zoo, and they are filling their bags with gold, jewels, new weapons, and even stranger things like kitchen appliances.

All the while they chat with one another, sometimes even laughing. I turn to Kelsea and Edihi for explanation. Kelsea is still holding Rixave's vest from when I gave it to her earlier, giving it a confused, surprised, teary look.

Guilt stabs through my chest, but then Edihi grabs my attention.

"This is the Oasis, also called the Gardens. It's the second to last stop of everybody's ride. Pretty much, it's the forest's reward for our hard work. That," she points to the singing woman, "is Lady Luck. If you step on the grass around her, you are paralyzed forever, but if you throw yer weapon into the grass in front of her, you get a few years of good luck. Well, only if you make it past the last clearing, that is. The closer you get it to her, the longer yer luck will last, but if you hit the stage, you're cursed, and if you hit her, you immediately die."

I glance at the groups of people chatting over snacks. One of them haplessly tosses a samurai sword into the air, and it lands around the midway point. His buddies laugh, pat him on the back, and continue chatting.

Yeah, I'm not taking my chances with that.

"What about that place over there with all the stuff?"

Edihi goes to explain, but then notices Kelsea still staring at Rixave's vest with that shocked expression.

"Kelsea," Edihi says loudly, "do you want to tell Matt and his sister what happens in that park?"

The shaolin blinks as if she just awoke from a dream, and a few tears absently roll down her cheeks.

"What? Oh yeah, um, okay. Well, this is the Oasis, also called the Gardens, and, uh, did she tell you two about Lady Luck?"

Sam and I look at one another, and then nod.

"Okay so," Kelsea wipes her eyes, "Um, that place over there doesn't really have a name but it's pretty much just a replenishing treasure chest. If you dig around in the piles of gold and junk long enough, you'll find what you really need. But if you're too greedy you might reach down and…" she looks sadly at Rixave's vest, which is placed beside her, "get pulled in."

Edihi puts her arm around Kelsea and looks at me blankly, studying my face. I look back at her with both shame and confusion in my eyes.

"Why don't we go over there and look around?" The assassin asks Kelsea, still studying me, "Come on y'all, we're bound to find some neat stuff…"

The four of us get out and make our way towards the park. As I approach, I can hear more clinking and conversation about people's finds. My eyes scan over the gold coins, random crowns, sparkling jewels, and silver ingots. Some people are dumping the valuables into their bags, others are digging around for that "important thing", and a few are doing a combination of both.

Everyone is keeping an eye on how much they take, though, and occasionally, a few people will put some of their gold and stuff back. Kelsea and Edihi hurriedly rush up to the rusty bars and kneel down with the rest.

I look at my sister with apprehension, but she shrugs and kneels down next to them. If Sam's doing it, I might as well tag along. I kneel down, then instantly spot a silver and velvet crown. That looks awesome! I reach for it and graze it with my fingertips.

Grunting, I painfully squeeze my shoulder just a bit further and grab it. To my surprise, it fits through the bars, and a second later, I'm holding it right in front of me. I stare at the crown, surprised that it was so easy to get, and then open my bag and place it next to the Peace Per. Oh yeah, I do have that, don't I?

I look back, then spot an emerald necklace not too far away. Mom would love that. At the thought of Mom, I suddenly get a sobering feeling and remember what Kelsea warned about greed. I can't let this forest take me; I've got to return to my mom.

I get the necklace with another rush of astonished euphoria, then decide that this next thing will be my last. I reach under the mound of gold coins in front of me, feeling around for something not cold and spiky. Suddenly, I find it: an oddly warm piece of paper. I keep feeling around it until I realize it's a scroll.

I grab it by the middle, then gingerly pull my hand out. As soon as I look at it, an instinctive panic rises up in me, making me freeze up. The ancient parchment rolled between my fingers radiates evil and power beyond anything mortal. Two weak, ruby red seals contain the document from coming open. Like a glow, deep and audible humming comes from this scroll. This is obviously evil, but for some reason, I pull it closer.

Maybe I should take it, I could open it alone later on. It's obvious this thing isn't a trick of the forest. Just looking at it feels much more grave and grim than anything I've seen tonight. This thing has to either be destroyed or leave this place immediately.

I look over at Sam, but then realize that everyone is looking at the scroll in my hands.

"What is that?" Edihi asks.

"I don't know; I was getting ready to ask you the same question." I reply, greeting some of the unnerved stares with honest confusion.

My sister and the assassin trade looks, and then Kelsea chimes in, "I say you keep it. If you leave it here, I feel like something horrible will happen."

I nod and stuff it in my pack. I can still feel its evil presence, but just like its humming, it's muffled to the point of being easily ignored. The four of us are soon back on the hayride, and once everyone returns and is ready to continue, we're pulled back into the forest's blackness.

It seems like as soon as we enter the void, we exit. The clearing we're in now is far bigger than any clearing I've experienced, even bigger than the Gardens. For some reason, there are mannequins in the field in front of us, rows and rows of them in fact. The hundreds of dolls surround a massive cloud of wriggling darkness at the very edge of the tree line.

But something even weirder lies here: the other three hayrides.

Survivors and our teammates greet us as our hayride eases to a stop. Sam and I jump out, along with everyone else, exhilarated by the sight of our friends. I embrace Cici; then look around at the others. There is only her, Ilone, and Dr. Keeko. Wait…

"Where is Yoseph and everyone else?" Sam asks.

The three of them get grim expressions and my heart sinks.

"Bacoj… lost his arm in the third clearing." Ilone admits.

I look at Sam, horrified, and she asks, "Did he survive?"

"Luckily," Ilone says, "but he's still out. Yoseph, Kabel, and Ellia the new person said they're going to spend the final fight with him."

"Final fight?" Sam asks.

"Yes, with the Puppeteer of Death." Dr. Keeko replies.

Both my sister and I stare at him, both lost and a bit intrigued.

"Oh, that's right, the whole alien thing." Cici says, which prompts a confused look from Dr. Keeko.

"So yeah," the drummer explains, "at the end of every trip into Drax Woods, all of the hayrides meet up to face the Puppeteer of Death. He's like this really big blue hooded guy with a scythe."

Cici takes a breath, and I'm reminded of the hooded figure from my nightmare all those months ago, where I was sent to the depths of Hell. Before I can dwell on that, Cici continues, "Um, there's a lot to explain, so I guess I'll give you the history first. So, the folk hero Teodusi was the first to find the Puppeteer and he sealed it in its grave to begin with."

At the name of the hero, I remember that I have the Peace Per in my bag. For a second, I let my thought die because the Peace Per needs sunlight to work, but then I remember Kelsea's on my side.

I shout for the shaolin, and she looks over at me, startled. In an odd little dance, I beckon for her and sling off my bag at the same time. By the time I unzip my backpack and pull out the Peace Per, the shaolin is right in front of me. Edihi is behind her, staring at me with an odd look.

"You called?" Kelsea asks, trying to keep her eyes in mine.

"Yes. This weapon here," I raise the heavy thing, "works on sunlight. You think you could help me with it?"

"Sure thing!" The shaolin replies, and Edihi silently raises an eyebrow behind her.

"Is that… the Peace Per?" Cici asks "Like, *the* Peace Per?"

"Yep." Sam answers for me.

Ilone and Cici look at one another, and then Ilone says with a shrug, "Honestly, at this point, I'm not even surprised."

Cici laughs and nods, but Dr. Keeko is still silently staring at the weapon with a mixture of skepticism and awe.

"Thinking about firing that at ol' Puppeteer?" Edihi chimes in.

I meet her eyes and nod, but I'm then greeted with a frown.

"Ain't got that good of a shot from all the way over here. You'd have to get much closer to hit 'em."

Edihi's right; even though the field kind of slopes downward towards Puppeteer's grave, it's too dark for me to make out just how big the cloud of hands around the grave is. On top of that, I have no idea how to aim this thing. Either way, I still don't want to approach the Puppeteer's grave. Something tells me it'll be a one-way trip to Hell, just like in my nightmare.

Kelsea then chimes in, "I mean, I can make as much sunlight as you want. We could run down there, but it won't hurt if we miss."

"Y'all go ahead then," the assassin says, nodding, "It ain't like the undead are here yet, and besides, it's better to stay safe.

Kelsea looks at me expectantly, and I heave the weapon onto my chest. Despite the tweak of pain in my shoulder, I try my best to aim the cumbersome thing towards the distant, swirling clouds, then I root myself and nod at the shaolin. She smirks at my stance and then flicks her wrist.

A spear of sunlight materializes out of thin air, darting straight into the middle of my weapon. Nothing happens for a bit, but just then, it begins rumbling and shining with its own blue radiance, letting out a low, building hum. I brace myself and let out a shout. The

Peace Per surges backwards, emitting a screeching beam of sky blue light. Force blasts from the beam, kicking back all of my friends and throwing me onto the ground immediately.

I hit my head and instantly get a spinning headache. The weapon thumps down in the grass next to me. There is a distant explosion, and testily, I sit up, my head swirling. Smoke drifts up from the smoldering crater in the field, and it's raining dirt over there.

The cloud of hands looks perfectly fine.

Embarrassment begins to set in. I… I missed? I shakily stand to my feet and pick up the Peace Per. Everyone else gets up too, looking over in the field before letting out a disappointed "aww". Other survivors are staring over at us, startled.

"What do you know; it is the real thing!" Dr. Keeko exclaims.

"Let me get another shot!" I blurt out, and then Kelsea is suddenly by my side again.

"Okay," she says, "but you might want to brace yourself better.

We go over to Winged Glory and I place the Peace Per back on my chest, ignoring the pain. I lean back onto the railing, then look over at Kelsea. The rest of the team, including Edihi, are standing behind the shaolin, curiously peering at us.

Kelsea flicks another ray of light into the Peace Per, and then she scrambles back along with everyone else. I brace myself again, and then a blast screams out, pressing the back of the plate deep into my chest.

I watch as the magnificent beam of rushing blue light streaks into a group of mannequins just short of the hand cloud, exploding into a blossom of fiery dolls and smoking dirt.

Another disappointed "aww" resounds, though this time, it's from even more people. Now I'm more embarrassed plus a little frustrated, too. How freaking accurate do I have to be with this?!

"Gah! Third time's the charm!" I shout, and speaking so loudly reminds me of this swimming headache.

Kelsea walks up to me, trying to contain a grin, and flings another bolt of sunshine into the Peace Per before rapidly backing away with everyone else. My grip tightens angrily, and I squat down a bit so that the beam will go up some.

After the building hum, the plate punches into my chest once more, piercing the night air with a blue beam of light. It darts, shining and bold, but then flies over the grave and explodes against the wall of trees. Horrific snapping cries out, and some of the trees fall with a swish and a crash.

Even more people "aww" in disappointment, followed by dozens of comments like "so close" and "come on man." Someone walks up next to me, but I'm so angry, humiliated, and in pain that I shove the Peace Per into their arms.

It's Cici, and instead of getting angry back, she laughs, "Looks like somebody's getting a bit grumpy…"

My head hurts too much to deal with this, so I just storm off next to my sister and let the anger steam out of my nose. Even Sam is picking with me, but I ignore her, glaring intently at Cici.

"Okay," she says, looking at Kelsea, "I'm going to try something a bit wild."

The shaolin was already approaching with sunlight in hand, but then she stops, "What is it?"

"I remember reading about the Peace Per in literature class. Teodusi had a friend that betrayed him… Calilier I think. Something about trying to kill Teodusi with his own weapon. But the Peace Per supposedly only hits a target if it's aimed vertically… so I'm going to point it up and see what happens."

The shaolin shrugs and throws light into the weapon once more. We all back away, and Cici raises the golden slab of a plate high above her head. It trembles in her hands, then releases a blazing stream of bright blue straight into the air.

We all watch the beam go higher and higher into the air, and then to my surprise, it begins arcing smoothly and slowly in the night sky. It continues to curve, tearing through the darkness above like a comet, until it beams straight down as if it were a solid pole of lightning. To my dismay, it crashes directly into the cloud of hands, engulfing it in a bubble of light for a second before vaporizing it in a shockwave of wind.

Everybody begins laughing and cheering, rejoicing over the fact that such an intimidating final fight was ended before it even began. I, however, just let the wind wash over me, too angry to acknowledge the countless insults coming my way from teammates and strangers alike.

After a few seconds, people begin to rush back onto the hayrides. I hop back on Winged Glory, but then remember Bacoj and the others back in Life Paladin. Before I can get out of the wagon, all four begin to simultaneously retreat into the woods. I guess they only give us a small window of time to celebrate.

We enter the black forest once more, but then suddenly, a dome rises over us, closing us off from the elements. For a moment, there is mutual silence.

Then suddenly, I realize just how exhausted I am, so I go ahead and fall asleep.

CHAPTER 23

NIMA'S SECRET

~ MATTHEW ~

I wake, confused, wiping the short line of slobber from the corner of my mouth. My head feels fuzzy, and a small headache lingers underneath. We're in a little clearing with rolling, harvested farmland to our left and looming, steel gates to our right. The sun shines bright overhead, glaring unopposed in a cloudless sky, and its heat beams through the translucent dome above us.

Though I am sleepy myself, I look around to see the other Earth Pirate members in a soft slumber. Everyone looks calm and peaceful as they lean on one another for support, and I can't help but smile. My memory seems foggy for some reason, so to help jog it, I try to remember everyone's names.

Those two girls leaning on one another are Ilone and Cici. That man curled up by some papers and a tablet is Dr. Keeko. The woman sitting cross legged with the orange robes is… what was her name again? Um… it started with a K… Kelsea! Right!

Sam's head rests heavily on my shoulder, an act that normally wouldn't happen. My sister would never show this much affection. This is hilarious; I wish I could take a picture of her right now. Is that everyone? Wait, no.

I look down to see a tan woman lying her head in my lap, peacefully sleeping. That's Edihi, my assassin. An air of confidence washes over me after the initial shock. This lady was trying to kidnap and kill me two days ago, but now look at her. I'm not sure what happened, but I like it.

I sit frozen for a bit, allowing the girls to rest, but then Dr. Keeko begins to stir, so I wake them up. Both sit upright, dazed, and when they realize they were laying on me, they both pretend like it didn't happen. Well, at least Sam does. I can feel Edihi's curious stare burning a whole into the side of my face.

"What happened?" Ilone mumbles.

"Something about a forest?" Kelsea suggests, rubbing her eyes.

"I remember spiders." Sam says.

"Don't we have the Peace Per?" Dr. Keeko blurts.

"Oh yeah. Matt couldn't hit the Puppeteer for the life of 'em!" Edihi says, and everyone shares a laugh at my expense.

"For some reason I feel like…" Cici takes off her pack, unzips it, and says, "So I *do* have gold bars in my backpack!"

Everyone scrambles for their packs and for a moment I do the same. As soon as I zip open my bag an inch, this horrific, overbearing aura of evil starts to seep out of it, and I immediately zip it closed again. Oh right; I got that scroll thing. What am I going to do with this?

Suddenly, Kelsea is in front of me. She stares at me with a crestfallen look in her eyes, and there is a black police vest in her hands. That's right, didn't someone die? For some awful reason, I feel like it's my fault.

Edihi notices my exchange with the monk and begins to reassuringly rub my back. It's rather comforting, and my assassin's kindness is actually starting to worry me.

Suddenly, the dome above us peels back, inviting in crisp air. I immediately spot the swarm of people near the exit. There are a bunch of people with suits and small boxes in hand, and there are others with clipboards and stretchers.

Seeing them makes me feel both dreadful and relieved. The medics with the stretchers descend upon the other three hayrides, but everyone on ours is fine, so we just watch. I spot two medics carrying someone familiar to the exit. Is that… Bacoj?

The thief looks awful, with flushed, balmy skin and a sleeping face contorted in pain. His right arm ends abruptly in bandages. Oh my goodness. Kabel rushes after the medics, his giant sheath slung over his shoulder, yelling something about a payment.

I watch as Kabel hops on the roofless cart with Bacoj and the medics, then the whole thing jets down a track and towards the town on the distant side of the farmland. Once all of the medics retreat, people begin to get up and leave.

I watch as streams of people go over to the exit booth and receive little black boxes along with hoodies. Everyone in our section of the hayride stays put, quietly watching the exodus. Suddenly, Kelsea stands to her feet, the black vest still in her hands.

"I've got to get going. I made a list of all the things I want to do in life, and I still have a few things left."

"Is one of them traveling the country?" Sam offers, "Because we're doing that right now."

Kelsea chuckles, "No, I've already done that. All that's left is finding a husband, becoming a medic, and trying out that other adventure forest in *Oxeimec*."

"Well, good luck." My sister replies, and everyone else wishes the shaolin the same as she hops out of the hayride.

Edihi abruptly stands too. No one says anything though, because no one knows what she's about to do. The assassin looks down at me with a sad smile, then turns to face the others.

"Y'all be careful on your adventure. There are many out there that do actually support y'all. But there are just as many who were like me, blindly believing what they've been told, thinking that y'all are a bunch of terrorists or villains."

She then looks at me with that same heart-wrenching expression, "But y'all can't be evil. It's impossible. You're the Crescent of Darkness, Matt. You're supposed to be a no-good fella, a ruthless menace, my target and sworn enemy. But you saved my life in those woods. I'm your assassin, and you saved my life."

Tears come to her eyes as we continue to stare at one another. I don't know what to do, so I just stay still and hold her gaze.

"And then you turned around a second later and risked your life to save that other fella. Y'all ain't got a drop of evil in you. Y'all deserve to be praised, not hunted. I can't keep stalking and planning and scheming. It just ain't right."

"So," Sam begins testily, "do you want to team up?"

Edihi sniffs, and then blinks away her tears, "My job won't let me. So, this is what I'll do. I'm going to leave today, and I'll stop following y'all. If I ever see y'all again, imma have to do my job, but I'm going to try everything in my power to avoid that."

The assassin jumps out of the hayride, then says, "Good luck."

We watch her walk towards the exit, collect her earnings, and leave with eyes downcast on one of the roofless carts. All the other hayrides empty out, and even the other half of our team has left by the time we decide to get moving.

The booths with the fancy people are actually where we pick up these fabled Unkillable Rings. With such an intimidating name, it's bound to look awesome. I receive my little black box (plus a free hoodie), then hop on the next roofless cart with the others.

As we whizz through the farmlands, I put my curiosity to rest. Inside the box is… wow. It's a ring made of pure gold with a glittering, shiny ruby on the top. Along the sides are delicate swirls and jagged bolts of fire. Inside, seemingly etched from lightning, reads "UNKILLABLE VICTORY".

Surprised, I touch it to my finger, and it widens to fit. I slip the ring on, and it's unexpectedly comfortable. I continue to gawk at my new jewelry until we get back into town, wondering how it might come into use later on in the journey. Once the carts slow to a stop, the six of us get out and make our way to Kabel's house.

All along the way, I catch glimpses of people in the streets. Some are partying, shouting, and swaying as if they'd already gotten drunk. Others, however, are curled up and crying. Kabel's front door is unlocked like normal, so the six of us invite ourselves in. Waiting for us are Nima, Chirus, Yoseph, and the newbie. Kabel, his mother, and Bacoj are nowhere to be found.

"Welcome," Nima says flatly, "There is a secret I have been hiding from you all for a very long time now, and once you sit down, I will reveal it."

That was a pretty abrupt greeting, so we all stand in the doorway, stunned for a bit before realizing that we should probably sit down. Nima surveys all of us, and once she realizes that everyone in the room is waiting, she takes a shaky breath.

"I'm admittedly unprepared for this, so allow me some time to stall. Um, Ellia, would you like to introduce yourself first?"

We all look at the hooded newcomer, whose face is now pink.

"Damn dude you're just going to put me on the spot like that?"

I'm taken aback, but then Ellia follows up with, "Sorry, it's a bad habit I'm trying to get over."

There's a pause as the newcomer twirls some of their kaleidoscope hair between their fingers, and then they speak again, "Um, so hi everyone, I'm Ellia. Bacoj and I are old friends, and Kabel… he's okay I guess."

"Are you a boy or a girl?" Chirus blurts out, sounding as though he'd been impatiently waiting to ask that question. I'm glad he did, too, because that's been bugging me for a while now.

The new person has their mask off, but I still can't tell if they're a girl or a guy. Their face makes them look like a girl, but it could easily just be a guy with a feminine face. Same with their voice.

Ellia looks at Chirus, smirks, then says, "I'm a boy. No wait, a girl. Maybe I'm both, maybe I'm neither! It's a mysteryyyy."

The newcomer follows that up by bobbing their head like a ghost and doing jazz hands. We all laugh, and then silence falls again as Nima regains the spotlight. She sighs and starts.

"Chirus and I were having a discussion last night about our quest and its origins. He asked me how the Mundatorite got into my possession, and how I got to Earth in the first place, and well, here is the truth.

"I am Yatniv's former housekeeper. For those of you unfamiliar with this position, it essentially means that I was the head maid of his castle. I would supervise cleaning staff, all of whom were your age, and I would assist the head chef with his duties. I would also oversee the hosting of parties and events at the castle, and it would not be uncommon for me to engage informally with Yatniv and other international politicians during these events.

"Yoseph, if you will recall our first interaction with Empress Rigm, you may have noticed that I introduced us using our last names."

"Yeah," he replies, surprised that the spotlight is suddenly on him, "I, uh, thought that was just some formal customs thing."

"At that time I was unsure of whether or not I wanted to reveal my identity. Even without my first name, the empress almost recognized me, though it had been many years since we'd last met. While on the Farewind, I admitted who I was to her, and she told me she'd been somewhat suspicious this whole time."

Everyone stays silent, so Nima continues, "I would have almost considered Yatniv an acquaintance. Many times, my reports to him would be over warm drinks and snacks, and he would even seek my counsel on occasion for some of his political decisions. I was aware of his nefarious idiosyncrasies, but he was rather kind to me, so… I must admit that I turned a blind eye. Well, until the day came where he destroyed my home village."

"My family was killed. He destroyed everything I'd grown to love, all of the schools and parks and attractions that I was raised by. Of course, I was devastated, because I was under the assumption that I had Yatniv's favor.

"I met with him again over refreshments, and armed with four vira, I confronted him on why he would commit such a horrible act. Would you all like to guess what his response was?"

No one replies, and the air is uncomfortably silent, so then Nima says, "*Because I can.* He destroyed everything I loved simply because he could. When I revealed to him that Bridge Town was the location of my upbringing, he apologized, but there was cruel amusement in his voice as opposed to genuine remorse.

"I flatly told him that I never wanted to see him again, and that I wished the absolute worst would happen to him, but he simply shrugged. When I got up to leave, he stopped me. We stared at one another for a bit, and then suddenly, he tossed me the Mundatorite along with a navy-blue box.

"Of course, I knew what the Mundatorite was, because he had kept me updated on the project as it continued. He claimed they were both parting gifts. Before I could throw it back at him, I was splashed with some sort of teleportation potion, and just like Bacoj, I was suddenly on Earth.

"The navy-blue box was indeed a parting gift. I kicked it angrily against a tree, and before my eyes, the box began to spread open onto the tree, slowly building what looked like some sort of house-tree hybrid. This is where I lived for several years."

Apparently, that's it, because Nima falls silent afterwards. We all look at one another, uncomfortable and unsure of what to do next. I mean, that certainly was a secret, but how should I respond?

"So…" my sister begins carefully, almost angrily, "is this journey really about getting Earth back?"

Nima looks up at her, "Yes. That will always be the purpose of our quest. I will not let my past jeopardize our goal."

She lets out another shaky breath, and Sam seems to relax a bit. Our leader continues, "This is why I want our meeting with Yatniv to be diplomatic. If an altercation starts, I'm afraid he won't be using any teleportation potion on us. To make things worse, he is much too powerful to fight without casualties. Even with the Crescent of Darkness, Yatniv's combination of physical strength, offensive magic, and tactical wits are going to make him a formidable enemy."

Everyone starts mumbling in disagreement, and then Ilone angrily sits forward, "Why do you think talking will work? Matter of fact, why talk? Let's do to him what he did to you."

"Totally." Cici agrees, and so does my sister and everyone else.

"Even if we manage to defeat Yatniv, especially if we kill him, we will only have a negative outcome. He is an awful person, but an admittedly wonderful leader. Although he does horrible things to his citizens, statistically speaking, the chances of any random individual being targeted by these events are extremely slim.

"By controlling the food and energy resources, the government can afford amazing free assets for the public, hence why transportation is so cheap. We are one of the most well educated and prosperous countries in the world, and even though Yatniv is ruthless domestically, he is outrageously charismatic when it comes to international affairs.

"Killing Yatniv, although it would be emotionally satisfying, would send our country into a systemic downward spiral in which our economic, civil, and international infrastructure would be thrown into chaos. We would essentially be responsible for the downfall of our own nation."

Ilone raises her eyebrows, "Well, never mind then."

"Hold up," Yoseph says, "can you explain what this Crescent of Darkness stuff is all about? I think Matt would appreciate that."

"I would!" I blurt out, excited to finally get some answers.

"Honestly, I am not absolutely certain on the abilities that the Crescent of Darkness holds. I remember Yatniv having nightmares for a few months, and when he consulted a soothsayer, they told him about the Crescent of Darkness.

"This entity is supposed to be a young warrior from a faraway land, wielding a blade of the same namesake. They should have a special vira bearing the symbol of an ancient principal, one that expresses the complementary balance of existence itself."

There is a pause, and then I gently ask, "So, um, what am I supposed to do?"

Nima shrugs, "The soothsayer was rather vague. You are to bring reckoning to Yatniv, to punish him for his arrogance by destroying his pride. Through what means, I don't know."

There is silence, and I thank Nima with a frown.

"So... if you grew up, worked for Yatniv, and lived on an alien planet for a while," Chirus starts, "then how old are you?"

"29, but in human years I'd only be 14." Nima replies casually.

"Oh." Chirus says, summing up everyone's response.

More silence ensues, and then, to our surprise, Dr. Keeko speaks, "What is next on our agenda?"

Sam and Cici both go to pull out their respective Ieri Tropos, but Cici is faster. The drummer shows Nima the map, and she speaks as she scans it, "After Bacoj's operation, we will continue to follow the Ieri Tropo on our approach towards Yatniv. According to it, we are to depart to Cayeuxi where someone will need to sacrifice their Unkillable Ring. From there, we will get... Necriox: the Key of Death?" .

Everyone looks at one another, both worried and intrigued, and then Nima continues, "We are not close enough for me to see what will come after that, but rest assured, we are approaching the Celestial Conference. I am unsure of how long Bacoj's operation will take, but once it is complete, we will proceed."

"Very well," Dr. Keeko says as he stands, "I will head back to my hotel and see you all tomorrow morning."

The doctor leaves, and then Nima addresses our newcomer.

"Ellia, would you like to join us on our quest to save Earth?"

The newcomer nods, and their colorful hair catches the light at odd angles, "You bet I am. I've been wanting to kick Yatniv's ass…ets for quite some time now."

We all laugh, and then Yoseph asks, "What'd he do to you?"

With a sigh, Ellia begins to talk in a sort of up and down tone, like they'd told this story a million times before, "So Yatniv had his way with someone from my school, and I didn't know her too well, but I still wanted to do something.

"One year he came down to Aplestroff to oversee the start of the hayrides, and I thought I'd confront him. You can probably guess how that went from looking at my eyepatch."

"Is that so? I wonder, has anyone else had any interactions with Yatniv?" Nima asks.

One by one, the others begin to tell stories about how they saw him in a parade once or how they got an award one time with his signature on it. From there, the conversation spirals into a casual political discussion, and I pretty much just tune out for the rest of the day. Nothing else eventful happens, save for lunch and dinner with Kabel's mom. We pretty much just relax and talk for most of the time.

Bacoj's operation is finished by the next day. When he returns home with Kabel, everyone rushes him to get a good look at what happened. Like Kabel, he has an arm that looks as though its skin is made of silver. Unlike Kabel, however, it's the right arm instead of the left. He can't move any of his fingers or the arm yet, but he still wants to continue.

Nima decides that would be best timewise, and so we say goodbye to Kabel's mother, meet Dr. Keeko at the front wall, and depart on the next lansit.

CHAPTER 24

BETRAYAL

~ NIMA ~

We woke so early this morning that everyone was lulled into sleep after a few moments on the lansit. I rest sporadically for about four hours, and soon enough we reach the providence of Cayeuxi. As we're slowing to a stop in the station, I walk about, waking all of my slumbering teammates.

Soon, everyone is ready, bright-eyed, and armed with their equipment. As the lansit slows, we gather around the exit and hold on to the walls of the vehicle. We finally stop, and as soon as the doors part, we are greeted with a station full of police officers.

Countless rings of officers in yellow jackets surround the exit of our lansit cabin, arms straight and *zecnos* at the ready. Soldiers, dressed in blotchy camouflage, are kneeling behind them, rifles poised to shoot. Green lasers swim all over my team and I, flickering across my vision and littering the sea of officers with emerald glimmers.

On Arret, the zecno is a type of firearm similar in popularity and functionality to the Earth pistol. The zecno comes in the form of a pod-like band that goes across the wrist. From the bottom protrudes the trigger, a small ball that causes the weapon to fire lethal red lasers when it is squeezed. If one points with a zecno on, it produces a green laser instead, which essentially marks the path for where the lethal one will travel should the wielder engage the trigger.

Typically, a zecno fires in bursts while a rifle fires single shots. Both shoot red lasers, which can effortlessly pierce or slice many substances. It isn't uncommon for red lasers to ignite flammable objects like foliage, paper, and clothes as well. One zecno is already a formidable threat but facing a sea of them essentially assures immediate death.

All I can do is freeze, and everyone else does the same. I quickly register the countless orders to put my hands up, and I do so, along with everyone else. Luckily Bacoj can operate his new arm, because if not, this situation could've gotten much worse. I continue to blink, trying to wake from what must be a nightmare, but this is somehow reality.

From the swarm of yellow jackets emerges a familiar face, one that I have not seen in four days but I may never forget. When I first saw this face, it was filled with false kindness and mischief, but now, it is oddly somber. It is the face of the kupua assassin, Edihi.

For some odd reason, her eyes refuse to come off of the ground.

"I thou–" but Cirovati is interrupted by dozens of officers telling her to stop speaking.

The assassin finally looks up, and her majestic eyes are filled with strange annoyance. She isn't looking at the drummer; the assassin seems to be glaring just off to my left. I would love to steal a glance, but that action could result in all of my friends and I instantly perishing.

Edihi speaks in a flat, formal tone, "Crescent of Darkness, you are under arrest for illegal entrance into this country, attempting to overthrow the government, defaming our supreme leader, plotting to assassinate said leader, creating an anti-government militia, and committing multiple acts of extreme terrorism."

A small swarm of police officers nearest to us surround Matthew, and within seconds, he is triple handcuffed. The officers essentially pick Matthew up, carrying him towards the front exit of the station.

My heart sinks as I watch the officers carry Matthew, the Crescent of Darkness, our only hope, out of the lansit station and presumably into custody. How is this happening?! How did they find us out? The others assured me that Edihi was no longer pursuing us!

I have no time for confusion, dismay, or self-pity, because as soon as Matthew is taken from the premises, Edihi speaks again.

"To the rest of y'all..." she pauses, surveying our shocked faces and the countless firearms trained on us, "I'll give you a three-minute head start."

What? On cue yet equally as confused, the officers and soldiers obediently lower their weapons, looking around at one another. Kabel immediately leaps into the crowd of gunmen, his hand firmly gripping the hilt of Sizzle Stick, but instead of being met with resistance, the officers dutifully step aside for him.

The bionic warrior stops, looks back at us, and then beckons. Apprehensively, the rest of the team sidles their way through the small army of soldiers, and once we've exited, I notice that everyone is now sprinting full speed.

"Where are we going?" Yoseph asks.

Even though I am unsure, I go to answer. However, Kabel speaks over me, "I just noticed that hover car rental place over there. We gotta get outta here!"

The nine of us thunder after Kabel, and after a block of sprinting, we reach the rental shop in question. Once we reach the entrance, I notice that everyone is breathing heavily from their exertion. Luckily for me, I used my vira's hover tornado ability, so I am coherent enough to speak for the group.

The lobby of the rental store is fortunately barren except for a few hover cars on display, some cubicles in the back, and a disinterested, petite, female clerk behind the welcome desk. Rates and fees are listed on a holographic billboard above her.

"Welcome to Evillorn Rental Company, where our prices are so low they should be illegal." The clerk recites unenthusiastically.

I would love to revel in the irony of her statement under different circumstances.

"My name is Teherah, and I'll be taking care of you today. Do you have a pre-order or would you perhaps be interested in our Savings of the Month deals?"

"No thank you," I say, persuasion in my voice, "Do you have any vans available for use? Preferably something rather swift that can seat around eight to ten?"

Teherah gives me an irritated grimace and spits, "Good afternoon to you too, then. As for your question, we have vans and we have 'swifter cars', but those are obviously going to be sedan models. And you'll have to actually *pay* for them, honey."

I'm taken aback by her rudeness as well as the fact that my persuasion ability was ineffective, but then I realize that this situation involves money and thus nullifies the ability.

Kabel speaks up from behind me, "Look toots, enough with the attitude. Do you have somethin' cheap or not?"

Teherah recoils in surprise, and then a spiteful grin spreads over her face, "The registry is quite big. It'll take me a while to look something up."

Instead of immediately engaging with her computer, she continues to sardonically stare at us, wasting more time.

"Alright lady we seriously don't have time for this." Samantha chimes in, her voice shaking with shock and annoyance.

"Oh I'm sorry, would you like to do my job for me?" Teherah replies, and Samantha is so stunned that she looks at Yoseph for confirmation.

He shakes his head and speaks, "We apologize for everything ma'am. We were wondering if maybe we could just rent something like that van right there."

He points to one of the vehicles in the lobby, which was apparently a large green van. I must've been so caught up in our impending time limit that I didn't notice.

"No, that's a show car sir," the clerk says in a demeaning tone, "Do you want a van like that? It will be…"

She actually does some genuine, helpful computing, and then says, "Thirty nummis per day… but then you'll need insurance."

"How much is insurance?" I ask, trying to keep my patience.

Instead of answering me, however, Teherah silently stares at me with an offended look on her face.

Suddenly, an alarm blares to life within the lobby, and everything is washed in red. The clerk shouts, and I follow her gaze to see that Bacoj has somehow gotten all of the doors to the van open, including the trunk. The van seems to be running as well, however, it is still not hovering yet.

Kabel quickly opens his briefcase, angrily throws a fistful of currency into Teherah's face, and then dashes with the rest of us to board the van. I see my teammates piling into the trunk and the side nearest to us, so I round the side and find a seat open on the second row.

I leap in, not giving a second thought to the screaming clerk or her alarms, and I slam the door behind me. I notice Ilone in the driver's seat and Samantha sitting next to her, Ieri Tropo at the ready. Everyone begins to shout for Ilone to drive, and to my complete surprise, Ilone shifts the car into drive without retracting the wheels from the ground.

She slams on the accelerator, and the vehicle lurches forward, slipping for a moment on the smooth lobby floor. A second later, we burst through the front glass wall with a showering crash and roughly bounce down onto the street.

Shockingly, Ilone continues contact driving, or driving with the parking wheels instead of the levitation maneuvering. I can audibly hear her stomp on the acceleration pedal, and the wheels screech momentarily before we're all pressed against the back of our seats.

The engine in the front roars as buildings and shops pass with increasing speed. Everyone is panicking, and for some reason, there is loud, bass-filled hip hop music blaring from the radio. This is both terrifying and exhilarating.

Samantha pads around for volume control, and once the beats have been quelled to an appropriate level, Ilone asks, "Okay, so what are we doing?"

We suddenly come up on a blotch of random traffic, and Ilone slams on the brakes, turning the steering harshly and causing us to slide on two side wheels for a brief infinity before we slam back down onto four wheels.

"Yo chill with that! Uh, ah, d-don't we have to get some type of gem or something?" Yoseph shouts from the trunk.

We race past an intersection, and I glance down the perpendicular road with a few others. Immediately, I spot a military convoy retreating to the edge of town. I am absolutely certain they have Matthew.

"Whoa whoa that was Matt right there!" Cirovati shouts from the third row.

"Right?" Ilone asks, but before anyone can answer, the next intersection is suddenly upon us and she makes another near-death turn.

As soon as we round the corner, we're met with a disgustingly long line of traffic. Ilone violently applies the brakes, forcing our seatbelts deep into our torsos. The vehicle squeals to a stop, centimeters away from the car in front of us.

"Alright so what are we doing?" Ilone asks, nervously gripping and releasing the steering wheel.

"Well, we *were* going to get Matt, but I'm quite sure the convoy blocked off the streets, so it's going to be like impossible to catch up to him." Cirovati reports.

"Yeah it'd be safer if we just went to go get the gem thing." Chirus peeps from Cirovati's row.

"No screw that," Ellia says, "We're getting the Crescent of Darkness back."

Even though I am just as eager to retrieve Matthew as everyone else, chasing him is an unwise decision. I notice Samantha in the passenger's seat, uncharacteristically reserved.

"Samantha, what do you believe should be our next course of action?" I ask.

"What do you think?" She replies coldly.

Everyone, especially I, immediately silences themselves, and the hip hop music playing now seems horribly inappropriate.

"No seriously," Samantha continues, her voice trembling with what I now realize is shock, "What do you think we should do? Honestly, I'm not in the best mindset to make decisions right now. I just want my brother back. I think you would make the best decision."

I sigh in relief and smile, for the dread and rue that I felt moments prior has now dissolved.

"Then I believe..." I pause, trying to sort logic from emotion. Unfortunately, the traffic light turns white, meaning traffic can now flow. I must make a decision.

"We will continue with our quest." I say flatly, disappointed with the entire situation.

Everyone takes my declaration with a surprising amount of silence and acceptance. Samantha shows Ilone the map, and then she guides the vehicle at a legal speed behind the rest of the cars. We follow the detour, driving parallel to Matthew's convoy for a while before splitting off to the left.

The Crescent of Darkness has been captured.

CHAPTER 25

WORD DUEL

~ NIMA ~

By the time we reach the outskirts of town, our mood has lightened considerably. For the past few minutes, I have been able to convince the others that Yatniv is not brash and basic enough to instantly kill Matthew. Honestly, Yatniv does not seem like the one to do such a thing; that would be too abrupt and anticlimactic for him.

What I did not mention is the fact that Yatniv is probably waiting for us with Matthew in hand, eagerly anticipating our arrival. Additionally, I decided to forego mentioning that the probability of things going diplomatically has sharply decreased, and now it is highly likely that some, if not all of us, will die. But I must remain hopeful; I may be completely overthinking this situation. Yes, that is probably the case.

Some of our younger or less invested teammates accept my reassurance at face value, but the more serious ones, especially Samantha and Yoseph, easily understand my doubts. When we arrive at the golden gates of the Necriox Mansion, the van is full of both plastic and genuine optimism.

"Is this the place?" Ilone asks, pulling our modest van to the curb of the empty expansive country road.

Countless hills roll into distant mountains, and the sky is light and littered with wispy clouds. Aside from the nearby manor with its looming, permanently green foliage, all the other trees for as far as I can see are still and nearly bare. The grass is honey colored, blanketed with sparkling frost and, further back, browning leaves.

"Yes." Samantha croaks. She hasn't been nearly as upbeat or talkative as she was when Matthew was around, but she too has emerged from her previous frank depression.

Ilone powers down the vehicle, but no one moves to leave.

"Indeed," I mutter, realizing that the others are waiting on instruction, "I have a feeling this particular excursion will be more negotiation-based as opposed to one dealing with physical conflict. In addition, I believe it would be best for fuel efficiency and for overall driving quality if the van was converted to its typical levitation maneuvering settings."

Everyone laughs and mutters in agreement.

"Therefore, I find it best that we split into two groups; one to venture into the Necriox Manor and the other to repair the van."

"Well, I'm the driver, so I should probably give the van a look." Ilone reasons from the front seat.

Kabel shouts from the trunk, "Ah, I do a little mechanical stuff here and there. Nothin' special, but I could lend a hand too."

"Somebody else join, I don't want him alone with my cousin." Chirus says, and everyone, including Kabel, laughs.

"I might be able to figure it out. I did do fifteen years of electrical engineering after all." Dr. Keeko reasons softly.

"I'll see what I can do too! I might as well start building my resume now!" Bacoj says from beside me. His new bionic arm is seemingly starting to liven.

There is silence, and then Cirovati speaks, "I'm, like, totally trash with mechanics, so I can go to the mansion."

"And I'm complete sh… um, *manure* with talking, so I guess I'll hang back." Ellia admits.

"I suppose the rest of us will go to the manor then." I say, stifling a laugh. That was a rather clever censor Ellia used.

Everyone gets out of the van, and then half of the team swarms the vehicle's hood while the others follow me across the street. We walk down the sloping driveway until we reach the looming, thin gates. I had never realized the biting cold until just now. I must have ignored it in our previous haste.

The five of us pad quietly across the gray street, and the others start to bounce down the driveway while Samantha subtly motions for me to slow.

"It was the spy." She reports, with her breath sending up a plume of vapor.

At first I am confused, but then I quickly infer that she is referring to the capture of Matthew an hour or so ago.

"Is that so?" I ask, inviting her to continue.

We have no choice but to make our way down the sloping driveway as well, lest we draw suspicion, so we do so slowly.

Samantha says a few quivering words, but then stops and starts over again, "Remember when we said that we met with Edihi during the Hayrides, and afterwards she said she was going to stop chasing us? Even if she was somehow acting or something, she still left earlier than we did, so there's no way she could've seen where we went. The spy must've tipped her off, so I think she was forced to come back and arrest us."

The gush of steam from her speech quickly dissolves in the air, but the two of us are now within earshot of the others and can't continue our conversation. I agree with Samantha. Even though trusting this assassin is most certainly a last resort, it does seem as if she has some reservations about her mission after us. If that is the case, which it appears to be, then maybe this spy dilemma is a lot more serious than I had initially predicted.

"The gates are locked and there's this security system thing that does a whole bunch of crazy stuff if you try to break in." Yoseph says.

"Have you tried the buzzer?" I ask, looking at the white button next to an intercom.

"Nobody wants to chance it." He replies.

I nod in understanding. Possibly alerting the authorities at a time like this would be extremely detrimental to our quest. Mustering up all the courage I have and clearing my mind as much as possible, I bring myself to press the cold button.

Faint fanfare rings from somewhere inside the manor, and in a few moments, a woman's voice answers our call.

"Welcome to the Necriox Manor. Do you have any business?"

"Yes madam," I reply, beckoning for the Ieri Tropo, "we are here to discuss possibly purchasing the Necriox Gem from this manor's owner."

There is a dishearteningly long delay, and then, "Does your name begin with an S?"

This question catches me off guard, so my answer stumbles a bit, "Oh, ah, well, my name personally does not, but one of my present colleagues' does."

Another long pause, and this time my small team looks at one another with questioning glances. Suddenly, the gates give off a lovely, odd chime before slowly swinging inward.

"Wait," Cirovati says before we can make our way onto the mansion's grounds, "How are we going to purchase the Gem?"

I palm my head and laugh, "You're right, we need an Unkillable Ring, don't we?"

"Dr. Keeko said he'd give his up," Cirovati says as she begins to skip up the driveway, "I'll go get it."

With that, she sprints away, and not 30 seconds later, she's returned with the ring in hand. Satisfied and now properly prepared, the five of us pass through the gates and approach the manor's front steps.

Curiosity and awe urge me to take a look around, so I do. The grounds alone are exquisite. The cobblestone driveway loops past the elaborate marble entrance steps, around the traveler's statue, and back to the hill again. A smaller, more solid path leads from the cobblestone loop to a secondary house, which must be where all of the owner's cars are kept.

I take yet another look at the statue as we pass by. It's of a middle-aged man with an adventurer's dress and groom, admiring a large stone in his hand. The entire monument is made of translucent crystal, throwing the mid-morning sunrays in a flurry of different directions.

The gem in the adventurer's hand, which is purple instead of clear, catches the light in a near perfect way, causing it to glimmer and shine as though it was authentic. The base of the statue looks as if it was made to be a fountain, but alas, it is dry.

The five of us reach the door, and it is suddenly opened for us. A tall, lean, cinnamon-colored woman in a maid's uniform stands to one side of the entrance, beckoning for us to enter. For some reason, Yoseph and Cirovati glance at one another, but the five of us hastily enter.

Immediately, I begin to feel the heat of the manor's interior, and my subconsciously tense shoulders begin to sag in delight. We all pause in the foyer for a moment, drinking in the warmth that melts through our clothes, and then we follow the maid through the main hallway.

For some reason, Yoseph and Cirovati continue to glance at one another in a seemingly panicked way, but we soon enter a great room area and are invited to sit on one of the many comfortable looking sofas.

There is a luxurious armchair positioned in front of the fireplace, facing the rest of the loveseats and couches. This is quite obviously the host's chair, so the five of us go with the other couches instead.

The maid nods politely, and then hurries off to attend to matters. Minutes pass as we wait for our host. Yoseph and Cirovati are impatiently jittery for some reason, looking around the great room with a bit too much speed to truly admire it. I'll make sure to confront them once we leave.

Samantha is staring blankly into the crackling orange flames behind the host's empty chair, undoubtedly thinking of her brother. Chirus, seemingly overwhelmed by the sudden surge of comfort, is very obviously fighting the urge to sleep. I scan over the mahogany and maroon interior of the great room, admiring the coziness and architecture, then allow my eyes to be consumed by the breathtaking view of distant blue mountains and shimmering frozen tarns off to our right.

"I apologize for the wait." Says a voice at the entrance of the great room.

We all look, and there is our host, sleepy-eyed yet dressed well with an elegant black and red robe wrapped around his body. On his left breast are a pair of aesthetic spectacles (for any real vision problems can be fixed with florma) and a large, cursive "S" embroidered in gold. He looks identical to the adventurer outside, save for his more professional groom and indoor clothing.

I stand, and everyone else confusedly follows my lead.

"Oh no worries. Please, sit." He replies in a kind voice.

We all do as he commands, and the others shoot me puzzled looks. Our host sits in his armchair, taking a moment to get comfortable before crossing his legs. He surveys the five of us, taking note of our dress, demeanor, and age, but instead of continuing with a condescending air, he does so with mild intrigue.

"Allow me to introduce myself. I am Sedrix Necriox, owner of, ironically, the Teslan Range Clickboarding Company. I believe you all are familiar with this sport?"

Everyone nods, even though two of my team members couldn't possibly know what he means. Clickboarding is a somewhat popular sport here in Arret, nowhere near as worldwide as kaxahhe, but mainstream in its own right. Essentially it is "snowboarding" but with a *clickboard*, or hoverboard, allowing for high speed, greater jumps, and more impressive stunts.

"I am also born from a long list of aristocrats who, as you all seem to have prior knowledge of, possess the Key of Death. I am aware that you wish to… purchase it from me?" He asks the last part with an amused grin.

"That is our intention, sir." I say shortly.

He nods, then looks off behind us, probably to his maid, "Yes, Taamré? Could you bring us some *druplaite*, please?"

He looks back at me, "A proper confabulation always starts over good tea."

I nod, trying to hide my eagerness for what seems like a rather formidable intellectual debate. Out of the corner of my eye I notice Yoseph's subtle, wide-eyed glance at Cirovati, and Cirovati swallows hard, her face turning pale.

Much faster than I expected, the maid brings out a large, clinking platter of ceramic cups, each filled with steaming, gray liquid. She lowers the platter with surprising control, and the five of us take our cups before the host takes his. Taamré then retreats from the room.

Chirus begins blowing and sipping his drink already, but the rest of us put ours down. Samantha looks disinterested, consumed in thought, while Yoseph and Cirovati look like they have no intention of drinking at all. Necriox, like I, is reserving his ammunition for our impending duel.

"Ah, my apologies. I never got your names." He starts, and we briefly introduce ourselves.

"Very well… so, Ms. Iyr, as you know, established currency, regardless of the amount, will have no effect on my subjective position. Therefore I ask; what sibylline notabilia do you possess that may persuade me to relinquish my heirloom?"

I take an unblown sip of the druplaite, letting the burning, tasty, bittersweet liquid stimulate my brain. I make sure to take a very small sip to make sure Necriox isn't misled. I will not be using my persuasion ability; this will be a true battle of minds.

"My company is in possession of a smorgasbord of exclusive paraphernalia, but what may catch your interest is the fabled Unkillable Ring."

Necriox's friendly yet steely glare is almost broken with surprise, and after a moment, he takes a sip of tea himself. I stifle a triumphant grin.

"It would be quite clever to play on the avarice of an eccentric connoisseur, and I do admit that such a serendipitous item would be rather satisfying to obtain…"

He pauses, and I begin to worry. It seems as though Necriox has already revealed himself, but that can't be true, because he seems too smart to do so. I brace myself for something unexpected, and it comes.

"However, are you able to prove that such a treasure is not merely a verisimilitude?"

I'm hit with a dull, internal shock, and it takes all of my will not to lean back or blink in surprise. At a loss for words, I have no choice but to take a sip of tea, which causes Necriox to smirk. How am I supposed to reply? There is no way we can prove that the Unkillable Ring is real, even though it is. There might be some scientific way, but I'm unsure.

I can't take another sip of tea, because that would be akin to accepting defeat, so instead I verbally analyze his challenge.

"Firstly, Mr. Necriox, your kindness and good nature suggests that your personality greatly divagates from that of a niggard."

The host nods humbly, and Yoseph shoots me a surprised look.

"Secondly, in regards to your inquiry on the indubitable status of our Unkillable Ring, I," suddenly I'm stuck with a wonderful comeback, "will have to admit that it is as equally assertible as to the claim of authenticity your heirloom possesses."

Necriox isn't fast enough, and I notice his eyebrows raise ever so slightly. He is silent, then takes a sip of his druplaite.

"I see that you are not puerile in your persiflage," more silence, then he adds, "nor are you a neophyte to repartee."

He stares at the carpet more, trying to think of a solid reply or challenge, and I make myself blow and sip the tea again so that I don't grin in victory. He blinks a few times, shifts uncomfortably, then takes another swig of tea.

After the drink, he seems to have realized his position, because then he says with a defeated smile, "Present to me the Unkillable Ring and I shall do the same with my heirloom."

I silently rejoice, and Cirovati hands me Dr. Keeko's award.

"Before our exchange, there is one thing that you must promise." Necriox says seriously.

"What is that?" I reply, a bit of worry starting to dampen my victorious mood.

"Make absolutely certain that only Samantha will have possession of the Necriox Gem at all times."

My companion starts at her own name.

"Since our family gained the Key of Death countless generations ago, only those with names starting in S have been able to possess it without befalling great tragedy and misfortune. For your sakes, you are to always follow this promise."

I look at Samantha, who looks equally surprised, and then turn back to Necriox and nod.

"Very well. It is a family tradition to wait a week before venturing out to find the heirloom once more. The statue outside actually chronicled one of my favorite previous excursions to retrieve it."

Necriox stands with a smile and pulls a deep violet jewel from his robe pocket. It is even more mystic than the statue outside portrays.

"Your visit has brought me great happiness. I wish you success on your travels, and may we one day cross paths again."

We exchange valuables, shake hands, and then the five of us leave Necriox sitting delightedly in his great room.

Chapter 26

Ambush of Vengeance

~ Nima ~

A grin remains on my face even as we walk the chilly grounds towards the van. That was by far the most satisfying conversation I've ever had. That tea was fantastic, and these grounds are beautiful. What a shame it is that we couldn't spend the night here. I really do hope to meet Mr. Necriox again.

My companions, however, are much less ecstatic. Chirus is rubbing his belly happily, apparently enjoying the tea as much as I did, and Samantha turns the Necriox Gem over yet another time, entranced with the jewel's mystic aura.

Yoseph and Cirovati, however, seem to be trying to inadvertently increase the group's speed.

"What's the matter?" I ask the two of them, half worried and half annoyed at their behavior.

Yoseph looks at Cirovati, but before he can say anything, she blurts out, "We'll tell you when we get to the van, for now let's hurry because it's super cold."

Cirovati's statement is certainly true, but despite the frigid atmosphere, the pride from my victory mixed with the druplaite tea serves to warm me.

"Then let us talk to keep us warm. Did you enjoy the battle between Mr. Necriox and I?"

All form of haste seems to leave their mind as we round the corner. From here, we can see past the wide-open gates and up onto the road, where the hearty banter of the other half of our party can be heard. This seemingly reassures them, so they relax and begin walking at a tolerable pace.

"It was cool or whatever, but I didn't understand, like, anything you were saying." Cirovati admits.

"Same here. It was pretty entertaining once you finally stumped that guy, though." Chirus comments, with the vapor from his mouth being thicker than everyone else's.

Everybody nods and agrees, and my smile, which was finally dying down, rekindles again.

"Yo Nima," Yoseph starts, "Remember the first part of the last thing you said?"

I think, then reply, "Oh yes, the compliment?"

"Right," Yoseph says, "What was it you said he wasn't?"

"Ah… that would be a niggard, or stingy person." I reply.

He leans back with a chuckle, "Oh! I thought you said something way different. Glad we cleared that up; didn't want any problems."

Hmm, must be some strange Earth thing.

Suddenly, a loud zap sounds a few meters to our right, and a splash of dirt closely follows a flash of light.

Startled, the five of us turn to find the maid, Taamré, standing at the head of the stairs with rage in her onyx eyes and what looks like a tome in her hands. She violently slashes her finger through the air, and a watery, glowing ribbon of yellow light seems to form as if she drew it.

It hovers there in the air as she draws more with her finger until she finally makes a star out of them. Furiously and ceremoniously, she encloses her shape in a circle, and then the whole thing solidifies and flashes out of existence. She performed all of this in a little under three seconds.

"*Deleterious*!" She shouts without warning, and suddenly a dart made of crimson and black light appears out of nowhere, beaming right into Cirovati's arm and causing the drummer to scream in agony. She drops to the ground, and Yoseph kneels by her side while Samantha switchblades her shield into existence.

There is an odd whining noise, and then Chirus shouts, "The gates are closing!"

I look back, and sure enough, the elegant, tall, golden bars are slowly turning to meet one another again.

"Try to stop them!" I advise, and then I follow Samantha's lead and call forth my twin sickles.

The maid begins to slowly descend the stairs, looking quite enraged. Her murderously cold eyes and intimidating frown completely contradict her well-made, wavy black hair and her innocent maid's uniform.

"What is your quarrel with us?" I ask, genuinely confused.

She doesn't answer, but then suddenly, I hear Chirus scream in pain. I look back, and he's violently shaking his hands as if he'd just been hurt.

"The gates are electrified!" He warns, and, seeing that his only option of safety is now almost gone, he slips through to the other side before they close.

Suddenly, the maid from behind me shouts, "*Caliginous*!" I wheel back around to see her attack. From the air around her, there is suddenly a daunting, swirling cloud of thick smoke zig-zagging towards Samantha and me.

It rushes forward, much too wide and fast to dodge, and before I know it, I'm briefly engulfed in rushing wind and complete darkness. I can't see anything, and suddenly, my blood feels as though it has frozen solid and is now stabbing my insides. That is the only way I can find to describe this extreme discomfort and pain.

Luckily, the darkness eventually dissolves, and throbbing soreness is left in the place of sharp agony. The maid is now much closer, almost within striking range, but I don't have enough bearings to attack.

She grabs me hard by the shirt, then surges me back with more strength than I had expected, causing me to land hard on my rear. I'm already sore from her smoke attack, so even more pain jabs through my body when I connect with the cobblestone driveway. Hurriedly, I try to think up a phrase where I can use my persuasion ability.

"The most effective way to solve–" but before I can finish, Taamré begins shouting shrilly, "You're friends with the Crescent of Darkness, and he's responsible for my fiancé's death. I don't know who you are, but if you're with the Crescent of Darkness, you deserve to die."

She begins to draw another magic circle, but I force myself to act and kick her leg out from under her. The maid falls hard on the cobblestone as well, and I command my aching body to get up and prepare for a fight.

For a moment I contemplate kicking her tome away from her, but she has it by the time I consider acting. Now armed again, she stands and swings the heavy book at me. I dodge it, surprised she'd go for a melee attack, but then she shifts her footing and spins, swinging harder and faster this time.

In a flash of rough colors, the book connects with my face, leaving me lightheaded and stumbling. I quickly take a glance around and see that Yoseph is flying a dazed Samantha over the gate. He must've done the same with Cirovati, because she's nowhere to be found.

Alright, it looks like I'll have to hold my own for a short time. I grip my sickles a bit harder and deepen my stance, ready for a battle. The mage, still not thinking correctly and overcome with misplaced anger, rushes forward, tome raised above her head.

I sidestep the attack and aggressively shoulder her back, and before she can gain her bearings, I land a solid kick in her sternum. My kick was rather weak now that I think about it, because she recovers almost instantly.

Taamré seems to remember that she is indeed a wizard, and thusly cracks open her tome. I go to knock it out of her hands with my sickle, but she pulls it back, still in close range. She attempts drawing a magic circle, but I swipe at her with my second blade, causing her to flinch and back up.

Now slightly out of range, the mage smirks. I lunge and take a vertical swipe, aiming more so for her tome, but she sidesteps the attack with a surprising amount of grace. With a snap and a "*Salvo*!" her next attack suddenly appears as a small, bright explosion between the two of us.

I'm thrown back, but instead of falling down again, I'm caught by someone; Yoseph. He whirls me around and turns around himself. Without thinking, I hop on his back, and in a few fiery bursts, we're over the gate.

We land a bit rough and when I hop off of him, I look back to see that Taamré is quickly retreating back into the house. I don't remain there to find out what will happen.

Yoseph and I run to the street where the van is already on and hovering. The door is open, and as soon as the two of us get in, Ilone presses hard on the accelerator. The vehicle speeds obediently towards the mountains.

We smoothly coast past rolling hills, and I watch as the mansion shrinks away, but then suddenly, the distant figure of Taamré runs out into the middle of the street. There is some sort of staff in her hand, and she puts it on her shoulder. Is that a rifle?

A few moments later, a javelin of red light slices the top half of the roof. Everyone lets out a scream and starts to rush one another with questions. The next two shots miss the car, and the third one dislodges our right side view mirror.

As we continue to race away, Taamré's shots begin to miss by more and more, until soon, she disappears from sight.

CHAPTER 27

QUEEN OF THE UNDEAD

~ SAMANTHA ~

A road trip with nine people is nearly unbearable. Despite the close quarters, everyone seems to be having a genuinely good time. At first, everyone was talking about what happened in the mansion with that maid-wizard lady and her gun, but it soon devolved into jokes, idle talk, and would-you-rathers.

I find a nice, calming radio station to match the background music of conversations and then promptly stare out the window for the next hour or so. I would normally be eager to sit in the back with the others and joke along with them, but the relatively quiet passenger seat, only interrupted by Ilone occasionally asking for directions, is what's making this ride doable.

It takes us a few hours of driving and pit stops to get to our next destination. The only thing that can keep my mind off of worrying about Matt or the spy is the Necriox Gem. I continuously turn the jewel over in my hand, letting its defined edges massage my palm. What are we going to do with this?

The infinite rolling hills outside my window eventually begin to even out. The distant mountains are now just dark lines on the horizon, and those eventually disappear too because of the increasing amount of homes out here. Before we know it, we've rode directly into a port town. For a moment I'm surprised because the map says we're nowhere near the ocean, but then I look again and see that we're just on the outskirts of a colossal lake.

We stop for fuel and then take a short ride to our destination. Initially, I thought we were going to stop at the maritime themed lansit station with the track that jets off into the lake horizon. But the map tells us to keep going, so we drive for a few blocks and stop at an oddly serene cemetery.

The brownish-yellow grass stretches uniformly across the expansive yard, and behind the rows and rows of circular, horizontal, plate-like tombstones is the shimmering blue lake. The winter sun paints everything in a still, calm light, and the sight of such a strangely beautiful scene helps to clear my mind.

The mood of the rest of the van somewhat dampens, though. There is a bit of silence before Nima says, "Again, I believe we should split into two groups. Boys, I would like for you to find the cheapest, most delicious eatery in town. The van is yours, and I ask that you meet us at this location again in 90 minutes."

"90 minutes?" Dr. Keeko, of all people, asks, "That seems like an excessive amount of time to hunt for a good place to eat."

The leader gives the doctor a look, "I want to make sure you find the best spot. Simultaneous high quality and low cost is very difficult to obtain in this area. Please do a thorough job."

Dr. Keeko still seems a bit unnerved by the time slot, but all the other guys in the group start to agree with laughter and one-liner jokes.

Nima continues, "Ladies, we will be assisting Samantha in her quest with the Necriox Gem."

I look at Ilone, who nods nonchalantly.

"And I guess I'll just screw off then, huh?" Ellia asks.

Everyone laughs, and Nima seems caught off guard. It looks as if our leader is about to retreat into serious thought, but then Ellia says, "I'm just joking with you, I'll be where the food is."

All the guys cheer, and then there is a bit of silence before Ilone abruptly opens her door. The back door opens too, and I soon realize that I should probably get out. As soon as I do, I'm hit with just how cold it is. The only warmth is from the sun; everything else from the wind to the grass is crisp and icy.

Once all four of us girls rally together on the curb of the road, we watch as Dr. Keeko takes the wheel and Ellia hops in my seat. The doctor readjusts the van's features to fit him, and as soon as he powers the vehicle on, Ellia switches the radio to the bass-filled hip hop from earlier. Dr. Keeko pulls off, and the vibrating van full of dancing boys gets lost in the tangle of the town.

I turn to Nima for direction, but I notice that the other three girls are looking at me.

"Oh, right." I say, and I take a look at the Ieri Tropo.

It says we need to go a few meters straight, and I look up to see a statue of a woman facing the glimmering lake waters. I start quickly walking towards the water's edge, but Nima stops me.

"No need for haste," she says in a soft tone, "the boys won't be back for another 90 minutes."

I look at Ilone and Cici, both of whom have equally sympathetic looks in their eyes, and then I register what's going on.

Instinctively, I let out a laugh and wave my hand, "Oh come on. I'm fine, nothing to worry about."

Nima looks at Cici, who frowns back at her in an '*are you kidding me?*' kind of way, and Ilone raises an unamused eyebrow, "Sam, it's fine, it's just the four of us."

My eyes scan the cemetery, and they're right. We're the only people here. Well, alive at least. I sigh, and out of my mouth comes a big cloud of vapor. I hate opening up, not because I'm super antisocial or secretive or anything, but because people can never be trusted.

Nima convinces me to sit on one of the cold metal benches, and I force myself to talk. At first, I thought I was making myself vulnerable, but as soon as I put down my guard, so do the other three. For the next hour, the four of us start to reveal more and more about ourselves.

Nima admits her uncertainties and ever-growing fears about our quest, and the rest of us admit to sharing those fears as well. Ilone reveals that she has never felt more devoted to a project than this one, and we agree with her. Cici tells us just how horrified she is about her life, our lives, and the livelihood of her family, and the rest of us share the exact same view.

I cried more with these three girls in this cemetery than I ever have with anyone else in my entire life. I agreed with every word they said, and I don't think anyone has understood me more than they have. But just like the frost on the golden grass around us, an hour melts away in the blink of an eye.

Somebody else enters the cemetery, and we realize that we should probably get moving. With a burst of laughter, we all stand from the now warm bench, wiping our faces and joking about how serious that was.

Nima makes us promise to never talk about this to the boys, and we wholeheartedly swear because her request is a no brainer. Finally, we start to head off towards the woman's statue.

I feel much more at ease with the girls at my side now, and the cemetery seems even more ethereal and beautiful in the warmer, noon air. As we pass tombstone after tombstone, I catch glimpses of a slew of weird Arretian names and nonsensical year dates. My eyes curiously flick over to the only other person in the cemetery, and he is staring at a tall white cylinder that seems to have taken the place of a tombstone.

"What's going on over there?" I ask Nima.

She glances over, then nods and nonchalantly says, "He is admiring his loved one's corpse."

Obviously, this takes me by surprise, and the other two laugh at Nima's abrupt explanation. Our leader looks back at us, confused.

"Okay Nima, let me explain," Cici says, "So I'm not sure how it is on Earth, but here on Arret, we have, like, a set up or whatever for after a person dies. In their will, they attach a picture of their favorite pose, and once they die, their body is, like, locked into that pose.

The graves here are made so that if you press the button beside them, you can see your loved one again in that pose."

"That's not creepy to you at all?" I ask with a shiver.

"I'm not sure about everyone else but yeah I find that, like, really weird." Cici admits.

"I feel as though once someone dies, making them into a pseudo-statue is a fitting way to honor both their life and their remains." Nima says, her eyes still lost in the glimmering lake and the approaching stone monolith.

"I think my pose is going to be something like this," and then Ilone proceeds to jump into some sort of funny kung fu stance.

The four of us laugh, and then we finally reach the statue. It's of a tall Egyptian woman in a simple dress and flowing coat, standing forward with one foot, arms outstretched, and hands cupped as if she's trying to get a drink from the cool midday sky.

She stands on a pedestal with a plaque that simply reads "SONYA VINTELLE NECRIOX". Above the words is a thin slot with a curvy stone lip. I fish the purple, beautiful Necriox gem from my pocket and routinely turn it over a few times.

"Well that was easy." Ilone says, solving the puzzle instantly just like everyone else.

I hop onto the edge of the pedestal, grab onto the statue's stone coat, and then lean on my tippy toes to see into Sonya's cupped hands. Unlike the rest of the statue, which is cut smoothly and realistically, this part seems almost unfinished. I stretch out with the Necriox Gem in hand, and sure enough, it fits perfectly.

As soon as the jewel sinks into place, a wall of shadow jets up from where the ground meets the water. In awe, I watch as it rises higher and higher, curving and meeting with other walls of darkness to form a dome above our heads.

Startled, I look down at the girls, who are just as puzzled as I am. Then, without warning, all of the tombstones in the graveyard jet upward at once, blanketing the once visible field with ominous white columns. The one other person in the cemetery jumps in surprise as his flat surroundings suddenly engulf him.

Without skipping a beat, Nima switchblades her sickles into her hands. A moment later, Cici calls forth two gleaming sais, and Ilone does the same with her wooden tonfas. This is the first time I've seen Ilone's weapons, which are a matte dark brown but have contrastingly glossy sea green ribbons dancing along the sides.

I go to hop off of the statue and help out my girls, but to my horror, it's as if I'm super glued to the thing. My hand is seemingly sealed onto Sonya's flowing stone coat, and the soles of my shoes feel like they've been morphed into the pedestal.

I struggle a bit, but then a calm, mature voice from right next to me says, "It's no use."

My eyes glance up and are immediately met with the dark purple ones of Sonya Vintelle Necriox. I instantly know it's her from her almond-shaped eyes to her angled face. Her skin is a warm tan instead of cement gray, and her hair is shiny and brown.

"What's going on?" I ask, much more confused than scared.

Sonya's eyes flash mischievously, "Why, this is your first and final test Samantha Jane Blue, Princess of the Undead."

Everything is happening too quickly and randomly for me to process, so I just let out a flat "what" instead of responding in an equally unpredictable way.

"Allow me to explain. Most historians know me as a former ruler of Fiponik, before the line of Yatnivs came to power. I was an adventuress before my time as ruler, and I found many treasures, one of them being the Key of Death, and another being the Inkwell of Torrents. Unlike my other finds, I named both of these after myself, as you can see.

"The Inkwell of Torrents, or the *Vintelle*, was so useful to me in life that I brought it with me to death, and only the Necriox Gem can be used to get it back. Those who use the Key of Death become the Ruler of the Undead, and so far, only you and I have done this. If you pass my test, I will abdicate my role as Queen of the Undead to you, since it is no longer of any use to me."

I am silent, still not fully understanding what is going on. Queen of the Undead sounds sick though, so I take her up on the offer.

"Alright then lady," I start, my confidence returning, "What do I need to do to pass?"

At once, there is a wrong-sounding, almost broken rush of air that simultaneously comes from all of the now towering tombstones. I notice that the girls have been calling for me, but I can't hear a word they're saying, and I guess it's vice versa.

"Look at the graves instead." Sonya advises.

I do so, and nothing happens, but then all of a sudden, I recognize bodies, frozen in noble and gentle poses, eyes and mouths sealed shut, unnaturally waddling and jerking their way over to us like amateur puppets.

Seeing such stiff, dead movement sends a chill up my spine, and then Sonya starts, "As Queen of the Undead, you will have influence over those already brought back from the afterlife, as well as living creatures of the dead. As your first and final test, you must prevent these corpses from killing your friends."

At first, the corpse-statues just seemed to be grotesquely teetering their way over to us out of some type of automatic command, but once Sonya mentions killing the girls, the things start to approach much more aggressively and violently. The girls take position around the woodish guy, who must've made his way over here at some point.

Bland, garbled voices rise up from the mute corpses, chanting "*Kill!*" over and over again.

"No!" I shout to them, "Leave them alone!"

To my surprise, the unnerving march comes to a confused halt.

"Continue marching!" Sonya shouts in an authoritative, attractive voice, "Bathe in their innocent, warm blood!"

A cry of agreement comes from the corpses as they begin to shuffle themselves forward again. I shoot Sonya an incredulous look, and she returns with a gaze of delighted, girly mischief.

"No! Please stop!" I shout out again, but I can tell my voice fell on deaf ears because the first of the zombie-statues, an old man in a fisherman's outfit, is soon in striking range of Ilone.

She could easily attack, but she doesn't, seemingly curious. The corpse's pose has outstretched arms, as if to welcome visitors with a hug, but instead of snapping them closed like I'd expected, his entire body leans back before suddenly twisting around, swinging its frozen right arm with a deadly amount of force.

Ilone ducks under the crushing blow, and the old man's frozen body continues to spin with his missed attack, teetering until it's finally upright again like a nudged bottle. Ilone kicks the corpse square in the chest, but it's as if she kicked an actual statue.

Horrified, she punches with one of her tonfas, and a startlingly aggressive blast of whitish gray water rushes forth, immediately engulfing the line of corpse-statues in front of her. Once the mist from the powerful spray settles, we see that the corpses are still standing, just pushed back a bit.

My confidence in the girls' safety is failing.

"Alright everyone let's think about this," I shout out into the undead army, trying to use my persuasion ability, "Why are you even attacking them?"

The responses come out much quicker than I had expected, "*Hatred!*" "*Despair!*" "*Abandonment!*" "*Lust!*" "*Retribution!*" And then they start to get too jumbled to understand.

"Okay, okay, my bad," I shout out, but before I can continue, Sonya shouts into the crowd, "So then release your suffering on these insolent mortals!"

The corpses begin twitching excitedly, and for a moment I consider slapping Sonya with my free hand until she can't speak anymore. I look up at her, and she grins cartoonishly, as if preventing me from saving my friends is absolutely hilarious.

The corpse statues begin attacking my girls, violently swiveling their bodies and trying to hit them with any outstretched limbs. I need to try a different approach if I'm going to stop this…

"Hey everyone," I say in a sultry voice mimicking Sonya's, "Will attacking my friends solve your problems?"

The shift in my tone catches both Sonya and the frozen zombies off guard. The undead army stops mid-swing, mid-shuffle, and thinks about my question. I guess it was a bit too tough for them, because they start groaning in what I assume is confusion.

"Yes it will," Sonya starts seductively, but before she can jeer on the one-sided crowd, I interrupt her, "For good? How so?"

I seem to have trumped Sonya, and I feel the same singular triumph Nima must've felt when she beat Mr. Necriox. The corpses moan even louder now, impatiently waiting for answers.

I smirk and teasingly say, "I'm not going to tell you. How about you go back to your graves? Maybe you'll come up with an answer that'll shock us both…"

Protesting, the corpse statues reluctantly waddle back to their graves, all the while muttering passive-aggressive things like "*Whatever.*" "*Fine.*" and "*Okay.*"

Sonya is silent the entire time, trying not to let a defeated smile come across her face like it did on her descendant's. The corpses eventually get back in their pods and stop moving, and the muttering melts into delighted sighs and eventually pure silence.

Sonya looks off towards the lake horizon once again, and her smooth Egyptian face finally gives in to the smile.

"This has been good fun. I bid you farewell and wish you good luck Samantha Jane Blue, Queen of the Undead."

In an instant, Sonya's face, still smiling, becomes heavy stone once more. The Necriox Gem in her hands is suddenly hidden by a stone cap. The dark dome around us melts into the brisk air, and sunlight pours onto the cemetery grounds. I can hear the town in the distance and water lapping against the graveyard's edge.

Sonya's coat is no longer sticky, so I hop down from the monument with ease. Now reunited with my girls, the four of us (and the woodish boy) take a moment to gather ourselves. I glance at the pedestal and notice a lavender pen resting on the stone lip.

This must be the Vintelle. I pocket it, and then the five of us realize that all of the graves are still up. For the next few minutes, we go around the cemetery closing graves and talking about how crazy that was.

As soon as the last grave is sealed, our green van full of boys pulls up to the curb.

CHAPTER 28

THE IMPOSSIBLE BATTLE

~ SAMANTHA ~

It is sunset by the time we board the lansit, but my smile from midday still hasn't disappeared. So far this has been a really amazing day. My brother was kidnapped in the very beginning, but the next place on the Ieri Tropo implies that we're on our way to go get him now. The road trip with friends, personal time with the girls, and becoming Queen of the Undead (which comes with this really cool tattoo on my shoulder blade) has also helped to keep me from thinking about Matt.

Apparently as queen, all I have to do is say "Queen of the Undead" and suddenly the power activates. I can't use my vira once it activates, but when it does, my clothes are instantly replaced with a ruby dress and a classy brown coat to match. Simply saying "Sonya" changes me back, so for the entirety of lunch, I was just randomly transforming back and forth.

The woodish guy in the cemetery, Nale, decided to join our group. Before we got on the lansit, we went to his house for a bit. He packed some essentials in his bag, including his *jetsuit*, which is like a jetpack vest, and his laser bow.

The glittering lake, now painted with orange and gold, glides past us as we blast towards a distant island. Our lansit tracks are on a small strip of rocks and bushes, and boats are the only other things out on the lake. As the vague splotch of dark orange on the horizon begins to solidify into shapes, I realize how oddly calm yet anxious I am.

****

We finally reach Gumwood lansit station; a serious silence has fallen on the group. The once distant castle, shrouded in afternoon air, is now right in front of us, hovering and grand. As the imperial, baby blue fort floats like the Skyling Stadium, an equally beautiful and high-tech city stretches out beneath it. At every edge laps the silky pink waters of the afternoon lake.

We enter the elegant welcome center and follow the signs to the castle staircase. A royal blue, fifty-foot wide staircase greets us at the edge of the concrete corridor, leading to the mouth of the castle's second floor.

The wind is cold and biting but surprisingly gentle. I should feel nervous about falling off, because we are *very* high above the city, but the stairs are sturdy and I'm mostly just awestruck. We ascend the stairs, and it's a pretty short climb to the first platform.

Instead of just a normal platform, it's a massive circle of rainbow glass that connects to our staircase on one side and a similar staircase on the other. The other, however, leads straight past a pair of giant white gates and into Yatniv's castle. Looks like we'll be meeting him before the Celestial Conference.

The eleven of us walk down the viewing platform and up to the heavily armed booth blocking the next staircase. The man working the booth greets us with trained enthusiasm and simply asks for our fingerprints.

Everyone else scans their fingers, and by the time Yoseph and I scan in, which probably showed that we don't even exist, the man and the soldiers around him are all padding through files on tablets and speaking in code through earpieces.

After a few minutes, the man speaks again, but his voice is flat.

"It will be a half hour wait."

At that, Nima suggests that we wait in the lansit station to get out of the cold, but when we turn around, there are now soldiers casually standing in front of the exit.

Our group of eleven decides to just wait on the viewing platform benches, which are slightly better than this vertigo-inducing glass floor. Everyone is silent while we wait. No jokes. No would-you-rathers. Just anxious silence.

I watch as the red sun slowly dips into the sparkling horizon, dragging gold from the sky and leaving behind chilly greens and sleepy blues. The two moons begin to appear, but before they come out of hiding, we're approached by a few soldiers.

"We're going to have to ask you all to leave your belongings with us. No shuzas, no wallets, make sure to put any non-clothing items in your bags. You will receive these after your meeting."

Apprehensively, we do as he said. I empty my pockets and, regretfully, take my vira off, tossing everything into my bag. We all receive a pat down, and after a few uncomfortable glances, the soldiers step back.

"Miss, the gloves." A soldier says out of the blue.

I look over to see an irritated Ellia staring back at a soldier.

"*Miss*, these are medical gloves. I have the shakes." Ellia insults.

Those are definitely Ellia's machine gun gloves, but of course we stay quiet, and they are keeping up a pretty good façade.

"The only condition your medical record suggests is that your vision is impaired." The soldier challenges.

"I got them yesterday after the Hayrides. It hasn't been processed on my healthcare yet." Ellia replies.

Luckily, the soldier seems convinced. Now he focuses on Kabel, who is the only one in our group who hasn't moved an inch. Everyone gives him concerned looks, but he continues to stand there, arms crossed, a light expression on his face.

"Sir, your possessions." The soldier's buddy says.

"Oh, I'll be stayin' behind to watch over everyone's stuff."

The soldier looks at what must be his superior, but she shakes her head, and so the soldier nods and steps back.

We all put our bags by Kabel, whose face is unreadable, and then follow the soldiers up into the magnificent castle. After winding through great rooms and climbing gold staircases, we finally meet the looming doors of Yatniv's throne room, emblazoned with lightning and swirling clouds.

The gates crack open just enough for us to file in one at a time. As

I shuffle in behind Nima, my eyes drink in the room. On the far wall is a massive panel of glass, looking out onto the city and lake far below. On the horizon is that familiar red sun, accompanied by its veil of gold. A new, dark orange line marks land on the other side.

This room is huge and bare, with nothing more than a marble floor, a fancy-looking wooden table with some comfy chairs around it, and cool streams of water that gurgle gently as they flow through their angled, stair-like troughs. They seem to start from where we are and go to where Yatniv's throne is.

The throne, which faces the window-wall, is fit for an emperor. Elaborate designs swirl around a sparkling, jewel-encrusted crest, and that's just the back. Beside it stands a ten-foot tall steel monolith, ominous and out of place in the elegant throne room.

The last of our ten-person group files through the door, and then it closes with a deep slam and a clicking lock. The sudden finality of the door closing sparks fear in my heart. Call it intuition, but a giant locked door plus ominous surroundings plus no weapons doesn't sound like a happy outcome to me.

The throne revolves slowly, revealing a smirking woodish teenager. His fingers are interlocked and his legs are crossed. He leans back comfortably, with a casual black tunic and baggy white pants on. His white crown sits straight on his bed of pink hair.

Those hazel eyes, once piercing, are oddly excited, and his smile is somewhat mischievous but mostly welcoming. This is actually Yatniv in the flesh, right in front of us.

"Ah, Nima! It's good to see you again! Is that Bacoj over there? And you, you're Ellia aren't you? Come, please sit."

His voice is like that of any other normal teenage boy, so having him in the middle of a throne room as a dictator of an entire nation is even more jarring to me. We do as he asks, and I notice as we sit down that the chairs are bolted to the floor.

Everyone looks terrified. Chirus chose the seat farthest away, Bacoj's eyes are downcast, and Nale continues to scan the throne room, caught up in the elegance of it all. Ilone is sweating, Cici is twirling her hair nervously, and Yoseph, who is sitting beside me, is trying to keep his leg shaking under control. Ellia and Nima are strangely calm, and Dr. Keeko seems almost angry.

"Well," Yatniv says, uncrossing his legs, "I have something I want to show you, but first I want to hear what you have to say."

There is silence, and then Nima starts, "Great Sir Yatniv… it is interesting that we should meet once more."

"That it is." replies Yatniv.

"There are two individuals with us today, Samantha and Yoseph, whom are from Earth. They came with Matthew–"

"The Crescent of Darkness." Yatniv adds.

Nima nods shortly, glossing over that, "Simply to retrieve their planet back, as the Mundatorite has taken its essence. Our objective is to see if you would be gracious enough to return Matthew and the Mundatorite ring."

"I could certainly do that for you." Yatniv says, nodding slowly.

An excited pause settles over the room, but when Yatniv doesn't fill it, Nima continues, seemingly prepared.

"Not only will Matthew, Samantha, and Yoseph never appear in or around Fiponik ever again, but those of us remaining will publicly denounce any political momentum we may have gained. I will also become a pro-government advocate to ensure the effectiveness of this initiative."

Hearing Nima say this makes my heart sink because I know that's the last thing she would want to do, but then Yatniv raises his eyebrows and my heart sinks even more.

"I wasn't expecting that! That actually sounds very enticing..."

Yatniv sits there for a long time in silence, thinking hard on Nima's offer. Everyone else just kind of nervously looks at one another or stares at the table.

"Your plan is pretty solid, Nima," admits Yatniv at last, "but I have something a bit more fun in mind."

A wave of goosebumps come across my skin as Yatniv reaches out and spins the metal monolith, which has my brother strapped to the front. Before his waist is a tray with a bag, but my focus is on Matt. His blue eyes are wide, and some sort of solid black goop is crammed into his mouth.

My sunken heart shatters.

"I'll give you two choices. The first is that you take that bag and leave. Inside is the Mundatorite, plus the other treasures the Crescent has collected. However, the bag lies on a panel, so if you move any weight, it will keep tightening the Crescent's restraints until he is crushed and eventually split in half.

"The second is to simply leave. If you do, I will make the Crescent my servant… and torture him regularly. Oh, and the Mundatorite, with Earth inside of it... I'll probably just end up throwing it away or something."

Almost immediately, Dr. Keeko raises his fist, and his hoodie sleeve pulls back to reveal a zecno. The doctor points, and a green laser suddenly appears between Yatniv's eyebrows.

"You will do neither. You will release Matthew and leave us be." Dr. Keeko declares in a threatening tone.

Everyone is stunned and confused, but Yatniv continues on as if he'd expected this.

"So, you turned on me, huh? Felt bad after what you did in Cayeuxi? I'm quite sure Edihi was very disappointed in you. I was wondering why both of your reports suddenly stopped."

Dr. Keeko says nothing, but he keeps his arm raised and the zecno pointed at Yatniv.

"Will you shoot me?" The dictator continues, "Would you take someone's life just like that? Do you know what will happen to your country if you kill me? Do you, Niejir?"

The doctor is totally unresponsive. He simply holds the green laser statue-still between Yatniv's eyebrows, his face intimidatingly emotionless.

Yatniv smirks, then waves his hand and says, "*Vinculum.*"

Faster than anyone can react, a small, whining, greenish-white crescent of light beams from Yatniv's wrist, darting through the air and landing right in between Dr. Keeko's middle knuckles.

There is a sickening combination of ripping noises and what sounds like eggs cracking. The doctor's zecno and sleeve are split down the middle by ghostly scissors, and at the same time, a line of crimson travels from his knuckles to his shoulder.

To my horror, I realize that Dr. Keeko's arm was… *split in half.*

The doctor looks down at his extremely bloody limb with surprise, then collapses dead on the floor.

The rest of us jet out of our seats, backing away from the coppery smelling mess and the insane magician dictator. Yatniv, seemingly unaffected by what just happened, actually laughs.

"I guess you're leaving then?" Asks the dictator.

The rest of us look to Nima, scared and confused, but then Ellia raises two gloved fists and unloads a storm of bullets. The invisible beams of hot metal immediately shred the wiring around Matt's death contraption until they are completely severed.

Once the shooting stops, a cotton-stuffed quiet overcomes us all. Everyone, especially Yatniv, is stunned.

"Damn, was I not supposed to do that?" Ellia asks.

"No," replies Yatniv, "I was honestly going to follow through with my word on either option, but now… now…"

The king stands angrily and picks up a large tome that he must have been sitting on. With a snap and a "*Sallet!*" there is a flash of light around him like a dozen flashlights flickering. After the flash, I notice a circle of pink light on the floor around him as if the marble beneath was glowing with embers. Magic symbols and rose petals litter the inside of the circle, almost turning the floor into stained glass.

Like the maid Taamré, Yatniv draws a glowing star enclosed in a circle, then he reaches through the middle of the floating symbol and shouts "*Acheiropoieta!*" As if he switchbladed it, a serrated sword appears in his hand, first white and then gleaming bronze.

He whips it through the air, turning the dangerous weapon into brief golden blurs, and his mood improves the more he swings his blade. With a sword in one hand and a magic book in the other, he descends the small staircase between his throne and our table.

Nima is having a complete breakdown, curled up and wailing not too far from Dr. Keeko, and one look at our group tells me that they're equally as freaked out as I am. Ellia still points their gloved fists at Yatniv in vain. We can't kill him for political reasons, and even if we tried, that pink circle on the floor will probably do something we won't like. On top of that, Nima is in no condition to lead right now, Dr. Keeko is dead, and we're locked in here without any weapons. We're screwed.

I look at my brother who is still tied up, his wide eyes alive with fear and anger, glaring incredulously at Yatniv. With a sigh, I bring myself to a resolution. Whether I die or not, I will stop at nothing to make sure my brother is safe.

Rashly, I sprint towards Yatniv. He is in mid-swing and he seemingly isn't looking in my direction, so by the time I reach him, I'll land a good tackle on him. Out of the corner of my eye I see Ilone and Yoseph rushing up behind me, but then I'm suddenly on the wizard dictator.

I surge him back into his throne, toppling off his crown, and before either of us can react, Ilone's tan fist comes from nowhere and slams into the dictator's face. Yoseph's dark arms reach for the tome, and then I see the silvery arm of Bacoj reach for the monarch's sword. In an instant, we've all dogpiled on Yatniv, scratching and punching and trying to rip anything we can from him. In a spit of blood, he suddenly screams, "*Voluminous!*"

A column of boiling white light pierces up from him and violently expands, throwing us all into the air with scorching, ruthless force. I soar, weightless, before painfully crashing into the table.

Weakly, I pull myself over the edge and take cover. Everything is still throbbing and my clothes feel like they just got out of the oven, but I try to pull myself together. The others are slowly getting to their feet as well, including Yatniv.

He smears his blood on his black sleeve, then spots Chirus scrambling away. The dictator grins, rests his tome in midair, outstretches a hand and says, "*Ecclesia.*"

Chirus' body begins to unnaturally glide backwards and towards Yatniv. Chirus tries to grab at something, but the invisible force is dragging him too quickly across the smooth marble floor.

Right before Chirus is pulled into striking range, Ilone rushes up and kicks Yatniv in the stomach. Chirus stops sliding as the monarch stumbles back, and then he takes a hearty swipe at my friend. My heart leaps in my throat as she barely dodges one, then two, then three swings before sprinting back towards the table.

Yatniv starts to run too, but then he realizes that we're all trapped, so he starts to walk menacingly instead. No one does anything because he's out of surprise attack range.

Randomly, Yatniv slashes a magic circle into the air and shouts, "*Efflux!*" A branch of hot blue lightning cracks through the air, blasting Cici off her feet in a splash of smoke. She tumbles down into one of the gurgling streams, absolutely motionless.

Instinctively, Ellia lets loose a hail of bullets, and everyone tenses up as the loud slaps ring through the air. All of the shots bounce harmlessly off the air in front of Yatniv, right where the pink circle starts on the floor.

The emperor locks eyes with Ellia, who then furrows their brow, trying their best at a playful grin and casual finger guns. Yatniv, amused yet unamused, raises his tome and retaliates with a thundering "*Conflagration!*"

A bolt of energy streams out from the top of the book, beaming into the floor between Ellia's feet and suddenly engulfing them in a towering tree of orange flames. The horrific and blinding attack fills the room with raw heat for a moment before all the flames disappear and Ellia is left smoldering and shriveled on the floor.

Yoseph rushes over to Cici and Ellia, Chirus is trying to get Nima to move, and everyone else decides to go for another rush at Yatniv. Now is a better time than ever to stop hiding, so I quickly creep out of my hiding space and join the other three.

Nale and Ilone dance right outside of Yatniv's sword range, and as I approach from behind Nale, I can see Bacoj is sneaking up to Matt's bag. Nale makes an empty lunge at Yatniv, but his unwillingness to hurt the monarch is too obvious and Yatniv whips his wicked blade across the other woodish boy's face.

Ilone, capitalizing on Yatniv's distraction, kicks at his tome. The emperor curves the heavy book through the air, dodging Ilone's attack, and then counters with a jumping, spinning slash. His serrated sword comes around with so much speed and power that it's pretty much a rush of sharp bronze air.

Ilone's chest is suddenly filled with a large crimson gash, and she spirals to the ground. I go to rush over and see if she is okay, but Chirus skates in from nowhere, instantly surrounding his cousin in a teary and horrified embrace.

I back off and glare at Yatniv, who is looking at me oddly. After studying me for a bit, the monarch smirks up at Matt, whose eyes are now filled with glossy hate.

"That's your sister, isn't it?" He asks Matt, absolutely ignoring Bacoj. My brother, mouth still clogged, begins trembling, his face turning beet red as tears of anger stream from his eyes.

Yatniv's grin grows wider as he turns his full attention towards me. I begin to back up and raise my guard. Yatniv throws down his tome, raises his sword to the side of his face in a jabbing angle, and begins to approach me in a slow, almost theatric way.

"Defile or decapitate? I'll let you decide."

We continue to stare down one another, and I go to duck around him but he swings his sword and dissuades me. Bacoj rushes for the tome, but his footsteps must've been too loud, for Yatniv shoots out a violent back kick and knocks the thief clean out.

"Try to hurry it up," Yatniv continues as he twirls his bloody blade, "I've got a ton of paperwork after this."

For a second, I'm absolutely flustered, and disgusted disbelief rises in me as I consider actually choosing between the two, but then a burst of inspiration hits me and I reply, "I think I'll choose de-screw off."

With that I turn and bolt away. The excited running footsteps of the insane emperor are right behind me. We sprint past a crying Chirus huddled around a bleeding Ilone. We pass Dr. Keeko and his pool of crimson, Nima and her pool of wails, and Nale treating his face in one of the small streams grooved in the floor. Dead ahead is Yoseph, who is kneeling in prayer between a motionless Cici and a motionless Ellia.

Tears come to my eyes as I watch Yoseph pray, realizing with growing hopelessness that I'm actually going to die here and so is my brother. How could Yoseph pray at a time like this?! What makes him think that would work?

More bitterness and despair begins to fester in me when… suddenly, light springs up from behind Yoseph. At first it looks like sunlight shimmering off water, but then it strengthens and grows brighter until I can start to make out a figure.

As the figure comes into focus, all the hatred I felt melts into oddly misplaced joy. I almost laugh at how weirdly pleasing this is; it's like a fountain of good feelings just cut on inside of me. I stop running. I know we'll be safe now.

The figure is finally complete; it's Junia, the beautiful angel with a river of bronze hair and a brilliant radiance. Her eyes, like soft green fields, look into mine with love but confusion.

The angel scans the bloodstained, smoldering throne room, and the more she sees, the angrier she gets. Her eyes are soon piercing emerald daggers, her radiance blinding and scalding.

With a nightmarish presence, she booms, "WHAT HATH THY DONE TO THESE CHILDREN OF THE MOST HIGH?!"

Yatniv doesn't respond, but I wouldn't blame him. Junia isn't even talking to me and I'm about to soil myself. The angel speaks out again, seeming a bit calmer now.

"Thou hath begotten sin, and beget sin, and shall beget sin to the end of your days. I curse thee with a curse, that thy shall be overcome by sin and swallowed up into the belly of darkness–"

She stops, looks up for a moment, and then nods reluctantly.

"Lo, I must wish thee only blessings instead. But be warned, Wicked One. Verily I say unto you, study thy steps, for they shall lead thee into the abyss."

Yatniv doesn't respond, and Junia continues to scold him with her glare for a bit before her entire demeanor shifts and she addresses the rest of us with softness.

"Sons of men, I pity thee. Thou hath been deceived. That it is not the will of our Lord to smite thy enemy through my own works, therefore thou shalt be taken up into the clouds and I shall comfort thee with a stone to sharpen thy sword. Come, children of our Father."

She claps, and everything rushes upward into darkness.

CHAPTER 29

QASIM'S STRONGHOLD

~ SAMANTHA ~

"Sam? Sam." Yoseph's voice fades away as I open my eyes, and so does his hand on my shoulder. The first thing I'm met with is a fresh, blue night sky, full of white pinprick stars and the glowing double moons. When I sit up, I'm met with the harsh beam of a military flashlight and about a dozen rifle barrels.

Confusion, along with many other emotions, must've surfaced on my face, because a Hispanic man holding a backpack instead of a rifle lets out an unamused chuckle. I don't dare lift my hand to shield my eyes, but instead I squint and look to my side, where I find Yoseph and Bacoj sitting cross-legged with eyes downcast.

"What's going on?" I whisper, but then the Hispanic man, who is dressed in pixelly camouflaged fatigues, barks flatly, "On your feet!"

Yoseph and Bacoj scramble up, but I react with defiant slowness. I expect to hear the shuffles of everyone else behind me, but there are none. Behind me, as I just saw, are simply more soldiers and rifles.

"I am Adrian Odahl, Senior Major of the 11th Brigade, 29th Explosives Division, Regalia. You… you…"

He stops, chuckles for real, and then says, "Follow me. Everyone else, at ease."

The rifles are lowered, and Odahl starts walking quickly towards a shadowy, looming building in the not-so-far distance. I would call it a stronghold, but it also kind of looks like a palace too.

"So I'm brushing my teeth," the major says in an annoyed yet frank tone, still walking briskly, "and Private Beauchamp comes in to tell me that a bunch of dead people and an angel are in the middle of the drillfield. Obviously, I come out to take a look."

Odahl's irritated walking pace is so fast that Bacoj and I have to nearly run to keep up with him. Yoseph looks like he isn't having a lot of fun either.

"Sure enough, only you three were uninjured. You wanna know what the funny thing is? All the injuries came in twos. Two disgustingly brutal sword slashes, two extreme third-degree burns, two completely incoherent sobbers, and then there was just one guy with the arm…"

We've cleared the dark, grassy field and are now at the side doors of the stronghold. Major Odahl looks at us with an expression of curiosity and pity.

"I don't know who you are, but I feel sorry for you."

The doors open, and Odahl leads us down a long, industrial hallway. The major is completely silent on the long walk through the winding palace walkways. We finally exit the industrial area and enter a more formal looking section, with hard-tiled floors that reflect the white overhead lights.

At the end of this one hallway is an intimidating door, and I realize with a bit of dread that we're heading straight for it. In a moment, Odahl is knocking on the door, and with a flat "Come in" the major opens it.

Sitting behind a large desk with a toothpick sticking up from her lips is a small Indian woman with a kind face but a serious expression. Plaques line the walls in her warm but stern office, and bookshelves are filled with documents and awards alike. A nametag reading "Captain Neha Hudait" rests under a lamp, right next to a stack of tedious looking files.

Odahl salutes, and the captain responds with, "That is all."

The major puts down Matt's bag and closes the door behind us. Hudait looks the three of us over, her friendly brown eyes covered with a scary layer of military strictness, and she finally brings herself to speak.

"Have a seat. It will be for a short moment but take it anyway."

Bacoj, Yoseph, and I comply. The seats are a lot less comfortable than they looked. There is more silence, and a clock that must be above the door behind us ticks softly.

"What are your names?"

We tell her, and she nods. A bit more silence, and it almost seems as though Hudait is waiting for something. She looks at the clock, then looks at the two boys, then at me.

"So Samantha, how did you get to know these two?"

I look at Yoseph and Bacoj, who are returning my gaze with small, curious smiles. Well, Yoseph is my neighbor, and Bacoj stole my

MP3 player, blew me up in the middle of the woods, then met me on a different planet and teamed up with me.

I lie and say they're both school friends.

Hudait nods, almost interested, and then a tablet that was on her desk lights up. She grabs it quickly, pads through it for about three minutes, then looks up and takes out her toothpick.

"I've got a lot of information but the general wants to speak to you, so I'll make it quick. Unfortunately, two of your friends are dead… Niejir Keeko and Ilone Lhu."

At the second name, I feel a breath slip from my lips and carry away all of my composure. No, that can't be right. Ilone couldn't have died, they should've easily been able to treat her wounds in enough time!

Silky warmth begins to rise below my eyes, and a wavering mixture of anger and sadness fills my chest. She was such a chill friend, one of my favorite people on the team… why did she have to die? Yatniv is a monster. He's a disgusting monster.

Hudait finishes what she's saying and leads us to the general, but I'm not paying attention. All I can think about is Ilone and how we can never have any fun memories together again. Dr. Keeko is dead too… he was the spy all along but in the end, he died trying to make things right.

Oh wait… Kabel and Matt are still back at Yatniv's castle, and so are our vira. I'm not sure where we are or where the others are either. Will anyone else die? Will I ever see my brother again? Will we finish this journey? Was it even possible to begin with?

By the time we reach the general's place, I want to die myself.

Hudait opens the door and I'm stunned by who we are greeted with. A mountain of a man, towering and muscular with a black cape and a formal military hat to match, gazes out of his office window at a massive field of soldiers. When Captain Hudait closes the door, the general turns around.

He's got a very handsome, Middle Eastern face with stubble neatly hugging his chin and some sort of innate mischievous twinkle in his brown eyes. His serious frown and poised demeanor suggests he's far from a jokester, though. The insides of his cape are fuzzy and bright red, and his white gloves both contrast and match his black military suit.

He was picking his teeth with a large, visibly sharp bowie knife, and he stops when Hudait salutes.

"You're good Neha. Go outside with the others, and make sure to bundle up."

With a small "Yes sir," the captain places Matt's bag down and backs out of the room.

"Sit." The general orders in his deep voice.

The three of us immediately comply. His seats are as comfortable as they look, and that's a good thing.

"I am General Qasim Qasim of the 29th Explosives Division, Regalia. Apparently, you all just *appeared* in the drillfield a few moments ago. Do you know where you are?"

We shake our heads. The general toys with his giant knife for a moment, and then continues, "This is *Koppia.* For all three of you, it borders the country in which you're enemies of the state."

A stunned, hard silence falls over the room.

"What I am going to do is place you in our facility's detainment cell until all of your friends have been healed, and then I will–"

Before the general can finish, the hearty roar of thousands of soldiers floats up from the fields below. Even through the large glass window, I can still hear the excitement in their voices. Qasim, apparently caught off guard, wheels around quickly to see what's going on.

A massive projector spreads some sort of sports broadcast across the side of one of the fort's walls. The camera is currently panning an indigo tennis ball court, and a bunch of monochromatic people with giant scoopers on their arms are staring down one another from either side of the field. The stadium is packed, and it's much bigger than any stadium I've ever seen. That's the really famous sport here… kaxahhe.

"Is that the Esto World Cup?" Bacoj asks.

I thought Qasim would reply harshly, but instead he puts down his knife and gives a soft, "Yes, finals."

"Oxeimec or Elvadra?" Bacoj tries.

"Elvadra, and I'm really banking on this win too." Replies the general absently.

The thief asks no more questions as the game begins. The room is silent for a number of different reasons. General Qasim is focusing hard on the game in front of him, Yoseph is consumed in dark thoughts just like me, and Bacoj is doing a bit of both. Despite the jeering and horns coming from the game, I tune out pretty much everything.

I can't believe this is happening. Ilone is actually dead. And… oh my goodness, who else is alive?! What if the others die too? What if it's just Bacoj and Yoseph and I left?! My gut wrenches and my vision is suddenly filled with tears, blurring the distant sounds of fun and sport. Matt is probably dead. Everyone is probably dead. This is absolutely hopeless.

For some reason, I try to fight back the tears. I don't want to cry, because if I do, then I'll no longer be tough. I've got to be the strong one, to fight and live on in memory of all of my friends. But why? Why should I even try? I feel Yoseph put a consoling hand on my back, and then the tears begin to pour out.

****

Halftime comes quickly, with Elvadra at 13 and Oxeimec at 11.

Many of the soldiers in the field scatter for food or the restroom, and the general finally stands again and begins to wring his gloved hands excitedly.

"Come on guys just a little longer…" then he seems to come back to the situation, "I apologize. As I was saying, after this kaxahhe game, we will go about the procedure of sending you back to Fiponik for processing. Not unless…"

The general stops, shakes his head, and sits back down behind his desk. He stares thoughtfully out into the field until halftime ends, and then his body stiffens expectantly as the news broadcasters pan and zoom into the field once more.

I've cried all that I can, and now I feel dry and empty. I want to think about something, anything, but my mind is full of silence. Everything is numb. Time seems to fade away into nothing, and all the motion in the distant sports screen blurs into one insignificant color. Why should I keep fighting?

"No... oh no..." General Qasim mutters as the soldiers in the field below begin to cheer.

For some reason, that grabs my attention. I look over at the screen and notice how much the night has deepened, how bold the stars are, and how cold the drillfield must be. All the soldiers are huddled around the base of the screen, pumping their fists and fruitlessly shouting encouragement.

On the screen, the kaxahhe players are doing flips and beaming the glowing ball at one another with so much force that it looks like a line. I take a look at the score. 1-1. This must be literally one of the greatest toss ups for pretty much everyone watching. Normally I couldn't help but get goosebumps at such an epic, down-to-the-wire game. But now I don't feel anything.

One of the green players scoops the ball from the air and rockets it toward his own teammates, it bounces around for a bit, then suddenly the ball is on the other side and the Oxeimec score is 0. The empty pit I've become is suddenly filled with surprise as the entire stadium erupts into green fireworks, flags, and confetti. At the same time, the drillfield full of soldiers explodes into manic cheering. I'm about to go back into sulking when I notice the mass of thousands of cadets and officers are now sprinting towards the palace.

General Qasim swears harshly, his face flushing of all color, and in a magnificent display of grace, he clears his desk in a single leap, slams his office door shut, and locks it.

"Help me move the desk!" He shouts frantically as he clears the furniture a second time.

I look at Bacoj and Yoseph with confusion. Qasim begins sliding the desk all by himself, so we decide to at least move the chairs out of the way. As soon as the loud grinding stops, I can hear the horrific sound of hundreds of footsteps running eagerly down the hallway outside.

"Get on the floor! Don't make a sound!" Commands Qasim in a whisper and he silently throws his body onto his office's expansive hardwood floor. His cape billows down after him, and then he violently beckons for the three of us to do the same.

We do, mostly confused. The stampede outside quickly grows from faint to thunderous, and then a machine-gun fire of knocking blankets the door, covering the entrance with sheets of noisy, terrifying rain. The door handle begins to jiggle viciously, as if maliciously waiting for a fool to unlock it. Screaming, hollering, and laughing from countless men and women bleed through the door.

I try to pick up on what they're saying so that I can figure out what the world is going on.

"General Qasim! Will we set off the royal fireworks tonight?"

"General Qasim! Will we never have morning PT again?"

"General Qasim! Will I get moved up three pay grades?"

"General Qasim! Will you streak across the drillfield tonight?"

"What is happening?!" Yoseph hisses at the General, pure terror caking his voice.

Qasim, once a huge, serious, and intimidating man, is now curled up in a ball using his cape like a little kid would use a blanket.

"I promised that if Oxeimec won, I would say yes to the first person who asked me any question," he curls up tighter, "I didn't think they were actually going to win! Elvadra always wins!"

"How long until the deal runs out?" Yoseph asks lowly.

"I didn't put a time limit on it." Qasim nearly sobs.

The knocking, jiggling, and shouting dies down to something even more terrifying; camping. We can hear the hundreds of soldiers now sitting outside of the door, scheming quietly with one another and waiting for the general to come out.

Bacoj nudges me and Yoseph, then whispers, "Where's the final place we need to go?"

"What do you mean?" Yoseph asks.

"Didn't we need to go to some sort of meeting so we could get back to your planet?" Bacoj questions, and the mention of Earth starts to call forth an odd mix of sadness, dread, and numbness.

"Um, it was the Constellation something." Yoseph suggests.

"Right, the Celestial Conference!" Bacoj realizes.

"Why do you need to know that?" Yoseph asks softly.

"We can use this bet in our favor and make it back to Earth!"

A startling rush of bitterness fills me, "So we're just going to leave my brother behind? If… if he's even still alive? What's the point of even trying to go back? You really think the three of us can beat Yatniv on our own? Without Nima? Without weapons?"

Bacoj grows silent, and I can tell by the look on his face that I hurt his feelings. For a concerning moment, I almost feel good about that.

"Have faith, Sam. Things will work out one way or another, because we're not going to give up, okay?" Yoseph reassures.

I go to glare at him, but as soon as we lock eyes, all of the fight leaves me. It's so naive to think we could ever actually win, but I can't seem to bring myself to argue with him. I wouldn't want to see the hurt that I feel come to his big brown eyes, to dampen the only hope we have left.

"Yatniv may have beat us once, but we're not going to let him beat us forever." He declares, breaking through my grief and speaking straight into my heart.

The directness of his command makes me shiver. Swallowing my pride, I simply nod.

"It's okay, Bacoj." Yoseph encourages, "Go ahead, ask him."

The thief nods and offers a fake smile, still thinking about what I said, then crawls next to the General and tugs on his cape.

"Hey General Qasim. Will you help us get into this year's Celestial Conference?" Bacoj asks in a voice low enough not to be obvious but loud enough to carry a threat.

The General looks up at Bacoj with incredulous shock, but before he answers, he pauses and starts to think. I can see Qasim mentally weighing his options.

"That sounds like a good deal to me," Yoseph peeps, "I'd take it if I were you."

"Yeah me too," I add, "you could lose a lot from this bet, if you think about. Your job, your house, your… l-little brother…"

The general looks at us with deep, sinister dislike in his eyes. Someone from outside suggests throwing ice cream at him while he streaks the drillfield, and then everyone laughs in agreement.

At that, Qasim's scary leer breaks into a defeated frown.

"Yes, I will help you get into this year's Celestial Conference."

CHAPTER 30

THE ASSASSIN TRAIN

~ YOSEPH ~

Our week at Qasim's stronghold was both needed and depressing. I think the circumstances were morbidly perfect, so that's why everything played out nicely. Shortly after Qasim agreed to help us, everyone from our group was unofficially drafted into the 29th Explosives Division, Regalia.

Of course, many of the soldiers were a bit cross with the idea of underage foreigners who were technically terrorists stealing their free promotions and joining their division. We were watched 24/7 because of this, and if I were to look around at any moment, I could quickly spot a pair of judgmental eyes glaring at me.

Our teammates healed rather quickly, and by our second day there, everyone was out of their florma and in their fatigues. Nima and Chirus were there at dinner the night of Qasim's decision, but it was almost like they weren't. Bacoj, Sam, and I sat with them and tried to converse, but that didn't work. Nima only replied in small, simple sentences, and Chirus didn't speak at all. Their eyes didn't come up from their food until they were done, and after that, they seemed to realize the world around them. Well, at least Nima did. Chirus' eyes remained downcast, even on our way back to the barracks.

Cici and Nale are at breakfast the next day, and a few of the soldiers' hearts must have softened, because three of them decide to sit with us as well. Nale seems like a naturally shy person, so he doesn't add much to the conversations, but the presence of Cici seems to improve Nima and Sam's moods.

After one of the most physically exhausting mornings of my life, we are greeted at lunch by Ellia. They, like everyone else, are not their normal selves. Instead of goofing around or cracking jokes on people, Ellia eats quietly, constantly surveying our faces and contributing softly to conversation.

Dinner is pretty rough. When we get to the mess hall, the only people waiting for us in our usual spot are the three friendly soldiers; Beauchamp, Onyeije, and Munda. They pretty much talk to themselves for the entire meal.

Shortly before the end of dinner, Captain Hudait comes in and takes us to her office. She has a lot of chairs this time, and all of them are comfortable. While there, she gives us the opportunity to see Dr. Keeko and Ilone one last time before they are sent to their families (Dr. Keeko would be going to his siblings). Outside of Nale, everyone goes to her office.

It's a lot less sad than I thought it would be. The girls got a little teary eyed, and Sam needed a bit more consoling. Ilone and Dr. Keeko stand like statues in their pods, with their eyes closed, their mouths in a smile, and their hands clasped respectfully in front of them. Their skin is full and healthy, their bodies normal and intact, with clothes on that are nice but not something they wouldn't normally wear. It almost looks as if they'd jump up and start laughing like the whole thing was a big joke.

But they don't, and it isn't.

****

By the end of the week, we're a much different team. Aside from Ellia, who has still retained some of their goofiness, everyone is quiet, serious, and almost humorless. If the others have the same reason as I do, it's because everything's pretty much at the lowest of low. I'd normally be the light-hearted, optimistic guy, but I know just as well as everyone else that any outside optimism would do more harm than good.

Yes, a few of us (me included) still have a small internal ray of hope that we can actually save the world and maybe even Matt and Kabel too. But if I were to say it out loud, it would sound too silly and childish to believe. Honestly, our task is so impossible that I'm not even sure why we're still trying.

"Hollingsworth." Says Munda, one of the soldiers.

I snap out of my stupor and realize that the next lansit has finally gotten here. Our group had to wait at the cold cobblestone lansit station for an extra 90 minutes because Ellia needed to use the bathroom. I board with Munda, and it seems like the initial car is filled with friends and strangers alike, so we have to find a seat on the one in front.

Onyeije, the black female officer, is here with Nima, so we sit beside them. This car is actually pretty empty; outside of us there are maybe five other passengers. We begin to glide off towards the capital city of Paris. Apparently, Koppia is a safe haven for a lot of people from Earth, so that's why everyone's names are normal and the capital cities are familiar.

We glide through fields and forests for a while, sometimes talking but mostly staring. Suddenly, there is a painful-sounding thud in the car behind us, and a bunch of people start yelling. I, along with the other three, look through the little door window at the rear of the car to see what's going on.

Chirus is beet-red, his face a terrifying blank slate of rage, his olive eyes empty and dark. He's walking towards something that must be on the floor in front of the car door. Beauchamp, one of the soldiers, is trying to pull Chirus back, but Chirus is walking with so much unyielding determination that Beauchamp is more like a backpack than an obstacle.

Suddenly, the two of them and the rest of the car are blasted with a violent gush of white water that seemingly shoots up from whatever Chirus was walking towards. I look back at the others in bewilderment. Munda and Onyeije get up to go settle things, and one of the passengers further down the car does the same.

I look at Nima, shrugging and standing too, but then suddenly the entire back wall of the lansit car is covered in a thick sheet of ice. The two soldiers jump in surprise, and Onyeije whirls around while Munda, whose hand is frozen under the sheet of ice, begins oddly kicking at it.

I turn around, trying to figure out what the heck is going on, and my eyes meet the burning black ones of Taamré. A shiver of surprise and fear runs up my spine, and then I feel my face grow cold with dread. We don't have our vira; there's no way to fight back.

The wizard smiles, "Would you look at the odds? I was just going out on vacation, but here you are again. You outran my anger spell at the concert and my rifle at the manor. Where are you going to run now?"

Nima and I trade horrified glances, and then Taamré swings a magic circle into the air. Before either of us can react, the wizard sends a "*Cosset!*" our way in the form of a swirling silver ribbon. The attack shoots right into my chest, and then suddenly I'm wrapped once, then twice, then three times in a thick sheet of… bubble wrap? What?!

My arms are stuck tight to my sides, so all I can do is look over at Nima. Taamré sends another "*Cosset!*" at my leader, but she ducks before it can hit her. Suddenly, Onyeije sprints down the aisle and heads straight for the wizard. Taamré is a second faster, and right before Onyeije can reach her, the wizard shoots out a "*Salvo!*" mini-explosion, throwing Onyeije to the floor.

The soldier lies there for a moment, more startled than in pain, but then she brings her knees into her chest and does a back roll onto her feet.

"Munda?" Onyeije calls, still staring down the wizard.

"Still stuck." He replies, kicking oddly at what must be a rather sturdy wall of ice.

"This is no time to study for Icicle Training." Onyeije replies, and then the two soldiers laugh at what must be an inside joke.

I'm pretty surprised that they can be so humorous in such a serious situation, but then Taamré goes for another magic circle. Onyeije's smile immediately disappears as she lunges to the side and ducks behind the wizard's "*Caliginous!*"

Instead of seeing what the soldier does next, the entire car is filled with a rushing column of thick black smoke. It spirals towards us, spinning up from thin air, and I force myself to leap out of its path, knowing that I won't be able to catch myself.

Sure enough, my face slams onto the hard edge of one of the seats. My upper lip immediately swells with heat and itchiness. Desperately, I wriggle and kick until I'm sitting upright, then shimmy-slide my way up the wall.

Onyeije has Taamré in a headlock, and Nima, who must've dodged the darkness attack too, is walking up purposefully to the pair. Taamré struggles for a bit in the soldier's steely lock, trying to get a few elbows or head-butts in, but when that has absolutely no effect on Onyeije, the wizard lets off a startling "*Corybantic!*"

Just as Nima was getting within striking range, the area around Taamré and Onyeije is suddenly filled with bright, screaming fireworks. The glowing balls of neon flame spiral in all directions, bouncing off of the walls and bursting into forceful displays of quick, colorful fire.

Deafening pops and booms fill the car with hot, short gusts of blue smoke. Nima has no choice but to back away, ducking down and covering her head. The attack, glittering and loud, is soon over, and before Taamré can draw another magic circle, Nima kicks her in the face with uncharacteristic brutality.

The wizard stiffens, then raises her arms and tries to struggle out of Onyeije's grasp. "*Frior-*" but then my leader stomps Taamré again and the wizard is out cold. As soon as she goes limp, the bubble wrap around me is suddenly gone. Munda runs past me, apparently free, and checks Taamré's vitals.

"Yeah, she's out." He reports.

Onyeije let's up, then gives Nima a high-five, which she receives awkwardly.

By the time we've reached our lansit station and the police are carrying away a woozy Taamré, we suddenly remember to check on the other car.

CHAPTER 31

CASUAL RENDEZVOUS

~ YOSEPH ~

Reporting back to Captain Hudait was awkward to say the least. The guys explained what happened perfectly on the way there, but once we arrived at our designated hotel, everyone seemed to be at a loss for words.

Chirus had spotted Edihi on the lansit and immediately went into attack mode. I'm not really sure why, and Chirus' only reply to our question was an expectant stare, so I'm guessing it's because she arrested us earlier.

Edihi, on the other hand, was travelling to Paris to try and make things right. She was planning on searching around for us so that she could apologize, give up her allegiance to IPSHA, and outright join our group. On the lansit she'd defended just as blindly as Chirus had attacked, and once enough people pinned the two of them down, she explained herself.

That was an easy enough story for them to tell us right afterward, but under the critical, unamused eye of Captain Hudait, everyone's words pretty much jumble together.

"Everyone with an injury is going to medics on the third floor. Everyone with wet clothes gets to stay at the hotel and dry them.

The rest of you can go ahead and use your travel allowance."

We all nod, and the others try to hide their bitterness as they follow Beauchamp to their rooms. Sam and I share a displeased look before she follows the others. She and I were going to try and stick close. Nonetheless, Nima, Munda, Onyeije, and I turn to leave, but then Captain Hudait speaks up.

"Onyeije! Where do you think you're going with that bruise? Don't look at me like that. Left temple."

Sure enough, there is a small, reddish lump there that must have come from the fight with Taamré. Onyeije presses it lightly with no reaction, then nods indifferently to the Captain and heads to the elevators. Huh, I guess it'll just be Nima, Munda, and I.

The three of us go out into town. For a while we just walk around, drinking in the peaceful late morning vibes, and then we decide to get something to eat. Neither Munda nor Nima have been here before (and I certainly haven't either) so we decide to be a little adventurous and ask a random group of teens for restaurant suggestions.

I'm not sure about everyone else, but the majority of my lighthearted bravery is coming from the fact that we're finally somewhere that's normal. People's names are normal, there aren't a bunch of party-colored aliens walking around, and for once in three weeks I'm not actively being hunted by an insane wizard dictator. Also, this uniform is pretty nice. I could really get used to this.

The group of casual teenagers smile and stay for a small chat, then finally recommend a place called Danyell's. The boy in the green hoodie heard a rumor that they closed early to serve a special guest, but they all figured that we could just go to a neighboring restaurant should that be the case.

After some directions and a moderately short walk down a few cobblestone pathways, we arrive at a homey looking restaurant with purple flowers swaying in hanging pots outside. A giant "*Danyell's*" is painted in cursive on the cobblestone in front of the eatery entrance. It's red-orange roof and white stone walls match the other buildings in the city, giving everything a peaceful Mediterranean village feel.

There is a roofed terrace surrounding the restaurant, but instead of normal customers sitting at the chairs under the umbrellas, there are armed guards. I mean it's packed, with guards taking up all of the forty something chairs out there. Yo, is that… no way!

Nima must've recognized him too, because she starts to quicken her pace. Munda just kind of follows along. Soon, the three of us are at the edge of the gated terrace, and Virrel is on the other side, still in his gray pajamas, eyes wide and eyebrows raised.

"What are you guys doing here?!" The ghost asks.

"I was about to ask you the same thing!" I reply, looking over at Nima.

She nods, "Is the empress nearby?"

"She's actually inside meeting with some others. They're having a bit of a discussion right now, so I'd just go in and wait if I were you. By the way, nice uniforms! Did you decide to throw in the towel and run off with Koppia's army?"

"Not necessarily. This is merely a more strategic approach to our original plan." Nima replies.

"I hear you." Says Virrel, and then he opens the door for us.

We enter the dimly lit, comfortable restaurant, and the inside looks exactly like I'd expected from the outside. Cushioned booths, candles, family photos on the white walls, wiry bronze chairs, and tiled floors.

Unlike outside however, the inside is empty save for one table. In the middle of the restaurant is a circle of people, talking casually over delicious-smelling meals. The table looks like it only seats four, so the fifth person had to pull up a chair.

The five people all stop talking and look up as soon as we enter. I immediately recognize four of the five. I've never seen the Black guy with the glasses and the crown before, but then there is General Qasim, Empress Rigm, Matthew, and Kabel.

"You're alive!" Nima blurts out, clearing the floor in three steps and wrapping Matt in a relieved embrace.

He accepts the hug, equally happy to see us but also somewhat surprised at Nima's display. I quickly salute to General Qasim, who nods shortly, then walk up and engulf them both in a big bear hug. It would be really good to let all of my emotions out right now. It would be appropriate too, wouldn't it?

The relief of Matt being alive, the hope of a shot at actually redeeming Earth, the fear of returning to our goal and having to face Yatniv again, just letting all that pour out. But I don't. Instead, I let them go, then give Kabel a bro-hug.

"Thank you Yoseph. At least somebody knows how to treat a fella around here."

Empress Rigm smiles, and the crowned dude gives me the traditional "*You straight?*" head nod. Just knowing that he also knows some of my struggle puts me even more at ease, and I fight back a grin as I return the nod.

We all relocate to a larger booth, and after Munda, Nima, and I put in our orders, the others start talking.

"Well," Rigm starts, "I'm quite sure you have a lot of questions. Ask away."

"Before I begin, it's good to see you again Pri… or rather *King* Howard." Nima says, looking at the Black guy in glasses.

He nods and smiles modestly, "Come on Nima, you don't have to be so formal."

Nima turns to me and says lowly, "This is the current king of Koppia, or the country in which we reside in now. He and Yatniv shared many discussions, and I got to know him well as a result."

There is silence, and then Nima starts again, "Kabel and Matthew, I cannot begin to explain to you how relieved I am to see you are well. However, I must ask, how did you survive?"

Kabel and Matt smirk at one another, and then Kabel starts.

"Funny story that one is. So I kinda figured it was a set up, but it was too late to say anything, so I was gonna wait outside and make sure a bunch of soldiers didn't try to rush you. Well in a bit, that's what it started looking like, so I whipped out Sizzle Stick and was getting ready to put a hurtin' on 'em but then Matt over here comes ducking and dodging his way outta nowhere."

"Yeah," Matt says, "After Junia disappeared, Yatniv just walked over quietly and let me free. Maybe he was scared? I don't know… and Bacoj had already taken my bag with the Mundatorite thing in it so I didn't stick around either."

Kabel resumes, "And so the two of us are holding all these vira and backpacks and we're, oh wait that's right."

He unzips his backpack and pads around, then casually hands Nima and I our vira back. Just holding the amulet fills me with strength. I can feel its familiar, buzzing energy and the promise of gushing flames to my heart's content. For a moment it feels unreal.

I look at General Qasim for approval, and he nods. Kabel continues his story as I put on my necklace.

"So, we had to fight our way to the station, past swarms of guards, and I honestly didn't think we were gonna make it, but then Matt did some transformation thing and pulled out a legendary something or another."

"It was the Crescent of Darkness, like you'd said, Nima," Matt adds, "I know how to bring it out, but it's really weird to explain. Anyway, go ahead Kabel."

"Right," the bionic warrior continues, "so he whips that out and we start making some great progress. We got to the lansit, rode it to Silpetro, used my gift card for some wings at Slushere, fought more soldiers, and then took the lansit over to the border."

"The hardest part was making sure to knock out all those people and not kill them. I felt really weird when I had the Crescent of Darkness out, and it took all of my focus to keep the blade backwards. How about you Kabel?"

"Oh, I didn't… I mean sure it was rough. Anyway, we luckily spotted Rigm's group, cheesed border patrol out of checking for ID, and took the lansit to King Howard's castle. He's a family friend and he goes way back with Rigm, so I was thinking he'd definitely be able to help get us outta this mess, and he did."

"You already know I gotchu man," King Howard says, "But your mom still better be making that cocoina."

Everyone chuckles, and then our meals are slid onto the table by our waiter. I don't hesitate to dig into my roasted chicken salad.

"Man, you guys are scarfing that down!" King Howard says with a chuckle, "I can't blame you though. I wanted to come out of the castle today and this was the first spot I thought of."

Munda attacked his Alfredo pasta with similar viciousness, so the both of us are trying our best to respectfully nod and smile while also stuffing our faces. Nima, on the other hand, seems more interested in conversation than in this startlingly delicious food.

"What have you all decided?" Nima asks, then takes a sip from her water.

The air of the table shifts into serious business. I'm not sure about Munda, but I immediately feel out of place stuffing myself with this unlawfully good dish.

General Qasim leans forward, and with him comes his strong, looming presence, "King Howard originally summoned our division to do security for the Celestial Conference, but he and Empress Rigm had the idea to conceal Kabel and Matthew in our army, just like you all have done."

The general shifts and his voice gets a bit stricter, "Of course with the same pretenses of not being able to kill Yatniv."

"Things will be more difficult now, because I just realized how recognizable you are, Nima." King Howard admits.

Nima tries her best not to look flattered.

"You've met many of the global politicians that will be there. Even though we haven't seen you in a long time, your presence is sure to stir up some speculations." The king adds.

"Huh," General Qasim says, "I guess we're sort of stuck then."

"If I may General, I think I already have a solution." Nima says.

"Proceed."

"Currently on our team, we have one woodish male in addition to the large number of humans and me. If I were to take a Mask Potion, I could also temporarily become woodish, and then the woodish male and I could dress in royal regalia and claim that we represent a small country. Although such a potion requires time to cool, we are currently in possession of an artifact that can expedite the process using wind."

"That'll work out perfectly," King Howard replies, leaving the whole magical potions part unaddressed, "Armilan is going through a socio-political reform again and they wanted me to stand in for them, but I'll just send you guys instead. I can look around for some royal regalia at the castle. I'm quite sure Grace's Specialty Emporium is closed for this specific reason, but I can probably convince her to whip something up for you. General Qasim, do you approve?"

The great man's face turns hard, "Yes, but only conditionally. If we don't act like this was an unexpected infiltration, we could risk war. Therefore, if any of you decide to return to Arret from the Conference, you will be arrested and sent to *Prisona Maxima*."

There is an oddly grim silence that overcomes the table as they nod in shock and understanding.

That place sounds scary to me and I'm not even from here. Finally, Nima speaks.

"I understand your terms, and I will ensure everyone else does."

There is some awkward silence, and Munda looks as though he is waiting anxiously for someone to start talking again so he can eat. General Qasim suddenly notices the soldier and smiles grimly. Munda meets his commander's gaze and immediately puts his fork down.

"Munda."

"Aye sir."

"The rest of the division will be leaving once the Conference is over. I'm going to need someone to stay behind and make sure these kids keep up their end of the deal."

"Aye sir."

"The consequences still apply. Will you accept?"

Munda takes a thirstless drink of water, then says as calm as ever, "Aye sir."

There is an uncomfortable, impressed silence from everyone. Did he just give up his position in the military to choose between an alien planet and prison?! This guy has guts.

Suddenly, Kabel says, "Alright enough with the serious talk. Nima, how's the team been?"

Our leader tells the table of our battle with Yatniv, how he gravely injured three people and killed two. At the death of Dr. Keeko, both Matt and Kabel were unsurprised. Of course, Matt was there, and Kabel said that while he was compiling all of our stuff together in a few bags, he found Dr. Keeko's tablet (strangely without a password) and read up on all of his spy files.

At the death of Ilone, however, the pair didn't take it well. Matt's face was smacked with shock, and Kabel was sad for about three minutes before being overcome with rage and storming out of the restaurant.

The glass door closes with the clink of a bell, and everyone left at the table sits silently.

"Well," General Qasim says as he stands, "We should get moving. The first day of the conference is tomorrow, and it starts at 0830, so we need to complete whatever tasks are necessary as soon as possible."

The general waits for the king to stand. Once Munda, Nima, and I salute to them, they both make their way out of the eatery. Rigm and Matt wait in silence for the rest of us to finish eating, and then we pay our bill and leave.

****

The others take the ultimatum surprisingly well. I'm actually really impressed with them, because I know I would be a wreck in their shoes. A little after noon, we're all sent to the castle to pick up our royal guard outfits.

We get fitted rather quickly and receive our uniforms with almost no turnaround time. The clothes are all white with flashing silver accessories, a decent upgrade from our normal navy blue, white, and dandelion yellow dress uniforms.

We carry them back to our hotel with nervous silence. Instead of going to our respective rooms, we all pile into Matt and Kabel's new one. There, we finally break our steely shells. We make jokes, we laugh, we cry, all without shame. Grief and confession are commonplace in that room. Even Chirus, who has yet to speak since we fought Yatniv, laughs and cries alongside us.

Sam has been nearly glued to Matt all day, and seeing them together and joking makes me want to laugh and cry even more. At first the conversation stays around the shock and horror from our run in with Yatniv, but then we end up reminiscing late into the night, talking about that one time Ilone beat Kabel and Cici in the spicy wing contest or the other time when the boys and I nearly died on that piece of junk motorboat with Rixave.

It's about 2AM when we decide to split up for bed. I have the shallowest sleep of my entire life.

CHAPTER 32

THE CELESTIAL CONFERENCE

~ YOSEPH ~

I'm lying on my back with my legs hooked around the lip of the chair. My team members and I sit quietly in columns while the other soldiers joke and laugh as they climb into their seats. It's like five in the morning, but I'm not tired at all. I don't think I can ever be tired, or hungry, ever again. All I feel is overwhelming nervousness.

I look over past Bacoj's solemn face and watch Arret's misty, golden sun rise with a dome of beautiful pinks and blues and greens. The unfamiliar constellations in the open sky fade as the winter sun slowly wakes, but we'll be long gone before the stars are. Wow. This is my last morning on this planet… forever. I've been here for a month and now I'll never be anywhere remotely close to it ever again.

As I do whenever I'm in a situation like this (though it's usually coming back from a different state, not a different planet), I immediately do a pat down. My vira is tucked safely under my all-white dress uniform. My Unkillable Ring is firm around my finger. I own nothing else but a long dead cell phone, a wallet, the Hayride of Doom hoodie, and some healing bandages, all of which are in the white briefcase at my feet. Come to think of it, everything from our bags is in our respective suitcases.

Everything accept the Peace Per, that is, because it's apparently a national treasure. Even the Mundatorite, the ring holding the essence of Earth itself, is wrapped snuggly in Bacoj's briefcase, and Matt's weird scroll is locked tightly within his luggage.

I tear my eyes from the solemn, beautiful, final sunrise and look across the middle aisle to my other special dressed friends. Chirus and Cici sit in front of (or I guess over top of) Munda and Edihi. Chirus is armed with his cousin's vira, and for once he looks well rested and healthy, but he's still unsmiling. All four of them have chosen prison afterwards. Just like the sunrise, after whatever happens today, I will never see them again. I've already wished them well, but I do so again in my head.

The others decided to come with us to Earth. This sunrise has to be all sorts of trippy for them, then. Bacoj has no family here, while Ellia, Kabel, and Nale surprisingly got the OK from their parents. I wonder what kind of values a lot of Arretian households have if this is how accepting their parents are.

Two additional people are joining us on Earth as well, and they sit two rows above me. The first is Virrel, who is determined to see to it that we are safe. The second is Yera, a pale, green-eyed, French-faced girl with short, red hair. She's also from Rigm's group of guards, and she got an ultimatum similar to Munda's.

Nima and Nale sit far above us, dressed so royally it's intimidating. Nale's crown (which he got from Matt who I guess just had a crown lying around) matches his burgundy suit. Golden ropes adorn his shoulders and stripes of the same color run down his legs. The only thing he's missing is a king's confidence, for out of everyone, he looks the most uncomfortable.

Nima, who looks absolutely nothing like her former self except for her gray eyes, has on a sparkling diamond tiara and a similarly flashy dress, also with a royal red blazer. Everything from her air to her vocabulary fits her disguise.

It's time. The odd, white, metal tower of a ship we boarded begins to rumble, and now it's really hitting me. This is it. This is really it. Everything that just happened, this whole adventure, it was all leading to this. I hope that Yatniv got sick and had to call out for the day.

Suddenly, the sad sunrise outside fades into obviously fake stock footage of an empty, sunny beach which is parallel to my view as opposed to perpendicular. I feel the ship tremble and jeer, and then in a hard punch, we're lurched upward. Instead of feeling the shaky blast of rocket thrusters cut on, we continue to glide upward at an oddly smooth, slow rate.

Fear clenches in my stomach as weightlessness suddenly overcomes me, and while the other soldiers are hollering in exhilaration, I'm trying desperately to keep my hat and briefcase from floating away. We glide in this uncanny, terrifying limbo for about ten minutes before all of my weight is shifted abruptly from the air to my butt.

I look around, bewildered, with purple splotches swimming

around in my vision. Fellow soldiers are standing up and sidling down the aisle casually, as if the wall becoming the floor is just an everyday occurrence.

Bacoj and I wordlessly scoot out into the isle, briefcases in hand, and make our way with the flow of the crowd to the exit. My gloved hands are cold and clammy, almost shaking. I look out the small windows as I pass them and watch as the water laps at the shore of the stock footage beach. It doesn't calm me at all.

I'm immediately overcome with awe when I exit the pod with Bacoj. This place is much, *much* different than I expected. The first thing I see is the calm, peach-colored sun just above the horizon. Then there is the massive wooden dome with artsy, crystal clear windows spiraling along the sides. That must be the Celestial Conference hall.

Circling the dome is a stone walkway, which branches out into oriental style wooden bridges. I follow the red railings with my eyes, and each one leads to a quaint stone cabin. Each stone cabin has a name floating in the air above it, and my eyes instantly catch "Earth" over to the left. I linger there for a moment before scanning some more.

Both the giant dome and the four stone cabins are suspended on small rock islands, and beneath everything is baby blue water. I look to the horizon, but I don't see any land. As we approach the dome, I look back at our ship. Instead of seeing the mouth of some white tower turned on its side, there's just another stone cabin with "Arret" floating above it.

In a startling jolt, I realize that everything outside of the wooden dome in the center is an illusion. The peach sun, the rolling clouds, the stone cabins, they're all just as real as the stock footage beach back on the ship. I don't even think the water outside these rails is real.

I follow the flow of soldiers into the wooden dome, which has a huge, spanning, marble floor ballroom with grand chandeliers dangling from the ceiling above. I look around at the high ceiling and shiny smooth floor, taking in the wall's elaborate art and windows, but then Bacoj nudges me.

For a moment I simply stare at the woodish royal couple standing in the middle of a circle of white uniformed teenagers. Then one of the teenagers turns and looks at me, and I recognize their strong green eyes. Not long after Sam looked at me, I'm at her side.

The woodish Queen Nima waits patiently for all of the soldiers in our regiment to file into the elevators. Once the majestic, polished ballroom is empty except for decorations and the fourteen of us, our leader begins speaking.

"Firstly, I am forever grateful for your sacrifice. Those of you that have decided to join us and stay with us until the end, I truly owe my life to you."

She pauses as the others smile and nod humbly, then she continues.

"Today is the day that determines our fate. Our three options are prison, a new life in a foreign land, and death. Let us not choose the last. But that is beside the point. Our main task is to restore Earth through as little confrontation as possible. Bacoj, do you have the Mundatorite?"

The thief opens his briefcase and takes out a wrapped parcel. To everyone's relief, the cloth is unraveled to reveal a glittering diamond bracelet. The entire world slowly spins inside of the glass pearl on top.

Nima breathes a sigh of relief, then frowns and says, "I apologize, but I have reached the extent of my knowledge. I am unsure how to operate the Mundatorite or return it to Earth, and actually, I've never been here before. I've merely heard about it."

Everyone looks at one another. This isn't good. No one in our group could possibly know where anything is; we would have all been maybe four years old when the last conference happened. Virrel smirks, then starts to speak.

"See? You young folks can't do everything on your own. I've been here twice actually, and where we've got to go isn't too bad. We're representing, what, Armilan?"

I can feel a bit of warmth come back to my fingers and face once Virrel reassures us. Some of the crushing, fluttering nervousness in my stomach disperses at his calm. There are sighs of relief from everyone, and then we realize that he asked a question.

"Oh, um, yes." Nima confirms.

"That's good. We'll probably be on Floor Ten, far below Yatniv. Hmm, but we'll have to act fast. I'm taking it that Earth's transport shuttle isn't even active, so we'll need to go to the bottom floor, convince System Control to turn it on, and then somehow figure out how to fix the planet from there."

"Isn't the conference a day-long event? Do you think such a process would take so long?" Nima asks.

"It's actually three days, and this is the first day, but that doesn't really matter. Anyway, after all of the world leaders get here within the next couple of hours, the conference hall is locked. We'd need a fire or something to get them to unlock the doors, and I'm quite sure you all know that starting a fire in a spaceship isn't a good idea."

So, this really is a spaceship and all of that scenery was 3D stock footage. Great, now everything feels even trippier.

"I think our best bet is for Nima and I to go down to System Control, use some inter-planetary hoopla politics to convince them to open Earth's transport shuttle, and then I'll go through with the Mundatorite."

By now, everyone knows that Virrel is a ghost, so going onto a barren planet without an atmosphere won't kill him.

"Excellent thinking, Virrel. What would you like for us to do in the meantime?" Nima continues.

"Stay clear of Yatniv and play your roles. By the time the conference hall's doors unlock again, I should have figured out how to work things out. Maybe. Hopefully."

It's a shifty plan, but I can't think of a better one.

"We're putting our faith in you, Virrel." Nima says with a nod.

"No pressure." Kabel adds, and everyone chuckles.

We make our way to the elevators, and I'm shocked to see that this place has a whopping eighty floors. There's a huge graph next to the wall of buttons listing which countries go where and which activities happen on which floors.

Behind the buttons is a fancy graphic of the ocean, with "01–The Surface" (the ballroom) and "00–Kitchen" (the floor above us) being above the silky water, and the rest of the floors going down into a darker abyss of blue until it finally reaches "80–System Control" and "BV–Bridge View", which has a background full of stars and inky blackness.

Floor Ten is still in relatively light water with colorful aquatic creatures around it. We press our respective floors and wish Nima and Virrel good luck once we get out of the elevator.

****

Nima returns, smiling with success, as the rest of the world leaders begin to enter, and soon, breakfast is served. Menus are distributed, and among the long list of unpronounceable alien delicacies, I spot *Belgian Waffle w/ Poached Egg & Lamb.* I'm more of a solid-egg kind of guy, but almost everything else on the menu looks like made-up words, so I just go for that. Since there are four countries from each planet being represented here, and they all have a small group of guards, the food takes a little while to be dished out. I already wasn't hungry, but as I see what some of the other tables ordered, I'm even less hungry.

I guess the dining staff got the memo that Earth was skipping out this year. The green, four-armed ambassadors, red, feminine-figured presidents, and pale, oriental-faced representatives all seem to brighten at what must be delicious meals to them, but the only thing that looks remotely edible are the waffles I got and a few dishes some of the others ordered. Sam and Matt also chose the waffles and water, but Bacoj, who's sitting on my left, got some type of burrito pie or something. I don't know; he must have recognized a few of the dishes.

Bowing my head and closing my eyes, I say a brief Grace before starting on my waffle. I force my utensils steady, taking empty bites of waffle, staring into the middle of the table.

"You gonna be able to finish all of that?" Sam's joking voice abruptly comes from my left.

I meet her green eyes and smile, "I'm just a bit… you know…"

She nods, "Yeah, same. I don't think anyone is *not* nervous."

"I'm not nervous." Ellia says flatly.

"Really?" Sam challenges.

"Yeah, I'm terrified."

Everyone lets out a little chuckle and returns to clinking their plates and scraping around their breakfast. Out of the blue, Munda of all people starts talking.

"So, how did you guys meet?"

We go around the table, telling the soldier about fatal airplane crashes, violent rock concerts, and venturing into the Forest of Doom. At the end of it, Munda seems really impressed.

"If you guys can survive all of that, then I'm sure we'll be just fine today."

****

The day crawls by. I entertain myself by watching the colorful sea creatures gently bouncing and swimming by the windows. The only way I can tell they aren't real is the fact that they don't cast shadows into the room despite the lights behind them.

Monotonous interplanetary politics drone on in the background, mostly talking about how good it is to see such-and-such's country or how effective so-and-so's policy has been. There might be the occasional passive-aggressive roast, but those are so rare that I don't even bother paying attention.

By the time lunch rolls around, I'm actually kind of hungry and sleepy. I was thinking about playing it safe with the *Cordon Bleu w/ Roasted Squash* but Kabel convinces me to try the *Elati Violette w/ Breadsticks* with him. Sam says she'll try it with me, then Matt, and then next thing I know the entire team has ordered it. The dish comes out eventually… it looks like fettucine alfredo, but the sauce is lavender?

Disappointed that I wasted my meal and a bit afraid that I might get sick, I follow everyone's lead and hesitantly start my pasta… goodness. Either I'm really hungry or this is amazing. I shovel and slurp noodles for a few moments before Bacoj nudges me. I look up at his smirk and then follow his gaze. As soon as I lock eyes with Ellia, they drag their tongue sensually up the side of their breadstick and then fiercely bite down on the end of it.

I let a grin come to my face and say, "Miss, I'm going to have to ask you to do that again please."

The three of us, with Kabel and Chirus included, let out a few stifled laughs. That's an insider from when the girls were off at the graveyard outside of Gumwood; this lady at one of the diners we went to tried to hit on a waiter by doing that, and the waiter responded with what I'd said.

There is a bit of silence, and then Bacoj peeps, "Call me an idiot, but I think today won't be so bad after all."

"I agree with you buddy," Kabel chimes in, "If we win, which we should, then we oughta be able to handle the consequences. If we lose, well, at least we go out together."

****

A lot of my energy comes back after lunch. The combination of my friends' reassurances and the good food serve to both wake me up and calm me down. My fleeting thoughts of failure and underpreparedness begin to fade as the conference goes on.

After a long bout of discussion and a short water break, the conference facilitators begin announcements and final thoughts. The facilitator goes on thanking everyone and summarizing today's progress, but my mind is elsewhere. Why are there butterflies in my stomach? Why is my mouth so dry, and why are my hands so icy? I haven't seen Yatniv all day, and speaking of all day, Virrel has had multiple hours of concentration to figure out how to restore the world. Everything should be fine, right?

There's a little snickering something, though, a nagging dread that assures me I will face Yatniv tonight. It even toys around with the idea that Virrel hasn't figured anything out yet. What if he accidently let go of the ring, and now the frozen essence of the world is doomed to drift in space forever?

Dinner time comes shortly. Some of the others thought it would be poetic to all order the same thing again since this is technically our last meal together, but we'd already done that for lunch. I was going to order the *Lobster & Rice w/ Seasonal Vegetables,* but with a sudden, melancholy jolt, I realize that this is for real the last meal I will ever eat with these people *ever.* I decide to try another Arretian dish, the *Shom & Imso Magar w/ Smoked Flatbread*, as the final taste of Arret in my life. Edihi ordered the same thing, and she reassures me it will be good.

My dish eventually comes out; a brothy, slightly spicy stew with pulled pork and spinach and a few other vegetables and spices I'm unsure of. Edihi was right, it does taste really good. I take a few more spoonfuls of the stew and eat a bite of bread, then survey the table. Everyone is, for lack of better words, lightheartedly serious. According to them, I'm not the only one feeling anxious. Who would've guessed.

We all eat in thoughtful, excited, scared silence for a bit before Sam starts talking.

"So, uh, I guess Nima would normally do this but she isn't here now, so I suppose I can do it."

Sam's right. Nima and Nale have been on the other side of the conference room for the entire day. Our only interactions with the royal couple were through water breaks.

"You're talking for Nima?" Bacoj asks, "Make sure to use big words."

Everyone smirks, and then Sam starts again, "My fellow vira-wielding companions have had a premonition on the possible events occurring this fortnight."

"Wait, so in two weeks?" Cici asks, and then the table rolls with controlled laughter.

"Alright so to the real thing. These vira sometimes give us dreams that kind of predict the future… it's really weird to explain. The point is, all of us vira wielders," she pauses, "Ilone included, had the same dream about fighting a skeleton army. Chances are, if we face anything, it'll be that."

"*Skelet'n* army? Now it just sounds like ya makin' stuff up." Kabel protests.

"It was with, like, Yatniv's magic or whatever." Cici replies.

"How big of an army is this? And are you sure they were real skeletons, or do you think they represented something?" Munda asks stoically, cutting his sip of drink short.

I see where he's going with this, so I decide to reply, "No worries Munda, I think it was a literal premonition. We won't be fighting our old regiment tonight."

The soldier seems to relax at that.

"To answer your question, it was like… maybe one fifty-ish?" Matt adds.

People stop eating and look up incredulously.

"One *hundred* and *fifty*? Well, we're dead." Ellia says.

"I don't know, Matt, that's kind of steep. I'd say maybe just 70 or so." Cici suggests.

"Mmm… no Cici it was somewhere in the hundreds for sure. Maybe not one hundred and fifty but maybe like 110 or 120." Sam reasons.

"That's still almost a 10-to-1 fight we're lookin' at. Do they all have rifles?" Edihi asks, dread heavy in her voice.

"No, they had axes and wooden shields and stuff." Sam says, and the whole table almost leans back in unison, sucking their teeth in renewed courage.

"No rifles? I could wipe 'em all outta here in no time." Kabel scoffs confidently.

"Yeah, I'd have to agree," Munda chimes in, "If they only have melee weapons then we have a serious advantage."

"Boy. These skeletons finna get wrecked." Ellia jokes.

"Honestly though," I say, feeling the optimism and hoping to draw from it, "at this point it'll just be a contest to see who can take out the most before they're all gone."

The table agrees with enthusiasm only stifled by our setting. Soon, the sound of conversations grows as people finish their meals and head to the elevator to leave. The first day of the conference is over… the time is now.

The table is quickly full of empty plates and bowls, but we decide to wait until everyone is gone before we move. This way, it won't seem suspicious that woodish people and guards from an Arretian country are going to Earth's stone cabin transport thing.

We make small talk while we wait for Nale and Nima to finish theirs. The more and more the others learn about our possible foes, the less and less they seem worried. As the last couple of presidents say farewell to Nale and Nima, the rest of us begin to gather our stuff.

I touch my chest reassuringly, and sure enough, my vira is still under there, now slightly warm with anticipation. I grab my suitcase with my spare belongings and head toward the other side of the conference room. I'm so ready.

When we reach Nale and Nima, the only other people in the room are the cleaning staff. Everyone has a hunch that people are still hanging around the stone cabins upstairs, so despite the cleaning staff's protests, we help them tidy up the room in preparation for tomorrow.

After about an hour or so of wiping, carting, folding, and sweeping, the room looks nice and neat. The cleaning staff begrudgingly thanks us but commands us to leave with them since the elevators have long since become staff-only activated.

At this point, we're almost certain that everyone, including Yatniv, is gone, so we gladly ride up with them. Sure enough, when we reach the top, the only other people there are other cleaning staff members heading to their respective stone cabins.

Excitedly, the fourteen of us speed walk across the smooth ballroom floor to the exit closest to Earth's. The ballroom is filled with a golden glow from the grand chandeliers, and outside the windows is a clear night sky with swirling, blue, cosmic clouds and beautiful, blanketing patterns of stars.

We click our way out to the stone pathway around the conference hall, and I look around to see that the bridges are glowing in the dark, which actually looks really dope. The water laps gently beneath us, and the sounds of goodbyes are now fading into silence.

Yatniv stands right in the middle of the bridge to Earth's cabin.

My heart immediately drops. We all freeze, surprised yet unsurprised. The dictator nods, smiling, and the glow of the light coming from under him makes him look even more evil. An image of Dr. Keeko's arm splitting open flashes across my mind.

"For a while there I thought you all had done the smart thing. I guess that wasn't the case now, was it?"

No one replies because no one has anything to say.

"You were pretty clever with the disguises, though. You had everyone, even me, not suspecting a thing. Nice touch with that Mask Potion, Nima."

"Great Sir Yatniv, we ask that you leave. We simply want to return to Earth. We do not wish harm upon you." Nima says flatly.

I take a glance around. Chirus is trembling with rage, Kabel has one hand on Sizzle Stick, Ellia's fingers are fluttering anxiously, and Munda's sleeved rifle is held calmly in both of his hands instead of on his back. Everyone else is holding their briefcases so that they can easily pull out their weapons.

Speak for yourself, Nima.

"Oh, come on Nima," Yatniv taunts, "I tried to kill you guys like, what, eight times? Ten? You seemed to completely avoid most of them, but I still tried… and hey, I killed some of your friends it looks like. Yeah, I must've gotten the cute mixed one with the dreadlocks. What a shame."

Chirus begins growling, and then Yatniv looks over at him.

"*Eruption.*" Says the dictator after drawing a tiny magic circle. Chirus lets out an animalistic screech before collapsing to the floor.

Yatniv bursts into laughter, "What?! He was already *that* angry? I was hoping he'd just blindly rush into death, but that was much more satisfying."

The girl from Rigm's group, Yera, kneels down to check on Chirus, and then the monarch draws another magic circle, mumbling an accompanying, "*Acheiropoieta.*"

His serrated, double edged sword appears white, then bronze in his hand, and he twirls it before setting it down on the railing. Reaching into his royal suit pocket, he pulls out a flask.

"You weren't the only one to go to Grace's Emporium, Nima. I've got a potion of my own."

He raises the flat, metal canteen to his lips and tosses back the contents. While he's chugging down whatever it is, Nima says lowly, "Retreat to the ballroom."

We don't question her. We all shuffle back until we're in the dead center of the huge, bare, golden ballroom. What a fitting place for a final battle. Suddenly from outside, there's coughing and the sound of metal scraping wood.

Heeled footsteps, astonished laughter, and hot, buzzing air approaches from outside, and soon Yatniv fills the exit, blade in hand and eyes oddly bright.

"*Acromion Patella!*" he says with a voice much more thunderous and booming than should be possible. The name of his threatening spell reverberates around the ballroom, running goosebumps up and down my skin and clinking through the crystals in the grand chandeliers.

The voice seemingly shifts into wind, which begins swirling the chandeliers but then forms into dozens of tendrils of dust, which touch down on the smooth ballroom floor like pencil thin tornados. The countless tendrils, now solid with dust, pour down from all around us, closing off everything but the single chandelier above us.

Nima switchblades her sickles, and within a few seconds, everyone is armed. I grip the wooden pole of my spear tightly. The fiery blade at the end is much bigger and angrier than I remember.

Matt shakes his machete violently, closes his eyes, concentrates hard, and abruptly, a horrific scraping sound comes from the blade. Ice sprays everywhere, and what's left underneath is a sharp, smooth, one-edged sword made of black metal. Translucent green waves of energy, like a mirage on a hot day, worm and fizz around the blade. When Matt opens his eyes next, the irises are bright red as opposed to blue, and the pupils are a disgusting milk white instead of their normal black.

I turn back around. Just like they said it happened in the dream, I'm quite sure he's going to go off and battle Yatniv, so no need for me to worry about him.

Suddenly, the tendrils from above dissipate, revealing the wooden walls, the night sky glass, and a ballroom floor covered in miscellaneous bone parts. They begin to assemble themselves perfectly as if they had magnetic ends, and as they do so, Yatniv draws a magic circle.

"*Phlegethon.*" He commands, and a bright, scalding stream of flame leaps from the tip of his sword, stretching out towards us, specifically Matt. Matt points his sword, what I assume to be the Crescent of Darkness, back at Yatniv. Almost too fast for me to catch, what looks like a silvery liquid rainbow beams out of Matt's sword and smothers the huge tongue of fire.

So, Matt has magic now?! The two begin to walk menacingly towards each other, but now I'm beginning to notice that the skeleton army is almost fully assembled. Munda and Ellia immediately go to town, spraying the nearly formed skeletons with lasers and bullets.

"Behind you!" Bacoj shouts, and I whirl around, cracking a skeleton's head off before even registering the danger. A group of them have fully formed, shields raised and blades flashing dangerously in the chandelier light.

The thief runs up and outstretches both hands like he's about to coat them in flames, but then I suddenly remember Virrel's warning about spaceship fires. I shout for Bacoj to stop, and as soon as he turns around, I kick him the axe from the first guy I hit.

The thief flips it up into his hand and twirls it, then nods. The skeletons look at one another, then begin to try to surround Bacoj. I immediately lunge forward, jamming my spear's blade into the first skeleton I see. It doesn't actually hit any bones, but instead gets lodged into a shield.

Another skeleton holding two sabers rushes up to me from my left, so in a panic, I pull my spear up. It cuts through the wooden shield like butter, drawing a thin line of charred black and glowing orange up the middle.

Once the weapon is in the air, I hop backwards and swing it sideways. The dual wielding skeleton raises both swords to block. My weapon comes around fast and slams hard into my opponent's, but aside from a considerable jolt, the skeleton seems to be just fine.

People always joke about skeletons being scary, but when actually facing an adult human skeleton held together by magic and wielding razor-sharp swords, it's not so funny. The skeleton with the shield tries to come around on my right, but I back off so that both of them are in front of me.

Through the startling pops of gunshots, the jolting clank of weapons, and the wavering variance of magic streaking through the air, I suddenly pick up on clattering footsteps headed my way from behind. Immediately, they're way too close for comfort, and I can feel the air pause as whatever's behind me rears back to strike.

Trying to use the element of surprise, I lunge forward with my spear diagonal, putting pressure on the two swords and the shield. Not a second later, there is a whoosh of something sharp inches away from my neck.

Panic rises in me as I debate whether it would even be worth it to scream. I look past the two skeletons and out into the ballroom. Before my eyes can go out into the starry night and brace for a biting death, they lock with Nale's.

The woodish archer raises his bow towards me and pulls back with a near professional smoothness, and then pecks off one, then two, then three javelins of ruby red light, all flickering past my vision for a fraction of a second before causing whatever is behind me to collapse.

Stunned relief and gratitude flood through me, but the archer dances back from a spiked club and I realize that we're still in the middle of a battle. I leap back from the two skeletons, confidence and adrenaline rushing through my blood.

The three of us stare one another down. I fight the urge to glance around, keeping my spear raised and my eyes fierce. Alright, so the one with the shield is probably always going to go defense. I'll fake towards it, reel the sword one out, and then take that one by surprise. After that the shield dude shouldn't be a problem.

I lunge at shield skeleton and it raises its shield in preparation. Just as planned, the sword one goes in for some type of fancy double slash. Oh, it messed up big time. I plant one foot down hard, then push my body weight, along with the shaft of my spear, into sword guy's ribcage.

It rams through, snapping some things on the way, and both of my enemies look as surprised as skeletons can. I plant both feet, violently twist my weight, and slam sword guy into its buddy's shield with enough force to send its bones splashing everywhere.

Shield guy blankly looks at its shield for a second, and then it raises the protection again, angling its axe and slowly backing away. I rush up to it and hit it with the smooth footwork. It's staring at my feet, trying to figure out where I'm going, and then I get a hilarious idea.

I stop juking around it, twirl my spear, and jab way off to the left, nowhere even near the skeleton. It quickly raises its shield anyway and I use my momentum to violently kick it out of the skeleton's hand. I can't believe that actually worked.

It grabs its one-handed axe with two hands now, waving it menacingly and still backing up. Suddenly, Sam runs up behind the skeleton and kicks it towards me. The blade of fire at the end of my spear sinks into its sternum, and I instinctively pull my weapon up, sending its skull and collarbone sailing into the air. Oh… that was a lot more violent than I'd intended.

Sam and I trade nods, then I turn around to see the rest of the battlefield. My heart leaps into my throat as I watch Cici, surrounded by skeletons, get bashed very hard in the head with a stone mallet, but then she disappears in a puff of smoke. Phew, it was just a clone. Ellia and Munda proceed to mow the circle of skeletons down.

A bit further off, I watch as Kabel brings his massive sword down like a guillotine on a shielding skeleton, sending splintering wood and bone flying everywhere. A quick scan tells me that all the other skeletons have already been taken care of. Wow, that was a lot easier than I'd first imagined.

Soon, the only sounds that are left are the clashing and zapping of Matt and Yatniv's intense fight. I watch in awe as flickering tongues of flame and dangerous branches of lightning cross one another, sending sparks and smoke spraying in every direction. I'm mesmerized by the skillful fluidity of the two of them. It's quite jarring to see my neighbor go toe-to-toe with an evil wizard dictator.

They cross swords once again, gritting at one another over their bouncing blades, but before anything else can happen, the bones on the ground begin to whirlpool towards the center of the ballroom.

"Now!" Nima shouts, "Retreat to your respective planets! Move with haste, before the next opponent forms!"

Immediately, people begin to quickly trickle towards the exit, and I'm certainly with them. Yatniv screams out towards us, but no rushing burst of magic comes spiraling our way, so we keep running.

I emerge from the golden ballroom a moment later, taking in the star-filled, electronic sky. Cici and Edihi scoop up Chirus and carry him off to the Arret cabin while everyone else makes their way to Earth.

Instead of getting on the bridge first, I stand by its mouth and beckon people towards it. I know, absolutely useless, but in the moment, I felt like I was doing something important. As familiar faces pass me, I look back into the ballroom to see what's going on.

Kabel holds Sizzle Stick like a baseball bat, shuffling sideways as he stares up at a towering bone monster with three arms. It must have been four at one point, but I guess Kabel already hacked one off. Sizzle Stick is glowing an extremely hazardous looking yellow-orange, and even from here I can see the heat coming off of it.

The monster swipes at Kabel, but he does a flip over the hand, and as he's raising his weapon to counter, Nima nudges me. I start, then follow her to the cabin. We pass through the strangely lit doorway, and I see what its weird light source is.

Staring me down is a massive portal, maybe forty feet wide, painting the walls with wind and bright neon colors. Standing in front of this thing feels like standing at the edge of a cliff. Nima, without hesitation, sprints right into the wall of light. Instead of disappearing or something, she drops off of an apparent edge, falling down into what I know is a river of pink dots.

I reach the edge and look over into the nauseating, swirling limbo of light. Before I can jump in, an image pops in my head. It's Ilone, calm and dead in her see-through coffin. No, the others should be fine. I need to just hop in before something bad happens. Ilone and Sam dance along happily to the beat of the music back at the Semparus festival, and then a second later, Yatniv draws his blade across Ilone's chest. I step back from the portal with a sigh.

I can't let Sam and Matt die.

Chapter Finale

Great Sir Yatniv

~ Matthew ~

Seeing the weakness in his eyes makes me want to kill him. Another wave of self-awareness hits me and I decide to will away the Crescent of Darkness. As soon as the blade disappears, I'm rushed with exhaustion from all sides. I wobble to my knees and sit down, almost exactly like Yatniv did once I'd beaten him.

Someone walks over to me, and I tiredly look up to see that it's Sam. She gives me a concerned look, but I return with a thumbs-up. A moment later, Kabel walks up to me from my other side. As soon as I spot him, I realize all the fighting noises have stopped. He must have killed that giant skeleton monster thing.

He walks right past me and Sam, looms over Yatniv, and spits on the floor next to the dictator.

"That… was for Ilone you punk."

He seems a bit too winded to do anything else, so he just limps out of the ballroom. I watch him go, noticing that no one else stayed behind. Once he leaves, the ballroom is empty aside from Sam, Yatniv, me, and a fallen chandelier. Suddenly, I'm struck with a brilliant idea. I could just talk to him one-on-one now. Of course,

Sam kind of ruins that, but I'm not even going to try and ask her to leave.

"Hey," I say to Yatniv, getting his attention, "Can we just talk?"

"Talk?" He asks, still propped up on his elbows.

Deep purple blood slowly trickles at his shoulder and his left brow. His royal suit is covered in burn marks, and his white crown looks damaged beyond repair. Despite his efforts, I can see his whole body rising and falling as he catches his breath.

The dictator looks at Sam, then me, then the empty ballroom, and shrugs, "I mean, sure I guess."

As soon as he says that, Yoseph appears in the far doorway, trotting over to the three of us.

"Everything cool?" He asks as he reaches us, and a pang of annoyance springs up in my heart. I wanted this to be a one-on-one, and Sam butting in was already frustrating enough.

"Yeah, Matt just wanted to get some answers out of Yatniv." Sam reports.

"Ah, this ought to be interesting then." Yoseph comments, plopping down next to me.

There is silence, and then the dictator says, "I'm listening."

I don't really know what I expected from this. Friendship? A truce maybe? Understanding? Let's go with understanding.

"Why did you steal Earth?"

"Well," he sighs, "Do you want the long or short story?"

I look at the others, both of whom shrug apathetically.

"I've got time."

Yatniv nods, casually patting himself down like he's looking for a wallet or business card. Quickly, he pulls a silver thing out of his coat, but then Yoseph switchblades his spear into his hands. I soon realize that Yatniv is holding another potion flask.

"Nope. We ain't doing that again." Yoseph says, angling the fiery blade near Yatniv's neck.

The dictator lets out a defeated laugh and moves his hands up. Sam snatches the flask from him a moment later.

"Alright fine," Yatniv says as he sits up, "So my dad, Great Sir Gentarh Yatniv, used to be ruler of Fiponik before me. He was a pretty decent ruler; made sure to keep everyone in check, had his fun from time to time, you know, normal stuff. But for some reason, he was always absolutely obsessed with humans.

"All his staff were humans. He always treated the human diplomats with the most respect and friendliness. He'd never shut up about you guys. It was pretty gross; he'd even have his way with human women only. Wait, no, my mom was woodish. Dad was always disappointed in the two of us for one thing or another, but I knew it was because we weren't also human."

I take an uncomfortable glance at the others before Yatniv continues, "So one day he decided that your planet was so fascinating that he was going to take it for himself. That's when he started the Mundatorite project. He gathered the best magicians and engineers in the country to help him with it. Raised taxes, cancelled conferences; he was really serious about it.

"At the same time, he'd set his eyes on this 'attractive' human woman. I forget her name, but he would never shut up about *her*, either. He was torn between having her as a second wife or just kidnapping her like normal, but then this ambassador-spy person from Earth came and swept her away with him.

"Of course Dad was angry over this, but he used his anger as more inspiration for the Mundatorite. After a few years, he was still thinking about that human woman a lot, so he sent assassins to track her down and kidnap her. He also wanted them to kill the ambassador she ran off with and make it look like an accident."

Yatniv shakes his head and laughs, "But the assassins accidentally ended up killing the woman and her kids as well as the ambassador, and my dad was beyond heartbroken. So he killed himself. Mom ran off into the woods somewhere and I was left with the kingdom and the Mundatorite project."

I look at Sam and Yoseph, who are looking off into the distance in thought. I almost feel bad for Yatniv, but the strange thing is, he doesn't seem very sad about the whole thing. He's just really… matter-of-fact about it.

"So… you finished the Mundatorite project even though you hate humans?" Sam asks.

"Well duh!" Yatniv says, "Billions of nummis went into that project, I wasn't just going to let it flop! And besides, I've had enough of humans and Earth. I figured I'd capture them in the ring and maybe bury it next to Dad for a little bit of irony. But for certain I was going to finish it."

"H-how exactly did you get that to work in the first place?"

Yoseph asks.

Yatniv chuckles, "Look man, magic is complicated. There are probably as many magic styles as there are languages. I don't really know the specifics of how it works–"

"Oh, I meant like how did it actually trigger and suck up Earth." Yoseph interrupts.

"Oh! Yeah, I just put a hex on it so that once it got on Earth, it would go off if two or more people got close to it. I figured Nima was going to try and get some help, so I thought that'd be the easiest way of going about things."

"Instead of it activating right as it got to Earth?" Sam asks.

"That would make sense, wouldn't it?" Yatniv says, "But I'd originally thought Nima was the Crescent of Darkness. Long story, lots of weird loopholes and stuff."

"I want to hear it." I blurt out, eager to learn everything I can about my power.

"Um… okay," Yatniv starts, "Ever since I started having those dreams about your weird symbol, I had a strange hunch that Nima had something to do with all of it. She was a really good maid though and I honestly didn't want to fire her, but I needed to get rid of her somehow. So I figured I'd destroy her village to make her want to quit, then send her to Earth with the Mundatorite the moment she resigned.

"The day of her resignation, she shows up in my throne room with four vira, one of which was yours, Crescent. Of course she never knew exactly what it looked like because I never specifically described it to anyone outside of the soothsayer. For a moment I actually thought she was you, which would've been really poetic, but then I figured that was wrong.

"The dream interpreter said you'd come from a distant land, and Nima was a citizen of Fiponik, so it couldn't be her. But then if I were to have sent her to Earth and had the Mundatorite immediately activate, she could have technically came from a distant land if she followed the Mundatorite back to Arret. I figured she would leave her vira when going to get help, so that way when the ring activated, even if she managed to get back to Arret, she wouldn't be able to come as the Crescent of Darkness. I didn't know she'd show up with the amulet, but I guess it paid off for me to be paranoid."

The four of us are silent for a bit, and then Sam peeps, "That's pretty convoluted."

Yatniv shrugs, "I'm not the dictator just for my looks."

"But…" I start, still not satisfied, "but why me? Why am *I* the Crescent of Darkness? And what does it all mean?"

The dictator lets out a chuckle and shakes his head, "You're overthinking it, man. Sometimes things just happen. It's really just the amulet that makes you the Crescent of Darkness. No hard feelings, but without it, you're just some normal kid. Why the amulet fits you, well, heck, why does anything happen? Random chance, probably."

I slouch, crestfallen. That can't be right… there has to be a reason. Yoseph puts a hand on my shoulder, and I look over to see him smiling reassuringly.

"Don't worry about it Matt. It'll all make sense someday."

I don't believe him, but I smile and nod anyway.

"Alright, so are you guys going to leave or am I just going to answer questions until I bleed out?" Yatniv asks casually.

"That doesn't sound half bad, but unfortunately, I don't have any questions left." Sam retorts.

"Me either." I admit.

Yoseph is silent, and then he apprehensively asks, "Do… do you have any questions for us?"

"What?" Yatniv and Sam reply nearly at the same time.

"I mean, I wouldn't want to be rude." Yoseph excuses.

"Yoseph," Sam starts flatly, "this guy is responsible for tens of thousands of his *own* citizens' deaths, including Ilone and Dr. Keeko. We should be stomping his teeth in right now."

"Harsh." Yatniv peeps.

"Well, he could always end up giving us info we hadn't considered." Yoseph defends.

"Fine. Go ahead and ask your question." Sam spits.

Yatniv thinks for a long moment, then grins.

"Can you call up that glowing bird woman that you used in my throne room?" Yatniv asks.

I look at Yoseph and Sam, who look at one another, their expressions unreadable.

"I don't see why not. It's not like she's going to hurt us or anything." Yoseph says.

"Sure. But any weird stuff and I'll make him even uglier." Sam warns.

Yoseph bows his head to pray, and the rest of us wait. At first it was just his low mumbles filling the scarred, golden ballroom. Then, slowly, there is a column of light that begins to shimmer into existence. Eventually, it solidifies into Junia. Her bright white robe floats in the air along with her flowing hair, and her eyes are as loving as her smile.

"Sons of men," her tone drops as she spots Yatniv, "and the Wicked One. From whence do thy troubles appear?"

The mere presence of Junia takes my breath away, and it seems like the other three are at a loss for words too. Suddenly, Yoseph finds his bearings.

"Um, we're actually good. It's *that* guy who wanted to talk to you." Yoseph thumbs over to Yatniv, who offers a little wave.

Junia scoffs and crosses her glowing arms, "Does a dog eat at the table of a king? Much less should the Wicked One be afforded the blessings of the righteous."

The four of us stare at her, dumbfounded, and then she starts again, "Very well. Speak out and I shall answer."

"W-what are you?" Yatniv questions.

"I am an angel, servant of the Highest to perform His will throughout the universe."

"Oh. Um, what can you do?"

"The Host of Hosts has blessed me with unending gifts. The gift of healing, the gift to take and restore sight, the gift of everlasting joy, the gift to call fire from the heavens, the gift to prophesy, the gift of light which begets destruction, and the gift to raise up plagues among the dust of the fields of men are but seven in my great storehouse."

"Prophesy? You can tell the future?" Yatniv asks, perking up.

"The Lord speaks and I repeat His will." Junia replies flatly.

"What's… what's my future look like?" Yatniv tests.

Junia glares at him for a long time, then says, "Thou shalt be taken in and given prosperous gifts."

I recoil in surprise, then look over at Sam and Yoseph, who are also surprised.

"Really?" The dictator asks with a smirk, "then what?"

Junia looks even more annoyed as she waits for an answer, but then suddenly, the most panic-inducing terror I've ever seen fills her face. Those shining green eyes swell with horror, and at once, her head snaps to the side. We all follow her gaze to see her staring at a white briefcase near the wall… my briefcase!

In a fraction of a second, she is standing over the briefcase, then looming over me with the briefcase in hand. Yatniv, Yoseph, Sam and I all recoil at the angel's sudden reappearance.

"Within this lies a great evil. Such darkness makes even the angels weep and the demons tremble. The scroll shall beget suffering and death beyond all that creation has witnessed. Mourn and lie prostrate before the Lord, for trials as many as the stars in heaven shall appear, and the future bears bitter fruits."

The genuine fear in her ethereal voice is beyond terrifying, so all I can do is take the briefcase from her.

"I shall only appear when times of unbearable strife cometh, that my presence be consecrated for the hour in which thou should need a shepherd. Do not open the scroll. Peace be upon thee, children of our Father." And with that, she is gone.

I look at Yatniv. He's stunned silent. Yoseph and Sam are looking at one another with fear and bewilderment.

"I think we should leave now." Yoseph suggests.

"Yeah," Yatniv croaks, "good talk."

My neighbor, sister, and I gather our belongings, then make our way out of the golden ballroom and into the starry night. Everyone is silent as we click across the marble floor, then the stony walkway, and then the glowing wood of the bridge. Yatniv doesn't attack us as we leave; he's either too tired, too scared, or both. The three of us give him one last look before stepping off into the giant, swirling, neon portal.

Something tells me this won't be the last of him.

****

My eyes slowly open to swishing, barren trees overhead. The branches softly click against one another. The white sun shines alone in the clear blue sky. I sit up, realizing at once that I'm in a fluffy, comfortable red coat and thick dark jeans, an outfit I certainly don't own. Wait, do I own this? It feels right…

I scan my surroundings, bewildered and confused. The barren trees rise high out of the brown leaf blanket on the forest floor. A sloping hill leads to a forest trail not too far away. Three bikes are by the road… I guess those are our bikes?

Lying on my left is Sam, curled up cutely in a ball of sleep. On my other side is Yoseph, also asleep. He wears the exact same thing that I have on but with a green coat, and Sam has a purple coat with light jeans.

With a loud shuffling noise, I stand up. No matter how many times I scan the trees around me, I can't find anyone else. No Nima in sight. Bacoj, Kabel, Ellia, Virrel, the blue archer, the woman from Rigm's group, all missing. Didn't they make it? This is Earth, right?

I can feel the cold on my face… where is my vira? Did it even exist? Where's my briefcase, my hat, my guard uniform? That couldn't have all been a dream. Bewildered, I look down at my sister and my neighbor to wake them, but a white business card stands out among the maroon and orange bed beneath me.

I pick it up; it reads:

> Griffin A. Voltaire of Team Spiral Thunder. IPSHA Certified. Tear for appointment.

Below that it lists a Canadian address, an email, and two phone numbers. I stare at the card, confused, then flip it to look at its back. In spidery, boyish handwriting is a message:

> Thank you, Matthew. I'm looking forward to meeting you.

Epilogue

~ ~ ~

For a moment I really do think I'm going to bleed to death. Sitting here has gotten comfortable, especially after all that scary stuff the angel was saying, and now that I consider it, I don't have the strength to get up. Luckily, a blond man in a royal guard's uniform trots up to me from the ballroom entrance.

He hoists me on his shoulder like I'm a rug, then begins heading towards the exit again, bouncing my stomach into his sharp shoulder again and again. He moves with a silence that implies he isn't going to speak, so I decide to say something.

"Who are you?"

"Mitchell Munda, sir." His voice is flat and dutiful, a soldier's.

"Were you with the Crescent?"

"Yes sir."

I see we're heading towards the Arret transport station. Good.

"So you just left once Acromion Patella was first defeated?"

"Yes. That boy, Kabel, wanted to face the giant skeleton alone, and Matt wanted to face you, so we let them. Those were their battles to fight, not ours."

"Ours?" I prod.

"Yes. The rest of us that are returning to Arret waited for you."

I'm somewhere between flattered and confused, "Why?"

"Strictly orders sir… *strictly* orders." The soldier says bitingly.

I would try to intimidate him with what his punishment will be, but he seems like a smart guy; he probably knows what he got himself into. Me on the other hand, I don't know what I was thinking, but I surely wasn't thinking ahead. Why did I summon Acromion Patella? I should have definitely went for something more tactical. Of course, the ballroom is still in one piece, but it's covered in laser burns and slash marks and stuff.

Oh man, how am I going to explain this to the Bukanarions? I destroyed your priceless interplanetary conference ballroom because… someone tried to kill me? No, that won't cut it. This'll cost a fortune. If I don't figure something out, the rest of my nation and I are going to be eating game and living in scrap huts for the next five years.

Mitchell ducks through the transport station and walks down the teleportation pod hallway. Before I can take note of the other people in here, he drops me roughly in a seat. After the painful jolt, I get a brilliant idea.

Earth wasn't at this conference… I'll say it's because they went rogue and no longer want to be a part of IPSHA, so they sabotaged our meeting space and tried to kill me. If I work off that, I'll get the blame off me, maybe get rid of the Crescent in the process… and maybe even wipe out the whole planet. Good.

This time will be different…

End Credits

Thanks God for blessing me to get where I am now; I hope this book was to Your glory, my King.

Thank you (yes, *you*!) for buying and reading this book; your willingness has helped me so very much!

Thanks Mom for reading and attempting to edit my very first manuscript; also for birthing me and loving me and stuff.

Thanks Dad, Courtney, and the rest of my family for supporting me; you guys are the coolest.

Thanks "Alice Green" and "Mad Chulo" for being big advocates for the original; I'm glad we got a chance to know one another.

Thanks Blake, Chris, Eloni, Jacob, other Jacob, Leila, Mackenzie, Mitchell, Victoria, and Xavier; hopefully you don't befall the same fates as your characters ;)

Thanks to everybody who bought the original two; I now those grammer, continuity and reelism mitsakes where ruff. *wink wink*

Find more info about the author and Crescent of Darkness at

www.weirddisciple.com

www.ingramcontent.com/pod-product-compliance
Lightning Source LLC
Chambersburg PA
CBHW020605310726
48979CB00008B/1347/J

* 9 7 8 1 7 3 2 6 5 4 8 7 7 *